Charlie's War

In September 2004 *Richard & Judy*'s Executive Producer, Amanda Ross, approached Pan Macmillan: her production company, Cactus TV, wanted to launch a major writing competition, 'How to Get Published', on the Channel 4 show. Unpublished authors would be invited to send in the first chapter and a synopsis of their novel and would have the chance of winning a publishing contract.

Five months, 46,000 entries and a lot of reading later, the five shortlisted authors appeared live on the show and the winner was announced. But there was a surprise in store for the other four finalists.

On air Richard Madeley said, 'The standard of the finalists is staggeringly high. All are more than worthy of a publishing contract.' Pan Macmillan agreed and published all five.

The winning books were *The Olive Readers* by Christine Aziz, **Tuesday's War by David Fiddimore**, *Journeys in the Dead Season* by Spencer Jordan, *Housewife Down* by Alison Penton Harper, and *Gem Squash Tokoloshe* by Rachel Zadok.

DAVID FIDDIMORE was born in 1944 in Yorkshire and is married with two children. He worked for five years at the Royal Veterinary College before joining HM Customs and Excise, where his work included postings to the investigation and intelligence divisions. *Charlie's War* is the second in the Charlie Bassett trilogy.

Also by David Fiddimore

TUESDAY'S WAR

DAVID FIDDIMORE

Charlie's War

PAN BOOKS

For

CHAS McDEVITT & NANCY WHISKEY,

and the generation who rode the last train

to San Fernando

First published 2006 by Pan Books
an imprint of Pan Macmillan Ltd
Pan Macmillan, 20 New Wharf Road, London N1 9RR
Basingstoke and Oxford
Associated companies throughout the world
www.panmacmillan.com

ISBN-13: 978-0-330-44656-3
ISBN-10: 0-330-44656-8

1 3 5 7 9 8 6 4 2

A CIP catalogue record for this book is available from
the British Library.

Typeset by SetSystems Ltd, SaffronWalden, Essex
Printed and bound in Great Britain by
Mackays of Chatham plc, Chatham, Kent

Charlie can't let this book pass without thanking the four people he consults as he commits his memoir to paper:

Marion, Andrea and Gwen,
who all live with his stories on a daily basis,
and Sarah Turner, his editor and guide. Bless you.

PART ONE

England: November 1944

One

I had three books.

One was a thrice-read Western by Zane Grey, one was an Edgar Wallace, and the third was a book of erotic poems by John Wilmot, Lord Rochester – given to me by Conners before my old aircrew split. I missed the old gang more than you could imagine. Grease, our Canadian pilot, had returned to the prairies, and the rest were up north in cushy training berths well out of the way of the war, except for Fergal, who had run away to be a priest. Part of me was glad of that. The other part damned the lot of them for being the jammy sods that they were.

I had given a bomber squadron at Bawne airfield, near Cambridge, twenty-eight trips, and when I drove away from it I took most of the clothes I had arrived in, a little Singer open four-seater I had inherited, and Piotr's big radio. Piotr was Pete, our rear gunner. Being dead since our last trip, he wouldn't need either for the time being. I was given two weeks off for good behaviour so I drove north to see my dad, who had evacuated to Glasgow. It wasn't a city I fell in love

3

with instantly: people seemed to evacuate all over it every Saturday night – mostly from bladder, bowel or stomach – and a girl I had met at St Enoch's for ten bob put me out of action for a fortnight afterwards. It may seem stupid but I reported for duty at my new station three days before I was due. I couldn't settle with the civvies.

I didn't fly: I had done my trips, and was being rested, or *screened* in a training job. Still on a bloody squadron though. That was unusual, although not completely unknown. It figured because it was an unusual bloody squadron. From Tempsford they flew all over unfriendly Europe in some of the oldest, slowest aircraft the service could find. My job was to house-train their radio operators if they arrived on the squadrons untrained or unwilling, and sort out their kit. I was supposed to deliver W/Ops briefings before their trips if a special briefing was called for. It never was. Anyway; that was the theory of it. They say you live and learn. A lot of the buggers I'd last flown with never learned, and didn't live that long. QED.

Frohlich walked in while Cab Calloway was singing away, '. . . a kiss ain't a kiss, unless there's a kick in it', on Pete's radio in the room they had given me. That was in a small farm servant's cottage down the dirt track from Waterloo Farm, which was one of the other names for Tempsford airfield. I was sitting in the armchair with my blankets wrapped around me because the previous night I had used up my coal ration for the week trying to keep the place thawed out. I wasn't going back into those sodding books, so was open to offers when he stuck his head round the door and called pub.

'Fancy a pint, Charlie?'

'Do you think they'll have a fire on?'

'Must do; weather like this.'

'I'm in then.'

'Good. We can take your car. Ours is running on hope and petrol vapour.'

'Steal some. Everyone else does.'

He gave me the sad look. He was OK with a pint in his hand, but he didn't like thieves. Bible basher. Jewish bible. I drove us all up Warden Hill to the Thornton in Everton village: me and Frohlich and his mixed-ranks crew. Tempsford being the funny place that it was, the officers and NCOs spent more off-duty time together than on other squadrons. The bosses looked the other way. Frohlich was a Sergeant Pilot. His Navigator, Klein, was a Flying Officer, and his Radio Operator was a Pilot Officer named Albert Grost. Both outranked him on the ground, but they called him *Skip* in the air. In my opinion Grost was cack-handed, so I rode him hard over his pathetic Morse signature. The first time I told him to practise he complained to the CO that I was anti-Semitic. Goldie pointed out that the whole of the rest of Frohlich's crew was from the promised land, and didn't seem to have a problem with me. I held him back as we all left the bar to hog the small fire in the snug.

I asked him, 'Look, can I call you Albert, or Al, while we're here in the pub? I know I'm not part of your team.'

He looked momentarily disconcerted, then, 'Of course. Albie. You're Charlie?'

'Right. I knew another Albie once.'

'Another radio man? Radio men should stick together.' Turd. The other Albie was an American tank commander. As soon as I met him I knew he was on the way to shake hands with Dr Death.

'Right. We got off on the wrong foot. I'm supposed to be the expert, and make sure you're up to scratch. Not much point if I don't tell you the truth.'

It had been a bit like fencing, and my last few words had been a definite touch. Touché. He gave me a rueful grin as a reward. He can't have been more than nineteen.

'OK. I know my Morse isn't much good.'

'I could help.'

'OK.' He gave himself a gulp of the hoppy beer. 'I'll come to see you tomorrow, all right?'

'Fine.' Then I told him. 'You were right though; I *am* prejudiced.'

'I thought so. I'm used to it.'

'Not this, you're not. I just hate fucking officers.'

He had that uncertain sort of laugh as we joined the others at the fire.

I slipped out for ten minutes between drink two and drink three, to visit Black Francie where he lay in the churchyard of St Mary's church behind the pub. He had been an air gunner cut into three pieces by unsociable Germans. We had buried him here about two months earlier. There was a small posy of fresh flowers on his grave. The rich earth on the grave seemed higher somehow, and there was a distinct crack in it at one side. I wondered if it was being lifted by his decomposition gases and moodily pressed it down flat with my foot. Sometimes I said a word or two to him, but on this occasion just being there was enough. The light was fading. Someone had switched on the flare-path lights of the airfield in the valley below us, and I heard the heavy growl of four Hercules radial engines throwing an aircraft into the sky. That would probably be a Hallibag. I felt stupid, a bit lost, and exceptionally lonely. I hated my new squadron, and decided to go and get crocked. The lights flicked off again.

My hangover the next morning was like a deep depression rolling in from south-east Iceland. I vowed abstinence for the rest of my life if God would take it away and give it to Hitler. God didn't listen to me.

The CO called me up at about 0900. The NCOs all called him 'Goldie' because of the colour of his hair and moustache. The officers called him Squadron Leader, knelt, crossed themselves, and wiped their tongues with toilet paper afterwards. That probably explained the toilet-paper crisis: there had been none on the station for weeks apparently. Each bog was hung with wads of cut squares of newspaper, neatly threaded on looped string. I used to look for the crosswords and the cartoons, but someone was always there before me, and nicked the drawings of *Jane*.

He asked me to sit down, which was never a good sign.

'Settled in, Sergeant?'

'Thank you, sir.'

'Any problems?'

'It's been a little difficult sorting my duties out, sir. There's nothing on paper, and I didn't meet the man I replaced.'

'Seen the squadron Radio Officer?'

'Not yet, sir. He hasn't been here since I arrived. No one seems to know where he is.'

'We can be a bit like that sometimes.'

'I understand, sir.'

'I don't think that you do, but you will, if you stick around long enough.'

Attack being the best defence and all that, I pressed on.

'Shall I just carry on then, sir? At present I liaise between the ground staff and the aircraft, and check new men who haven't flown with you before.'

'Sounds spot-on, Sergeant. Initiative.'

'It can be a bit difficult because I don't actually *know* what they do on these sorties, sir. I was thinking of hitching a lift on one of them. Bat myself in, so to speak.'

'Good idea, Sergeant. I shouldn't be surprised if your predecessors didn't do the same. Anything else?'

One of us was being a twerp. I wasn't sure which one.

'When I left Bawne, sir, my old CO put me up for canonization. They wanted me to continue as an *officer*. I think that it was a reward for living long enough.'

'Yes; I've read your papers. Nothing's come down from Wing yet. Worried?'

'Only the principle of it, sir. If they think I'm worth more, they should pay me more.'

He gave me a fiver from his desk drawer as if it was a tip. It probably made him feel good.

'Don't ask me where it comes from; my clerk gives me more whenever I ask. It seems that the War House thinks we need more filth than most outfits.'

I couldn't tell him that I didn't need it, once I'd opened my mouth: I would have to talk to Frohlich, I thought. I buttoned it into my right top pocket, saluted and about-turned; I felt a party coming on. Or maybe I should speak to the American Master Sergeant guy I knew at Thurleigh Field, and make him an offer for a box of toilet paper.

Tommo Thomsett from Thurleigh told me that the Kraut and his U-boats had deliberately targeted vessels carrying toilet paper, and torpedoed them in the Atlantic. This had led to what he described as 'a little supply side difficulty'. I got a box of flat packets for three quid, which was extortionate. Then he told me he was glad I was back. He didn't like to lose an old customer.

Later that week I shared a breakfast table with Frohlich. He gave me his bacon, and asked me, 'Have you noticed that some beggar is stealing all of the *Jane* cartoons from the arse paper?'

'Yes. I saw that.'

'Wonder who?'

'Some spy, I should think.'

'*I* should have thought of that,' he told me.

They operated the *need to know* system at Tempsford, so naturally nobody ever knew anything. The squadrons didn't consider that I needed to know much at all. I was surprised to find it rather suited me. My mum used to say that what you didn't know couldn't hurt you. The flue from her kitchen stove had leaked, and she didn't know about that. It killed her and my kid sister. I suppose you can't be right about everything.

There were two resident squadrons, 138 and 161, who clandestinely flew people and materials to the parts of Europe that Adolf was still in love with. They also brought people out again. The aircraft they operated varied from small Lysanders and twin-engined Hudsons, which actually landed over there, to the big Halifax and Stirling bombers: four-engined jobs like the Lanc I flew on my tour.

A week or so after my arrival I had stood at the WVS canteen lorry behind the converted parachute store in which they kitted out the passengers, who they called Joes, and watched a Hallibag limbering up its engines for a trip across the Channel somewhere. It looked very old, and huffed and puffed a bit. It made a lot of smoke. There was a scruffy Flight Lieutenant with a full set of wings alongside me, blowing on his tea. He was probably fifteen years older than me, and his uniform, although clean, hadn't seen an iron since it had been issued to him – it gave him a curious boneless look. He'd borrowed his moustache from Douglas Fairbanks, but it didn't give him the edge he'd hoped for, and he wore his Irvine flying jacket over his shoulders like a cape. I thought that he'd seen *The Dawn Patrol* at his local fleapit too often at Saturday morning pictures, but he was the only one left to talk to. I asked him how long they would be out. Stupid question: my speciality.

'As long as a string of bangers, old son. Could be going to the bloody moon and back, couldn't they?'

'Sorry. I'm new here.'

'I guessed. It's bad form to ask about a trip on this station, but I won't tell on you. I'm David Clifford. Most people call me Cliff.'

'I'm Charlie Bassett. I was sent here as a radio instructor, but I can't find anyone to instruct.'

'Don't knock it. Let *them* come to you.'

'I'll remember that. I can't seem to find my boss either; he's the Station Radio Officer. Stan somebody.'

'He went out on a trip to Never Never Never Land three weeks ago, and he's walking back.'

'What's Never Never Never Land?'

'Never ask. Never go there. Never *land* there if you do.'

He took a thick gulp of tea: he must have had an asbestos throat.

'Do you really *know* that he's alive and walking back?'

'Yes, we do, actually, old son. You'll learn the form quick enough.'

'What do you do?'

'I call myself the odd-job man, but the Group Captain calls me an Intelligence Officer. But I can fly a bit as well: it's what we like here — sort of jack-of-all-trades. Someone must have picked you out for the job.'

'I can't believe that.'

'You'd be surprised.' Then he spun the chamber on me. 'Fancy a bevvy? They won't be back until tomorrow. There's a good bar at Blunham, just down the road, that I'd be pleased to introduce you to – and I understand you've got a flash little car at your disposal. If *I'd* been running your security checks, the first thing I would have asked was how a humble Sergeant could afford that.'

'It was inherited. From a good rear gunner who ran out of luck.'

'Ah. One of those. It's an ill wind, and all that.'

'Yes. I suppose so.' I think that that was the first time I really believed that Pete the Pink Pole was dead, and wasn't about to turn up from another irregular couple of days' leave in London, with a new bird on his arm.

I didn't tell him that I already knew the bar at Blunham: it was where I had first met Albie Grost. When he got drunk he recited reams of beautiful poetry, and the whole bar fell silent to listen to him. That's why I kept on leaning on him, and that's how I ended up teaching him how to palm Morse code when your fingers stopped working. What goes around, comes around.

There was still no sign of my missing officer a few days later. I badgered Cliff, but eventually he pulled rank and told me to bog off for pay parade. Everything comes to him who waits, he told me. Then, 'What's the hurry, old son?'

'This doesn't feel like fighting a war.'

'I told you before: *don't knock it*. The old man will call for you when he's ready.'

'Which old man?'

'The one with the scythe and the long grey beard.'

I asked Frohlich if I could fly with his crew, using the excuse of checking Albie out after I retrained him.

'No.' Just like that.

'No. Just like that? Why?'

'We like you, Charlie. You fixed up Albie just right.'

'Thanks.'

'But your trips have run out. Maybe your luck has. We think that you should stay on the ground until you've earned more karma. Maybe you used up all you had, going to Germany last month. Leave it out.'

'What's karma?'

'It's like directed luck; only you have to earn it, it doesn't come free.'

'How do you earn it?'

'By being good.'

'I *am* being good.'

'Be good for a bit longer. Then we'll take you.'

'Is that Jewish. That karma?'

'No, it's universal. It's Buddhist.'

'But you're not a Buddhist.'

'How do *you* know? Perhaps everyone is Buddhist.'

'They can't be. We're fighting a world war: several of them. Buddhists don't kill people.'

We were in the recreation room at Hazells Hall, which was our HQ building: it had a nice little bar. Frohlich was thrashing me at billiards. The rest of his crew were sprawled in and

over comfortable old leather armchairs with books and magazines. He extended his left arm, and moved it around to
include them all.

'Neither do we,' he said.

His navigator looked up from his book and smiled at me.
He'd heard it all before.

The next pilot I asked was a small guy, like me. A dark Taffy
named Tippett. He said, 'Good idea. Tomorrow night if the
light's all right?'

'Thanks, sir.' He was an officer type, and I was doing the
asking, after all. 'This will really help me.'

'And then you'll be more help to us. That's the idea.'

I thought that I could put up with him for six hours.
Just.

Frohlich's crew touched me by coming to see me off. Then
Frohlich said, 'This is a mistake, Charlie.' In that preacher's
tone I'd come to recognize.

'That's what my dad always said I was.'

In the timber-clad parachute shed disguised as a barn, they put
us crew through the same routine as the two Joes with the
one-way tickets. We had to prove that our clothes bore no
labels, and that our pockets were empty of anything except
escape gear. I was left with just my old fibre ID tags, and my
pay-book, to say who I was. Then we had to wait for the Joes,
because the packers had already loaded stores containers into
the aircraft. The two Joes, a scared-looking man and a woman,

were taken behind canvas screens for the business. I was surprised to hear them both being offered the option of walking away from it. I heard the man say, 'No. It's fine,' too loudly. I didn't hear the woman.

The telephone rang in the shed whilst they were being checked, and I was called over. It was Goldie, the CO.

'Sorry to butt in, Bassett, but I thought you'd want to know your papers have come through. We'll get them ticked up, and you'll be an officer by the time you get back. Party tomorrow night. Congrats.'

'Thank you, sir. I'll have to spend all that money you gave me.'

'. . . and the rest of it. Good luck tonight.'

I said Thank you, and put the receiver down. I suddenly tasted bile in my mouth: that was the fear. On my last squadron no one would have dreamed of wishing you *good luck*, for fear of bringing down the other thing on you.

We trudged to a bloody old Stirling which was more patches than aeroplane. The pilot was cheerful: I'd picked a cretin for my first operational sortie from Tempsford. The pretty WAAF had given me a peck on the cheek and had said *adieu*: no one had done that to me before, either. I trooped out to the heap with the two Joes and the crew, which included a wisecracking Dispatcher. *Nerves.* I was last to board and turned instinctively to dog the door shut behind me. Their rear gunner, who hadn't said a word to me so far, nodded, and double-checked the door. I liked that: always go to war with a cautious man alongside you, not a fucking hero. The Joes were strapped into side-by-side seats against the fuselage skin. I had to sit on the floor of the blanked-off bomb-bay with the Dispatcher, our backs to a bulkhead.

The pilot started and ran up the four Hercules engines one after the other. The last one fired up rough. He shut them down, and then tried again. This time they ran perfectly. I could sense that the Dispatcher was tense. He leaned towards me and shouted, 'It's the mag for the starboard outer. Always was a shit. No worries.' Aussie.

I think I must have nodded. I felt the aircraft begin to move – away from its hard-standing, and around the peri-track. This part of the trip had always seemed the longest to me: I was all right once I was in the air. Through the small square window to my right I got occasional flashes of the full moon over the trees towards Tempsford village. At the end of the huge strip the pilot ran the engines up again, against the brakes, and then there was the sensation of launch: the jerk and the slow thrust forward against the bumps, and the grumbles of the Stirling, as it prepared to throw itself at the sky.

The Aussie leaned forward, and pushed my loose radio connection into a small jack on the bulkhead behind me. I could suddenly hear the pilot's mumbled monologue above the howl of the motors. The sense of movement ceased, and was followed by the staggered thumps of the main under-carriage wheels into their spaces under the inner engines. At that moment I think that I heard two things separately but together: one of the engines screaming faster and louder than the others, and also the pilot's unhurried voice.

'Pilot to crew, take . . .'

Then there was a huge concussion, and my world became

yellow and red – I saw the woman Joe, her head on fire. Finally it was black. All over.

For the time being.

Two

If I had dreams, I didn't remember them. There was a tune running through my mind, somewhere just below the pain threshold. That first time it was 'Tiger Rag' played by Bunny Berigan. *Mind that tiger . . .* it told me, over and over again. It reminded me of a Hindu proverb: *Do not curse your god for creating the tiger; bless him for not giving it wings.* The music is there every morning now, and although the tunes are different, they linger all day.

My new world was full of shining dazzling hospital whites, which made my eyes water. That was my excuse, anyway. A man's voice, slow and with that Bedfordshire twang, asked, 'Can you hear me, son?'

When I didn't reply he said, 'You've had a bit of an accident. You were in an air crash.'

I shut my eyes. My brain issued orders to move my tongue and my lips, trying to make, 'How long . . .?' but my voice dried up. My lips felt dry and brittle, and parts of my mouth seemed stuck together, and not to work too well. I had a raging thirst.

'Days. You've been ill; but they tell me you're through the worst. You breathed in flames.'

'Must give up smoking.'

'That's the ticket. Hang on half a mo, I'm going to get the nurse.'

I tried to tell him, 'I'm not going anywhere,' but my voice croaked out to nothing halfway through.

I must have drifted off again. When I reopened my eyes they still weren't too useful. There was a nurse in whites fussing about me. She smelled of soap, so at least one of my senses was functioning, but I couldn't focus on her. I didn't know if she was plain or a looker. I was pleased to realize that I could still wonder about that when my face, mouth and shoulders hurt so bloody much. I could see the Bedfordshire accent alongside her in outline, and I could see his khaki clothes. Bloody brown job.

He told me later that he was a veteran of the last bash – more than thirty when he was demobbed in 1919. He had presented himself at the hospital in his old Yeomanry uniform during the Battle of Britain, and installed himself as a part-time nursing attendant, despite various medical objections. He just adopted individual fallen heroes, and nursed them through to their discharge – one way or another, if you get my drift. When my eyes started to come back a few days later I saw his stripes: a Sergeant like me. So that was all right then. Once, when the pain of my face overcame me, and I couldn't touch it for fear of damaging the scorched skin, I cried. I couldn't help it. He sat

and held my hands. After a couple of days one of my periods
of sensibility coincided with the bedside inspection of Herr
Doktor: I didn't know her name at that stage, but learned
later that her name was Hildegard. She spoke with a husky,
strained European accent, like Marlene Dietrich. She smiled
a tired smile, sat on a chair beside the bed, and said that my
face was all right and that only my shoulders were bad. She
said that even they should heal quickly, but that they would
always be ugly and scarred and twisted. She didn't hold back.
In later life, she told me, they might give me a spot of
trouble.

'Face?'

'Not so bad. People might think that you were an inefficient
schoolboy boxer, but the skin still looks like skin. You only
had a light grilling. I was more worried about your eyes, that
was once you had started breathing properly again. You might
have to watch your chest for a few years.'

I tried to smile without cracking the crust the skin around
my mouth had grown into.

'I'd rather watch yours.'

The light in her eyes went out: I knew immediately that I'd
said the wrong thing. She said flatly, 'I'm fifty.' As if that meant
anything.

'Where are you from?'

'Germany. A big town: you won't have heard of it.'

'What is it called?'

'Krefeld. Why? Do you know it?'

'No.'

At least I was feeling well enough to start lying again. I had been to Krefeld three or four times and left it burning. Left some pals there too.

The Sergeant's name was Bernard. He told me afterwards, 'Some of the men won't let her near them because she's German.'

'Idiots. If the bus-driver has a heart attack, you don't ask the man who grabs the wheel if he has a driving licence.'

'That's quite clever, son.'

'Someone told me. I can't remember who. Am I going to get out for Christmas?'

He shook his head.

'Definitely not, but there'll be some sort of a party for the walking wounded, and some of the nurses are goers. You want a beer?'

'Yes. How?'

'You got a crate of it under your bed. Some Yank rolled in with it for you a couple of days after you arrived. That, and a big box of flat bog paper: the hospital staff nicked that, I'm afraid. We've been short for months.'

'Are you on the squares of newsprint like the rest of us?'

'Aye.'

'Does someone always nick the *Jane* cartoons off them?'

'Aye. How did you know?'

'It must be some sort of crime epidemic.'

'You're talking crap again, Charlie, instead of shitting it. You must be ready for your snooze.'

My father got time off and came south, and was in the room with me during the worst times, a week after the crash . . .

turns out that he and Bernard were in adjacent trenches in 1916, and they got on famously after they found that out, swapping trench-foot stories. The RAF sent me a new uniform with a decent walking-out jacket, peaked cap and the proper badges for a newly promoted officer. Perhaps they'd awarded me the accident in revenge for my having lived long enough to become an officer.

The Christmas party was a light-hearted, gay affair in an indoor squash court. There was dancing to a wind-up gramophone, and a bar. Most of the booze was home-made. My father came down again for it, and when he and Bernard sat in straight chairs out in front and sang 'The Charlie Chaplin Song', instead of laughing, everybody started to cry. I disgraced myself by fainting while I was dancing the Beguine with a spotty Irish redhead. Bernard told me that it had looked quite comical, because she had continued dancing with me well after I was out of it: flinging me about like a corpse. Then she realized that I might be, screamed and dropped me.

Bernard told me that when I awoke, which was days later, sometime near January. Dad had gone home earlier, a bit shaken up. As soon as I opened my eyes Bernard slipped out to telephone him. He must have tipped Dr Hildegard off, because as he left she swept in. She made me drink a half pint of water before allowing me to sit up, or speak. When I looked down I could see that I was skin and bone; my pyjama jacket hung off me. I asked her, 'What happened to me?'

'If I was a foul-mouthed Englishman I should say *Buggered if I know!*'

'But you're not. You're my doctor; for which I am grateful.'

'I am glad we have cleared that up. But it doesn't alter the case: I don't know what happened to you. You passed out, and slipped into a coma. We tried for the best part of a day to bring you round.'

'No good?'

'No good. You just lay there with a nasty grin. Several eminent doctors from other hospitals have visited you. They didn't know what to do either, so I feel better about it. Now that you're back I shall consider you one of my successes.'

'What do you think happened to me? Your best professional judgement.'

'I think that you banged your head in the accident, and that we didn't notice. Bad internal head injuries are often revealed by severe swelling of the head: haematomas.'

'Yes?'

'By the time you were brought in here your head was badly swollen anyway – by the heat and your burns. I think that that concealed an impact injury – I missed it.'

'Will it happen again?'

She shrugged.

'I don't know. I don't think so, but there is a dying Australian next door who has a phrase for it.'

'What's that?'

'*No guarantees.*'

'Situation normal,' I told her. Then, 'I think I'll get up.'

She smiled. It took years off her, but she shook her head, 'Definitely not. This time we go slowly. I asked Bernard to bring you a perambulator. He will push you about.'

'But he's as old as my father.'

'. . . and he doesn't go around crashing aeroplanes.'

Bernard walked in preceded by an ancient wooden wheelchair.

I said, 'Jawohl, Frau Doktor,' and earned a scowl from the woman who had kept me alive since December. Bad one, Charlie.

Bernard took me visiting the larger wards, although they depressed me. There were a lot of people with bits missing, and sometimes, when you looked behind their eyes, you realized that there were bits missing there as well. The only positive note was that a nurse sat with me through each night. The night nurses were young, and some of them pretty; and when I couldn't sleep flirted with me until I felt drowsy.

The spotty Irish redhead was one of them: she wasn't spotty any longer. She had long, wavy and lustrous red hair, and when I told her that I was in love with her she laughed it off. Late one night she leaned back in the uncomfortable upright chair they used to keep my nurses awake in the wee small ones, kicked off her shoes, and rested her feet on the edge of my bed. I could have touched them, but I think that that would have spoiled it. The small radio the girls had smuggled into my room was burbling away to a dance station in the background. It was the Glenn Miller Band and 'String of Pearls'. I asked her, 'When will they move me out of here, and into the general ward?'

'I'm not sure they will: you're too unusual.'

Then I noticed the tears running down her cheeks. My heart gave a huge scared lurch.

'Don't be sad. I don't mind.'

'What?'

'That I'm going to die.'

'Don't be soppy. What are you talking about?'

'Then why are you crying?'

She wiped her cheeks with a slightly used handkerchief. 'I always cry when I hear "String of Pearls", stupid. I remember him when he was alive.'

'Who?'

'Glenn Miller, of course.'

'Is he dead?'

'Yes. His plane went down in the Channel in December. Didn't you know?'

'No. It must have happened when I was hibernating . . . I'm *not* going to die then?'

' 'course not. Don't be daft. We'll discharge you in a week or so if you don't faint again.' She sniffed, and prodded my hip gently through the blankets with her stockinged foot. A reprieve, and what's more things were looking more promising.

'Does my face look good enough to kiss yet?'

'Getting there, Charlie Bassett: I'll tell you when it is.'

The next night she brought me a newspaper she had saved; its front page announced the band leader's loss in big black words, around a large publicity photograph of him wearing the Major's cap I had last seen him with. You may not believe this, but the face I recognized was that of a Major I'd once seen going into the American Red Cross Officers' Club in Bedford with a girl I'd met. Then again, snoozing in the seat behind me, a fellow passenger in a light aircraft, in which he'd offered me a lift to Manchester. I had flown a trip with Glenn Miller, and hadn't known it: that must have amused him. I told her, and she went all snotty.

'You don't have to shoot a line with me, Charlie Bassett; *everyone* has a Glenn Miller story these days.'

Privately I agreed with her, and decided to leave it at that. Anyway, that was the night she gave in to my jokes, slipped the small bolt on the door, and into my bed. She had long milky white legs, and smelled of Lifebuoy. It had been a long time, and I wasn't too handy, but she didn't seem to mind. When I hugged her into my sore shoulder after the event I told her, 'I don't even know your first name.'

'Give me one.'

'Again? Let me get my breath back, love.'

'Don't be silly; give me a *name*. Make one up.'

'Gloria.'

'Like Gloria Swanson. I like that; I'll keep it forever for whenever I'm going to be bad. *Now*; give me one.'

'Seriously?'

'Seriously.'

'Even if it kills me?'

'I'm a nurse. You're in good hands.'

*

Bernard went a bit odd at the end of January. In '45 we were a nation of people going a bit odd. It must have been something to do with the war. He'd been in a secret specialized Home Guard mob before and told nobody about it. Now he had to go back to parades, and carrying his rifle openly, although still wearing his 1914–18 uniform. They were bloody awful days. I read a hundred books, and didn't remember a word of them.

David Clifford began visiting me about then. The first thing he said was, 'There appears to be a soldier from the Great War sitting outside your door: rifle, bayonet, puttees, gas mask round his neck; the bloody lot. Bloody strange. He asked me for a pass before he'd let me in.'

'Got one?'

'As a matter of fact I have. Signed by your CO.'

'I didn't think he knew I was here.'

'Not *that* one. Your German doctor, Doctor Hildegard somebody.'

'Where the bloody hell have you been? I've been here for ages, and no sod from the squadrons has been anywhere near me.' I tailed off sort of lamely, '. . . it's a poor bloody show. That's what I think.'

Cliff looked smart; well, as smart as he could. He had his sheepskin-lined flying jacket over his uniform. I felt disadvantaged: I was sitting in a cane chair they had brought me, but was still in pyjamas and a dressing gown. They had hidden my walking-out clothes in case I did.

'You haven't been listening, have you? Visiting, except next of kin, was verboten. Frau Doktor's orders: kaput.'

'That means *finished*: it looks as if it's just started again, if you're here.'

'That's the style, old boy. The bang on your head didn't do permanent damage then?'

'You know about that too, do you?'

'Yes, the Colonel told me when he briefed me to come down for this little session.'

'Colonel?'

'My boss.'

'I thought you were in the RAF.'

'See? You picked it up: I knew you were feeling better as soon as I walked in the room. Can I sit down?'

He pulled the hard upright chair towards him: it didn't look as if I had much say in the matter.

Bernard put his head round the door. He was wearing his helmet. He ignored Cliff but asked me, 'Everything OK, sir?'

'Fine Bernard, but don't call me *sir*: we were both still sergeants when I arrived.'

'You won't overdo it, sir?'

'No, Bernard.' I sighed. 'I'm fine. I'll call you if he gets difficult. A couple of cups of char wouldn't come amiss.'

'I'll get one of the young ladies to see to it, sir.'

Cliff asked, 'What *would* he do, if I got difficult?'

'Bayonet you, I think.'

'You're serious, aren't you? Why would he do that?'

'We haven't established that. He adopted me when I arrived here: it's something we haven't discussed. *Have we, Bernard?*' I directed the last three words at the open door. Beyond it Bernard barked, 'No need, sir.'

Cliff said, 'I suppose that closing the door is out of the question?'

Bernard's next bark beat me to it.

'It is.'

I told him, '*OK, that's enough, Bernard.*' Then I told Cliff, 'But he's right; the door stays open.'

Bernard brought the tea in. He gave Cliff the one with tea slopped into the saucer.

Cliff said, 'He wasn't here when you came in.'

'How do you know?'

'Because *I* was.'

'How come?'

'I travelled in the meat wagon with you. In case you had any famous last words; that sort of thing.'

'Was that important?'

'Yes: there was no one else, you see.' He looked away, regret on his face, but not grief. For some reason that struck me as very professional.

'Thank you.'

'Think nothing of it. You were in a bit of a state. It took us about half an hour to find you. The old cow had veered hard to the west as she went in . . .'

'That was because the starboard outer went mad, and pushed her that way. I was in a Lanc that did that once: my pilot fought her all the way back from Germany.'

'That's what I came today to find out.'

'Don't you *know* what happened?'

'You're not listening again, Charlie. I told you: no one else made it.'

A picture came into my mind.

'I saw the female Joe. Her head was on fire.'

'Don't tell me any of that, Charlie. I don't need to know.'

'Squeamish?'

'No. It's just a matter of taste. Don't forget that the silly sods made you an officer.'

There was one of those gaps in the conversation until I asked him, 'You said I looked in a bit of a state?'

'We found you sitting up against a grave stone in Tempsford graveyard. Initially I thought that that was quite appropriate. You'd been blown about twenty yards into it by the last explosion. Your face was puffed up, and black. You had strips of curled skin hanging from your shoulders . . .'

From outside the door Bernard coughed once.

I said, '*It's OK, Bernard.* I want to hear this.'

Cliff said, 'I can't get over the way your face has healed. You don't look burned too much.'

'Frau Doktor says that I was lucky. My shoulders are worse. When I move you can see exactly the way the muscles expand and contract: I can make them dance to Dorsey Brothers tunes. Want me to show you?'

'No thanks, old boy. Sounds ghastly; sorry.'

'She tells me that the greatest effect on my face will be to the hair follicles: something goes wrong with them when they're burned up. I won't ever have a moustache or beard: probably won't have to shave again.'

'Handy.'

'Yes. I thought so. Why did you call your Boss *the Colonel*?'

'Sometimes I think you radio ops can't take anything in

unless it's coming through a pair of headphones. I told you before that the people down there are more flexible than your usual service wallah. My boss is a Colonel because the brown jobs run the security. They run the security because they run the operations out there that we deliver to. We're only delivery boys: don't forget that.'

'Seems odd.'

'I'll tell you something odder: they want you back for something when you're ready. They must be even stupider than we are.'

'Your Army takes itself too bloody seriously. Can Frohlich visit me?'

'No. He's gone.'

'Where?'

Cliff shrugged. I pushed him.

'What happened to them?'

'You don't need to know,' he told me. And that was that. Funnily enough I felt better after that. I'd always thought that Frohlich would visit, and I was miffed that his people had forgotten me so quickly. I wondered if they were lying in a prison camp, hospitals or deep in Mother Earth. I turned away from it: Cliff would never tell me.

'That Yank,' Bernard told me a day later. 'He's back, sir.'

'Then let him in.'

I felt better. They let me wear my RAF jacket over my pyjamas: it made me feel as if I was still part of something.

'He hasn't got a pass.'

'Sell him one.'

Tommo slouched in a couple of minutes later, and crash-landed on the upright chair.

He said, 'Your guard made me pay him for the privilege of visiting. I thought that *I* was supposed to be the gangster back here. Not for long, though.'

'Thank you for coming to see me, Dave, and what does *that* mean?'

He tossed a carton of Luckies and a package of pipe tobacco on the bed, and told me, 'Shipping me home. I been here since 1943, and now we're winning they're shipping me home.'

'What did you do?'

'Nothing: they say I've done my bit. Uncle Sam says, *Thanks; but you can go home now.*'

'That's great.'

'No it ain't. What about my business?'

'Being a gangster?'

'Don't be funny. I've a good number here. Back at Fort Nowhere I'll be up to my arse in non-com officers who spend their time in the john reading the rule book. Then they'll pull up their pants, pull the chain, and throw the goddam thing at me.'

'They'll wipe their arses first,' I told him.

'What with? I just arranged the whole year's sanitation paper allocation shipped over here to fill your needs.'

'I'll phone Winston, and tell him there was a mistake. Get him to send some back again.'

'Truly?'

'He wouldn't know what it is. He has aides-de-camp to wipe for him.'

'Yeah, we got those in the US too.'

This took about thirty seconds it seemed, and then we were both grinning. I could grin now without my face cracking in half. Dave said, 'You're looking almost human. Time you got a nice English girl.'

'I had one, thanks, Tommo. Are you serious about leaving?'

He sighed as if he meant it, and looked at his funny peaked olive cap, as he twisted it in his hands.

'Yeah. It's a shit; so I came to ask a favour. There were some things I couldn't arrange to sell off or move: they don't give you all that much notice – they're in two kitbags outside with your mastiff. Will you stash them for me until I come back for them?'

'Is that likely?'

'Christ, yes: I'll find someone's palm to cross with silver once I'm back over there; I'll try for a posting in Germany – that's where the money will be when it's all over.'

'It's not knocked-off gear that I'll go to prison for if I'm caught with it?'

'Christ, no. I wouldn't do that to you. Not without telling you. We're buddies, ain't we?'

'We're *buddies*,' I confirmed. It made me feel very old. 'Of course I'll keep it for you. How long have you got?'

'A few days. Then they're flying me out to Ireland – Nutts Corner or the Lodge – then a big boat home from Belfast Loch.'

'I always thought that an appropriate name for an airfield –
Nutts Corner. Can you make a few telephone calls for me
before you go? See if you can find out where Grace is; I can't
ask the people here – they don't know her.'

Tommo Thomsett knew Grace – a girl I knew. She'd
known me, and a lot of other men that I knew, if you get my
drift. She was an ATA pilot I'd last seen about six weeks
before my accident. At that time she was pregnant and
deciding what to do about it. I'd asked her to marry me a few
times: at that time it was a compulsion I had every time a pair
of knickers hit the deck. The point is that Grace was the only
one to have said *Yes* so far; albeit in a vague sort of way.

I'd asked her, '*Marry me?*'

She had said something like, '*OK. Yes. Once the war is over.*'

'*OK.*'

'. . . *if you can find me.*'

That was the nearest I got.

The American said, 'Amazing! You still hankering after
her?'

'Yes; stupid, isn't it? I'm going to miss you too, Tommo.'
I meant it.

'Not for long you won't.' I could take that two ways,
couldn't I?

He called me back a few days later to say that Grace was
AWOL: nobody knew where she was. He'd attracted some
heat, he said, even asking the questions. And her father would
like to see me when I got out. That was her stepfather. He

34

had as much reason to worry as the rest of us. Not many people knew that.

Early February drifted in. Bernard was putting bets on for me with a runner he knew at his local. I always lost, but I was training for after the war: I was going to be a racing journalist. I didn't know much about the horses but I liked the idea, and I'd seen Prince Monolulu on the cinema newsreels.

A few days before Frau Doktor signed my movement order Bernard strolled in unannounced, took the upright chair to its limit with his mass, and told me, 'Your dad's looking in tomorrow, sir. Him and your uncle.'

'Good. I was wondering how Dad was.'

'Most people write letters: you could try that.'

'I'm going to get paid for what I write.'

'You're a mercenary little bugger, sir, and useless with the gee-gees. Anyway, he's just popping in to say *goodby-ee* for the present. Him and your uncle.'

'Why? Where are they off to?'

'France. Then Germany most like; I almost envy them.'

'Don't be daft, they're old men.'

There was a bit of a hiatus then: because they would have been round about the same age as Bernard. He asked me, 'They were in the trenches, weren't they? During the last lot?'

'You know Dad was. You swapped trenchie stories with him over Christmas, didn't you?'

'So I did. What did he do over there?'

35

'Pioneer. They both were. Dug holes for other people most of the time. They probably dug yours.'

'There you are then. His Country needs him again, and all that; only as a civvie on better wages. Loads of the old fellahs are doing it. Loads of spondulicks around, apparently. The front is moving so fast they need people who can dig trenches quickly. Your old man spotted his chance.'

'Silly sod! What if he cops it?'

'I don't think that he cares much, sir. Like father, like son. Why *is* that?'

'He evacuated my mum and my sister with him to Scotland when our house was doodlebugged last year. My uncle found them a flat. Dad found a job. There was something the matter with the stove in the flat. He got home from night shift one morning to find them dead in their beds. It changed him. Changed us both.'

'Is that what you fell out over, sir?'

'Yeah, but only for a couple of weeks. No point staying mad at the only one you've got left.'

'But he still feels it, I'll bet. Him and his brother both. So they've gone to take it out on the Jerry, by digging trenches all over his allotments.'

I wanted to leave hospital in my uniform. Frau Doktor was there to say goodbye. She had to lean down to kiss me, and I was surprised when she did. When Gloria did the same I felt her hot little tongue slide briefly into my mouth, like a wren in a hedgerow.

She asked, 'Will you come back and show us how you are?'

'Of course.'

'I know you'll never write.'

'How?'

'You haven't written to anyone from here, have you? You'll not come back either.'

'Give me another kiss.'

She obliged. She was an obliging sort of girl.

'Yes I will,' I told her. 'I'll come back for more of those.'

It was a lie, but her smile was half worth it. Cliff thumped my half-filled old leather case and Tommo's two heavy kitbags into the space behind the front seats of the Singer.

'Strewth. What have you got in these?'

'Don't know. I'm minding them for a friend.'

I drove and crashed the gears all the way to Bedford, until I got the hang of it again. Cliff rested his arm over the low door and watched the grey-green countryside sliding past, pretending not to notice. I told him, 'We should have put the hood up, it's bound to rain before we get back,' and of course it bloody did.

Three

'. . . I don't need it, sir. All I need is a week for what I've got to do.' Goldie had been asking me about the two weeks' crash leave I was entitled to.

Then he said, 'Good-oh,' and '. . . Famous,' and noticed me looking at a patch of sticky tape covering a piece of skull where a hank of his famous fair hair was missing. He patted it gingerly. 'Left a bit in Holland. Bloody Germans, I think. You'd think they'd give up.'

'I keep on wishing they would, sir. They've *lost*. Where shall I report when I get back?'

'Motor pool. If you need a car choose yourself a good one. One of those big Humber staff cars should do the trick.'

'Motor pool, sir? What about the radio workshop?'

'Christ no, old man. Old Stan was back in time for Christmas, like Santa Claus – walked over the front line in Belgium somewhere. You're an officer now, and one squadron radio officer is more than enough. We found him a new Sergeant: we had a bit of a run on Sergeant W/Ops last year, didn't we?' I understood that I wasn't supposed to reply; I had been one of them, after all. '. . . so we're lending you to Major England. Liaison. He's probably over the other side right now – he has a batman he calls Raffles. You'll find them good value: altogether a cushy number to let you get your eye back in.'

'What will I be doing with Major England, sir?'

'Buggered if I know, the brown jobs never tell us anything, but it's something David Clifford has cooked up. He said you were a handy driver. Know anything about cars?'

'Very little, sir.'

'Piece of cake. Earth, fire, air and water: they run on the same principles as medieval magic. You'll soon get the hang of it. I was a medievalist at Cambridge; that seems like half a lifetime ago now . . . Anyway, enjoy your seven days, and enjoy your little trip.'

'Sir?'

'Your little trip. We're throwing you back up into the wide blue yonder for an hour to see if you can still cope. You know the idea: if you fall off a horse get back into the saddle as quick as you can. Some can't, you know; not after a serious crack-up.'

I couldn't resist it.

'I wonder why?'

I deliberately left off the *sir*, and Goldie just as deliberately ignored it. He had my open file on his desk. He closed it with a snap, gave me the big eye and muttered, 'Dismissed.'

That's what the umpire used to say to me with such relish at school cricket matches. Bastards.

*

Would you believe it? It was another fucking Stirling. And Cliff was going to fly the bloody thing. We walked out to it with Strainer, who was a buckshee Flight Engineer, and a nineteen-feet-tall Navigator. Cliff referred to him as 'Big Job': he filled a comfortable space below the Skipper. Strainer looked, frankly, as if he wasn't all there. He reminded me of some of the types in the big ward. I shook hands with them both, remembering briefly how courteously Sir Thomas More had greeted his executioners.

Cliff asked me, 'Windy?'

'A bit, sir, I think. I usually am until we get going.'

'That's all right then.'

'Yes. What's the form?'

'Air test. Then some other poor sod gets to fly it tonight.'

It was painted overall black, and had no squadron codes or other numbers. The only other colour was provided by the red, white and blues, and they still looked too much like gunnery targets.

'Anything else I should know, sir?'

'The MO wants us to wind it up to five thou or so, and then put you on oxygen to see if there's any permanent damage to your lungs. Don't worry: if they collapse or blow up on you he's told us what to do.'

'Which is?'

'Pull your parachute ripcord and sling you out apparently: get you back on terra firma before us.'

My feet were on the rungs of the ladder by now. No way back. The two sergeants had preceded me into the kite, and

Cliff pushed me up the steps in front of him, eager to get going, before he missed too many pints.

Strainer sounded bored as they pre-flighted the Stirling, and yawned between calling back the checks. Cliff paused and said, quite casually, 'Wake yourself up, cunt, when you're flying with me. Otherwise Charlie here will take you back, and drown you in the Elsan. He's murdered two types already; a third won't make any difference to him now.'

He sounded very believable. I wondered how much he knew: I'd witnessed one murder on my old station, and knew of two others. Even helped dispose of a couple of the bodies. It didn't seem like a big deal when you set it alongside the number of people we'd killed with our bombs every night. The problem was that I couldn't recall ever mentioning it to Cliff.

As usual I found I didn't mind the take-off so much as long as I was up at the front looking around. It was a clear, sharp day, and some of the trees and hedgerows were showing off a faint blush of early green. The tall buildings, like the manor and the church, threw exact shadows on the grass. The Stirling lifted off slower than the Lancs I had been used to, and Cliff seemed to hold her on a lot longer than Grease, my old Canadian pilot, would have. Nevertheless he pulled her off smoothly, with none of that sideways yaw that radial-engined aircraft are notorious for. I noticed at once that there was something ominously competent about his flying. He flew in shirtsleeves, with the mask and mike dangling at his throat, holding it up with one hand when he wanted to speak. He addressed Strainer again.

'OK, cunt. Get lost. Go down to the dispatcher's berth and strap yourself in there.'

'Aye, Skip.' That was Strainer. He had an odd glaikit grin. Made him look not all there. After he'd left the flight deck Cliff called me forward to fill his seat. I asked, 'Why do you treat him like that? What's he done?'

'Nothing. Other ranks. Thickos. I bloody hate them.'

'Funny. I used to feel like that about officers. Did you hate me when I was still a Sergeant?'

'No. I knew you had it coming. Do you want to talk, Charlie?' But before I could answer he pulled up his mask, and called the Nav.

'Hey, Big Job . . . give me a course.'

'Where to, Skip?'

'Out around Cambridge somewhere; that'll do.'

'Roger, Skip. Fly 0030 for now. I'll give you a correction.'

'0030,' Cliff said into the mask, and then let it drop. 'Why doesn't the silly bugger say *nearly north*, which is what he means?' he asked me.

'It's the way we train them. What do you want to talk about?'

'The two guys the RAF thinks you killed. One at Bawne, and one in London somewhere. Did I get that right?'

'How did you know about that?'

'Does it matter?'

'I suppose not. I didn't bump them off, as it happens. That was Pete, our rear gunner: you probably know all about him. He blew them away with a Colt .45 that an American friend had given me. You probably know all about him too. If Pete hadn't killed them they would have murdered him, and me. He did them in first.'

'Like self-defence before the event?'

'You could call it that.'

'A court martial won't. They'll hang him.'

'They'll have to find the bits first. He got blown to pieces over Holland by our own trigger-happy flak gunners. Now you know why I won't join the brown jobs.'

'So we executed him anyway, in a manner of speaking, and you inherited his radio and his car?'

'Someone had to.'

'The two dead men were policemen. Did you know that?'

'One was English and one was a Pole, like Pete. They weren't proper policemen. Did you know *that*?'

'Why would they have killed him?'

'He once told me something about the death of General Sikorsky: he was there. On the plane. It was some sort of political thing. Now that the war's as good as over, and governments-in-waiting are popping up all over the shop, I think that someone was cleaning their stables. Pete was just a piece of horse shit that might have been stepped in.'

'You really think that, Charlie?'

'What?'

'That the war's as good as over?'

'Don't you?'

'I think it's just beginning. Ask me again in 1950.'

Then he leaned forward and tapped the altimeter, which

had stuck stubbornly at 175 feet. The indicator hands spun up immediately to over six thou, and he said, 'On oxygen, Charlie; let's see how you do. Big deep breaths now.'

I noticed that he didn't, and had a quick moment of distrust and misgiving, before I thought *Oh hell*, and *Who cares?* and filled my lungs to capacity. Cliff pulled his mask up again, mumbling to me just before he did so, 'OK. Let's put you under some pressure.'

Then he spoke into the mask for everyone's benefit, and said, 'Hold tight chaps. Here we go,' and dropped the bugger's nose until we were pointed at the ground.

What I learned that day was that Stirlings fall very fast. We still had a thou on its unreliable clock by the time he pulled her out of it, but he must have had 350 knots on the speedo at some time in that dive, and Stirlings weren't designed for that. Neither was I. The old kite creaked and trembled. By the time we were flying straight and level again I was breathing deep breaths. Cliff said, 'Off ox, Charlie,' and, 'You'll do. Your lungs didn't burst.'

'No thanks to you.'

'That's no way to thank the officer who's just saved you from an internal inquiry and a court martial, Charlie boy, is it? Anyway: the sun's over the yardarm – fancy a bevy?'

We walked back from dispersal to the sheds. I was remembering I had seen the ground coming up to meet me at more than 300 knots, and on it was the big accommodation hut at Bawne where Pete had shot one of the policemen who'd come after him. It was from Bawne airfield that I had paid numerous nocturnal visits to the Thousand Year Reich.

How could Cliff have known exactly where we were in that big sky? How could he have known that? I told them a long and complicated joke about Don Bradman, and was pleased to raise the dutiful laugh. Bravo Charlie.

As we dumped our parachutes and flying clothes he asked me, 'What do you want to be when you grow up?'

'I fancy being a journalist on a sports paper, living some-where where the sun never sets. My mum always had her heart set on one of the professions – doctor, teacher, civil servant. That would never work out though.'

'You'd make a good civil servant.'

I said, 'Fuck off, Cliff.' It wasn't to be the last time.

Whenever I think about Cambridgeshire or Bedfordshire I think of rain: oceans of the sodding stuff. In Cambridge they have more names for rain than Eskimos have for snow. Which is why it is so odd to remember that during all the visits that I made to Crifton House – during the war, and since – the rain held off. Crifton is a honey-gold Palladian mansion bigger than the Admiralty Building. It straddles the county boundaries like your childhood: a place in your memory where the sun always shines.

It was also where Grace lived. The last time I had arrived there I had been a strung-out Sergeant on a borrowed motorbike, wearing a tatty collection of RAF uniform parts, and giving sweet f.a. about anything. Herr Death in Germany had been knocking on my door, and reorganizing my values. Now I came back as an officer with his own car, and money in the bank. Grace's mother also lived there, with a few

45

vintage retainers who dated to the turn of the century, I'd guess. She kept court, and suffered the occasional visit from her husband, Grace's stepfather, a bullets millionaire. The phrase we would have used about them in those days was 'They didn't get on.' The old man got on with making money though: if there is a surer recipe for success than making the bullets for the winning side in a major war, I don't know of it. Grace's mother got on with visiting heroes. It was a complicated household because her husband had rogered Grace before he got round to the old lady, and that was all of six months after he had killed Grace's original old man in a drunken duel in Germany. That was before we fell out with the Kraut, of course. You see what I mean. Complicated.

Barnes, the butler, was about seventy and divided his time equally between the house, the lady's maid, and listening to the radio traffic from our bomber raids on a cat's-whisker radio he'd built himself. He usually looked shagged out. He said, 'Good morning, Mr Charlie,' and, 'Nice car.'

'Thank you Barnsey. Has Miss Grace shown up yet?'

'No, sir. It's been some time now. We hoped that you would turn up sooner or later, to look for her.'

I let that lie.

'Is Mr or Mrs Baker at home?'

'Mrs Baker, sir. Sir Peter is at the *small* office at Blunham, and asked me to call him if you came by.'

'Would it be too difficult to stop the *sirring* Barnsey? It's making me twitchy.'

'I expect it goes with the new uniform, Mr Charlie.'

'Bugger off, Barnsey.'

'At once, sir. I'll take your case from the car. Mrs Barnes and the staff will be pleased to know that you're staying again.'

I hadn't exactly intended to. Damn him.

'What about Mrs Baker?'

'Not as pleased, Mr Charlie: she's grieving for her last American.'

I had met the man. He was another one with the 306th at Thurleigh, a USAAF station. I had known his navigator too, a slow-spoken, funny man named July Johnson. I liked them both a lot. I guess that I turned my head away, because Barnes added, 'Oh no, sir. Nothing like that. He's taken up with the postmistress in the village, that's all. Madam's nose is seriously out of joint.'

That was all right then; except that I had known the postmistress as well. So had Glenn Miller; I mentioned her earlier but you didn't notice. Barnes turned to get my bag and gave an unexpected little skip, like a child. I realized that he was drunk. As he walked away, he told me that Madam was in the Orangery.

I knew the way: ninety degrees banked turn to port from the square Jacobean hallway, and down a corridor a half-mile long. The last time I had met her in the huge, empty room, with its symphony of light, and floor-to-ceiling windows, she was pounding around it as if it was an indoor exercise track. She was still exercising, but this time on a great black high-stepping horse. They had spread sand on the floor to prevent it from slipping, which had been stupid because it made things worse. Black Beauty was making a fair old mess of the fine pine boards with its iron shoes. The noise was tremendous, and the beast skidded from time to time as I watched them. I wondered how long before they crashed out through one of the vast sheets of glass. When she tired she walked the steaming beast over to me. It shoved its face in mine and showed me its teeth. I showed it my teeth back, and pushed its head firmly away. The only animals I've ever been truly afraid of fly Messerschmitts.

Adelaide Baker held her hand down to shake mine. I said, 'Men are bastards.'

'We agree on something at last, Pilot Officer Bassett. How nice of you to come.'

'I'm sure you say that to all the men.'

'Only when I'm in the mood. I'm in the mood a lot less often than you'd think these days.'

'Like Grace. She said something like that.'

'You've come to find her for us?'

'Actually I'm looking for her, for myself – if you see what I mean . . .'

'Adelaide. You can call me Adelaide or Addy, now that you've been made an officer. How does that happen by the way? A solemn ceremony with an Archbishop and a sword, or something?'

'Not quite. Another officer signs a piece of paper that says *You are now an officer*. Your pay goes up, and your brain boils away into space. Just like that.'

'Grace told me that you said that all the time.'

'What?'

'*Just like that!*'

'I suppose that I do, really.'

'She liked it very much.'

'Yes. I liked her too.'

She was off the horse by now, which wandered away to steam in another part of the room. Adelaide Baker and I looked at each other, neither breaking the silence. The horse broke the silence with a long and pungent piss. Addy said, 'Balls. Who's going to clear that up?'

'Your Mr Barnes, I suppose. He seems to do almost everything else here.'

She scuffed at the scarred and sanded boards with the toe of an expensive riding boot.

'I guess you're right.'

I thought that she had been spending too much time with the Americans.

We walked around the outside of the house together. The coarse gravel path was as golden as the stone house, and crunched under our feet. Adelaide Baker flicked her riding crop lazily against her boot as we moved. I hoped that she wasn't about to start on me with it: I'd heard of women like that. I told her, 'It's odd. I don't feel much like an officer yet. It's as if I'm pretending, and will be found out at any minute.'

'Don't worry. You'll find that other people treat you as if you *are* one. Then it fixes itself. It was like that when I married Peter. People treat you differently when you're rich, too.'

Lunch was cold beef sandwiches. The beef was old. I was glad that I still had all of my teeth.

'Your American, Washow: he liked you for yourself. And he liked your body.'

'I know. They're not bad, are they?'

When Peter Baker breezed in later he was followed by Cliff.

He said, 'Don't get up,' to Adelaide, and bent to drop a kiss on her upturned cheek. You'd think they were Darby and Joan if you didn't know better. He asked me, 'She given you a drink yet, young Charles?', but before I could answer, bellowed, 'A bottle of whisky, please, and three tumblers,' over his shoulder. Barnes must have been lurking outside the door.

I asked Cliff, 'What are *you* doing here, Cliff?' then, before Cliff had time to reply stuck in, 'Nice to see you again Sir Peter,' for Baker.

They lined up on me like a half section of Kraut fighter planes; taking turns.

Cliff said, 'Sir Peter's place is just round the corner from the Blunham pub; I offered him a lift when I heard he wanted to come back to talk to you.'

Baker said, 'So you've come to find our Grace for us?'

I wished they wouldn't keep saying that. I didn't know where the hell she was. Anyway, if you're wondering where this is going, Adelaide withdrew, and left the men with a bottle of ten-year-old. You'd think that there wasn't a war on.

My old skipper once told me to always expect the unexpected. I should have listened to him. If I had I would not have been surprised when Cliff and Baker told me what they'd arranged for the next few months of my life. Nice. These people were like icebergs: ninety per cent was under the surface, waiting to rip you to pieces. I'm surprised it wasn't sealed with a special handshake. Maybe it was, because they didn't even bother to smile.

First of all Cliff said, 'You haven't got a proper job any more, Charlie, and you won't want to get back into a Lancaster, not this close to the end. Your Tempsford berth's been filled. They needed a living person in it.'

'I *am* one.'

'But not a Sergeant any more. Cheers.'

We echoed him, and swilled down some of the whisky. It was fiery and over proof.

'Anyway, everyone expected you to die. That's why no one came to see you. Too depressing.'

'Thanks.'

'You're welcome. Cheers.'

We did it again. Baker topped up our glasses, and I rounded mine off with water. Then Baker said, 'They do that in the distilleries, you know: top off their whisky with water. They wouldn't dream of swigging it down neat, English fashion.'

'How did you learn that, sir?'

'I think we can dispense with the *sir*, Charlie; you're almost one of the family now. I have a small island and its own distillery. It's why I chucked my lot in with Winston at the start. Couldn't bear the thought of Jerry getting his hands on it, you see.'

'I tried to get Mr Barnes to stop calling me *sir*. It didn't work.'

'It wouldn't. He's a bloody Red. He secretly hates you for selling out.'

I took in what he'd just said.

'Have I sold out?'

'Definitely.' Cliff eased himself back into the panto. 'Officer and a gentleman. I was just trying to explain.'

I took a deep breath, and told Cliff, 'Then try again. I didn't get it the first time round.'

'First of all there's Grace. Sir Peter's daughter, and she's had a good war. Probably get a medal for it, or something. A legend in her own lifetime.'

'Bedtime,' I corrected him. 'A legend in her own *bedtime*. If she gets a medal it will be a Distinguished *Service* Medal.'

'Unkind, Charlie,' Sir Peter said. 'Very unkind.'

'Loving Grace doesn't blind me to her eccentricities.'

He smiled when I used the word *eccentricities*.

'You *do* love her, then?'

'Of course I do. Why the fuck do you think I'm here?' Sir Peter winced, so I hurried on. 'And now she's got herself pregnant and buggered off; leaving everyone worried sick about her.'

Cliff said, 'Exactly. That brings us back to Sir Peter. Not only worried about his stepdaughter, but with enough clout to do something about it. We need his bullets, and his whisky is just about the only export currency the government has left. He has what others wish for: Winston's ear. Sir Peter and Lady Adelaide want Grace back, and Winston expects that a grateful nation will do its best. You have no idea how many folk think that you're just the man to find her.' He paused, but couldn't resist sticking on, 'Alternatively, I can order you to.'

'You'll have to, Cliff. It's a barmy idea.'

'Then I just have. Go across the water, bloody find her. Bloody bring her back; kid too, if she bloody has one.'

'Bloody stupid.'

'Bloody way of the bloody world.'

Sir Peter sounded a bit tired. He said, 'Shut up the pair of you. Pour another drink. Who's going to find her is not the question; that's decided. The *how* is the question.'

Just like that. I asked them why they thought I should do it. Sir Peter said, 'Grace loves you.'

'I'm not sure of that. No one could be, with Grace.'

'Adelaide says so . . . and you don't have the nerve to argue with *her*.'

'You're right there.'

'There you are then. Grace told you something like she'd marry you if you could find her. We know that. All you have to do is find her.'

'She said *after this lot is over*, meaning the war – and it isn't, yet.'

'In the West it will be in four months. Maybe sooner.'

That was Cliff sounding more sober than I felt.

'How can you know that?'

Sir Peter looked away, and out of one of the library windows. Then he looked back at Cliff and nodded, as if he had just given an order.

Cliff said, 'The war will be over in a couple of months,

Charlie. Hitler's dying. His doctor is slipping him a slow poison that will kill him in months.'

'Why is his doctor doing that?'

'His doctor wants the war to finish. Anyway he's one of ours.'

'Why is his doctor ours?'

'Because Martin Bormann has told him to be.'

'Why has Bormann done that?'

'Because Bormann is ours. We bought him. The war will be over in months, and it won't be anything to do with the military. The industrialists, the spies and the bloody doctors run the show now. Some Nazi bigwigs will get killed, some will do it themselves, and some will bloody swing for it. Brother Bormann will disappear with a big fat cheque in his pocket. Bloody way of the bloody world. We bought the end of the war a month ago, only Nazi Germany is a bit like a dinosaur: the brain is more or less dead, but the rest of its body doesn't know yet.'

I thought about that, and I believed them. There was a weary authority underlying the way they spoke.

'What if I said *no*?'

'If you chose to disobey orders you'd get a few weeks of jankers that you won't like, and then you'd be back on a squadron as a Sergeant again; blowing women and children to bits for the greater good. What's more, it would probably be in some sort of death or glory mob where there's a chance you'd get chopped before hostilities cease. Far safer to go to Europe and find Grace.'

'I thought you said the war was going to end at any time.'

'It will still have time to kill you, Charlie.'

'You see his point, old man, don't you?' That was Baker. 'Another snifter?'

Then I realized that they had told me Grace was already in Europe.

Bugger them. Bugger Europe. Bugger Grace.

I asked Cliff a couple of inconsequential questions.

'I thought you once told me that the war wasn't going to end so soon: that it was going to go on for years to come?'

Peter Baker cut in for him.

'Different war, Charlie. Look at it this way. The first part of the Second World War is nearly over. We'll still have to stop the Ivans if they get much closer.'

'For God's sake, doesn't anyone up there know when it's time to stop?'

'Apparently not. Neither do the top Russians. It's power, you see: the top dogs have never exercised so much of it before, and they're loving every minute of it.'

'You sound like Hitler.'

'That's why Hitler was so dangerous: he sounded just like us.'

'. . . and like Stalin.'

'Yes: and like Uncle Joe. Sad, isn't it? Have another?'

I was ready for one. The New World Order was beginning to sound too bloody much like the old one.

The other inconsequential question was about Grace. Why did they think that she was in Europe?

'I've spoken to her ATA people,' Cliff told me, and asked,

'You know that she couldn't make up her mind whether or not to have the kiddie?'

'She'd done it before, apparently,' I said, and fixed Sir Peter with my best Iron John stare. Sir P wouldn't meet my eye. 'So, yes: I knew.'

'She lay around here for a few days. Then she went to London for a break. Has some friends there; in all of the Services.'

'I would never have guessed.'

Cliff gave me the look: something was hurting him.

'Apparently she was driving a borrowed car down some street in West Ken when a building next to her was hit by an A4.'

'What's that?'

'A rocket bomb fired from Germany: big things that arrive and explode before you hear them coming. The first you know of it is waking up dead. The Ministry of All-Things-to-All-Men is telling the people that they are gas boiler explosions, or some such nonsense, but the *Daily Mirror* knows what they are.'

'I've heard of them: I just thought that they were called something else. We were supposed to smash them up at Peenemünde last year.'

'Grace was OK, but she was either brave then, or disoriented, because when she climbed out of the car she walked towards the bomb site.'

'Is this the bad bit?' You sense some things coming.

'I think so. It had been a primary school. There were bits of children everywhere. Someone saw her standing there with a child's arm in her hand. Just the arm.'

None of us spoke for what seemed an age. Peter Baker splashed the last of the whisky into our tumblers. His hand shook. Finally I said, 'Poor Grace.'

Baker finished the story.

'It gets thinner from then on. She met some American tank crew men, who were in London for a few days' leave after a bad patch in the Ardenne. She disappeared at the same time they returned to Belgium. She's not in London with anyone she knew. There's no evidence that she's living down a hole somewhere with the rubble rats, and no dead body so far remotely matching her description . . . although that doesn't necessarily mean anything. She hasn't contacted anyone in the ATA, and she hasn't turned up at an airfield.'

'Who told you this?' I asked him.

'A Sergeant Fabian. Metropolitan Police. He investigated it for us.'

'Is he reliable?'

'Very, we're told. Hunts spies, murderers, that sort of thing. Very good at it. He says that his instinct tells him she's not alive in London.'

'You trust him?'

'I trust *you*, Charlie. Enough to ask you to try to find her.'

I got up and walked over to one of the library windows. It looked out over a gently sculptured hill, lined by trees, which Crifton called the Long Ride. It was scarred where a B-17 had smacked it a year before.

I said, for no one in particular, 'I *hate* my life at the moment.'

And Grace's father said, 'Thank you, Charlie.'

Four

I met the man Goldie had referred to as Driver Raffles for the first time in my room at Tempsford the day I returned from Crifton. When I walked in on him I thought I was being burgled. But he was sharp: he spoke first.

'Mr Bassett, would it be, sir?'

That's the first time I noticed his joint services uniform, tank jacket and the Sten gun on a piece of rope around his neck. By *joint services* uniform I mean that he had a Navy battledress blouse, Army trousers, a small black beret without a badge and the high lace-up boots with canvas tops that the Germans wore in the desert. I noticed the Sten first.

'Yes. Who are you?'

'Private Finnigan, sir: Major England's man. I was taking the liberty of getting your things together, sir. We won't have a lot of time.'

'For what?'

'Stowing your spare gear at the Major's club, sir, getting you kitted out, and getting over to France.'

'*Just like that?*'

'Funny you should say that, sir. I saw a comedian just last week who used that as his new catchphrase.'

'What was he like?'

'Can't make my mind up, sir. He's either effing useless, or an effing genius: sometimes it's hard to tell.'

Private Finnigan was a small man, in the vertical – like me – but he had a prize fighter's shoulders and arms. His face was a bit bashed up, and topped by an unruly thatch of curly light brown hair. I thought I could place his accent within a few miles. I said, 'You're from somewhere south of London, say Morden or Sutton.'

'Not bad, sir; you've obviously an ear for it. I was brought up at Belmont, like in *The Merchant of Venice*. That's near Banstead, in Surrey.'

I said, 'I come from Surrey myself. You don't *sound* like a Finnigan to me.'

'And *you*, sir, if you forgive my saying so, ask too many bleeding questions.'

'Sorry, Private.'

Finnigan nodded, and carried on packing my gear. Everything I owned fitted into an RAF kitbag, and an old leather suitcase I'd inherited from Pete. Then there were the two US kitbags I was stashing for Tommo, the Yank. I pulled them from under the bed. Finnigan hefted one of them. He asked, 'What's in here, sir, *War and Peace*?'

'Would you believe me if I said I didn't know? I'm minding them for an American pal who has just been shipped back to the States, and has promised to get back to Germany before it's all over. He says that Germany is where all the action will be when the shooting stops.'

'He'd be some kind of businessman, then? This friend of yours.'

'What was that you said earlier about people asking too many bleeding questions, Private?'

'Just testing, sir,' he told me, and grinned.

'How are we travelling to your Major's club?'

'In your car, sir. Understand you have a little corker.'

Who had been talking?

'Mr Clifford is a bit of a bastard, isn't he?'

'Not many would disagree with that, sir.'

'The Squadron Leader led me to believe that you were already in France.'

'So we were, sir. Now we ain't.'

As we filled the small back seats of the car the Private looked up at the cloud base, licked his right forefinger and held it up. Then he turned to me and said, 'Shall us have the hood up, sir? It'll rain before we reach London.'

The little sod was right, too.

'Are you driving, or am I?'

'You, sir, if you don't mind. I'll keep an eye on your driving, if I may? The Major said to look you over.'

'Oh he *did*, did he?'

'Yes, sir. Definitely.'

After half an hour he said, 'OK, sir. That's enough. If you'd care to pull over I'll drive the rest.'

I'd managed thirty-five miles without grinding a gear: no problem.

'OK, am I?'

'Frankly, sir, you're effing useless, but nothing a bit o' practice can't cure.'

There endeth the First Lesson, and commenceth the Second. I studied him all the way to the big house in Highgate we were bound for. I hadn't realized the little Singer was a racing car. From time to time he whistled as he drove. Always the same tune. 'Lili Marleen'. Note perfect.

It was a huge old red-brick Victorian terraced house on Highgate Road, a wide, gently undulating road looking out into Highgate Woods. Through the trees I could see a late cricket match was under way, and hear Australian voices. A neatly painted sign on the door said, *Officers' Club*. There was a three-house gap in the terrace about a hundred yards further on. Finnigan told me, 'That's where the first bomb fell on London. Poor bugger was lost. I wonder if he got a medal for it?'

'We staying here?'

'Yes, sir. Don't bother to unpack much. We'll be moving on in the morning. There's a big garage round the back: I'll put your car up on blocks for when you come back, and stick the keys in the tail pipe, just in case you don't.'

'You're very thorough.'

'Smashing little car, sir. It would be a pity to waste it. It reminds me of a Clyno I had before the war. My missus sold it to some RAF bloke when she was short.'

I couldn't stay angry at him for long. Not when I agreed with him. It *was* a smashing little car.

The airy front room of the house was a bar. There was only one person in it: a tall, round-shouldered soldier with black-rimmed spectacles, a thin dark moustache and a bit of a stoop. He was wedged into a utility armchair, and looked about 190 years old. He was probably one of the 1900 vintage. A uniform jacket with an Intelligence Corps shoulder flash was gracing the back of an upright chair. He was wearing a Fair Isle sleeveless cardie over his uniform shirt. I decided that I liked that. He looked up from a small notebook he was studying, and said, 'Oh. Hello. You met Raffles then?'

Raffles? Private Finnigan said, 'The Major doesn't like *Finnigan*. He calls me Private Raffles, instead. Lots of other things as well.'

The big chap stood up, and held his hand out to me. He had to drop it a couple of feet before we could shake hands. He said, 'You're Bassett, and I'm England.'

I was quite glad that he'd got that right. I'd always heard you had to be quite sharp to get into I Corps. He'd caught my glance at his jacket and added, 'Don't let the badge fool you. I'm an agronomist: farming and nutrition. College lecturer before the war, and doing more or less the same now.'

'I don't understand.'

'Don't worry about it. I'll tell you about that when we get along.'

'My last squadron were always telling me that.'

'Maybe they wanted to get to know you first,' Finnigan told me. Or was it Raffles?

He showed me where I could kip for the night, and where the kitchen was. We made a stack of sandwiches from tombstone-sized cuts of bread, and cut slices from the largest piece of cheese I had ever seen. Butter didn't seem to be the usual problem, either. I had the weekly cheese ration for a family of four between two wads. The Private caught my look and said, 'It's a shitty war.'

'Yeah, but the only one we got. I've heard *that* before. Do I call you Private Finnigan, or Private Raffles?'

'Private anything.' He shrugged. 'Raffles: the Major rarely calls me the other.'

'Why does he call you that?'

'You'll have to ask the Major that yourself, sir.'

There weren't any other people in the place. We joined the Major back in the bar. The Private opened a couple of bottles of beer – drinking his own from the bottle, but pouring mine into a glass. The Major was on scotch and sodas: eventually he sighed and tucked his little notebook into a jacket pocket and buttoned it in. The conversation was a serious war conversation. Who was in what show at which theatre, and whether the Troc was worth what they were charging for it. Raffles excused himself after the one beer, and headed for his room. The Major held up his glass and asked, 'Would you oblige? Get yourself one if you'd rather.'

Behind the small bar were a dozen bottles of the precious commodity, and a couple of lead-wrapped soda siphons, part full. I didn't take a second asking.

'Is anyone else living here, sir?'

He slurped the scotch and soda I gave him before replying.

'No. It says Officers' Club outside, but there are only two supply-side officers in the Corps in the European Theatre at present, and Willy – my opposite number – is away. Bandit country, I should think. So it's our place really. We both have driver-batmen, and they lodge here with us: downstairs, of course.'

'Of course.'

'And now there's you. Another officer. At least we out-number the bastards now.'

'Why do you call *your* bastard Raffles, instead of his real name?'

'Who, Les? Because I want to, I suppose. You don't care for that?'

So: Raffles. Raffles or *Les*.

'Not very much.'

'Commie? Cliff did hint that you might be a bit of a free-thinker.'

'No, sir. I'm not a Commie yet.'

'Forget the *sir* when Les is not here. I'm James.'

'OK, James. Who am *I*?'

'If you don't know that by now, Charlie Bassett, I'm not going to tell you. Cheers. 'nother?' This time he moved for the bar himself.

'Thank you. How do we pay for these? Is there a slate?'

'Doesn't work like that in the Corps. Need to know and all that. You don't need to know where the stuff comes from, nor who pays for it, as long as *we* don't. OK?'

'Fine. What happens to the place when you're away?'

'If Willy's not here then one of Les's brothers keeps an eye on it – he's dozens of them: there's always one back on leave from somewhere, and they all look hideously alike. One's even a Brylcreem boy, like you.'

'Cliff told me that they were lending me to you as your driver. It was also a way of getting me over to Europe to do . . . something else.'

'A little private enterprise I hazard?'

'Something between that and public duty. It's not *my* private enterprise, anyway.'

'Anyway, young Charlie . . .'

'Do you know that no one calls you *young* Charlie if you're six feet tall?'

'Point taken. Anyway, *Charlie*. Change of plan. You're not really a good enough driver to get me out of the trouble I sometimes get myself into, are you?'

'I wouldn't know.'

'Take my word for it.'

'OK. What next?'

'So become my passenger. Fellow traveller. Help Raffles out when and where you can, and toddle off about your own nefarious bit of business when you have to. Sound OK?'

'Yes, James. Yes it does. It beats bombing the hell out of the poor buggers. Do you want another?'

'No. Lights out. I want to be on the road by 0530.'

'That won't be a problem.'

'Nothing I tell you to do ever will be, old boy. You mustn't worry.'

I didn't like the word *tell*. No one ever does.

*

We were driven that morning by a WAAF driver with a big RAF Austin staff car: each of us had a half-empty kitbag in its boot. The pick-up was at Croydon airfield. Nobody told me, but I recognized it from a visit I had paid with my father before the war. We had watched the old silver Imperial Airways biplane airliners flying the England–France route. My mother had told me that she and the old man knew that the war was definitely on a month before they announced it, because from the top deck of a passing bus one Sunday they had spotted a dozen little brown and green aircraft partially under tarps near one of the boundary fences: it was the first time they'd seen a Spitfire. We passed a big corner pub named The Propeller on the way to the main gate – the last time I had seen it I was too young to drink there.

I sat in the front with the WAAF, and fell in love with her, watching the way her calf muscles tensed and relaxed each time she changed gear. It took more than an hour to get across London, and she was smiling by the time we got to our destination. Just before we slowed for the main gate and the guardhouse, I sensed Raffles and the Major settle down in their seats, and pull their collars up to obscure their faces. I copied them instinctively.

'No telling who's watching these days, Charlie,' the Major told me, and, 'No point Jerry knowing I'm coming over if he doesn't need to.'

The girl drove us to a smallish blister hangar a long way from the main buildings. She seemed to know the form: I was glad somebody did. When we stepped out of the car and stretched, I walked around the car to the driver's side, and bent down so that my head was level with hers. I said my thanks, and then asked, 'Can I see you after I get back?'

She smiled, and after the significant pause, said, 'I don't see why not. My name's Wayne. That's Dolly Wayne. Section Officer. I'm at the Central Car Pool at Whitehall.'

'I'll find it.'

'And you are?'

'Sorry.' I offered her my hand to shake through the opened car window. 'Charlie Bassett. Pilot Officer, but I used to be a Sergeant.'

She gave my fingers a little squeeze before she let them go.

'So did I. Happy landings, Charlie Bassett.'

After she drove away Raffles stretched again, and said, 'You don't waste much time, do you, sir?'

'I don't have much time to waste, Private. What about you?'

'Married man, sir. Three nippers – the last was born at Christmas.'

'What are they?'

'All human beings, as far as I know, sir.'

'You know what I mean.'

'Yeah, sorry. Sometimes I can't resist it.'

'I know what you mean: once I couldn't stand officers either.'

'What did you do, sir, if you don't mind my asking, that was so bad that they punished you by making you be an officer?'

'I lived. I survived. I made it. This is the RAF's revenge.'

'Ah. There you go, sir. They wouldn't like *that*, would they?'

'I suppose not.'

'And my kids are all boys. Three elevenths of my own football team. Thank you for asking.'

We were standing on the tarmac with our kitbags at our feet. England was staring out across the airfield at England, if you see what I mean; distracted. I don't think he was even aware of us.

'What next?' I asked Raffles.

'You stay here, and take care of the Major for me, sir. Make sure no harm comes to him while we're waiting for our aeroplane. I'll pop inside, and rustle you up some decent clobber.'

'Say that again?'

'I'm not driving you over any border in *those* clothes. It may not have occurred to you, sir, but men in RAF blues aren't exactly greeted with open arms by a citizenry you've been bombing shit out of for the last five years.' *Clobber*: brown-job speak for walking-out dress, apparently.

It suddenly dawned on me that if there was only one person running this operation, then maybe it was neither me nor the brave Major. Inside my memory my dead friend Black Francie smiled at me. About ten minutes later Raffles called to me from a small office stuck on the side of the blister hangar, and waved me over. Inside it was like a second-hand clothes shop. He picked me out a couple of smallish pairs of battledress trousers, one khaki and one navy, and an oversized khaki bum-freezer jacket. I was joining the Army.

'Put these on, sir, and stick yours in your bag: they still might come in useful, despite what I said earlier. Keep your boots, it'll save you wearing gaiters, and wear your old flying jacket over the lot. A lot of us have got them; filched of course, but bloody good against the cold.' When I paused, he added for effect, 'If you could get a move on, sir? The plane's due any min.' Then he glanced out of the open door and said, '*Sod it!* Where's the Major got to?'

I followed his gaze. Our kitbags sat on the tarmac like three small sheep, grazing. Where was the fucking shepherd? A comedian could have said that England was everywhere, but nowhere within sight. Raffles said, '*Jildi* – get a move on!' to me as he trotted out, and, 'You understand?'

'Yes, sir,' I told him, and began to move. Force of habit, I suppose.

When I walked out in my new kit, Raffles was standing by our sad bags of luggage, hands on hips, radiating impatience. There was a small gold cross in each lapel of my new battle-dress jacket. My new regimental shoulder flash said *Seaforth Highlanders*. It had been thoroughly spruced up, and the two holes I noted in its back panel, and one above the breast pocket, had been neatly mended. Not only a brown job, but a dead brown job, a fucking Jock, and a fucking parson to boot. Then I remembered that a Chaplain had a Captain's rank in the Army: I'd been promoted again. I told him, 'I'll need a Bible and a prayer book if we're going to carry this off.'

He swung on me, and Private to Captain or not, I would have got the rough edge of his tongue if James England hadn't ambled around the other side of the small humped building buttoning up, and said, 'Sorry about that. Got took short. Weren't worried, were you? Would that be our transport just bounding down the airfield now?'

Bloody Tempsford. They always had to get in on the act. It was a 158 Squadron Hudson, and it turned out David Clifford was driving the bloody thing. *Flying* would have been a more appropriate description of what he was doing with it: I wondered if he had flown the type before. He was still laughing as he climbed down from the small fuselage door.

'Did you see that, Charlie?' he asked me. 'Bounced like a fucking kangaroo! I hope I haven't upset it, or stuffed the oleo legs.'

I said, 'Hello, Cliff. Yes, I saw that. It really gives me bags of confidence.'

'Don't be such a dismal little sod. I'm much better with the heavies. How's your head?'

'Less burned, thank you. But I still have a trace of the hang-over I brought from Crifton.'

'Great people, aren't they?'

'No, Cliff; they're turds. They're exceptionally rich turds, and they might get me killed.'

'Said it before. Dismal little sod.'

'This is Major James England, and Private Finnigan or Raffles.'

'I know. I knew them before you did. What ho Beginagin.'

'Hello, sir,' said Raffles, and gave him a salute that was like touching his forelock.

'Hello, Cliff,' said England. 'Shall we get going then?'

There were eight forward-facing seats in pairs in the accommodation of the Hudson. Raffles stretched himself across two and went to sleep. England strapped in three rows back, and began to study rows of figures in his small notebook. Cliff pushed me into the seat alongside his own.

'Don't touch anything unless you know how to fly.'

'I know a bit.'

'What bit do you know – getting up into the sky, or getting back down on the ground?'

'Neither. The bit in between.'

'In that case don't even think about it.'

'You're the boss.'

'No, I'm not, but you don't need to know who is.'

I think that the problem was that the Hudson was so much lighter and more sensitive than the Stirling he had shown me he was good at. All of his actions seemed heavy-handed. I think we were flying sideways as we actually unstuck. He told me, 'That was fucking horrible.'

'I wasn't going to mention it.'

'Good.'

'Grace's dad said I'd get a briefing before I went over.'

'This is it, and there's damn-all to tell. Just a couple of hints. After that you're on your own. Well, not quite on your own. You've got *ITMA* back there, for backup.'

'I got the impression that it was the other way round.

Don't they expect me to help *them* out? *Look out!*' Cliff had turned to me as he spoke, trying to gauge the impact his words made. That meant that he wasn't looking at the Waddon Gas Works chimney coming towards us at about 180 knots. He hauled us round it with a girlish giggle which didn't suit him. The Major called forward, 'Everything OK up there?'

'Grand, Major. I'm just teaching old Charlie the rudiments of flying.'

'Do it from a bit further up, old chap.'

Cliff laughed, and pulled us into a steep circling climb. He didn't speak again until there was eight thou on the clock.

'What do you really *know* about Grace?' I asked him.

'I know she's jumped ship. You knew that she was a civvy pilot for the Air Transport Auxiliary: a ferry pilot?'

'Yes, of course I knew that. I'm her intimate. That's how I got into this mess.'

'Somehow the ATA Command found out that she was pregnant, and grounded her until after the happy event.'

'She wouldn't have liked that. I wonder who told them.' I looked away: it had been me.

'Understatement. She threw a bleeding Dodo: tried to skewer her boss with his own walking stick. OK: grab the wheel now – both hands – and be gentle with her . . .'

'Like you are . . .?'

'Feet on the pedals, please; no sarcasm. OK: you've got her.' He held his hands up to show me that I was flying. 'Watch your artificial horizon – that job, there.' He rapped one of the dials. 'Keep the floating white line horizontal, and along the line on the face of it. Then you'll be flying level.'

'What did she do afterwards?'

'Took some old war-weary Spit without permission, and thrashed it down to Great Gransden, beating up three RAF airfields in the process, abandoned it there, and went home to Mummy and Daddy in a huff, leaving the ATA and the RAF to argue what the charges should be.'

'Good for her. Interesting though: I never her saw her lose control.'

'Look, fly the bloody thing straight can't you? It can't be all that difficult.'

'Sorry. Good for Grace, though.'

'That's what I thought, until Sir Peter called his markers in.'

'When did it all start to go wrong?'

'Lady Baker says that Grace seemed to settle back home quite quickly. She thought that she'd decided to *have* the baby. Actually I think that Mummy and Daddy were quite chuffed at the idea. Then Grace went to London, and you've been told about that, and something happened because she pissed off with some American cavalrymen, and the near Continent got its first bona fide English tourist since the start of the war.'

'Any idea why?'

'Obviously something to do with that bombed school, wasn't it? Any other ideas?'

'You know that Grace flew half a dozen trips to Germany with us, as rear gunner?'

Cliff said, 'Christ!' and grabbed the aircraft back from me. We immediately lost about fifty feet in a great lurch. Raffles shouted, 'Oi!' from the back, and Cliff shouted back, 'Sorry!'

Then he asked me, 'Does her old man know?'

'Maybe. He won't make a fuss about it as long as I'm around.'

'How come?'

'He was rogering her before the rest of us got there. I know, and now *you* know too. He won't want to take a chance on that getting out. For all we know her baby could even be his.'

'When was she due?'

'About now. Maybe. I lost track of time a bit after the accident.'

'It makes some sense to me now,' Cliff told me. 'One of the people she stayed with in London said that after that rocket nearly killed her she talked about *putting it all right again*, and told them she had pals in the American Red Cross in Paris who could do with a hand. They were the hints I mentioned earlier. Seven months pregnant, having recently helped you bomb Germany, she wanders into a bombed primary school in pieces, full of children also in pieces. Poor cow.'

'You're being glib, Cliff. She's more complicated than that.'

'Makes sense to me, too.' That was James England. He could move stealthily when he chose: he had moved up to stand behind the seats we were in. 'I can get you into Paris, Charlie, never fear.'

'Thanks.'

'How long now?' England asked us.

I could see the South Coast swimming towards us ten thou beneath. Cliff said, 'We'll be on the ground in an hour.'

'Good; I'll take a snooze then. Fly smoothly.'

'Jawohl Herr Major,' I told him. If he noticed he didn't show it. He said, 'Jolly good. Carry on then.'

I thought that I ought to bottom it out with Cliff while I still had the chance.

'So I'll start at the Red Cross offices in Paris. That's your idea?'

'Can't think of anything better, can you?'

'How do I report back?'

'Don't. Find Grace; get her to come back with you.'

'Why is that important?'

'Winston says so.'

'I don't like Winston.'

'That's *not* important.'

'Explain please.'

'Charlie. Elections cost money to fight and the first one after this war's not that far away. Winston has no money at all, and few friends. You produce Grace, and a grateful Baker Small Arms Company bankrolls his next election campaign. It's the only chance he has of beating Clem Attlee for the top job.'

'So I'm over here to get the next Conservative government elected?'

'That's the ticket. You're quite sharp when you try.'

'But I can't stand the bastards.'

'So what old chap? Take this; whilst no one's looking.'

He pulled a bulky envelope from inside his beat-up flying jacket, and pushed it into my hands. I made sure it was stowed down in a pocket.

'What's that?'

'Spending money. Some dollars and pounds: they'll get you anywhere. There are loads of invasion francs and deutsch-marks, but don't depend on them, they're forgeries. About three and a half grand in all. That should get you through.'

'How do I get back?'

'Initiative. Hallmark of the officer class.'

I probably sulked. Then I asked him about Major England, and Raffles.

'Darby and Joan. He's not really an Intelligence Officer; he's some sort of food and drink wallah. Les looks after every-thing else.'

'He told me about being a food expert. I didn't quite see what he meant.'

'His job is to be just behind the point of the Army's advance all the time, make an assessment of what food and rations it needs. It sounds safe, and it is unless Jerry decides to come back at us with a counter-attack, as he has a few times already. Then he can find he's the wrong side of the lines, or in the middle of the shooting war. He's been wounded twice, and Raffles three times. They're bloody inseparable.'

'I suppose that to do their job safely he'd have to be an ace navigator.'

'What? Sure. An ace. Why?'

I don't think that he realized why that worried me. I'd seen the Major studying a map before we set out. He had been holding it upside down. I heard Raffles stir in his sleep, and snort.

Cliff asked me just one more thing before we started the let-down over Abbeville. 'That thing you just said – about Grace flying some trips with you. How come?'

'The rear gunner – the one you were interested in – you remember I told you how he killed those policemen? Then he went over the hill. Pissed off. Grace had become attached to us earlier. She was billeting with us between delivery flights: they were sending us a lot of new Lancasters down from Ringway. She just stepped in, and took his place. No one noticed the difference. You have no idea how stupidly easy it was.'

'The ATA must have realized that she was missing?'

'No, Cliff. That's the irony of it, now. She'd been grounded by them for beating up Bawne airfield in a bloody Spitfire. They thought she had the twitch.'

'So that business with the two phoney coppers: Grace was there all the time?'

'You could say that. Out there on the edge. She helped us cover Pete's disappearance.'

'Bollocks.'

'Indubitably.' I hadn't used that word since I'd left the squadron.

'Good gunner, was she?'

'Yeah. She got one. Bloody good shot.'

PART TWO

France: March 1945

Five

The airfield outside Fécamp had been a grass field used by German fighters during the Battle of Britain. We asked for it back again some time after D-Day, and laid a prefabricated metal runway, made up of steel links. Cliff got it almost right this time, but the track was wet from a morning shower, and caught him out. His approach was a shade too fast. Halfway down the strip, with all three of our wheels on the deck, he applied the brakes and slid out immediately to the left. One main wheel slipped off the metalling and dug in, while the rest of the plane tried to fly on. We did the handbrake left turn, then stopped with a distinctly loud metallic cracking noise, at right angles to the track. This all took place in less time than it's taken to tell you.

Raffles, not strapped in, ended up on the floor. He muttered, 'Effing hooray!' but I'm not sure whether that was out of anger or fear. My strap had dug into my shoulder, almost dislocating it.

Cliff said, 'Balls!'

An American female voice came over the radio, 'Cliff, get

DAVID FIDDIMORE

your heap off the edge of my runway. I have 47s due in twenty-five minutes.'

Airfield control was from a caravan like the one I had known at Bawne: it seemed a long way away, but within a couple of minutes a jeep was moving away from it. A blonde girl in USAAF duds waved to us when she bailed out of it.

Cliff said, 'Hello, Wendy.'

She replied, 'Hi Cliff, hi Major . . .' but she made for Raffles, and gave him a hug saying, 'How's my man?' Then she spotted me, and said, 'New boy.'

Raffles unwrapped her and said, 'No. Nothing like that. We're just giving him a lift to Paris. This is Charlie.'

I said, 'Hello, Miss.'

'Hello yourself, Charlie. Welcome to France.'

'This is my first time over.'

'Watch those girls in Paris. Come on.'

While we were climbing into the jeep Raffles told her, 'Mr Clifford did well to keep us on our wheels.'

'I didn't doubt him for a minute.'

'Pleased to hear that, Miss.'

'You wanna drive me, Raffles?'

Raffles drove. She sat alongside him unwrapping the small brown parcel he'd magicked from somewhere, while James England, Cliff and I squeezed in behind them with our three bags. I looked over her shoulder at her tits, and the parcel on her lap. As far as I could see her tits were great, and the parcel contained several pairs of stockings, a couple of half-bottles of gin and a couple of packs of fat Turkish cigarettes. There was also what looked like an irregular lump of shiny dark brown

82

ear wax, about the size of a thumbnail. The American girl said, 'Thank you, hon. Will you all be staying tonight? They've opened a small estaminet down the road.'

There was a pause. Then, 'Maybe on the way back, Wendy.' The Major; at last. That was good: I'd begun to wonder if he'd died. 'Charlie's in a hurry to get to Paris.'

'So was I, when I was his age.' She turned and gave me the full blast of her smile: her lips were the colour of pumping venous blood. I'd seen some of that splashed around in aeroplanes. She must have been all of twenty-five years old.

Cliff said, '*I'll* be staying if I can't hitch a lift back. You can take me instead.'

'OK,' the woman said. There was something careless about it. False gaiety.

Halfway back to the control caravan Raffles stopped the jeep, got out and walked away to vomit on the grass.

'He's scared of flying,' Major England said to me. 'I don't know why he does it.'

He wiped his mouth on a great handkerchief before he got back in. Wendy leaned over and gave him a hug again.

The caravan was crowded, so I stepped outside. Thirty feet away there was a concrete dispersal pan up against a perimeter hedge. One of those huge *Queen Mary* trailers sat on it, its load shrouded by a torn camouflage tarp.

I wandered over to it, trailed by Cliff, and pulled back the tarpaulin for a closer look. It wasn't a large aircraft, but it was more or less all there, except for the radial engine. Its wings and struts had been disassembled and laid on the trailer, strapped to the fuselage. I recognized the horrible little

Norseman. Cliff wasn't paying close attention. The aircraft looked knocked about a bit, but not in bad nick. There were a couple of holes in the front screens which could have been bullets. Nothing big had touched it, unless the missing engine had copped it.

I told Cliff, 'I think I know this aircraft.'

Cliff looked up, and then there was something funny. He looked rattled. That was a first. He said, 'No you don't. Can't do: it's been here for months.'

'You're wrong, Cliff. I've flown in it. I was given a lift in it up to Ringway, just after my tour ended.'

'No, Charlie. That must have been another one.'

'Don't be an arse, Cliff. I *know* that I've been on this plane. I'm in the RAF too, remember. I was on this one and Glenn Miller was snoozing just behind me.'

He pushed me out of the way, and hurriedly started to drag the tarp over it again.

'Charlie, I know that if you say that again, I'll have to take out my revolver, push its barrel into your mouth, and pull the trigger.'

'Are you *serious*?'

'Want to try me?'

It was such a stupid thing to get steamed up over, but there was a vein pounding on Cliff's temple, and his cheekbones had gone white. I nearly said it, but then Major England's voice cut in calmly.

'Leave the boy alone, Cliff: you'll scare him.'

He had ghosted in again. Cliff relaxed. Had he been prepared to do it? I asked him, 'Have you got the twitch?'

He gave me a very thin smile, which went with his moustache. Then he said, 'Yes,' and laughed. 'All the time. Sorry.'

The Major told him, 'I'll sort Charlie out, OK?', put his arm around Cliff's shoulder, and shepherded us both back towards the caravan.

An Army Humber saloon was rumbling up: it bore an Army Service Corps flash on its wings. It looked low on its springs and very second-hand. On the narrow area of scuttle between the passenger cabin and the engine, the name *Kate* was painted in army stencil white. The Major told me, 'You'd better get acquainted with Raffles's mistress: you're going to be inside her for a few weeks.' He laughed as if he had said something amusing.

Cliff walked away, and climbed back inside the caravan. When Les climbed out and opened the boot there appeared to be another half car in pieces inside it. Also the contents of a small bar, and a corner grocery shop before rationing. We squeezed our bags around the machinery parts. The Major told me, 'It was something he learned in the desert. There's nothing much on this old bus he can't replace if he has to.'

Raffles had both wings of the bonnet up. I asked England, 'Is there much to do before we leave?'

'Buggered if I know, old son. I don't think that he *trusts* anyone else to work on her. If I was you I'd stretch out on that groundsheet and get the last of the sun, while you can.'

'What about Cliff?'

'I'll sort him out, OK?'

'That's what you told him about me.'

'Exactly. Toddle along now. We'll call you when we're ready to move: won't leave without you.'

I picked a spot that put the caravan between me and a gentle breeze. The sun was getting some iron into it again. I must have dozed, until I sensed a movement, and Wendy's soft American voice.

'Shove over, bud.' I did, and she sat on the edge of the groundsheet just not touching me. 'Mother Wendy's medicine . . . here, I brought you this.' *This* was an opened bottle of red wine. She said, 'I've dozens of them.'

I propped myself up on an elbow to drink. We took alternate draughts from the bottle until it was half emptied. We watched Raffles working on the car. She held the bottle up to the light and asked me, 'Tell me, Charlie Nobody, is it half empty, or half full?'

'Half full. Definitely.'

She rested her head on her drawn-up knees, and moodily watched the Humber coming to life.

'I was your age once,' she told me; then got up and walked less steadily back to the caravan, taking the bottle with her.

Sitting in the car with Raffles, with the galloping Major behind me writing spells in his little notebook, felt better than being shouted at by Cliff. I asked our driver, 'How far are we from Paris?'

'About a hundred and thirty miles as the crow flies; about a hundred and eighty, two hundred, the way we'll go.'

'Say five hours then.'

'Say two days' – that was the Major – 'if we're lucky. You should see what you blue buggers did to the roads.'

'I think it serves you right, sir,' Raffles told me. 'Your lot made the holes; now you get to drive round them.'

'Thanks a bunch.'

'Don't mensh.'

'Will there be somewhere to stay?'

' 'course there will, Mr Bassett. We came this way before.'

'Would you mind keeping it down lads.' That was the Major again. 'Man in the back trying to get his sums right.'

Raffles and I grinned at each other. I was happier when he was looking at the road.

The first roadblock was after about six miles. A Redcap in battle gear waved us down at a pole across half the road. He had a stick with a white wood circle on the end; *traffic, for the directing of*. Raffles drove with his Sten in his lap. He pulled up a few feet short, and the hairs on my neck stood up as I saw him flick the Sten's safety before the copper reached us. The Major didn't even look up. Raffles wound down the window. I sensed that he was smiling at the man.

'Wotcha cock. What's up?'

'UXB. That field down there, about twenty feet from the road.' He turned and pointed away from us, and to the right. 'Some Sappers are looking for it.'

'One of ours or one of theirs?'

'Theirs. The Sapper Sergeant said it was a five-hundred-kilo job, from the entry hole it's made in the ground.'

'What were they bombing, French cows?' Raffles gave his

little relaxed laugh, and asked, 'Wanna fag?' He took off his beret, and offered the copper a roll-up from about thirty ready made he kept in there. I always noticed how careful he was replacing his beret; I never saw him drop one.

'Thanks. Don't mind if I do, and you can slip that safety on now.'

Raffles laughed again.

'That's what all the French tarts say.'

They lit up. Raffles blew out the match and tossed it on the verge. As it touched the grass there was the flat thump of a close explosion, and in the field an immediate small cloud of that odd yellow-grey coloured smoke that the Kraut ordnance always generated. The car rocked. The policeman staggered. We were showered in mud, grass and small clods of earth. The copper swore. Then he said, 'Found it.'

'Do you think you'll find them?'

'Doubt it. No one's screaming.'

'Can we move along then?'

'Yes. Take care until you're clear of the lane. Thanks for the fag, mate.'

'Pleasure.'

Raffles eased us carefully along the country lane. It was bordered by high hedges. There was a hole in the hedge on the right-hand side, and the smoke drifted through it. On the windscreen in front of him was a small red splodge. He tapped the glass to draw my attention to it.

I said, 'We once came back from somewhere – Lübeck, maybe – with fifteen feet of human guts draped over the wingtip. Lanc just blew up in front of us and we flew through the remains.'

'The trouble with you RAF johnnies,' Major England said, just to prove that he didn't miss much, 'is that you always have to cap a good story.'

'Sorry, sir.'

'Don't worry, I'll give you detention tonight. You can stay at home and look after *Kate*, if Les and I are on the town.' I thought that this had been a slip of the tongue until he added, 'Sod it, Les; I can't keep up the Major baloney much longer. Are we far enough away from England yet, do you think?'

'Yessir.'

'You tell him then.'

'This is a small car, Mr Bassett, and we're a small team, so from now on, if it's all right with you, sometimes I'm *Les*, and sometimes the Major's *Jim*, or *Jimmy* or *James*.'

'What about me?'

'*Charlie*; that right?'

'Yeah: pleased to meet you. It makes life easier, doesn't it?'

'So say thank you to Jimmy for saving your life.'

'Thank you, Jimmy. I didn't know he had.'

'That shows you how good he is.'

'When did this happen?'

'Back at Fécamp. You were stupid. Cliff would have killed you.'

'Oh, that. I wasn't sure.'

'We were.'

We were stopped at two more blocks before nightfall, and diverted off our route three more times. When I asked Les why, James answered for him.

'Mines. Jerry left them as a going-away present. We must have driven down that last lane about . . . how many times Les . . .?'

'Four.'

'. . . four times, without seeing them or setting one off. Funny, ain't it?'

'Yeah; very funny,' I told him. 'Remind me to laugh.'

'That's the trouble with you RAF johnnies,' Les said. 'No bloody sense of humour.'

We stayed at a small inn just outside a place named Gournay-en-Bray. It was showing no lights, but that was because they had a good blackout. Up close to the iron-studded front door you just got a glimpse of the light feeding out beneath it. Raffles hammered twice, with the flat of his hand: it sounded thunderous. Then he shouted, 'It's Mr Raffles, and the Major.'

Then he hammered again. The door opened immediately. He turned to me, and said, 'I arranged with them how many times we'd knock, and what I'd say. It's worth your remembering, in case you're on your own on the way back.'

'I couldn't remember the way here, and I don't know what the place looks like. It's dark.'

'That solves that problem, then, doesn't it?'

He nosed inside, the Sten held vaguely at the port before him. In the small panelled reception we were met by a tall, thin woman and a boy of about fourteen. The boy had bulgy eyes of the palest blue-grey colour, and a massive goitre. You knew immediately that he wasn't the full shilling. The boy had admitted us, and bolted the door behind us.

Raffles said to me, 'This is our friend Madame Defarge.'

The woman laughed. It was a bitter sound, but she held her hand out to me.

'Madame Demain. Your friend Raffles is droll.'

'Not my friend. My driver.'

'Make him your friend, Monsieur . . .?'

'Charlie.'

'. . . Monsieur Charlie. You will find him a useful friend.' She paused and then added, 'And a *good* one.' The smile she directed at Raffles seemed genuine enough.

He asked her, 'How is the boy?'

The boy's right hand had begun to tremble. She took it in her own.

'As you see him. Perhaps a little better.'

'You have had news of Monsieur Demain?'

'None since January . . .'

James England seemed to have nothing to add to the conversation.

The boy's trembling increased. His shoulders shook. Madame hoisted the sails of the most beautiful language in the world, and gave him a dozen or so sentences as fast as Browning machine-gun fire. He stuttered a couple back.

The Major had squeezed in behind me, and said, 'That's the trouble here. Neither Les nor I were picked for this job for our fluency in French. I can just get by in German, and Les even has problems with English. I don't know whether she said something reassuring, or told him to cut our throats in our sleep.'

I told him, 'The boy's terrified of me because he hasn't seen me before. He thinks that I'll attack her. She told him that I was a friend of Les's and wouldn't harm them because they were too useful to you. She also told him not to make any trouble because they need the money.'

'Good God. Why didn't you say you spoke the lingo?'

'Nobody asked. It's something I'm learning from people like you.'

'What is?'

'Need to know.'

Raffles guffawed. Then he said, 'Tell her that you speak good French.'

'Fairly average French,' but I did. Her raised eyebrows told me something about how Brits were regarded by their geographically closest ally. Thickos.

Raffles spoke again.

'Tell her that I have tinned meat for her this time, from the Americans; butter and cigarettes. I'll get them from the car shortly.'

I did. She looked curiously downcast, almost ashamed. I told her that we appreciated her accommodating us, and that we wished to put her out as little as possible. I also spoke directly to the boy, and told him that I wouldn't harm his mother.

The woman smiled at last, and murmured, 'Grandmère.' At least I'd said something right.

That night I slept on a soft mattress between stiff, clean

sheets, in a room that I could lock from the inside. It was as I did that, that I realized I was the only one without a weapon of some sort. I slept with the curtain open, hoping to let in the starlight, but cloud had blown south-westerly along the Channel in the evening, obscuring them. You could never have it all.

In the morning Les produced enough bacon sarnies for the five of us. The makings had been in the boot of the Humber, scattered among spare parts. That accounted for the vague whiff of petrol as I bit into one. The boy smiled shyly at me. I gave him a bobby-dazzler in return. When he took my hand he said nothing except, 'Monsieur,' but made it plain that he wanted to take me somewhere.

In the full light I could see that the building was timber, framed in narrow red bricks: probably medieval. It had steep roofs and tall gables. On one gable end was a faded painted advertisement for Citroën cars, which included a legionnaire and a distant *tricolore*. It was even more distant now, because at some time since it was painted it had received a burst of small-arms gunfire. There was a large, partly cared for garden behind the house, with unfamiliar vegetables in hopeful rows . . . and an unkempt apple orchard, in a corner of which was an unmistakable something the shape of an adult's grave.

The boy said nothing. He stood in front of the mound with his hands crossed; his head bent, praying. I copied him. Then he took my hand again, and led me back inside. Les, Jimmy and the woman were washing the sarnies down with clear, home-made cider – the family's only contribution to the meal.

They'd saved a share of it for me. As we left Les gave her some dollars, a small tin of coffee beans, a pair of stockings, and a small raincoat that would fit the boy. These were parting gifts. It was as he passed her the last item that she started to cry; silently. The boy put his arm around her waist and leaned in closer.

England muttered, 'I *hate* this bloody war. Absolutely.'

After an hour the gloom had lifted. Les whistled 'Lili Marleen' again, and drove with his elbow out of the car window. I worked through my logic for them.

'The boy . . .'

'Mathieu: Matt . . .' Les told me.

'. . . Matt. He was scared that I was going to attack the old lady. That means he's probably seen someone else attack a lady. His mother perhaps. That's her grave in the orchard.'

England gave a wry little chuckle. Les told me, 'No. That's all right as far as it goes, but almost completely bloody wrong. You would never make a good tec, would you?'

'Where did I go wrong?'

'Almost everywhere.'

'I'll tell him.' James England took over. He was *James* or *Jimmy*, again.

'The Jerry took Demain's son, Matt's father, away to work in 1941. He didn't come back. Someone told her that he was some sort of trustee at the camp at Natzweiler: there are mainly women there, so your average Frenchman will probably feel quite at home. After that, nothing. Now old Matt's not too bright . . .'

'I noticed that.'

'About six months later he saw what he *thought* was a man attacking his mother in the orchard. Only the chappy *wasn't* attacking her. They were having the horizontal meeting of parts.'

'I see.'

'I think that maybe you do, this time.'

'What happened?'

'Matt brained him. Gave him one over the napper with a ruddy great sledgehammer they kept for killing the pig. Every orchard had its own pig before the war.'

'Was it some Jerry?'

'Good Lord, no! It was his father's brother. His uncle. The old lady's second son. They buried him in the orchard to save fuss, and soon after that his mother left them.'

'How did you find all this out, if you don't speak the language?'

'We know someone who knows someone who does. It's how this business works.'

'What business?'

'Spying, of course. What else did you think Cliff does?'

Oh, I see, I thought, but I didn't say anything.

'That reminds me.' It was Les this time. 'I need to stop for a slash. Anyone else?'

We stopped overnight at another grass airfield: Beauvais. Goering had watched the Battle of Britain from there, until he got bored with not winning. A squadron of Typhoons had arrived before us, and there seemed to be a lot of grumbling about nothing going on. There were no permanent messing facilities, but they offered us a big tent with a kerosene heater, Tilley lights, camp beds and blankets. There were eateries in the village. I looked over England's shoulder at the map, and couldn't help myself.

'Beauvais. Look, Croydon was almost as close to Paris as this!'

'Paris tomorrow, Charlie. Les knows what he's doing. We piddle around these bloody side roads because the main roads have either been blown up by your lot, or are blocked to buggery by priority traffic. Trust him.'

Les chose where we ate. From the outside it was the least promising eating house in the town. There were chairs and tables on the paving outside some of the others, with drinkers and diners spilling out on them. Mainly servicemen accompanied by young women. I say *mainly*, because I saw one large elderly officer in German field grey, with all the silver buttons, dining at a small round table with a pretty woman in her thirties. The officer sat very erectly to table. A neatly dressed lad of about five stood patiently alongside the woman.

I asked, 'Wait a mo' – did you see *that*?'

'Naw,' Les said. 'I'm off duty.'

'It was a bloody Hun, sitting there.'

'I've seen him before,' Jimmy told us. 'There must be a story behind that.'

'Didn't either of you ask?'

'None of our business, old boy.' He sniffed. He made it plain that it was none of mine either.

It turned out that Les was looking for a cafe where we

could eat inside, and as far from the front window as possible. He found a place at the end of a terrace of more or less intact houses. Inside it, the tables were clad in red and white checked oilcloth, and the room was warm. It was dominated by a montage of three large national flags on one wall: American, British and French. The *tricolore* looked a bit tired and faded, but the other Allied colours were fresh and clean. From the nail marks in the wall behind you could see that the display had recently displaced a predecessor.

Les got us a table by the far wall, near the kitchen door. He sat with his back to the wall, whilst England and I sat at the ends of the small table on either side of him. They asked me to negotiate the eatings, and Les passed me a roll of dollars which made the fat Frog who owned the place's eyes water. I gave him five eventually. Les said, 'Jimmy wants to know what we're going to have.'

'Rabbit. Stewed with carrots and onions. It's almost impossible to eat French without onions.'

'How do you know? You've never been here.'

'I read it in a book. It must be true.'

'What else?'

'Blackcurrant puddings. The blackcurrants will be last year's leavings: pickled.'

'Didn't you ask him for a bottle?'

'I didn't pay him for the wine. I said that we'd taste it first.'

'Oh, my lovely boy,' Les told us. 'I'm going to like travelling with you.'

I asked Les about sitting so far from the front of the building.

'The Frogs aren't as friendly as they're cracked up to be. Some of the Maquis commandos want us out of their country even before all of the Jerries are gone. There've been drive-by shoot-ups at cafes with Allied soldiers in – just to encourage us, if you like. Then there are numerous Frog Pétainists who feel betrayed, and do the same. This is far from a liberated country, Charlie, despite what the nobs say. I like to sit where I can see what's what.'

'Wild Bill Hickok used to do that. I saw it in a film. The only time he didn't sit with his back to the wall someone shot him.'

'He was bloody right the first time then, wasn't he?'

The Major regretfully licked his dessert spoon into submission, put it down, and informed us, 'Nobody called him *Wild Bill* Hickok when he was alive; that was the invention of a journalist. His peers called him *Duck Bill* Hickok – because he had an enormous hooter. Not many people know that.'

'They say that guys with big noses have big pricks. I wonder if women know that?' That was Les. I couldn't resist the opening he'd left me; perhaps I wasn't supposed to.

'Don't worry. You've a nice, neat, wee nose, Les.'

'Our boy is getting bold, isn't he?' he told our friend Jimmy.

It was that sort of evening.

The heater must have run out sometime in the night. When I awoke my joints were stiff to breaking point, and my blankets hard with frost.

We joined an all-ranks queue for breakfast, which was bangers and mash – although the bangers were only soya links. The tea was good: brown as a Jamaican, and stiff with condensed milk. We visited the Beauvais petrol dump on the way out. Les did the deal with the Redcap guarding the stuff, and I gave him back his roll of dollars to finish it. We toured away with a full tank, two full jerrycans in the boot, and one lashed to each running board. That would turn us into a fireball if anyone shot at us, or get us to the border if need be, Les told us. I asked the silly one.

'Which border?'

'Germany, if necessary.'

'And you're ditching me in Paris?'

'We'll see. The Major's decided to go wherever you want to go; so long as you're travelling in the same direction as us.'

I looked away from him, and out of the window. The sun was shining, and Les had got quite a lick on, so the French countryside was dashing past. So England had become *the Major* again; there was a behavioural code at work here, which I couldn't read. When I turned to look over my shoulder at the Major he was smiling a secret smile, and scribbling magic formulae into his small notebook again. He looked like a bloody alchemist. He was also whistling a tune under his breath so that you could only just hear it: I'll swear it was 'The Galloping Major'.

Six

Why did they call Paris an open city? Because it wasn't; not if you were looking for somewhere to kip for the night it wasn't: it was as closed up tight as a nun's harmonium. Everyone seemed to have a girl and somewhere to stay, except us. England had a prewar Michelin street map. When he started to unfold it and fill the back of the car Les said, 'Put the bloody thing away, Major. You can't read it, and thanks to the war half the places marked on it aren't there any more.'

I asked him, 'Are you blaming that on my pals too, or is it down to Jerry?' I noticed I had started referring to the Germans as *Jerry*, the way the brown jobs did. The odd thing was that there was a sort of grudging respect in the way that they said it. Anyway, Les told me, 'Neither, I think. Once Jerry began to pull out of Paris, the Resistance came over all manly and onto the streets. They opened up on anything that moved. They used big stuff too: that's why some of their own houses are missing. Funny, we'd been parachuting bombs and guns in to them for years, and they waits till after Jerry's gone to use them. Then they uses them on each other. Remarkable how brave folk are when Jerry's got his back to you. I've seen that before. That's when the generals and politicians suddenly arrive, and start saying brave things about brave new worlds.'

'How long did the shooting go on for?'

'About four days proper. Me and Jimmy arrived on day one. We didn't fancy all the bullets flying around, so we found a widow with a little house over in the Tivoli. We had a jeep then, so I hid it in her back garden under a tarp. I slept for three days. When we came out again, De Gaulle and Leclerc's heroes were facing down the Maquis in the Place dew Concorde: each claiming they'd finished the war and beaten *les Boches* on their own – that's what they call Jerry. *Les Boches.*'

'I knew that.'

'Not many people do,' the Major told us, still wrestling with his map.

'Why does he sometimes say that?' I asked Les.

'It's something he does. Don't let it worry you. He gets a few words fixed into his head, and worries them to death.'

'On the squadron ours was "Just like that", like that comic you told me about.'

'I like that,' England said. 'I really do. I'll remember that.'

'Now look what you done,' Les told me.

The Major put the map away, and Les drove us to three places they had stayed at before. No go. There were liberators everywhere: it cost you three dollars to sleep in someone's garden. They'd even taken over a couple of the grand old churches for billets.

James England said, 'No bloody good, Les. What d'y'reckon? Push on, and see if we can get something further out?'

'How about a drink?'

Les stopped the car alongside an American Snowdrop who looked grateful that we'd distracted him from his duel with the traffic.

'Aw, fuckit,' he told us. 'They can drive on whichever side they wants. I'm up to here with them.' He held his white night-stick up to chin level.

'We were looking for a drink,' I told him.

'Come far?'

'From 1942.'

The Yank grinned.

'Two blocks up, take a left. One block on, take a right. You're on a wide avenue with trees, running parallel to this. So far?'

'Yes, so far.'

'You'll come to a small square at the junction of three roads. There's this guy there who sells vino from a sort of pushcart.'

There were two clumps of chairs and tables, under trees coming into early leaf, and a man with a small handcart – like an ice-cream cart – was parked between them, dispensing ten-cent glasses of wine from big, greasy jars. We parked up at the empty bunch of seats. There seemed to be a party from a heavily laden jeep going on at the other. American brown jobs and a couple of noisy civilians. The old man who sold the drink had moustaches which drooped to the floor and stringy yellow hair. He sold us a plain white wine, cooled by sitting the glass carboy it came in on a block of ice. He thanked me gravely for liberating him. I told him to thank General De

Gaulle, and he told me that his grandfather's oldest pig smelled better than De Gaulle. I held my hands up and surrendered to him with a grin. I wasn't arguing with him, I said. He said, 'Bon,' but after he returned my smile, looked down into his cart. I followed his glance and found myself looking at a revolver. Lying just to hand.

'I protect my customers,' he told me, and shrugged.

'What's all the Froggie talk about then?' Les asked me.

'He wanted to know whether we wanted white or red wine. I told him *white*.'

'I thought I could hear you talking about De Gaulle?'

'He named one of his wines after him. I chose the other.'

'Just so long as he keeps his mitt away from his gun.'

'You saw that, did you?'

'I *looked* for it. You and I are going to have to have a little chat about self-preservation.'

'Yes, Les.' I said it meekly.

'. . . and stop taking the piss.'

'Yes, Les.' I said it even more meekly.

England laughed. He had a big deep laugh.

Halfway through the second glass I had that nervy feeling that I was being watched. Without thinking I said, 'Someone's watching me.'

Les said, 'Get ready to jump, then,' and casually moved his Sten onto his lap, as if to make himself more comfortable. Then I looked up at the other party. A woman in an olive drab boiler suit was staring at me from twenty-five feet away, a big wicked smile on her face. I knew her short, dark blonde hair. I knew without looking that she had a flash saying *War Correspondent* sewn sloppily on a place above her left tit, and that she had crooked teeth. She waved. Les tensed.

'OK chaps,' I told them. 'Panic over. I know her: she's an American journalist I met in England. Sorry about that.'

'Never say you're sorry,' Les told me. 'It's a sign of weakness.' He relaxed.

'That's good enough to be in a film one day,' I told him.

'I thought so, too,' the Major said. 'I'm going to write it into my notebook.'

I waved back, and she sauntered over, rolling her hips like a Clydesdale.

I stood up to shake hands, but she gave a little laugh, and kissed me on both cheeks, Froggie fashion. I probably blushed. She said, 'Hi, Charlie. Taking some rays?'

'Rays?'

'Sitting in the sunshine, dummy. How *are* you? Stopped flying yet?'

'Temporarily.' Then I told my mates, 'This is Lee Miller. She's an American photographer and war correspondent. She took my photograph mixed in with US aircrew, in October, I think.' Then I told her, 'I was in a bit of a crash. Got myself singed. They want my feet to stay on the ground for the time being.'

'Best place for them, soldier, unless they're kicking up in the air. What are you doing here?'

'Looking for somewhere to stay, and looking for Grace Baker — you remember her?'

'Sure. She was through here a few weeks ago. She was travelling with Albie the tank man. Remember him?'

'Going where?'

'I didn't ask. She had some orphan kid with her, and she was wet-nursing it: ugh!'

'How old was the kid?'

'Few weeks, I guess. What's the matter? She steal it?'

'No, Lee. Nothing like that. Her family are worried about her, and I've been given time off to find her and take her home. Want a drink?'

'You got absinthe?'

'Where did you get absinthe?'

That was James England getting into the act.

'One of my friends over there.' She nodded back to the other table. 'He makes it from paintbrush cleaner.'

'He drink it himself, Miss?' Les asked her.

Lee laughed. Her laugh was an awful lot like the Major's, I realized.

'No. He sticks to wine. He gives the absinthe to women, and undresses them once they're out of it. He's a sneaky sort until you get to know him.'

'I'd like to meet him, Miss.'

'Come on over. Who are you two?'

'Ham 'n' Eggs.' That was the Major again. He meant to be funny. He actually sounded deranged. She trailed us over to her pals as if we were the train of her wedding dress. We picked up three more glasses of the white stuff en route. I suppose I felt like a tourist before I really knew what one was.

Up close I didn't realize that you could load that much luggage on a jeep without bursting its tyres. It had the word *Hussar* painted on the bottom frame of its windscreen.

Lee said, 'Ignore it. Some guy has promised me a Chevy saloon. I plan to get to Greece with it.' Then she said to us, 'This is Pablo, and this is Boris,' and in French to them, 'This is Charlie, and Ham 'n' Eggs. I knew Charlie in England: he's OK. I don't know the others.'

'They're OK, too.' I switched to their lingo. 'Only they can't speak French.'

'What about their English?' Boris asked me back in English, extending his hand for a clasp.

'Clumsy, but adequate,' I told him back in French.

Les said, 'What was all that about?'

'Introductions. They're cool about you now.'

'What does *cool* mean?'

'It means you're OK.'

'Then say OK the next time.'

'OK,' I said, and he gave me the look.

'When you've finished? . . .' Lee said, and raised her glass.

I can't remember Boris; isn't that odd? Only that he was something to do with the ballet, and seemed an improbably masculine type for it: you must have heard all of the stories. Pablo was a small, rounded man with short-cut greying hair, and the blackest round eyes you ever saw. He was what the working class would have looked like if they had been designed by Arthur Rackham. He looked rotund and muscular, even though he was probably thin under his clothes. Most Parisians were in 1945. Being fat was like wearing the label *collaborator* around your neck. Lee pronounced his name in a slurred, Frenchy way: it came out almost as *Pavlo*.

Pavlo proposed the first toast, which was, 'Death to the French!'

I asked him, 'Aren't *you* French?'

'Sometimes. Usually I am Spanish. Sometimes I am Basque. A world citizen.'

'There are a lot of those, these days. Half of Europe is on its feet and moving around.'

'I thought all Englishmen said, *Death to the French*? I thought that would please you.'

'We haven't said that since Trafalgar . . . and you don't have to please me.'

'Good. I can tell you that you are short and ugly then?'

'Yes, you can. You are even shorter and uglier than I am; and, what's more, you're old.'

'Ah, but you are *English*. You still have a lot of catching up to do.'

The Major enmeshed him and Boris in an argument about art, of all things, and soon they were all waving their arms at each other, and shouting insults. Even Les had an opinion.

He told them about an exhibition he'd seen by a man named Harold Larwood, at a place named *The Oval*. Boris didn't get it, and argued hotly. Pavlo did. He sat back in his chair and with his feet swinging just above the ground, grinned over his glass. His eyes twinkled wickedly. Lee was sitting next to me. She linked her arm through mine, and raised her glass for a clink. The greeny-tinged fluid in it moved lazily, like uncut disinfectant.

'Welcome to Paris, Biffo.'

'That's what you called me when we met in Bedford,' I remembered.

'Suits you, doesn't it?'

'We're looking for somewhere to stay for a couple of days.'

'When you see the pigs fly over, give me a call: I'd like to get a shot of them. You got contacts?'

'Tweedledee and Tweedledum *thought* they had. They were wrong.'

'Who *are* they?'

'Two guys giving me a lift. They're sort of supplies staff. They estimate how much food we need to lift into an area when we liberate it, if everybody isn't to starve. The older man is James England, he's the expert.'

James picked up on his name.

'Say *Hello*, James,' I told him. He waved lazily, and raised his glass. Alcohol gave him a great smile. '. . . and the other one's Raffles, his driver. Only his name's not Raffles, and I wonder if James's real name is England, as well. I'm keeping funny company.'

'Don't let it worry you, Biffo. Everyone's got more than one these days. Lee Miller isn't all my real name, either.'

'What is?'

'Lee Penrose, I suppose. Do you like it?'

'Not as much as Miller. Penrose sounds too English for you.'

Her eyes had a sudden sad cast to them. She looked away and quietly said, 'Bravo, Charlie.'

'Sorry. I touched a nerve there.'

'Not the one you wanted to, Biffo . . . want to come to a party? We're drinking at Pavlo's studio. He's an artist, in case you hadn't guessed. You might meet someone there who can put you up for a few days.'

When I looked up Les was looking at me. He hadn't missed a word of any of the conversations. He nodded almost imperceptibly. I said, 'Yes please. That would be lovely.'

If you ever asked me what an artist's studio looked like I would tell you that it was several rooms so filled with people and booze and tobacco smoke that you couldn't see the walls. There was a small kitchen with a chipped square sink. I got stuck with my backside against it, and people looking for water had to wriggle past me all afternoon. One thin girl in a summer frock — her eye make-up made her look like a vampire — stood with her right hand, with its cigarette, on my shoulder, and her legs astride mine as we talked. She used the press of the crowd against me. I lasted a delicious five minutes or so. She studied my eyes all the time. Immediately afterwards she said, 'I was watching for the moment. I love men's faces at that moment.'

I said, 'You're another American. You must be an artist.'

'No. Pavlo's the artist, and so is Paul. I'm not an artist.'

'You're an artist.'

'No. You need a cock to be an artist. All great artists paint with their cocks.'

'Who told you that?'

'Some artist.'

I could have said *See*, but it wouldn't have made any

109

difference. Lee must have noticed. She moved in on me, and said, 'I see you met Mariel. She was a friend to Papa once.'

'You mean your father?'

'No; Hemingway, stupid. He lived here in the Twenties.'

'You knew him, of course?'

'Not in the way you've just known Mariel.'

I looked down for the damp patch, and must have blushed. It wasn't there. She laughed. I laughed. I heard James's laugh over the buzz of the crowd somewhere. Part of my mind said, *So this is what peace is like.* I could live with that. England muscled over with Les not far astern. Les had a girl on his arm: a drunken redhead with a wicked great mouth. James said, 'Do you want the good news or the bad news?'

'Try good news first,' I shouted at him.

'I've done a deal with the artist. We can sleep in his studio after the party's finished.'

'. . . and the bad news?'

'It may not finish.' He shouted that back. I could live with that too. I wished that Les would put the Sten away. Lee Miller hadn't drifted off. I asked her, 'Where do you stay when you're in Paris?'

'Sometimes with a pal. But if I'm working it's usually the Hotel Scribe. Room 412 is Lee Miller's room.'

'Where's that?'

'Near the Opera. Near the Place de la Concorde. One Rue Scribe.'

'Naturally.'

'You're making fun of an old lady, Charlie Bassett. That isn't fair.'

110

'I know. I'll do whatever you like to make it up.'

'Drive me home.'

'Seriously?'

'Drive me home seriously. I'm too crocked to do it by myself. My time fuse tells me I'll pass out in about thirty minutes.'

She leaned very close, and blinked her eyes slowly at me several times. It wasn't a come-on: it was to show me that there was nothing much going on behind them. I believed her.

A jeep isn't as easy to drive as it looks. God knows how *she* managed it. Carrying about six cwt of kit up to room 412 of the Hotel Scribe when you're a drunk was even harder. Her room was a tip; like the inside of a junk shop. Old clothes everywhere, old food, weapons, a million cameras, and a strong smell of developer solutions and booze. She was flying straight again: more or less. We said a bit of this and a bit of that, probably wondering how to get away from one another, when she blurted out, 'I don't want to fuck you, Charlie.' She sounded more like one of my aunts.

I said, 'Good. I don't want to fuck you either.'

'In that case you can stay. You can wrap in a blanket and sleep on the other side of the bed. In the morning you can tell people that you spent the night with the famous Lee Miller.'

After a couple of glasses of something that came out of a battered jerrycan we turned in. I wrapped myself in a rough horse blanket I found on the floor, and lay alongside her. She turned towards me, and tucked her head over the arm I offered. But that was all. When I awoke during the night, she murmured, 'I met your Grace in England, didn't I? What's the matter with her?'

I said, 'I think her stepfather shagged her a lot.'

'Oh, that,' Lee said. Almost a whisper. She didn't speak again until the morning.

You'll remember that I wondered how Lee ever managed to drive a jeep. The answer was *well*. The next morning she piloted it like a racing driver, her elbows high and wide and moving like wings, her every movement smooth and coordinated. Back in Pavlo's studio it looked as if the night had ended in a fight. Everything was broken. I said, 'Cripes!' and Lee said, 'Don't worry. It looked like this before we started.'

There was a gendarme in the kitchen, asleep on an overstuffed armchair; a half-filled wineglass by his side and an empty bottle on the floor between his feet. He had probably arrived wearing a cap, but there was no sign of it now. He stirred, and said, ''allo, 'allo', to me. He had a lisp, and a very odd accent. He asked me my name, and produced a notebook for it.

I said, 'Bassett. Charles Bassett. Royal Air Force.'

'Ah, oui. English?'

'Yes.'

'Rank?'

'Wing Commander,' Lee said.

The policeman gave my ragbag of uniform parts a sceptical once-over: Lee added, 'with the *Resistance*.'

'Ah.' He made a great show of scribbling over what he had

112

written, and disappeared the notebook again. Lee asked him, 'Was there trouble here?'

The policeman answered in English, very slowly and concisely, for my benefit, because everyone knows that the English can't communicate with foreigners.

'Someone was shot. With a small automatic weapon.'

'Who?'

'A woman.'

'Fatally?'

The gendarme shrugged.

'For her pride. A clean and honourable buttock wound. She will tell her grandchildren she received it resisting the *Boche*, not servicing the British.'

'Who did it?'

This was wholly Lee's conversation: I wanted nothing to do with it.

'The artist. It appears there were two British soldiers staying here last night. When the artist had retired with his woman, one of the soldiers played a childish trick. He tied a bicycle saddle to his head, and a pair of handlebars behind it. In the half-light, once his head was bent forward, he looked like the Minotaur. Delicacy does not permit me to fully describe the moment – but imagine yourself the artist; your woman is above you when the Minotaur looks over her shoulder. He screamed, grabbed at the gun the soldier wore, and in the struggle a round was fired which pierced the backside of a person in the next room. She demanded a judicial investigation.'

'Where is Picasso?'

'Fled. That has happened before. He is a bull around women, but not around other bulls.' *Bulls* was French police slang for policeman. That wasn't a bad pun, I decided. I asked about the two Englishmen.

'Arrested.'

'Where, Monsieur?'

'At the Police Office. One of them took my cap, and gave me his own.' He handed it to me. I recognized James England's battered headwear. Bollocks.

The Police Office was the size of a small shop. It had three cells. Les was in one, pretending to be asleep. His beret was tipped over his eyes, and the Sten still around his neck: no magazine, though. Major England was in the next cell, cuddled up to the redhead I'd last seen with Les. She was wearing a gendarme's cap.

From the corridor outside I asked Les, 'What's with the bird? *Droit de seigneur?*' It was one phrase from French history that English schoolboys remember.

'She wanted second helpings,' he told me. Then, 'You took your time.'

'What do I need to do to get you out?'

'Ask the copper?'

The policeman looked uncomfortable when I asked him.

'You could promise that they will keep better company in future?'

'I could.'

'That they will refrain from shooting our citizens in the arse.'

'That too.'

'. . . and that the gallant Major returns my hat.'

'Certainly. Would there be any paperwork? Any embarrassing documentation?'

Only the French understand the word *embarrassing* better than the English. He shrugged.

He suggested that I move the Humber discreetly round the corner, and wait there. After about ten minutes the Major and Les appeared, the latter clipping the magazine ostentatiously into the Sten, the former under his own battered cap again. I had moved to the passenger seat to give Les his due. The Major settled into the back with a sigh. He said, 'Impressed, young Charlie. You know Picasso, and Paul Éluard; you spend the night with Lee Miller; you bribe the police to get us out of poky, and apparently they think that you're a hero of the Resistance.'

'I deny all that,' I told him. 'Where's the girl?'

'She's staying,' he told me. 'The gendarmes want to photograph her backside. There's such a wonderful bullet hole that they've all gone home to get their own cameras.'

Les asked, 'Where to, Guv'nor?' and it was startling to realize that he had addressed the question to me.

'Can you find the Grand Central American Red Cross Club?'

Seven

There was a big Snowdrop on the door, whacking his nightstick into the palm of one hand as if looking for someone to practise on.

I said, 'I'm looking for a Miss Emily Rea.'

He glanced down briefly at me, then looked away with, 'Officers only. Beat it.'

'I *am* one. Pilot Officer. RAF.'

'An' I'm Betty Grable's left tit. Beat it.' He spat. It hit the driver's side door of the Humber, and ran down the side. That wasn't a clever thing to do. Les smiled at him. You may already know that I'm leery of men who smile when something bad has happened.

I tried, 'It's all right. I'm on government business. I can identify myself.'

He laid the stick horizontally across my chest.

'Only one government's business behind these doors, son, an' that ain't yours. Now beat it. New York cops don't ask no four times.'

I shrugged and walked back to the car, leaning down to speak with Les and the Major.

Les said, 'I heard him. There's a cafe across the road, a hundred yards back. See you there.'

He was moving away from the kerb before his lips had stopped moving, pulling a left U-turn in the face of the oncoming traffic.

We sat at a table outside the Café Libération in violation of Les's rules. I could see that he felt uncomfortable: he was moving about in his seat all the time. Had it been the Café des Allemands until the Germans sloped off?

James said, 'That wasn't very helpful of him, was it? Although I suppose all sorts of Allied yeomanry tries to get in there. I've heard that they have a free bar. What are we going to do next?'

Les said, 'Wait here, and shoot the bastard?'

'That won't help me.'

'It isn't supposed to. It's supposed to piss him off. With dicks like that representing the occupying powers no wonder the French are still shooting at us.'

A waiter with a narrow, twirled moustache came out to the table. I ordered bread, small pieces of smoked fish, and glasses of wine. The wine here was fifteen cents a glass: I suppose that the owner had bigger overheads.

Les said, 'Shocking.' Then, ''allo, 'allo. Where's our friend off to?'

The Snowdrop outside the ARC Club had been joined by another: a black man who carried two inverted stripes on his arm. Maybe that's what had pissed the white one off. They crossed the road, and walked that measured policeman's walk towards us. They carried their nightsticks, and the holster flaps of their big American pistols were unbuttoned.

Les muttered, 'Wankers.' He kept his Sten in his lap, and an innocent expression on his face. They weren't coming for us. The big white cop had probably already forgotten me, the way you forget a fly you've waved off your food, which didn't mean that there wasn't a problem.

The problem was that Les hadn't forgotten *him*. As he reached our seats, and was about to pace past, Les stuck out his desert boot and brought the man down, neatly hooking his legs away from him. He twisted as he fell and his head ended up on the pavement close to Les's right boot. Les bent over and stuck the muzzle of his Sten in his victim's ear. The other cop was the first black cop I'd seen. He was quite good. He instinctively dropped into the fighting crouch, his hand to his holster, before he heard the neat clicking noise – Major England cocking the old Webley .38 he kept on a lanyard. He said, 'Please don't do anything precipitate, old chap, and please join us.'

England was good with his feet too. He used one to hook out a fourth chair for the man.

The cop on the ground gulped for air. There was a smear of blood on the paving where his chin had met it. Two Parisians, and a mangy old dog, stepped around him as if a military policeman lying on the path wasn't an unusual occurrence.

The black cop sighed, as if depressed. When he asked, 'Would you mind telling me what this is all about, before you kill me?' he had a melodious, cultured voice. James smiled. It was a smile that veiled something else.

'It would be helpful if you first placed your truncheon on the ground, and buttoned down the flap on your holster. But please move very slowly.'

The cop moved so slowly, and in jerks, that he was taking the piss. He wasn't scared.

'That's nice,' James told him. 'We can all relax now. I'm afraid that when we paid a visit, your man there made the mistake of spitting tobacco all over our car. It disturbed my driver.'

'Is that serious, sir?'

'It could be. I don't always have him fully under control.'

'That's the problem with Bassett. He's the man about to clean off your car with his tongue.'

'Bassett?'

'Yes sir. PFC Bassett. Passed out bottom of his class at Fort Benning. Now passed out in the gutter by the looks of it.'

'He could be one of my relations,' I told him. 'I'm a Bassett too.'

He gave me a shrewd look.

'I hopes not. One is more than enough. So what was *your* problem, Mr Bassett?'

'I need to meet with a woman named Rea. She asked me to look her up over here.'

OK. So it wasn't quite true. It was just the best I could think up at the time.

'Miss Emily?'

'Yes. That's right.'

'Emily's up at the Front for a couple of days. How come you didn't know that?'

'It wasn't that kind of appointment. I last saw her in the ARC Club in Bedford. She said to call on her if ever I crash-landed in Paris. It's become important because she's also a friend of a friend of mine: someone who just happens to be important to someone important, and who may have run away to join the Red Cross somewhere in Europe. Am I explaining this badly?'

The coloured said, 'I've heard better, but I think I'm following you.'

'I've been sent over to find a Miss Grace Baker, and Emily Rea is a person over here she might turn to.'

The Negro stared off into middle distance, and then asked Major England, 'Can I make a call? There's a phone back in there. I could make a few checks.'

'If you left your gunbelt at this table you could,' James agreed. The man draped his white belt and holster across the back of his chair. He grinned us a set of teeth even whiter. James asked as an afterthought, 'What's your name?'

'Simmer, that is Simms, McKechnie. My father came from Scotland. Who's the dame you're looking for again?'

'Baker. Grace Baker.' I told him. 'She was a delivery pilot. English girl. She's about twenty-eight. Dark-haired and pretty. I went to Scotland once,' I added. 'Glasgow. My family had been evacuated up there.'

'You see any black folks?'

'Some merchant seamen. That was all.'

*

The telephone in the bar made that god-awful sound that French telephones still do, and the man with the corkscrew moustaches picked it up, and called out to us.

'It's for you,' I told the Negro.

'I know that. Je parley. I was waiting for the man with the gun to say I could go fer it.'

'What gun?' James grinned.

When McKechnie came back to us he said, 'We have a Lieutenant Kilduff. People call him *Binkie*; I don't know why. He asks if you can come back tomorrow after lunch.'

The Negro coughed, looked uncomfortable, and looked away. James said, 'What's he do, this Binkie?'

He looked England in the eyes; I'll give him that. He replied neutrally, 'Same sort of thing you do, sir, I'd guess. Only in my army we call it *liaison*.' Then he asked James, 'You would be Major James England, and his driver Private Finnigan, sir?'

'Yes. How did you know that?'

'We got a signal that you were out. There were photographs with it: I should have paid more attention to them. Lieutenant Kilduff thinks that it's very amusing, us sitting here and waiting for you to give us permission to go.'

James positively beamed. I didn't ever like him in that mood.

'Have another drink.'

He said that to include everyone. That included Sweeny Todd and his demon moustaches, and even PFC Bassett sitting on the kerb cleaning the car door. I remember that it was several glasses later that McKechnie told us that he was a medical student before he was called up — but the Army had made him a policeman. The Army had no prejudice against black doctors. They had no black doctors either, because they thought that their smashed-up white soldiers might not like that. Wrong again. I noticed that the pads of his hands were as pink as mine. My namesake finished with the car door. The only time he took his eyes off Les was when he waved away a glass I offered him. There was a smear of dirt on one cheek, and he dabbed at the blood on his chin with a grubby khaki handkerchief.

Eight

Later, back in the car, Les asked, 'Do you trust the black bastard?'

Major England came back with, 'Not wholly. But not because he's black, because he's cleverer than me.'

I asked them, 'Aren't I holding you back? Aren't you supposed to be going somewhere?'

England told me, 'No. We're still ahead of schedule. We came back early to facilitate your little trip: Cliff arranged it.'

'That's the Cliff newly revealed to be a spy?'

'A facilitator of spies. That's the one. The Front's static at the moment anyway; we don't need to move until *it* does. Then we need to be up there with it. Monty's stuck, Simp's stuck, Horrocks is stuck, Brad's stuck, they're all stuck. Useless shower of bastards. Who's not stuck, Les?'

'The Russian General Zhukov. He's not stuck, sir: it's positively running out of him.'

'How d'you know that?'

'I have my sources,' Les said huffily.

James then summed up for me. 'So we're in no hurry at present.'

'What happens if you fall behind schedule?'

'Ditch you, and steal all your money I should think.'

Then they had this conversation as if I wasn't there.

'Shall we show the boy the Elephant bet?'

'Yes, Les. Why not? As good a way to spend the afternoon as any; then go and see Mrs Maggs. She might put us up – should have thought of her before.'

'Pushing your luck there, sir, I should have thought.'

'We've been pushing our luck for months.'

'About the Elephant, sir. Are you on for five bob again this time?'

'Not this time, Les; half a crown. Half a crown says they're gone.'

'Half a crown says they ain't.' Then, 'You're a lucky little bugger,' Les told me. 'The Major and me don't share the Elephant bet with everyone, you know.' They both appeared to find this excruciatingly funny.

I had noticed the whip aerial sticking up over the near-side rear wing before. Now was the time to show me what it did, or 'earn your corn,' as the Major put it.

He and I swapped places. I was put in the back seats, and given a small leather suitcase. When I opened it I found a small transmitter/receiver.

'German job,' Les told me. 'Smashing, isn't it? Bosch and Schmelling. Its transmit is *Morse only*, but you can tune it to receive anything: it has a very nice little speaker. You can even hear the Brylcreem boys dying over Germany on it, if you want to.'

I didn't rise to the bait. In truth it was the neatest job I'd ever laid eyes on; and I'm a professional. I wanted it immediately. It connected to two small glass-cased batteries in a battered old doctor's bag.

'We borrowed it from a Jerry agent who parachuted on to the Isle of Wight by mistake.' That was James again. 'The Home Guard got him. I am afraid that they were rather robust with him; hence the stains inside the lid.'

'It's smaller than anything we do,' I said, 'and its build quality is amazing. What do you use it for? I mean what kind of message? Clear or code?'

'Encrypted. One-time code pads. Nothing special. Old Raffles here drives me about a bit. I make a note of how many people I can see, and how much food's lying about – usually sod-all. Then I do my sums, adding in soldiery and prisoners. Encrypt it, and tap out my shopping list back to base. They send it forward on five-tonners the next day. Couldn't be simpler.'

'That's what Cliff told me. He also said that whenever it went wrong you got shot at.'

'Cliff's an old woman.'

'What do you want me to do with it, James?'

'Can you check that it's OK? Then tune it to some decent station, and get us some music. It blows the knickers off the Froggie as we cruise past her with music pumping away like some portable orchestra.'

The aerial lead plugged into a neat jack plug above the rear seats. It only took a minute to warm up, and then we were in business. I got them an American Forces station from Spa, in Belgium, in the middle of a Tommy Dorsey programme. I hummed along with 'After You've Gone', until the Major turned and frowned at me.

Les drove us onto the Bois de Boulogne and somewhere beyond. Somewhere around the Bois we overtook a pretty woman cycling at the head of a short column of Boy Scouts. Her skirts billowed up as her knees pumped, and seeing us looking at her legs she waved and laughed. The boys laughed and waved as well. I had that thought again: *This is what peace must be like*. I turned to watch them out of the oval back window, but they were already stopping, and turning off the cobbled road.

I met the Elephant at the other end of the Bois: a few miles on. You've heard that joke – when is a something not a something? When is an Elephant not an Elephant? In this case, when it's a fucking great tank: the biggest you've ever seen. It was on the grass verge facing Paris, and had a strip of its metal track stretched out behind it. Grass was growing through that, so it must have been there some time. Its huge, long gun barrel pointed vaguely upwards in a sad show of defiance. Les drove past, pulled up and parked. I was still looking at the beast. I said, 'Strewth!'

'A few Tommies have said that. Big bastard isn't it?'

'What is it?'

'We told you: Jerry calls it *the Elephant*, an' it's not really a tank – it's a self-propelled gun: the biggest fucker in the world. It doesn't have a turret: just has that bleeding great gun built into the rear superstructure pointing forwards. To aim the gun proper you have to aim the vehicle, although the gun has a bit of lateral tracking, and it *can* elevate.'

'It's twice as big as anything we've got.'

'Not quite. But it's big enough. The Major and I got behind one by mistake on the last trip. We hid in the field next to it until they decided to retreat. That gun is so powerful that every time they fired it, the fucking thing leaped back about ten feet. That's more than fifty tons of tank going backwards. Come an' 'ave a butcher's.'

Les walked out on the smooth cobbles, and not on the grass verge. I reckoned he knew what he was doing, and copied him. Major England brought up the rear. Up close the tank was blackened by burning, but you could see that the circular door in its back plate was still closed, and in places some of its original ochre paint was blistered but still showing. There was already rust at the welded edges of its massive armour plate. As I walked alongside it I thought, 'What the fuck does it take to stop one of these?' and must have spoken aloud, because England said, 'A gang of fourteen-year-old French boys with wine bottles full of petrol, apparently.'

He pointed out a mass of twisted metal around the front driving sprocket. 'It's so bloody big you can't see what's going on alongside, unless you're hanging out of the top waiting to get shot. That's what you call an original design flaw. Someone told me that the kids just walked alongside, fed a short length of iron girder between the track and the drive sprocket, and waited for it to throw its track.'

'What then?'

'They scrambled on top, and waited for Jerry to open the hatches. As soon as he did they tossed home-made firebombs inside – that's soap which has been boiled up and liquefied, added to petrol in a one to two solution, if you're interested – slammed the lids, and sat on them till Jerry stopped screaming.'

That explained one of the smells I'd picked up: gasoline. I wasn't as familiar with the other.

'That smell . . .' I said.

'Old dead things,' said Les. 'I didn't think you'd have met that before, and you're going to have to get used to it where you're going. Look . . .' He was already up on its scuttle, and reached out a hand to pull me up after him. I stood with him looking down into two small open hatches that once covered a driver and a machine-gunner. The inside of the vehicle was coated with a greasy black substance that smelled of petrol and burnt pork fat. The mainly black things sitting on the seats inside smelled of putrefaction: something rich and dusty that caught at the back of your throat. 'It makes some folk throw up,' Les told me.

'I think I can understand that. Flying sometimes does that to me these days.'

'. . . and I can understand *that*,' Les said. '. . . It ain't natural.'

I was fascinated despite myself. It felt oddly intrusive to be looking down on the corpses. The crown of both the skulls gleamed white as if polished, but elsewhere they were things of darkness: flesh and clothing, black and one substance. I tell a lie. The uniform was peeled back off the gunner's shoulder. There was black stuff which could have been flesh or muscle, and then that sudden gleam of white again . . . ribs.

Les said, 'When we first came by, they were untouched. Like little black jockeys sitting in here. Curled up like babies, and strangely shiny, an' the smell was worse. Real tart. I guess the rats are getting into them now. I can see grooves in the skulls, can't you?'

'Yes.'

'They're gnaw marks. I've seen that in Italy too.'

'What was all that about half a crown, that you and the Major were arguing about on the way here?'

'He always bets me that the Frogs will have taken the bodies away and buried them. I always bet him that they won't have done. Three—nil to me so far.'

Back in the car I switched on the radio again as Les turned us around on the cobbles without touching the verges. I tuned into the same US station at Spa. I heard the last few notes of 'Weary Blues', and when they started up again it was that fellow Sinatra singing 'I'll Be Seeing You'. I knew immediately that, whenever I heard the song again, what I would be seeing in my head would be the inside of that damned tank and its foetal corpses. My dad brought memories like that back from the first lot: he used to call it *going down nightmare alley*. I knew that road now, and wondered where he was, and if he'd passed this way. Les drove slowly, as if he was watching for something, which, of course, he was. He stopped the car close to a jumbled heap of bicycles, which was a few yards off the road, and in the trees. He looked across at England, and said,

'I'm not sure that the area's been properly cleared yet. Would you mind if I strolled over and warned them, Guv'nor?'

'No. Take Charlie with you, and show him the *walk*.'

'What's the walk?' I asked him as we stood out on the road. We had to wait to cross because a column of light stuff – ugly little scout cars, and bren gun carriers – went bouncing past. It seemed to take forever.

'Watch me,' Les said, 'an' I'll show you. It's the way you walk through a minefield, if you haven't a choice. Just let me go about six feet ahead of you, watch where I walk, and place your feet where I do. The walk'll come naturally.'

We set off across the trampled grass the Scouts had left behind them. The ground sloped down, and through a screen of trees. Les had a slightly longer and slower pace than mine, so I found copying him I had a loping movement. It was strange, but quickly comfortable. As we broke through the trees I could see the ground still sloped away, to a small pond in a natural basin, surrounded by thick grass . . . maybe fifty yards away from us. On the other side of it the ground climbed away again, and into thick woods. The Scouts were skylarking. Les didn't go any further: he sat down in the lee of the tree ring. I dropped alongside him, sweating slightly. Some of the boys had stripped off, and were swimming. I supposed that the boys who'd killed the Germans in the Elephant can't have been much older than this. The woman must have been swimming. She lay face-down looking away from us. Her bottom was very white, like the skulls of dead German soldiers.

'It's their Boy Scout Field Studies badge,' I told him. 'The

French have a different approach to biology. It's why they end up with less queers than us.'

As we stood up to walk away one of the boys waved lazily to us. Why the hell should they care?

I asked Les, 'There never were any mines, were there?'

'Oh, yeah. One time there were. It was one of the first areas they cleaned up. So many kids around here, see. A sapper got chopped down there. Blown to mincemeat.'

'So why did we go through all that stuff about *the walk*?'

'So you learned it, sir: I'm not going to be around forever, you know. Now you know how to walk through a minefield. Sometimes when you see a file of soldiers crossing a minefield from the distance, all doing the walk set out by the guy in front, it can look quite comical; like some old dance, with Death leading the way. Then the guy in front runs out of luck, and it doesn't.'

'I'll remember that.'

'And remember that more men get maimed by mines than killed by them; so if you find yourself in a minefield, don't panic. The odds are favourable – if you can get along without a foot that is.'

'I'll . . .'

'. . . I know: you'll remember that too.'

By then we were back at the Humber. The Major looked up from his little notebook and asked us, 'Anything doing?'

'No,' Les told him. 'Just those Scouts.'

James had retuned the radio, and I could hear Tommy Handley from London.

*

I felt at home in Maggs's place: it had the mid-upper turret from a Lancaster bomber in the back garden, and she was growing things in it. The aircraft's rear fuselage now attached to the back of a small house was her kitchen. She had created another small room with packing cases, and she showed me with pride the Elsan inside.

'Before that,' she told me with a disarming smile, 'I had to go outside come rain or shine. It wasn't funny sitting out there on a pitch-black frosty night, I can tell you.'

She made me laugh.

'Where are you from? Originally?'

'Stepney. You?'

'Carshalton in Surrey. Why didn't the Jerries round you up and lock you away?'

'Dunno really, but my old man was a copper in Vichy on and off. That probably had something to do with it . . . to tell you the truth I think it was just that I amused them, an' they thought I was 'armless. I wasn't the only one.'

'Were you?'

'What?'

'Harmless.'

'If you're with Les and the Major you know better than to ask me that!'

'Yeah. Just testing. Where did you get the Lancaster from?'

'I woke up one morning, and most of it was in the garden. The Boche took some of it away; the engines, the guns . . . things like that.'

'I'm surprised they didn't take the rest. Haw-Haw keeps

saying that every British bomber that crashes in Germany gets turned into fighters to defend it with.'

'Is that what it feels like up there, son?'

'Yes. The buggers are still coming up at us. How did you know I was RAF?'

'Because she's a bloody witch,' Major England said. Like Dracula, he'd glided out from what was once her back door, into what was now her kitchen. 'Meet Mata-Whory: the only woman in France not punished for sleeping with the enemy.'

'You've got a bad tongue on you, Major,' she told him, '. . . and one which could still get me hung from a lamp-post. Remember there's some round here still throws their right arm up when a soldier blows off. They haven't thrown away their Jerry flags, you know, just folded them carefully and put them in the bottom of their blanket boxes, waiting for the next time . . . and to answer your question, young man, you got the look. You don't look Army, and we're a long way from the bleedin' sea!'

I plugged on. 'What happened to her crew?'

'We stuck two at the end of the garden, poor sods, under the cabbages now. I expect your lot will dig them up eventually.'

'What about the others?'

'I expect they got away.' She set her lips in a stubborn line, and crossed her hands in front of her like a nun. I wasn't going to get any more in that direction.

The Major added something else.

'Mrs Maggs's husband must have heard it fall, and went

outside to investigate. She found him out there the next morning too, didn't you, love?'

She smiled. It wasn't exactly a smile.

He finished off, 'Deuced unlucky. One of the guns on the Lanc must have popped off as it ploughed in. Killed the little beggar. Smack between the shoulder blades. From the back of course.'

''e always was an unlucky man. I never know why I married a Frenchie in the first place,' Mrs Maggs told me, and then kept going. '*Mean* an' unlucky, an' he never knew whether he was comin' or goin', if you foller me?'

I said, 'I don't.'

'Then it don't matter.'

'Talking to Maggs,' James told me, as if she wasn't there, 'is like wrestling with the sea: every time you think you've tied down what she means, you find it's slipped out of your grasp again.'

'I see,' I said.

'You don't,' he insisted. 'That's *exactly* my point.'

'Well; that's all right then.' That was Mrs Maggs. It was like trying to learn a different language using familiar words in unfamiliar places.

The small house was a severe cottage made of large, polished, grey stone blocks in a wide avenue of otherwise enormous houses. It had two rooms downstairs, bisected by a passage front to back, and a narrow staircase leading to three bedrooms. The room I was given was small, and filled by a three-quarter-size four-poster with red velvet moth-eaten draperies. I looked in the larger room that Les and Jimmy were to share. It was the same, but the bed was bigger, and it smelled of stale perfume and disinfectant. The third bedroom was Mrs Maggs's, and I didn't have the nerve to look in that, but I guessed it was the same, because worn red velvet seemed to be the house's theme. Later, when James told me that he and Les had to go out that evening and didn't particularly want me with them, I mentioned the red velvet, and said, 'It sort of reminds me of a . . .'

'Brothel. Well *done*, Charlie. Mrs Bassett had a bright baby, didn't she?'

'I'm sorry, Major, it's not an area I'm particularly familiar with.'

'Well, you bloody *should* be. The only alternative's getting married, and you'll find that too expensive, although old Les has strong views on that.'

'If that's where you're going tonight, perhaps I should come with you then: in the interests of acquiring a well-rounded education.'

'Nice try, Charlie.' He grinned. 'But no go. We're looking up old pals. They wouldn't be old pals any longer if we took new pals along with us. No offence intended.'

'None taken,' I told him. 'Not much, anyway.'

'The witch'll feed you, and anyway I need someone to look after *Kate*. We won't be moving her tonight, and if I leave her here alone Maggs would probably have a couple of friends round and have the wheels off her. Think of yourself as on guard duty.'

We were standing at the bottom of the stairs in the geographical centre of the house. Before I could say 'OK',

Mrs Maggs's voice needled out of the kitchen, 'The *witch* heard all of that, so you can make your own bleedin' breakfast in the morning.'

If James was embarrassed it didn't show.

Supper was a surprise, as it turned out; dark brown, spicy onion soup, and a potato dish called stovies, which she said she'd learned from a passing Scots soldier. She didn't say *passing Scots soldier*, she said, 'Fucking great Highlander.' I guess it meant the same thing. This *stovies* thing didn't look too appetizing when it hit the table in a steaming serving dish; grey food never does. It was a small mountain of mashed potato, flecked through with small pieces of potato skin and small red lumps. The red lumps were smashed-up corned beef. She slapped it on my plate with a dollop of soured cream on top. I thought that it looked like something served up in the poor house a century ago, but was shamed into a first forkful. After that it was roses all the way. Bloody brilliant; a load of pepper, which was supposed to be as scarce as hens' teeth, just topped off the flavour. We finished it between us, in the narrow kitchen that had once been a Lancaster, and washed it down with the last of Les's cider, which I swiped out of *Kate*'s boot. It was strange, sitting comfortably and eating a meal inside the sort of aircraft I'd been over Germany in so many times. Swords and bloody ploughshares. I've told you before: what goes around, comes around. Mrs Maggs didn't speak with her mouth full, so it was a peaceful kind of meal. Even though we were paying I felt obliged to offer up something. I offered to do the washing up. The old lady threw up her hands, and laughed. Then she lowered the laugh to something respectable. But it was still a laugh. She shook her head.

'Why not?'

'One of the girls will do it in the morning.'

'Why not me?'

There was a pause for a three-beat before she told me, regretfully, 'You wouldn't do it to our satisfaction,' and that was that.

She had neither tea nor coffee, she told me, but made us two stone mugs of a herbal infusion from something she grew in the gun turret. She said that it could be a tender plant, and that during the frosts she sometimes left a shrouded oil lamp in there to take the edge off the cold. We took it to the smaller of the two front rooms, which had a small iron stove. The combination of a glass of cider and this strange spicy tea relaxed me. I was comfortable: the conversation flowed naturally. It was like being with an old friend, or a favourite aunt.

'What really happened to Mr Maggs? The Major was talking so much tosh earlier, wasn't he? He and Les talk in some sort of code around me sometimes. It's like parents talking in front of a child.'

Mrs Maggs's accent had changed. Either that, or I had become attuned to it. She was still London English, but most of the East End had gone. She said, 'Mr Bonnet, pronounced *Bonnay*. I shot the swine, took up with a Jerry an' opened a brothel.'

'So how did you meet the Major?'

'A few days after the Liberation. My Jerry — he was a Major by then, too — was hiding here, looking for someone to surrender to. The Resistance wanted to hang him, but Major England knew he was here an' came an' collected him. Surrounded the house with a patrol o' Redcaps at about six in the morning, and then knocked on the door as bold as brass. I hit 'im with a skillet. You can laugh about it now.'

'What happened to your Jerry?'

'I had a card from Beauvais last week. He's waiting for transport to England, with his wife and son. Turns out he's a spy been sending information to England since 1942. There was I, part scared and part ashamed because I'd thrown my lot in with the Jerries, an' my Jerry was spying for our lot all along. He was sending them details of the food that the Nazis were moving around France: from that they could work out what kind of unit, and how big, was being supplied. Silly, isn't it?' I noticed that *ain't* was now *isn't*.

'Why did you shoot Mr Bonnet?'

'For what he was doing: he was rounding up Jews and poor folk for the Black Riders. I wasn't standing for that. What a tosser!'

'Who are the Black Riders?'

'The SS. Freemasons with a bad attitude. They're a mad, bad bunch keen on black underwear, and cloaks down to the ground. Stay away from them.'

'How did you meet *your* Jerry?'

'He came the morning after the Lancaster dropped into the back garden: to take it away. Fancy another cup of this stuff, or a little glass of wine?'

'The wine would be good.'

The small stove radiated heat, and I felt very comfortable. It's the only word I can use. The wine she brought back with her was thick and heavy and sweet. Like port. She said that it was Madeira, or from Madeira; I can't remember which. You drank it in small half-glasses with thick stems. Mrs Maggs said, 'Your turn. What's the fine Major and Mister Finnigan up to?'

I can't remember any more. Until the morning.

It was a Hollywood hangover, but not a classic. My head felt as if it was full of cotton wool. There was a nasty dry taste in my mouth: a mixture of the herbal tea I had taken the evening before, and that heavy wine. Raffles wasn't best pleased with me. In fact I was almost certain that he was angry. I knew that from what he did and said. I must have slept on my back fully clothed. Les scooped me up by my shirt front with one hand, dropped me on the floor and snarled, 'You're an effing idiot, Mr Charlie; officer or not.'

'I'll take your word for it, Les.' I just wished that I could care.

I noticed that the stale perfume I could smell from his clothes wasn't the same stale perfume I noticed in his room. Somewhere in the house Sam Browne sang 'Let's Face the Music and Dance' from a reedy radio. The Major looked a bit washed out. He was sitting at the table in the aluminium kitchen, with a glass of water in front of him, trying to work up the nerve to drink it. He said, 'Good morning, Charlie,' then winced, and added, 'We owe you an apology, Private

Raffles and I. Sometimes we fail to take account of the fact that you and we have been fighting different wars.'

'Sorry, Major. I don't quite follow you.'

'Not like you followed Evelyn's herbal tea last night?'

'Evelyn?'

'Maggs.'

'I still don't follow.'

'Les and I should have warned you about her herbal tea: it's not quite what you imagine. Her husband, Bonnet, was once a Legionnaire, and brought the plants back from North Africa when he settled down. I understand that jazz musicians are quite attached to it.'

'You mean . . .?'

''fraid so, old boy . . . that interesting and profoundly illegal stuff you've seen the War Ministry film about. Don't worry: it won't make your knob drop off, or anything like that, but it does make you unco' chatty.'

'How did you know?'

'This morning. Mrs M told me all about your little errand, then asked me a favour – you'd been babbling like the proverbial brook. Donald Peers. That worries me, because you must have picked up bits and pieces about us, if you've half a brain. Les and I are seriously secretive about our business affairs.'

'That had occurred to me. Can I have that water, if you're not going to drink it?'

'Get your own.'

Les said, 'I'll do it. Sit down before you fall down.'

I asked them, 'Where's all this leading to?'

'A decision about whether Maggs lives to collect her Légion d'Honneur, or joins the other two, under the cabbage patch.' That was Les.

'You cannot be serious,' I told him.

England said, 'I quite like that. I might write it down later.'

Les came back at me with, 'Try me.'

And the Major explained, 'It depends on what you told her. I know you told her all about *you*, and your bint, but I don't know what you told her about us.'

'Nothing. I don't know anything about you, do I?'

'That was what she said. I don't know whether or not to believe it. Did she ask?'

A light went on behind my eyes.

'Yes. I told her I didn't know.' I drank the water Les had stuck in front of me. It was icy and sweet.

The Major went on, 'She told us she *didn't* ask.'

'She's scared of Les,' I told him.

'So am I,' he said.

'Where is she?'

'Safe. Locked in her bedroom contemplating her sins. Bugger it, Les: what do you think?'

'Fuck knows. Toss you for it, or leave it to Charlie? He was here. We weren't.'

England started in on his water, wincing with each sip. I decided to let him lead. He asked me, 'Look, is this thing we're sitting in *still* a Lancaster bomber?'

'No; it's part of someone's kitchen.'

'It's an example of nothing being what it *seems*, Charlie. Mrs Maggs is not just a friendly old Madame. Nor is she only a sad old murderess, collaborator or Resistance fighter. She's all of those things, and more besides. She swaps information for favours, with anyone she needs to. That includes me, the Yanks, the Maquis – in other words the Commies – and the Folies Bergère, for all I know. What you have to decide for us is whether you're happy that what you gabbed out to her last night ends up with a third, and possibly unfriendly, party. Because it will do. In other words are you, or are we, compromised?'

'And if my answer is *Yes*, then Les kills her?'

'If you don't want to do it yourself, *yes*. Although I am firmly of the opinion that one should take responsibility for one's own decisions.'

'I won't kill her, or let Les do it,' I told them.

'Decided by default then.' That was the Major. He sneezed, and after a production with a grubby khaki handkerchief muttered, 'Let her out, Les. She can rustle up a bit of breakfast, and count her stars lucky.'

Mrs Maggs looked a bit dishevelled, but not scared. Les said, 'Charlie says you can live.'

'If that's what all the fuss was about, Mr Raffles, you coulda asked me. He ain't no lad to go killing old ladies.'

England said, 'No. He's the type that turns his back on them: far more dangerous.' They actually smiled at each other.

She'd made up enough stovies for all of us the night before, and hadn't used them. Now she fried what was left as thin meat and potato pancakes. They were delicious.

*

I was the last to get into *Kate*. Maggs had the nerve to give me a peck on the cheek, and whisper, 'Good luck, Charlie.'

Driving back to the ARC I had the chance to sort a few things out with the Major. One was, 'The man she refers to as *her Jerry* was one of yours, wasn't he? You and he are both in the food business. That's how you knew where to come to fetch him.' I turned in the passenger seat to look at him. He looked up from his notebook, and smiled. That was all.

The next was, 'And he was the German at that cafe table in Beauvais; with the woman and child.'

This time he looked out of the window. He was still smiling. Raffles said, 'Well done, Mr Charlie.'

And the last was, 'What was the favour Mrs Maggs wanted from you?'

'She thought that they'd hung about in Beauvais long enough. She wanted them safe in England: today. Said it would probably be safer for you, too.'

'What did *that* mean?'

'What do you think?'

'What are you going to do about it?'

'Already made the call. They're on their way. I was going to save them for a trade later. You're an expensive friend, Charlie Bassett.'

I asked him again, 'He *was* your spy, wasn't he?'

This time he answered me. He was still smiling, but there was something else in there somewhere.

'He's my *cousin*, Charlie. On my mother's side.'

What do they call it? Endgame. I guess that there was something he hadn't needed reminding of: the look on his face said that it would stick around all day. The two policemen weren't at the cafe, so we drove on. As Les drew the big car up to the kerb outside the ARC he told me, 'Things to do myself. Meet you at the cafe along the road about 1900 hours; OK?'

'Yes. If I get bored I'll go sightseeing, or shopping.'

'Buy yourself a gun,' Les murmured as I opened the car door. They were moving before I had turned away.

Nine

McKechnie and his number one man were on the steps outside the ARC club, lounging like lizards. Bassett Major, as I had started to think of him, showed me his teeth. They weren't very good teeth. McKechnie smiled and said, 'Hi,' holding out his soft pink and brown hand for a shake. 'I thought that maybe you weren't coming back.' There was a worry line behind the smile.

Bassett Major didn't smile. There were bruises on his face: smiling probably hurt him.

'Is it late?' I asked him.

'Chow's long gone. But we didn't set a time, did we?'

'I didn't think so. Does your man have anything for me?'

'Search me, bud. The Lieutenant don't tell the hired help nothing. Just to show you in when you gets here.'

My instinct was to make some excuse and walk away: I still wasn't set up for verbal arm wrestling with an American intelligence officer. I needed a cup of char and a wad to set me up. Instead I followed the black policeman into the ARC, wondering when Emily Rea, the woman I knew, was due back.

The lobby was polished brown marble; as old as Napoleon and as big as the Albert Hall. A huge, wide staircase on my left spiralled flatly upwards to the next floors. Joe Loss walked down it, and past me. I think that my mouth must have dropped open. I asked, 'Was that who I think it was?'

'Yeah. His band is at the hop around the corner tomorrow. The tickets all went a month ago.'

'I'm not surprised. We go up there?'

'No: us nasties live beneath.'

He nodded to the right. The wide stair swung away, and down into the gloom of a false dusk. He led off, and I followed him after Bruised Bassett gave my elbow a little steer. He trundled behind us: presumably it took the pair of them to make sure I didn't get lost. I'd noticed the music as I had stood in the hall; now it followed us down the stairs into a wide, badly lit corridor. Hutch was singing 'Deep Purple' on some old record from some radio station. I said, 'That's neat. How do you do that?'

'Speakers every twenny feet. It's a club, after all. Folks are supposed to enjoy themselves.'

'That's Emily's speciality. She makes people forget the war for a couple of hours.'

'Maybe she's *too* good at that. The whole fucking American Army forgot the war on New Year's Day, an' the Kraut flung *his* whole fucking Army right back at us, didn't he?'

'Did he? I missed it. I was in a hospital bed counting my burns.'

'The Battle of the Bulge. It was just a B feature, unless you happened to be in it. Don't worry, Mr Bassett, you'll still be in time for the main picture.'

'You still think he'll fight?'

'Yeah. Don't you?'

There were enough shadows for a Boris Karloff film. I didn't like that. We were walking along a corridor of offices with steel doors. Most of the doors were open, but it still looked like a fucking prison. I didn't like that either.

'Kraut had it before we did,' was the only thing McKechnie would tell me.

Kilduff had a small office. There was no window, and just enough room for a desk, two chairs and a tall filing cabinet with a combination lock. He'd tacked a Coca-Cola calendar on the wall. Rosie the Riveter was bursting out of an improbably clean boiler suit: she had muscles like Joe Louis. He must have only just moved in, because another officer's name was on the door. The neat notice said *Lt Vallance*. You remember things like that. Kilduff was my size of officer – about five four. He pulled the door closed behind me to shut out the music.

The Intelligence Officer was one of those competent little men you take an instant dislike to and don't know why. He looked you in the eye when he talked, and from time to time touched a small dark Führer moustache which hung below a broken nose. His hair was salt and pepper, and his eyes brown. Everything about him shouted *Trust me!* Even his handshake was firm and dry, the way a man's is expected to be. Everything about me shouted back *Like hell!*

'I'm Kilduff. The men call me Binkie behind my back, but I don't mind that.'

'Hello. It could be worse, I suppose.'

'Yes. That's the way I see it. You're Charlie Bassett. Pilot Officer Charles Bassett of the RAF?'

'Yes: pleased to meet you.'

'The feeling's mutual, you're under arrest . . . although I fail to see why you're being so fucking dumb, Charlie.'

'I beg your pardon?'

'Granted. You're under arrest. But I expect you knew that.'

'I beg your pardon?'

He uncapped a nice Swan pen – everyone seemed to have them – and pulled a several-leafed form to him. It had a lot of blanks waiting to be filled in. He sighed.

'I hope that you've more than *I beg your pardon* in your vocabulary, Charlie, or it's going to be a long day.'

'I . . .' I started, but then thought better of it. 'What for?' I asked him. I've told you about me and obvious questions before.

'AWOL. You did a runner, Charlie. The RAF put you on the wires a couple of days ago. They want you back. They don't like people borrowing seats on aeroplanes for free.'

'That's silly, Lieutenant.'

'No. *You're* silly, Charlie. You could have stayed out of sight until the war was over, instead of walking up to our policemen and giving yourself up. What's the matter; war get too much for you?'

'How could it? I wasn't fighting it. I'd done my trips, and was in a training section.'

'In Tempsford? Setting up the spooks and assassins for their flights into Europe?'

'That's right.'

'Doesn't sound to *me* as if your War had ended, Charlie: it was just a bit more sneaky than before. SOE and OSS and that sort of thing.'

'What's OSS?'

'Like your SOE. Our agents instead of yours. You worked at Tempsford. The Funny Farm.'

'How did you know that.'

'I told you. The RAF told us. Look at this.' He gave me a typed-out two-page flimsy from an American signal pad. I felt my face going red as I read it. It was headed up with my name, service number and date of birth. It asked for me to be apprehended on sight. Then it contained a précis of my training and service details, including the fact that I had witnessed our Polish gunner shoot someone dead, and that I had conspired to smuggle a woman onto an aircraft for flights over Germany. It also said that I was believed to be involved in the black market, politically unreliable – whatever that meant – and implicated in the theft of an aircraft: to whit, one Stirling bomber. The last paragraph but one described me as AWOL after discharge from hospital, having smuggled myself onto an aircraft at Croydon. I was now thought to be on the run in France. The last paragraph asked again for my detention and return to the UK, and warned that I could be dangerous.

Little Charlie?

'That's you, isn't it?' Kilduff asked me. 'I can get a photograph brought over from your service police HQ.'

'It's me.' I told him, 'but I'm buggered if I understand it.'

'What do you mean?'

'I'm on a mission. Something special; it's all been officially arranged.'

'On a mission for whom? The Pope? Tell me please, Charlie.'

'I don't think I can. I've probably told too many people already.'

'Uh huh.'

'What does that mean?'

'That means I have a two-page signal from your people saying that you're a really bad man, whilst you tell me it's cool; you're on a mission; but you can't tell me anything about it. Right?'

'I'm sorry. Yes. That's about it. What are you going to do?'

'Not waste any more time until you begin to whistle in tune, Charlie. Welcome to Paris.'

He must have had a method of signalling outside because the door opened behind me, and Bassett Major dragged me off my chair backwards by my collar, and tossed me into the corridor as if I was a bantamweight. He probably enjoyed doing that. He kicked and pushed me about two doors along, and through one of those open steel doors. I was right the first time: it was a bloody prison. The big bastard tripped me as he pushed me into the cell, and then set about me with his nightstick. He beat me carefully on my burned shoulders. He knew exactly what he was doing. Bastard. The pain was exquisite. My lights went out after about the fifth blow. The music from the speaker just outside my cell door was 'You Are My Sunshine'. That was Harry Roy. What had the black, McKechnie, told me about the music? – *'It's a club, after all. People are supposed to enjoy themselves.'* Well, Bassett Major did.

When I opened my eyes again I was flat on my back on a thin pallet mattress on the raised concrete ledge that was the cell's bed. A black man in a white coat was bending over me. He said, 'Trust me, I'm a doctor.'

The wheels upstairs began moving. I tried the cynical grin (it probably looked like a rictus), and said, 'McKechnie says that there aren't any black doctors in the US.'

'He tells lies. All coloureds do. You speak very good English.'

'Of course I do, I *am* English. RAF.'

'Lordy! In that ragtag mixture of a uniform you're in I thought you were a Kraut stay-behind, trying to evade. What did you do to annoy Uncle Sam?'

'I haven't worked that out yet. I came in here to ask some questions about a missing Englishwoman, and your Lieutenant arrested me for things I hadn't done.' I looked instinctively at my watch, and saw the wrist where it usually lived. 'What's the time?' I asked him.

' 'bout 1430.'

I was also missing my flying jacket, which contained my pay-book; and my ID tags. I was nobody.

'I had a flying jacket on when they threw me in here.'

'You won't see that again.'

'My watch . . .'

'Nor that.'

'Can I see the Lieutenant who arrested me?'

'No.'

'Why not?'

'Because I gave you a shot to knock you out, which you already can't remember. It will keep those bastards off your back for a few hours, and give me the opportunity to examine those shoulders of yours. What did you do to them?'

'Burned in an air crash. Your shot wasn't much good,' I told him.

'How come, Mister?'

'I don't think it's wor . . .'

There was a small piece of graffiti scratched into the plaster at my eye level. The initials read AGM, and a date which had been scratched out, but might have been January 1945. Maybe that was why I dreamed about a girl I had met in a post office in England. Don't worry; you'll work out the connection. She was still in my head when I opened my eyes.

They call it déjà vu, don't they? I woke up in a bed in a hospital room. Now I was in pyjamas, and from shoulder level a faint smell of something aromatic was emanating. My shoulders tingled, but weren't painful. I could move them about. Maybe the black man's medicine worked after all. This differed from the hospital ward at Bedford in two ways: there were bars on the window, and I was handcuffed to the bed frame by my left wrist. Kilduff sat on a chair near the foot of the iron bed, reading a paperback novel. It was the same Zane Grey I had started out with. He put it down when he sensed me stir.

'That doctor had me over. I brought him down to see that you weren't dead, and he slips you something to buy you a few hours.'

'Arrest him then.' Whatever was in the shot had dried me out. My mouth was parched and stiff, like the first time.

'I can't. He's a Captain. We're very rank-conscious in the US Army. You gonna talk to me now?'

'I always was. This wasn't necessary. If I get out of here there'll be an official complaint that will tie you up in paperwork until the day you draw your pension. I'll have your arse. Bassett's too.'

'I'm very scared. Terrified. I guess Bassett will shit himself. Now; what was your mission again?' He added, 'What's so funny?' after I laughed. So I did it again, and then:

'I was in an air smash last year; November, I think. I woke up in hospital, days later. One day I woke up and there was an RAF officer sitting in a chair where you're sitting. He was a creep like you. He arranged all this, and now, before the ink's dried on the orders he gave me, here I am back in hospital again and the job is all fucked up before it's started.'

'He gave you written orders then? This officer?'

'No. It was just a figure of speech. Forget it. This is a cock-up: situation normal.'

'*Snafu.*'

'What's that?'

'We turn it into a noun in my army: a *snafu*. It says Situation *N*ormal *A*ll *F*ucked *U*p. Who was this officer?'

I saw no reason not to tell him; after all the bastards had dropped me in it.

'Clifford. David Clifford. He even *looks* like you, except he has a fiddly Douglas Fairbanks moustache.'

'Never heard of him, but there's no reason why I should. You told McKechnie that you were over here looking for some English girl who may have taken a Cook's tour of the war zone. Is she important?'

'To me, *yes*. I made her some promises once. To her folks, *yes*. They have influence. That's why we're trying to get her back.'

'Who is she?'

'I probably shouldn't tell you any more. Not until I've spoken to the woman you were supposed to let me meet.'

'Emily?'

'Yes. I met her in Bedford. She knows the woman too.'

'Emily's further forward. I won't bullshit you: I don't know exactly where she is, or when she's due back. She makes the arrangements for the visiting artists who entertain the grunts. Oils the wheels for them. Meets the generals, and kisses arse. We are all very fond of her.'

'Does that mean you believe me?'

'Nope. Jest keeping the conversation ticking over.'

I didn't know what to say. Eventually I turned away from him, and said something like, 'Oh for fuck's sake!' and stared out of the window. The bars spoiled the view. I asked him, 'Are we still at the ARC?'

'No. I talked to someone who told me the same story about you that I already knew, so I moved you. We're in a military hospital in the suburbs. This is the security wing where they keep the suicides, nutcases and murderers. They let me use two or three rooms here if my customers have accidents. They often have accidents. Sometimes they even have accidents after they arrive here. Now, tell me about Frank and Jesse — the two desperadoes you're travelling with. There's a tripartite agreement between the occupying forces that we tell each other whenever we deploy that sort of officer in the field. Your guys turned up a week early: kinda spooked us.'

There was something too casual about the way he slipped them into the conversation. I bought time with, 'What does *tri-partite* mean?'

'Three-way. Us, your people and the Frogs.' After a respectable pause he prompted me again. 'Major England and Private Finnigan. That's not their real names, is it?'

'I don't know, Lieutenant, and I don't care. The bastards have apparently abandoned me, haven't they? Even so, I know hardly anything about them, and even if I did I wouldn't feel inclined to tell you.'

'That's a pity, Mr Bassett. I might be instructed to send McKechnie and the Thing back to ask you the same questions. They can be particularly insistent.'

'If my people have asked you to send me back to England, Lieutenant, then bloody *do* it. I'd be better off sorting this out with them, anyway.'

He got up; left me a deck of cheap Gauloises, and one of those French books of paper matches. He said, 'I wouldn't be

too sure about that,' and left me wondering how I was supposed to perform natural functions chained to the fucking
bed.

There were white orderlies and black orderlies. I noticed
the difference. The black ones were the ones who talked to
me. Life wasn't too bad for twenty-four hours if you call
being chained to a bed not too bad. Then there was Kilduff
peeking in through the wired glass window of the door
periodically. I was an exhibit in a sodding zoo. Eventually
he was there showing me to a tall, concerned-looking Bird
Colonel with a sad face. I thought that I had seen him in the
flicks. About fifteen minutes later McKechnie breezed in doing
the Ostrich Walk, with my clothes over an arm. He was the
all-over-happy man. He said, 'Hi, Brother. You OK?'

'Brother?'

'Jive talk. All black folks talks jive talk.'

'Stop taking the piss and talk normally, McKechnie, for
God's sake.'

'Just trying to keep things light. It's *show time*. Time to go
visiting. I'll get your cuffs; then you can get dressed. I threw
that old shirt away. I got one of Binkie's for you, from the
laundry. He don't know that yet.'

'Can I get a wash?'

'No time.'

He took the handcuff off. I rubbed my wrist where it had
chafed. Although my clothes hadn't been washed or pressed,
my cap had been brushed: that was the American way.

'Where's my namesake?'

'We gave him time off. Guessed it wouldn't have been a fond farewell between you two.'

'Right.'

McKechnie laughed.

'I'm almost sorry to be giving you back.'

He left me to get dressed. The shirt was a good fit. In the institution's main corridor I looked around for my minders. My legs didn't feel too strong – but that was a combination of the beating, the dope and a day's enforced bedrest. McKechnie was standing with Colonel Film Star and Kilduff, down by a set of double doors. Binkie's lips were set hard and white: he no longer loved me.

McKechnie beckoned me to them using only his right forefinger. All he said to me was, 'Walkies.'

They put me in the back of an olive drab Chevrolet staff car. I sat alongside the Bird Colonel, who offered me a cigar. Kilduff sat up front; McKechnie drove. The Colonel's drawl was melodious and home-spun; just like he sounds in films.

'Sometimes they pull me in when there's a snafu to be sorted out. You jest sit there, son, and don't worry; the Air Force is on your case now. The other fellahs . . . aargh, that is the United States Army, are mighty . . . sorry they made this mistake over you.' Then he said, 'Aargh' again. It was a quiet, meditative sound. At first I thought that maybe he was in pain, then I worked out that that was the noise with which he finished most sentences. We both lit up. I asked, 'Where are we going?'

'You're going back to your own people . . . and we're getting one of our own back in return. I've done this sort of thing before; don't worry.'

'You keep saying that, sir. Don't worry about what?'

'Don't worry about the fact that when your people found out you'd been arrested by mistake, they kidnapped an Army Colonel from out of an off-limits cat-house, and threatened to go international with the fool unless we produced you. The Army is very good at creating diplomatic incidents, you see . . . aargh . . . but never as creative about solving them.' I found that his voice had a calming effect on me. I wanted to be his friend.

I asked him, 'Haven't I seen you in films?'

'Might have done.' He went on to tell me, 'It helps with this sort of thing.'

'What have you flown?' That was me again.

'B-17s and B-24s. Big bombers. Over Germany.'

'Me too. Lancasters.'

'Interesting, wasn't it?' That's not how it sounded. It sounded like a sentence of twice that length.

'What happens to me now?' A thousand ideas were seething in my mind, but I was strangely unafraid. *Gott mit uns*, this time: definitely.

Kilduff said, 'We get to give you back to your own people, and I hope they throw the fucking book at you.'

He was a bad loser. Real men are bad losers. That's what they say, anyway.

'When I walked into your place I had ID tags, and a pay-book.'

Kilduff said, 'We'll give them to the officers they send to collect you.'

'. . . and my wristwatch and flying jacket. I'm not getting out of the car without them.'

'You're being very awkward, son,' the Bird Colonel told me, but then he spoke to Kilduff. His voice was suddenly sharp and curt and commanding. Someone you didn't fuck with. 'Give him your watch, Lieutenant.'

I felt bold enough to break in with, 'No. I'll take the nigger's watch. I'm already wearing one of the Lieutenant's shirts. That just leaves my flying jacket. I was attached to that.'

McKechnie said, 'I wondered when the N word was comin'. Someone always has to remind me. Sometimes I think that white folk are on a duty from God just to remind us blacks that we are *black*. In case we missed it.'

'Thanks,' I said, and, 'What about my jacket?'

The Colonel said, 'I don't suppose you would consider accepting mine in exchange? I get them made privately, and flown over. Quality's good.'

'So's the exchange,' I told him, and shook hands on it.

You've seen the film. The two cars drawing up on the country road a hundred yards apart; the space between lit by their searching headlights. Part of me was asking, *Haven't they heard of the fucking blackout?* There was a big black mass on the side of the road where the headlights met. After a few seconds I realized that I'd seen it before, and that there were the bodies of dead German soldiers in it, and maybe a couple of dozen rats. That's why I wasn't surprised when Cain and Abel stepped into the light alongside it. Cain had the Sten around his neck on its string, and his right arm was resting on top of it, as if it was a sling. The USAAF Colonel stepped out to meet them, handing his leather A1 jacket back in to me as he did so. He took McKechnie with him. I thought that that said something. I asked Kilduff what they were doing. He said, 'Negotiating.'

'Is there anything to negotiate?'

'Nah.' He was turned from the driving seat to look at me. There was less anger in him now. 'It's just form really. We been doing this a lot longer than you Brits. Capone an' Legs an' Lucky: they been doing it all the time till they got caught.'

'Who're they?'

'Charlie,' he asked me, 'where you been all your fucking life?' There was genuine pity in his voice.

The Chevy engine rumbled on, so I couldn't catch what was being said: perhaps I wasn't supposed to — you never know. Eventually the Bird Colonel came back to me and drawled, 'It's all right now. Just get out, and walk up to the light. You'll find a US Colonel there. Stop, shake hands with him, then walk on by to your own folk.'

'Why shake hands?'

'We . . . ll.' It sounded like *waal*. 'I don't know, rightly. Perhaps it's just a matter of politeness, and no one will shoot you if you do that.'

'I'd better do it then.' Then I said, '*Goodnight*, Colonel,' as I scrambled out into the night, and, 'Thank you.' Although I don't know why.

He said, 'You're welcome, son,' and, in a lower voice, 'Why don't you get away from these bums as soon as you can? They're not your kind of people.'

'I'll remember that, sir,' I told him. I had been right to say *Thank you*, after all.

'If we meet again, you call me *Jimmy*, most everyone else does.'

'Yes, Colonel.'

He was a big man, so his leather flying jacket fitted nicely over my battledress: I pulled it on as I walked. The man I shook hands with asked me, 'Is that Jimmy Stewart back there?'

'I think it was, sir. It is a film star, anyway. I've seen him.'

'You don't have to call me *sir*, boy: it seems to me that we've both been in the same boat.'

'No, sir. Why are we having this conversation anyway, instead of just walking on?'

'Just to irritate the mother-fuckers, son. I don't suppose you know what the fuck this was all about?'

'No; sorry.'

'Thought not; me neither.' He sighed, then he said, 'Good luck, son,' and walked on. I guessed that he'd be in trouble when they got him back, so I offered, 'And you, Colonel.'

Out of the light was *Kate*, with a jeep parked up behind her. There were three men standing around her: England, Raffles and Cliff. Cliff moved out of the dark, and snarled, 'Can't you stay out of trouble for a minute?' at me, before stalking off to the jeep without another word. He started it savagely, fucking up the gear change, and tearing off down the road behind the Americans, who had already turned the Chevy and powered away into Paris. I had to jump out of his way.

In the car I asked them, 'Before I say *thank you*, would someone mind telling me what the fuck is going on?'

'Say *thank you* first,' Les advised me, 'while we work out the rest. Nice jacket by the way.'

'Was that bloody great charge sheet about me accurate? Kilduff said he got it from the RAF.'

'I would imagine that the Yanks embroidered it a bit – just to make you talk. *Did you*, by the way?'

'No. They gave me a bit of a beating first, just to encourage me. After that I found a stubborn streak I didn't know I had. I told them Cliff's name – I didn't reckon I owed him any favours.'

'He won't like that if he finds out.'

'He *won't* find out.' That was Major England taking part for the first time. 'We won't tell him, and neither will the Yanks. Who beat you up?'

'Their thug Bassett, in the library, with a stick. He was careful to choose my shoulders.'

'You need an MO?' That was Raffles again.

'No. Some American doctor at the hospital spread some jallop on them. They feel better than at any time since the accident. I must find out what it was.'

'What are you going to do about it?'

'I'm going to get a gun, go back and do the sadistic bastard in.'

'No you're not,' the Major told me. 'We're off to Belgium

before anything else goes wrong. Les and I have got to go back to work: the armies are on the move again. Let's hope the Duke of York isn't in charge this time.'

'What about Bassett?'

'We could always look in on the way back . . .'

'And Grace Baker? I don't suppose that Cliff would have left me here unless he expected me to finish the job.'

The road turned from cobbles to tarmac: the noise the Humber made on it changed from a rumble to a hiss. There was a gentle drizzle falling, which reminded me of Cambridgeshire. Les's left hand lifted from the steering wheel from time to time to activate the screen wipers. The car lights showed against the straight tree-lined road like narrow pencil beams. Into the silence he said, 'We asked around a bit. I don't think she's in Paris. The American bird you wanted to see about her certainly isn't. I don't even think the Yanks have told *her* that you're here. That leaves the American tank crews you told us about. You said she might have contacted them again.'

'Did I?'

'*Someone* did,' the Major told us. 'Anyway. They took a bit of a hammering from the Jerry apparently, and they're back in a rest area . . . and that rest area is directly on our route to catch up with Monty's finest, who're probably racing across Germany at this very moment. At about two miles an hour.'

'Oh, what a coincidence!' I told him.

''tis rather. Lucky. Maybe you're a lucky soldier, Charlie.'

'I'm not a soldier at all.'

'I rather think that you are *now*, old son.'

I believed him. Bastard. I couldn't see that he had any reason to lie about it.

'Does that mean that the charges the RAF might be alleging against me can't be proceeded with?'

'I hadn't thought about that.'

'What's this garbage about stealing a Stirling? I've only been in two. One crashed and burned, and the other was flown by Cliff: rather well, as it turned out.'

'It was something to do with a bunch of conchies from Tempsford who nicked their aeroplane and pushed off out of the war. Clever sods.'

'What's that got to do with me?'

'Friends of yours, apparently. Your old CO, Goldilocks . . .'

'Goldie.'

'Goldie, then . . . he thought it must have been something to do with you because no one would tell him where you'd gone. He reported you. Cliff thought that it was very funny until you were lifted. So did we, afterwards.'

'I really appreciate your worrying about me, you and Les. Do you know that?'

'Don't mention it.'

'Anyway, if you hadn't left me in that Yankee loony bin for twenty-four hours I don't suppose that I would have got to meet James Stewart.'

The Major smiled. 'Is that so? Pansy, was he? Most of them are, you know.'

'No; he flew bombers. Probably with the 8th Air Force: that's their Bomber Command.'

Les said, 'I'd always wanted to know how to tell Pansies from other men. Now I know.'

I felt too tired to tell them to fuck off.

Les drove through the night. I slept. At one time I awoke as the car lurched, and found my discs and pay-book in my hand. One of them must have given them to me.

Les muttered, 'Sorry. Shell hole, I think.'

I asked him, 'What month is this?'

'February, March or April. Does it matter?'

'No. Do you want me to drive?'

'No. I'm fine. I've got some blue peters to keep me up to the mark. When we reach our next stop I'll bomb for twelve hours. Go back to sleep.'

'Where are we?'

'Still in France, heading for Belgium and Holland. You'll be safe when we get you over the border.'

It hadn't occurred to me that I wasn't. The Major groaned and moved in the back seat,

'Belt up, you fellows. Let the only brain the outfit possesses get some kip.'

'You heard him, Les. Get some sleep.'

We both laughed. It was companionable. I slept again soon after that.

Ten

I woke again in daylight when the car stopped moving. Les was stumbling around outside like a man in a dream. Major England was snoring in the back with a splinter-camouflaged cape pulled up to his neck. I think that it was German. We were parked up against a brick wall, out of sight of the road, in a shell-shocked farm courtyard. The three-storeyed farmhouse which formed one end of an open square was burned out; its roof caved in. I extracted myself with difficulty: the running board was almost up against a wall. Les was piling pieces of wood and dead branches around the car, mumbling to himself. He noticed me – a bit late, I thought – and said, 'Camouflage. We don't want the jabos to spot us.'

'What are they?'

'Jagdbombers: fighter bombers. They can be a bit of a nuisance.'

'They won't attack us, Les. There's a fucking great white star on *Kate*'s roof. You could see it for miles.'

'Not *our* jabos: *theirs*. Welcome to the real war, Charlie.'

Even the last sally had almost been beyond him. He was out on his feet.

I said, 'Get in, and get your kip, Les. You're beat. I'll finish this. Where are we?'

'Still in France. I had to make a couple of diversions in the night. Look . . .' He pointed vaguely forward and upwards as he slumped back into the driving seat. The farmyard appeared to be set at the bottom of a small fortified mountain: a massive castle wall ran around it in both directions, climbing out of sight.

'Windsor Castle,' I told him. 'I've seen pictures of it. You've taken us home again by mistake.'

Les yawned. He couldn't keep his eyes open. He said, 'Laon. About eighty mile north-east of gay Paree. Don't go up there; we're still in France, and I don't know if the natives are all that friendly.'

'Couldn't be less friendly than the fucking Americans, could they?'

'Wanna bet?' Les yawned again, collapsed down behind the steering wheel, and pulled his beret down over his eyes. He was snoring before his hands had fallen back.

I finished hiding *Kate* as well as I could. To my unpractised eye it still looked like a car under a heap of wood when I'd finished. Perhaps it wouldn't look the same if you were overflying the farm at 300 knots. The morning sun was drying out a short dawn shower. The ground glittered with light reflected back from water. I sat on the thick greystone doorstep of the farmhouse, took out and filled my pipe, and smoked in great contentment. An hour later three Mustangs armed with rockets belted close overhead heading north. They curved around the walls of Laon and didn't give me a glance.

It took me twenty minutes to walk around the wall of Laon, along a muddy farm track I chose to avoid the vehicular traffic. I had learned at least one thing from Les, and that was how to recognize the sound of a Sten being cocked as someone worked the bolt. My boots were heavy with mud, and I was passing between two dilapidated farm buildings. I froze. That may have saved my life, because the armed twelve-year-old in the doorway to my left didn't seem to know what to do next. Maybe he'd only trained on moving targets. The old man behind him coughed, spat into the mud and said '*Enough*,' in guttural French, and asked me if I was a deserter. I said, 'No. RAF aircrew. I lost my clothes in a crash.' I tried to make my French sound less efficient than it was. I remembered that the English were supposed to be cack-handed at European languages. He spat again.

'You speak good French.' So much for that.

'My school was keen on it.'

'You have proof of identity, of course, or did you lose that in the crash, as well?'

I moved my hand, and the boy twitched. The old man pushed him not too gently to the side. This time I fished my ID discs from around my neck. I told him, 'I have a pay-book as well.'

The old man nodded, and didn't speak for at least thirty seconds, then he sighed. Regretfully, I think. He would have preferred to have killed me. The interrogation took a new route. He asked, 'You are a socialist?'

'I am a nothing. I have no time for politicians.'

'Ah.'

'Is that bad?'

'In Laon it is better that you are not a socialist in these times.'

'Then I shall not be a socialist in Laon.' I thought that I was being amusing.

'So young, and so wise.' He thought he was being ironic.

'Can I take my feet out of the mud now?' I asked him.

He jerked his head. I moved. He asked, 'Where are you going?'

'I was looking for the way into Laon. To buy food and drink, if I can.'

It must have been the word *buy* that bucked him up. His smile showed gaps in his teeth you could get a pipe stem into.

'For one?'

'For more than one.'

'Ah . . . you mean the two brave British soldiers sleeping in the car you so badly hid in Modoc's farmyard?'

The old man had me. I grinned.

'Yes, those. One, at least, *is* a brave British soldier. He has fought in France, North Africa, Italy and now France again.'

'I know a man like that. He says that he has been in every retreat the British Army has made in this war.'

'That is cruel, M'sieur.'

'But it is also funny.'

'Yes,' I told him, and grinned again. 'How do I get into Laon? Is there a gate in this long wall?'

He said, 'Uh,' and, 'We will walk with you.'

He joined me in the mud. So did the child. The child sank up to his ankles. When he smiled happily at me I saw he had the same gaps in his teeth as the old man. We squelched on together until we reached a metalled road; the old man alongside me, and the child behind. Even through the mud I could smell the old man's feet. I asked him, 'Is it still necessary to guard the track?'

'No,' he told me. 'We stopped that the day we were liberated.'

'What were you doing then; back there?'

'Rabbits.'

'With a machine gun?'

'Big rabbits.' It was all he'd say on the subject.

The road passed through the wall, and turned immediately to starboard, following the curve of the hill upwards. It had been constructed as a defended causeway: there was always a wall on each side of you until you climbed out into a square, and a couple of weird churches. One was as big as York Minster, made of gold-grey coloured stone and washed by the sunlight. It staggered under the weight of thousands of small Gothic sculptures of grotesque animals and mythical beings. The other was small and circular and squatted in its shade. It had an open porch with pillars. The old man rested us there. On a piece of level ground covered with coarse sand a group of men played bowls with stone cannonballs, and drank from greasy wine bottles. A lot of staggering about seemed to be going on. Finally a fat man with thick black hair came into the porch, and plonked himself down alongside me. He mopped his brow with a clean, red handkerchief, wiped his hands with it, and offered one to me. The ritual shake. He gripped my hand a funny way, and frowned when I did the wrong thing.

'Rey. Mayor,' he said. 'I was two years the Mayor when the Boche came. Then there was a German administrator. I still have two years left to do. I start them now. Are you a socialist?'

'Not this week. How about you?'

He laughed at the challenge.

'This week I am a Gaullista.'

'Is that a good choice?'

'This week it is. You are the Englishman who speaks good French. Clément thinks that you are a spy. It is Clément who you came in with.'

'We weren't introduced. I am not a spy. How did you know what he thinks?'

'His daughter told us.'

'I saw no daughter.'

'She stayed behind in the barn, and then ran up here the quick way. We have been waiting for you for fifteen minutes.'

'The old man slowed me down.'

'I doubt it. He can walk all day without breaking a sweat – you say that in English?'

'Yes, M'sieur. We do.'

'I think that you are out of condition, Englishman: like a man newly out of hospital.'

Then he laughed a big pealing laugh that filled the small porch. The bowls players joined in. The boy and old man joined in. Bastards. When His Worship had had enough of the joke he wiped his brow again, and said, 'What do you want? Food?'

'Yes. For three. I have companions.' No harm telling them what they knew.

'I know. I have two men watching over them. They will be safe. Are you in charge?'

'No. One of them is a Major.'

'No matter. It is the rule of some people's lives: no matter how high in the ranks you rise, you still end up making the coffee, and fetching the supper. Maybe you are one of those.'

'Maybe.'

'No matter. I am one. Look; I am their Mayor, and yet the lazy swine expect me to deal with you myself. Maybe you be Mayor one day.'

'I would be honoured.' He smiled when I said that. A little inward smile. It was the first really clever thing I'd said all day. He called over a man he called Gaston, took his wine from him and pressed it on me, saying, 'You stay here, and toast the République. *Stay here.* I will bring food for your journey. You will be safe if you stay here. You have money, of course? 'Then he asked me, 'Why are you smiling, my friend?'

'There is no right answer to your question, for me. If I say *yes* you might steal my money; if I say *no*, you might say, *no sale.*'

'I think you can pay,' he told me. 'Clément's daughter told

me so. I will get you what we have most of: bread, wine and cheese. OK?'

'Fine.'

'No eggs, no meat – unless you eat rabbit.'

'Fine.'

He threw me an insulting mock salute as he strolled away. And winked his left eye. Its purpose was either to keep face in front of his subjects, or to warn me not to panic. I began to panic. There was a notice in *Ancien* French on a brass plate on the door which led into the chapel. I could just make it out. It told how a local laird, the Duc du something or other, a Templar Knight, was *discomfited* at this very spot (probably by distant relatives of the people I could see around me) in defence of his religion and the chapel. Only our Gallic neighbours would use a word like *discomfited*, when they meant that the poor bastard had been chopped to pieces with sharp agricultural instruments. Maybe the panic I began to feel was a residual of what he had left behind him in his last moments, sunk into the stone, like his blood. That had happened in 1307. It can't have been a very good year to be a Templar.

A pretty, dark-haired girl turned up hauling three bottles of wine and a big stone jar of what turned out to be water. Then she went back and returned with flat loaves of bread and a round cheese. I could have fancied her if I hadn't been so nervy. That, plus the Luger pistol she wore in a holster on a stout leather belt cinched in around her waist like a corset was a discouragement to the amorous. The Mayor didn't return

with her; he went back to his game of bowls. Sir Francis
fucking Drake. I asked Clément, 'Is that his daughter?'

Clément gave me his gaps, and laughed.

'She's *my* daughter. *Clémentine.* He wants her, but all he can
do is look. His wife would geld him.'

'Who do I pay?'

'Me. I found you.'

'How much?'

'Fifty invasion francs or fifteen dollars American.'

'That is a lot, M'sieur Clément.'

He shrugged. They call it the Gallic shrug. It's what the
French do when they've fucked you over, and want to lay the
blame on God. He said, 'You're still alive.'

I paid him. I got it at last. These folk were old-fashioned
bandits, lurking beneath their castle walls to waylay careless
strangers like me. He escorted me away from the cathedral
with its grotesques, and back down the way I had come.
Giving him sly sideways glances, I was sure that they had been
carved from life. The boy with the Sten had disappeared, but
the girl with the Luger walked at my other side. As we neared
the gate through the walls Clément spat in the road, and laid
a hand on my arm to slow me. He was carrying the wine, me
the food, and the girl the water jar. He said, 'I think that
you're going to make me an offer, either for the girl, or for
the Boche gun she's wearing.'

'Which would be best?'

'An offer for the gun would not offend.'

'Ten dollars?'

'Done.'

'The food cost more than that.'

'Food and drink are short. We have hundreds of Boche pistols. Officers can't fight. They threw them away as they ran. Give him the gun, girl.'

She unbuckled the belt, and passed it over as if she was granting me a bodily favour. Who knows? Perhaps she was. She thrust her hand into a pocket in her skirt and came up with a fistful of 9 mm bullets for it. I buttoned them into my Chaplain's battledress blouse pocket. I couldn't help watching the way her breasts moved under her shirt. Her father couldn't help watching me watching.

It took another half-hour to drag the vittles back to *Kate* on my own. Clément's duties had ceased once he saw me from the premises. England was standing alongside the car sharing a cigarette with a mad-looking youth with a Schmeisser machine pistol. It didn't look as if his rudimentary French had dented their relationship. Raffles was still asleep at the wheel; or looked that way.

'There you are!' the Major said to me. 'I think that this johnnie wants some money not to kill me.'

'How much?'

'Five dollar,' said the man. His gaps matched Clément's and the kid's. I was glad the girl hadn't opened her mouth as she smiled. I told him, 'I'll think about it.'

Clément Three – that's how I labelled him – helped us to unbury the car. I got Les to move over, dumping the goodies in the back with the Major. I put five miles between us and the small walled citadel before stopping to eat. That was in a small unwalled town with a flat, open square and no bomb sites that

I could see. I parked the car in the shadow on the up-sun side
of the square. The people smiled and passed by. We woke Les
up, and ate a long lunch in the sunshine. He admired my new
gun, and showed me how to strip it, and clear a jam. He told
me he wouldn't swap his Sten for it: I hadn't asked.

With my mouth full of greasy bread and cheap cheese I told
them, 'I'm sure the bastards knew who I was. Somebody's
been spreading it around. They dropped hints, but didn't
come right out with it.'

'A wanted man,' the Major said. 'How damned colourful.'
Then he said, 'You can't say I didn't warn you. They were
probably pals of Maggs.'

It was late afternoon. Les told us, 'I need another forty winks.
Come back for me in an hour or so, and we'll move on. I
want to be in Blijenhoek the day after tomorrow.' I didn't
know where Blijenhoek was, but what the hell? Grace was up
there with the tanks somewhere . . . or had she already been
passed on to somebody else?

England and I sat away from the afternoon sun at the back
of a darkened bar, the way Les had taught us. We kept the car
in view all the time, although I doubt that we could have
reached it in time if some bastard had decided to have a go at
Les. A flight of four P-38 Lightnings passed low over the
square, with one flash git waggling his wings at the local
popsies. The aircraft were all painted drab green, and had
black and white invasion stripes around their wings: the
wriggler had a big, smiley, orange and yellow sun on the
aircraft's nose. Their twin supercharged engines whistled as

they beat us up. England said, 'Saying *hello* to his girlfriend. They must be based close to here.' Deductive logic.

The wine was thin and watered, and dearer than better stuff in Paris. The waitress who flashed her chests at us probably was as well: Paris seemed a thousand years and a million miles away. I wondered where Lee Miller was – up ahead of us probably – and if the artist had come back yet.

'I didn't like the way I got into this,' I told England. 'When I joined up they told us how the service was supposed to work. That was training stations, until you were ready to go to war, then crewing up at an O.U.T.'

'Don't you mean an O.T.U?'

'Perhaps I did. This wine is getting better . . . after that you had the squadron and thirty trips to Germany, and if you survived that, a posting to a cushy number for six months, before coming back on ops.'

'Didn't it work out like that?'

'Only until I finished my trips; then it went wrong. After my posting to Tempsford, and the crash, everything got very unofficial. Goldie, that was my last proper CO, told me I'd been lent to Cliff, and Cliff lent me to the Bakers – that's Grace's parents. They sent me looking for Grace. First with Cliff's help, then yours.'

'What's so worrying about that?'

'No papers. No orders. Nothing. If I'm picked up by the MPs, and Cliff denies all knowledge of me – which he could just do, on his current showing – what have I got to prove that I'm not just AWOL?'

'Nothing. But their need for a commonsense explanation will direct them. Very straightforward folk, the rozzers: even Army ones like ours.'

'How come?'

'Most deserters travel away from the Front: not towards it, like you. You're bound to find some Redcap bright enough to at least listen to your story.'

'Then there's another thing. That charge sheet the Yanks said they got from my people.'

'I told you: they probably embroidered it to give you the shits. I should imagine your CO just issued something innocuous to cover his own back, and Cliff probably monitors signal traffic about you as a good way of keeping tabs. Maybe he even provided some of the lurid embellishments. If so, he fucked up: he gilded the lily and our American cousins thought they'd do us a favour by picking you up . . . especially if they put the word out on you, and Maggs picked up on it. That's why Cliff came out to get you back.'

'What about the theft of a Stirling bomber then?'

'I thought that that was a good touch, too. How much is a Stirling worth?'

'Thousands and thousands.' The thought depressed me.

'If they ask you to pay that back out of your pay you'll be fucked.'

'I get the feeling I already am.'

He leaned over and tapped me on the arm. He said, 'Ask her what her name is . . .' He meant the waitress.

The girl told me, 'ortense. No H, the way she said it. I told him, and he asked me, 'Look old boy, if you're *not* going to roger her . . . and she's begging for it worse than Fay Wray does . . . would you mind awfully if *I* did?'

I left him to her, or her to him, whichever way you care to see it, and strolled back across the square to *Kate*. Seeing her in the subdued light of lengthening shadows I realized that I was fonder of her than any man had the right to be of just a simple car. Maybe she wasn't so simple after all. Anyway, I hadn't better tell Les about it.

Just as I was about to climb in the front passenger seat alongside him, and kip until he woke up, the flight of Lightnings crossed the air above me again, on their way back. The racks on their wings, which had contained armour-piercing rockets for the low-level stuff, were empty now . . . And there were only three of them: not the four seen an hour earlier. The one that was missing was the one which had the big, friendly sun painted on its nose. Inside me I gave that Gallic shrug: maybe the flash git was walking home. You never know. I woke up when I felt the car shift under me as the Major settled in the back seat. He pulled the door shut. Les yawned and stretched, nearly braining me. James told me, 'I *told* you so.'

'Told me what?'

'That girl. Her boyfriend is one of those fighter pilots who flew over the square this afternoon. She says he always shakes his wings at her.'

'What was she like?'

'Excessively agricultural.' He coughed one of those weak apologetic coughs. 'But any port in a storm, and all that.'

*

Some distance out of town, with the light all lost, Les stopped us on one of those straight, tree-lined Roman roads that criss-cross northern and central France. England radioed a check into his HQ, wherever that was, and Les filled our tanks from a jerrycan. When we got going again James soon fell asleep, whilst I performed the little navigation feats that were required under the light of one of those right-angled WD-issue torches. The miles sang under *Kate*'s wheels. Les whistled 'Lili Marleen'. Life was OK, but I remembered an evening I had once spent in a field with Grace, when I had never been happier.

PART THREE

Belgium: March 1945

Eleven

Les stopped the car once at about 0430. I awoke with a start. Someone was talking to Les from outside the car. A torch flashed briefly in my eyes, and on England's sleeping face. When I focused on the stranger's voice I found that it was reassuringly English – a Brummie, I think – and we were at some kind of checkpoint which was lit by subdued half-lights. I heard a match striking, and smelled tobacco smoke. Les said something I didn't catch. I was too busy trying to get my body to move from the curled-up position it seemed to have set in. The stranger laughed, and his torchlight flicked briefly on my face again. The white and black pole in the narrow gleam of our shrouded headlights lifted, and Les got us rolling, winding up his door's window as he did so. It was chill; I could feel it getting into the car.

He doffed his beret, with one hand still on the wheel, and handed it to me, saying, 'Dig us out a couple of fags.'

So I did, selecting a couple of roll-ups from his store. He put the beret back on one-handed. I lit the fags with my American lighter, and we smoked companionably in the darkness. I asked him, 'What did you tell that frontier guard about me?'

'That you were a Chaplain on his way forward. I think there's a lot of burying to be done.'

The sky was lightening a little a long way to the east. I said, 'I didn't realize that dawn would be as early as this.'

Les gave a grunt. It might have been a laugh, or it might not.

'It isn't. That's Monty's moonlight. You never heard of it?'

'No.'

'They do it on nights of low cloud. They shine hundreds of searchlights forward and upwards, until the light is reflected back down by the clouds. It means there's enough light for the poor bastards to fight under.'

'Monty's moonlight?' I said, not quite believing him.

'That's right. You still never heard of it?'

'No.'

I rolled the window down an inch, and ditched my dog-end. I hunched down in the seat again, and dozed.

Les woke me at about six. The roads were wet but I had missed the rain.

'I want to get off the road and laager up – preferably with someone nasty near by to look after us if Jerry decides to come back. A nice snappy light tank squadron would do. Look for hedges that have been arseholed by something big and recent. You can follow tanks across the country by the flat stuff they leave behind them.'

'Flat stuff?'

'Like I said: 'edges, flat houses and flat people . . . flat everything.'

'There!' shouted England, who was fully awake. He was pointing to a signpost leaning crazily to one side at a point just in front of us, where the road was crossed by a country lane.

'Tank spoor!' the Major yelled. 'Knew it! Tally ho!'

We turned left onto a lane which wasn't much more than a track, and followed what they assured me was a tank trail of broken tree branches and scarred verges.

I asked them, 'What if they were Jerries heading the other way?'

James gave me the withering idiot stare before he answered, 'Well: the signpost would have been knocked in the other direction, wouldn't it?'

They were usually right. We turned right, off the road, when we found a hedge with several large holes smashed in it.

'Told yer,' says Les. 'If they'd been coming towards us there'd be shite and mud all over the road. There ain't.' After two more fields we found them, grazing like cows, and steaming in the weak sun. Most of them had parked up around the edges of a humped meadow. A couple of them had their engines running and were crowned by tell-tale plumes of thin blue exhaust smoke. Les gunned us up alongside one which had two limp pennons on a radio mast. *Kate*'s engine block ticked as it cooled and contracted. A brown job Captain about twelve years old was lounging against the tank. He straightened up, but not by much, when James England unfolded himself from our Humber. He touched his black beret with a leather-covered swagger stick, and said, 'Major,' and England said, 'Captain.'

I thought that it was about time somebody introduced them to the idea of verbs, pronouns and adjectives. Les turned and grinned at me.

'Don't worry,' he said. 'They'll get down to business eventually.'

Breakfast was taken alongside a curious tank without a turret. When I asked about it a tankie sergeant said, 'It's a Kangaroo: that's a Sherman without a turret. The Canadians make them. Our Skipper got it out of a Canadian squadron. We use it for dragging our nappies round in.' He put a mug of tea in my hands that was so large I needed both my mitts for it. It was sweetened with condensed milk: wonderful. The tankies had rigged an awning out from the side of the Kangaroo to cover the field kitchen they cooked on: the officers – the Captain, two Lieutenants and Major England – stood underneath it. Les caught my eye, and flicked his head towards it. He was saying, *You're a bleedin' officer; behave like one, and mix with the buggers!* The plate of grub their cook pushed at me looked grey and familiar. I had to balance my mug of char on the Kangaroo's track before accepting the food. The Captain told me, 'I know that it looks like fifty-seven varieties of stewed snot, but it's really quite tasty.' It was a tankie joke. I smiled for him, and asked the cook, 'Don't you call this *stovies?*'

He said, 'Aye, sir. How did you know that? A Scottie showed me how to cook this up, some place out of Caen. He was wandering on his own, and trying to join up with his unit. We lost him somewhere along the line. I wonder if he found them.'

I thought, *He got as far as Paris, anyway*. Another tank had fired up its engine. It differed from the others in that it sat in the geographical centre of the field, on a small hump. The rich smell of its exhaust drifted back towards me. I asked, 'Why is it doing that?'

'Dodgy engines. We have to run them up every few hours, otherwise the gremlins get into them.'

'Why is it sitting in the middle of the field? Surely that's a bit risky – every one else has hidden against the hedgerows.'

'That's the Judas Goat. If we get bounced by the Jerry fighter-bombers they get just one chance to hit us at three hundred knots before we start to shoot back. If you was Jerry, sir, who would you choose to go for in that split second – an easy target in the middle of a field, or indistinct, uncertain targets dispersed around it, who are going to start shooting back as soon as you circle to line up on them? The Captain is willing to sacrifice the one in the open for the others.'

Hard bastard, I thought.

James told Les, 'Get the car undercover when you've finished your scran. Then you can get some rest. You might have forgotten you've been driving all night, but I haven't.'

Les's shoulders suddenly dropped.

'Aye. You're right.' There was a pause that wasn't quite long enough for insubordination before he added the 'sir' that we waited for, and sloped off.

He produced a camo net from *Kate*'s cavernous boot. It had

coloured canvas leaves sewn all over it. He cut two long staves from a pollarded willow in the hedgerow, and standing them out from the wheels at forty-five degrees, draped the net between them and the car. That gave us cover, and an awning of our own. Les curled up on the back seat under James's German cape, and was soon snoring.

James and I sat on *Kate*'s running board and smoked: the sun through the netting over us splashed us with shadow patterns. I was really getting the hang of the pipe now, but was worried about running short of tobacco. I hadn't brought near enough with me. We talked war, and we talked personal. I felt comfortable with him the way I had never felt with officers before, so I didn't mind when he said, 'The trouble with being an Intelligence Officer – even if you've got a speciality like mine – is that you get asked to pick up any other intelligence tasking that might occur wherever you might find yourself. That's how I picked you up. I was just in the wrong place at the wrong time.'

'Sorry about that, James. I try not to get in the way.'

'Know you do, old boy. Don't mention it. You've actually been an amusing diversion, in a naive sort of way.'

Behind us Les gave an enormous snort in his sleep. James abruptly changed the subject.

'How are you getting on with that pipe? Never got round to one myself.'

'I like it better than fags now, but you can overdo it. It can sort of lie heavy on your stomach.'

'I'll remember that.' He asked me about *after the war*. A lot of folk were beginning to talk about *after the war* these days.

I remembered that Cliff had told me he didn't believe it: he saw a bigger war around the corner. I told James England about wanting to emigrate to Australia to be a sports journalist. He asked, 'Why? What started that?'

'Because I don't want to stay in the services and be ordered around for the rest of my life, and because the Aussies speak English, the sun shines, and sport's the only thing that interests them outside of beer and sex.'

'But you'd have to spend the rest of your life among Australians. Difficult.'

'Yes. There were a few on my squadron.'

'*Ghastly*, aren't they?'

'I suppose they were, come to think of it.'

'You wouldn't consider Wales, say Glamorgan or somewhere, would you?'

'Christ, no! Have you ever *met* anyone from Wales, James?'

'From Glamorgan, myself, matter o' fact.' He sounded moody, so I said, 'You see my point then?'

'I suppose so. Depressing, isn't it?'

I asked him about his *after the war*. He said, 'You'd probably laugh at me.'

'So what? You laughed at me.'

'There's a small port near Chichester, in Sussex. All the yachty types anchor there in the summer: crumpet everywhere. It's called Bosham; heard of it?'

'No, James. Sorry.'

'Don't say sorry all the time. You don't have to.'

'Sorry.'

'There you go again.'

I opened my mouth, but shut it again with a small pop. He said, 'Don't worry. Not many people know it: it's where King Canute ordered the tide to turn. Anyway, I want to buy a small place there, and open a really good restaurant. I want to serve meals so good that people will talk about them the other side of the Empire.' James added, almost as an after-thought, 'You shouldn't say *Christ, no*, you know; not while you're a Padre. God won't like it. Not seemly. Out of character.'

Before I could reply the tankie Captain mooched over. His name was Charteris, and naturally there was a white match-stick-man with a halo painted on the side of his tank's turret. Before he could speak we were disturbed by the sounds of high-pitched aero-engines in the air near us. Until then the tank laager had had a languorous, sleepy air about it. Now everything changed. From the turret of the Judas Goat a head wearing a bugle poked up, and blasted a two-phrase bugle call: then it popped down again. Charteris spun to face the field, and used a fifty-foot voice.

'*Stand to! Stand to!*'

He was behind the action though. Most of the tanks had Brens or Fifties mounted on their turret tops, and there were two on flexible mountings on the Kangaroo. Now each was manned by a trooper in a battle bowler. Some hadn't had the time to put jackets on, but no one had missed his steel helmet.

They swept across the field: the three American Lightnings we'd seen the previous day. They were all hooked up with wings full of rockets. They were so low that when one of the pilots looked in my direction I'll swear we had an eye lock.

They were so low that they couldn't miss the stars on the turret tops of the Comet tanks if they looked for them. In an eye blink they were half a mile away, but then they circled back.

'They're looking for something,' Charteris murmured, but that was more for his benefit than ours. They circled slowly out of our Brens' effective ranges, and when I sensed a relief and lessening of tension among the tank gunners, Charteris racked it up again by shouting, *'Fucking stand to, I tell you.'*

The Lightnings did another run near the field but their noses were angled up. Whatever their point was, it escaped me. When they were another blink away some nervous sod caught his finger in a trigger guard and pumped three or four rounds after them. Charteris said, 'Bastard!' and then bellowed, *'Stand down! Stand down!'* in his parade-ground voice.

The bugle attached to a small head popped back up out of the Judas Goat again, and gave us the benefit of the two-phrase call once more. This time it held on to the final note until it died of air starvation. I could immediately sense things calming down. Except the fiery little Captain, who bellowed, *'Sarn't Cummings. To me. Sarn't Cummings.'*

Cummings, who'd been the first of the tankies to unwind to me, doubled over from a hedgerow Comet. He was obviously Charteris's first man, even though there were two Lieutenants. Cummings skidded, and saluted.

'Who was the cunt then? The one with finger trouble?'

Cummings looked pained; he blinked before he answered, 'Trooper Wyatt, B troop, sir.'

'Then Trooper Wyatt just became the Judas Goat, didn't

he? Get those bloody tanks switched over, if you please.' He gave a quick little salute. Cummings didn't move fast enough for him, so he said, 'Sergeant?'

Cummings snapped out of it, saluted, and doubled away. By way of explanation, Charteris said, 'Wyatt is Cummings's gunner. Now *he's* out in the middle until someone else drops one.'

James didn't say anything, and I couldn't think of anything intelligent to respond with. The little Captain looked briefly puzzled. He muttered, 'They *were* looking for something, you know.'

It may have been my imagination, but I thought that he looked at us with a quizzical interest . . . but the moment passed. Behind us Les let out another great snort in his sleep. He'd slept through the whole damned thing.

Some time later the Major fell asleep as well, his head on his chest. One crew scoured out the barrel of their tank's gun with a solution of hot water and piss, and others slept by their tanks. Cummings walked around on an informal inspection. Someone had tuned in to the services station and Vera Lynn was quietly doing her stuff. I never liked her singing, but like everyone else I fancied her to death. That's an unfortunate phrase for a serviceman, isn't it?

After Cummings had returned to his own tank he couldn't seem to keep still: every few minutes his head would stick out of the lid, screw three-sixty degrees around and then jerk out of sight again. After my second pipe of the morning I tapped it out on my heel. The saliva in the stem made a hissing sound as it ran into the hot bowl. I cleaned it out with a screw of grass, buttoned it into my jacket pocket, and wandered over to the Cummings vehicle. It had the name *Fred* painted on a cast steel wing above the track, alongside a cartoon picture of a hound with floppy ears. The dog appeared to be taking a crap. Cummings didn't see me the next time his head popped up – he was looking north-east, towards the enemy. When it got round to me I said, 'Hello,' and he jumped out of his skin. I remembered then what Les had told me about the Elephant on the Bois de Boulogne: he said that tanks were blind to what was happening directly alongside them.

The Sergeant gave me a weak grin, and responded with, 'Oh . . . hello, Padre.' Then there was a pause which embarrassed both of us. Eventually he said, 'That may not be the best place to stand, Father. If Jerry comes over we're likely to be the first one clobbered.'

'So I heard. I thought I'd stroll over and maybe bring you the luck of the Devil.'

'Thank you, sir, but it would be best if you just moved on.'

I sensed that he was just about to shake his head when his little Captain did something to prove that he was psychic. Or maybe he just heard us. We both heard his voice booming across the field at us.

'*Mr Cummings . . . move that fucking tank into cover before Jerry gets his sights on you, and does the bold Padre a mischief. Look lively now!*'

I felt it was prudent to get well out of his way. The Comet's engine gave great bellowing gouts of sound and smoke as it turned in its own length, and got niftily under a thick willow. Blackbirds and larks sang; they hadn't paused for a minute.

Fred's smoke drifted away on the breeze. Cummings was out and on the ground as I pushed into the shadow of the great tree. The hatch above the driver opened; he leaned into it and said, 'OK boys, secure her please. Then you can get some air.' To me he said, 'Thank you,' again.

'Don't mention it. I was getting bored.'

'What I will mention, sir, if you don't mind . . . is that you're a bloody odd sort of Padre.'

'It's a new line for me. Six months ago I was a wireless op in a Lancaster. I probably flew over your head a couple of times. Who's *Fred*?' I pointed at the picture of the defecating dog. Cummings laughed.

'My dad's dog. Shits anywhere; like us.'

Before his crew dismounted he leaned towards me and said quietly, 'There's a village less than a mile away. I was thinking of wandering over for a looksee. It will help to kill the time.' When I failed to respond he added, 'You said that you were bored, sir?'

'Good idea, Sergeant.' I shoved out my hand, feeling a bit stupid. 'My name's Charlie Bassett, what's yours?'

'You know it's Cummings. It's Alfred. Alf, or Fred. Like the craphound.'

After a hesitation he shook my hand. It's bloody socialism for you; I called him *Fred*, and his driver *Doug*, and they called me *sir*, and it was me that was supposed to feel uncomfortable. Doug toted an empty pack, an empty gas-mask case, and a .303 short Lee Enfield rifle with a full magazine. He looked as if he knew what to do with it.

*

The village was called Brond. It had its own road sign.

'I knew a fat Scotchman called that, once,' Cummings told me. 'We could be in luck.'

We walked into it from the south. It was a single wide street which was split by a spired church into a narrow Y at its north end. Cummings waved us back, and Doug and I fell in behind him, a six-foot gap between each of us. Cummings walked the walk, and we matched him. I hoped that no one was watching. What the hell had my curiosity got me into this time? Halfway up the street it opened out into a small square containing a huge and ornate bronze fountain. A big house on the square had been the Gendarmerie. It was burnt out; the rest of the place was relatively undamaged, if empty.

When I looked up I saw the other soldiers. They were moving down the road towards us in open order. Four Yanks. They closed to a single file to pass us, but never looked up as they walked through. No eye contact. Their uniforms were clean, and they were freshly washed and shaven. Even so, I knew immediately there was something not right about them. Something that made me shiver.

Doug said, 'Aye, aye chums,' to them as they trod warily past, but they ignored us.

Cummings muttered, 'Eyes front,' as if he bloody meant it. Then, 'Don't look at them. Don't look back.' The last bit was in an urgent undertone. I've had to do this before: write down something I've seen, and still don't believe in. I'd seen something like it before, you see, so I knew what they were, that American patrol with the faded red triangles sewn to the shoulders of their uniform jackets. I knew they were dead men, walking to nowhere. Some people call them ghosts. I suppose Cummings knew that too: I suppose that he, too, had seen something like them before. Twenty paces further and Cummings said, 'OK, lad,' to Doug, and to me, 'You'll say something for those Yanks, Father? Once we reach the church, if it's safe to go in?'

'Of course I will,' I told him.

We went into three houses, and then gave up on it. The houses weren't knocked about at all; just empty. No furniture, nothing. Early vegetables in the back gardens needed thinning, and front gardens were overdue for attention. In the third and largest house we went into there was a modern Bakelite telephone in the hallway. I picked it up, there was that activity sound, and a sweet woman's voice asked me in halting French which number I wished to reach. I told her I didn't have the number, but could she connect me to the ARC Grand Central Club in Paris? She asked me where I was calling from. I told her Brond, and gave her the number on the phone cradle. The girl who answered at the ARC was a cheerful American. I asked, 'Is Emily back yet? Miss Emily Rea. This is Pilot Officer Bassett, RAF. She asked me to contact her.' It wasn't exactly a lie.

The girl said, 'The Programme Director is still out of Paris, sir, can anyone else help?'

'How about Mr Kilduff? He's a Lieutenant with your Military Police I think.'

'We have no one with that name here, sir, but if you'll wait a few seconds I shall connect you.'

Kilduff was laughing as he picked up the phone. He said,

'You're a cocky little bastard. I can't believe that you're still running around loose. What do you want?'

'Nothing. I just picked up a telephone to see if it worked.'

'They all do. Right across Europe. If you have the number you can phone up the bunker and speak to Goebbels.'

'Have you done that?'

'We all have. It really pisses them off – they're still trying to fight the war. I've been doing that a lot since I met you: trying to piss people off. You give people really bad ideas.'

'I don't understand. What do you mean?'

'You were born with the words *I don't understand* dribbling out of your mouth; probably in a talk bubble, like in the comics. You remember my Scotch nigger McKechnie?'

'Yes, I do. What happened to him?'

'Done a runner, just like you, Charlie. The bastard even left me a letter, resigning from the war. You found that woman yet?'

'I'm getting closer. When I do I'm coming back for you and your lunatics.'

He laughed at that, 'Maybe they don't *want* you to find her any more? Ever thought of that?' Then he laughed again. *Really* laughed, and put the phone down on me.

Cummings was standing beside me, moving restlessly. He wanted to move. Something that Kilduff had said had registered with me. I told Cummings, 'You go up to the church without me, if that's what you want.'

He nodded.

I added, 'I want to make another call while I can. This might be the only phone line in Belgium still working.'

'OK, sir, but please don't touch anything else. These spaces could be wired.'

'OK, I won't take any chances.' But I already had, just by lifting the phone without thinking. Stupid.

He and Doug moved down the tiled passageway, and out into the light again. I picked up the telephone handset and the same girl answered. My French sounded better than hers. I gave the telephone number for Crifton – the big house in Bedfordshire – and asked if I could call there. She asked if I had an authorization for calling England. I said I didn't know, and she asked for my service number. She went to silent running for about a half minute, and then came back and said that that was OK. Barnes answered. I told him, 'It's Charlie Bassett.'

He said, 'It's good to hear from you, Mr Charlie. Where are you?'

'Somewhere in Europe. Is Mr or Mrs Baker at home?'

'Mrs Baker's standing alongside me, sir. I'll put her straight on.'

Even over a crackly line Adelaide's voice was unmistakable. Unless you mistook her for Lauren Bacall that is.

'Hello Charlie. Any news?'

'No. That's what I was going to ask you.'

'No. Except that creepy policeman from London came back to visit, and leer at me. He said that she's definitely not in London.'

'She's been in France, but she's not there now. I found someone who met her here. It sounds as if you have a grandchild, by the way, but I don't know the details: congratulations. I'm heading north.'

The line was noisier now; and having phoned Grace's home out of curiosity really, I now found that I had little to say. So I closed it down.

'I must go now.'

'Take care, Charlie.'

'I will. Take care yourself. Look after Barnsey.' Why did I think that she sounded odd: or that there was something different in her voice? Maybe that bastard Kilduff had spooked me.

I stepped away from the telephone; and then back to it, and picked up the handset for the third time. After a ten-second buzz the same operator answered.

I said, 'This is Pilot Officer Bassett of the RAF. Somewhere in Belgium, I think.'

'I know. I checked your number against our list. Serving officers are authorized for telephone traffic.'

'I'm pleased. I telephoned again because I really like the sound of your voice, and wanted to know where your telephone switchboard is and if I could meet you. What town do you work in?'

After a pause she said, 'I probably shouldn't tell you.'

'No. You probably shouldn't. What's your name then?'

'Ingrid.'

'Tell me where you work, Ingrid.'

There was a ten-beat pause again, before she said, 'Bremen. At the International Telephone Exchange. I speak four languages.'

'You're *German*?'

'*Ja.*'

'In *Germany*?'

'*Ja.*'

'Crikey!'

'It's funny, isn't it? Do you think that the war is nearly over?'

'Yes. Yes; I hope so.'

'I hope so too. I am frightened. Frightened of the bombing and the occupation. Frightened the Russians will get here first.'

'So am I. Frightened, I mean. I'll find you if I get to Bremen. What's your other name?'

'Knier. We spell it with a *K* and an N. That is *K-N-I-E-R*.'

'And where do you live?'

'Here; at the telephone offices. My own house was bombed. This is a silly conversation, Pilot Officer – you are not writing down what I am saying.'

'I have an exceptional memory; trust me. You are Ingrid Knier, with a *K*, and you live at a telephone exchange. You are very pretty – I can tell that from your voice. You're frightened of the bombing, and the occupation. I'm going to find you in Bremen.' All my life I have been good at girls who are good at conversational pauses. Then she said, 'I think not, Pilot Officer. I must go now. Take care of yourself, and live long.'

Then there was a click. I put the handset down in its cradle, and picked it up again.

The line was no longer live. For the first time since I had joined up I had spoken to the enemy, and the enemy had spoken back to tell me to take care of myself, and live long. Funny bloody world.

I walked out onto the road, and caught Cummings and Doug outside the church talking to a man who was about eleven feet tall, and thin and blond. His hair was unfashionably long. It needed a good wash. Come to think of it, everything about him was long, and needed a bit of a wash.

Cummings said, 'Meet Henk. He's the Pastor here. The Dutch Unitarian Church.'

I said, 'They're Lutherans, I think,' and our new friend said, 'That's right. I am very pleased to meet you. I'm Henk Lammers.'

He held out his right hand for a brotherly clasp. When we shook hands his fingers wrapped around me like small pythons. He wore the dress black cassock of a French Abbé – which didn't look terribly Unitarian to me. Doug and Cummings were smoking his cigarettes. They said that they'd found him in the church, asleep on a pew near the door. His English was very good – better than Doug's come to that – and I asked him about it. He paused before saying, 'Cambridge. Then I went to a church school in Wales. Do you know it?'

I said, 'No: not even the Welsh know Wales. It's not knowable.'

At least he was bright enough to recognize a joke when he heard one. Either that or he was a halfwit: because he smiled. Every time you spoke to him there was a small deliberate pause before he answered. Then he smiled.

Cummings asked the question.

'*What happened here?*'

The Pastor drew deeply on his cigarette, exhaled, then ground his cigarette butt out on the church step before replying. He said, 'I don't know.'

I asked him, 'All the people? Their animals?'

Pause.

'I don't know.'

'Their vehicles? Their furniture?'

Pause.

'I don't know.'

'What *do* you know?'

Pause.

'Nothing. I arrived yesterday. It was like this.'

Cummings tried again. He was a more sympathetic interlocutor than I. He spoke gently. 'Where did you come from, Father?'

Pause.

'Den Haag. My Bishop sent me. He didn't say that all of the people had left. I came by bus and walking. It was a long journey. Last night I waited, but nobody came, except the Americans. Did you see the four Americans?'

Cummings said, 'Yes, we saw them.'

Pause.

'They wouldn't speak to me.'

'They wouldn't speak to us either. So no one came back last night?'

Pause.

'No. This morning I knew that I would have to decide what

to do next. I was hungry. So I slept – I get a better decision from a rested mind. Then you came.'

Doug had moved into the church. When he came out he said that it looked untouched, but empty. He brought out three suitcases tied up with string. Two were those nice leather travelling jobs that moved all over the Continent when people still travelled for pleasure. The third was smaller. I'd seen one like that before. Doug dropped them at our feet on the church steps. I was standing slightly behind Cummings facing the big Dutchman. I gave Cummings a small dig in the back before I spoke.

'Sergeant, I think that the Pastor should come back with us to the squadron, don't you? It's not safe for him here.'

Lammers asked, 'Squadron? You have aircraft near here?' For the first time he hadn't paused.

Cummings didn't want me to answer, but I said, 'No. Tanks. We can take care of you there.'

Lammers had taken a pace away, which put him a step above us, with Doug to his right on the same level. He replied, 'Thank you, but no. I should wait for my people to return.'

I spoke softly, 'I am afraid that I will insist.'

He said, avoiding eye contact this time, 'It is not possible. I cannot come with you,' and as he spoke his right hand dropped slowly. Maybe he was going to cry, and was going for his handkerchief. I got an eyelock on Doug, and dropped my glance to the pastor's hand. Doug was bright enough to pick up on it. He let the hand almost disappear into the pocket before he casually swung the .303 he carried. Casual, but fast, and with some force. The brutal impact noise made me wince. Flesh and bone against metal. Doug said, 'Sorry, sir. My mistake.'

The Dutchman screamed. That's just the sort of noise I'd make if a clumsy Tommy had just crushed two of my fingers between the barrel of his rifle and my own gun. Doug's hand dived into the pocket, and came out with a small pistol. He said, 'How very naughty,' and then, 'Nice job. German Walther .30. Good souvenir.'

The churchman held one hand in the other. Blood dripped between his fingers. Cummings had drawn his own pistol by now. I'd once seen what an American Colt could do up close. He was refreshingly formal when he said, 'I'm taking you into custody, Mr Lammers. My Captain will want to talk to you. If you answer his questions satisfactorily I'm sure that you will be allowed to return.'

The Dutchman looked at Doug and his .303, then looked steadily at Sergeant Cummings and his Colt pistol, then looked at me. He lifted a lip in a sneer, and spat on the step between us.

'Piss off, yer gouk,' he told one of us. I never worked out which one.

Before we left, Cummings asked me, 'Would you mind going into the church, and saying a few words for those Yanks, sir? Don't worry about chummy here. I'll drop him if he so much as twitches.'

The church was dark and cool. They had left nothing but the pews. The altar was now just an uneven block of stone. I walked up to it, put my hand on it aware of a hundred years of prayer in this place, and silently asked the forgiveness of a being I didn't believe in, for four American soldiers whom I didn't believe I had seen. The sudden move into the sunlight out of the church made my eyes water.

Outside, Lammers had a bruise starting to show around his right eye. He was prodded off in front of us carrying his large cases. I took the smallest one because I didn't want to let it out of my sight. It was a high, bright sun again, and I stopped at the fountain in the square for a drink, but it was dry. Cummings urged us on.

I sat on the ground in the shade with my back against *Fred*'s front plate. Twenty feet away from me Charteris sat with James under the awning that stretched out from the Kangaroo. Between them, and slightly forward, an old drum with a blackened skin was sitting on a small stool. There was a small book resting on it. Doug told me that it was the KRs. Lammers was sitting on the ground in front of them, his arms clasped around his knees. His fingers had been cleaned and bandaged. He wore iron handcuffs. Cummings stood at ease in front of the officers, clearly giving his report. From time to time I caught Lammers looking around the field. *Counting us*, I thought. *He still expects to get away with it.* Every time someone addressed a question to him he shook his head. I still had the small suitcase under my left hand. Eventually they waved me forward. Lammers didn't even look up at me. James asked me, 'What was the problem, Charlie?'

'He was. He's not right, sir. The village is like an army of cleaners have moved through it.'

'That's hardly his fault.'

'Every time I asked him a verifiable question, where he went to college, where he trained for the church, he told me – then asked, *Do you know that?* I think he's trying to work out how detailed his lies need to be.'

'Well done, Charlie. I like that.' James was being sincere, but he sounded bloody patronizing. Charteris frowned. I told them, 'He says he's a Lutheran, and then says his Bishop sent him here. I'm not sure that Lutherans have bishops in their mob. I'll have to check that, sir.'

James asked me, 'What else?'

'He had this in the church.' For the first time I gave him a decent butcher's at the small suitcase I had lifted. 'To me, it looks the same as the one you have: and you said that you got yours from Jerry.'

The Major's eyes gleamed.

'Well, well, well.' I think that he addressed that to Charteris, not me. 'What have we here?'

Charteris had Cummings open the suitcase.

'. . . over there somewhere, old chap: just in case.'

He waved him over to the centre of the field. Doug went with him, without being asked. That impressed me. It was locked, but responded to one of several small keys found around the Dutchman's neck on a piece of string. We waited for the discreet explosion that never came. After a decent interval they brought the case back to us. His papers and ration book had looked OK, and the other larger cases had just contained civilian clothes: some of them for a woman – that was interesting. It was the small case that got James's attention, of course, but he fretted over it. He asked me, 'Come and have a shufti at this, Charlie. If it's a radio it's like none I've ever seen.'

'Me neither,' I said, when I got alongside him. It was electrical all right, with ammeters and a voltmeter, and a small integral glass-cased battery, but James was right – it was never a radio.

'I wonder what that does?' Charteris asked us, and depressed what looked a bit like a Morse key, but wasn't.

The concussion almost knocked me over. The sky went black. The noise deafened me. The wind stripped leaves from the willows, the awning from the Kangaroo, and wrapped *Kate* up in her own camouflage shroud. I had instinctively crouched, and when I looked to the source of the explosion saw a massive black cloud boiling over Brond. A shower of fine rubble, dirt and dust fell on us like a summer storm. Lammers must have made his move, because he was flat on his face with Doug astride his shoulders, pinning his neck to the field with his rifle. Cummings, crouched by me, said, 'Effing hell!' which seemed appropriate at the time, and James, picking himself up and dusting his uniform down, said, 'Detonator, I think. It's a remote detonator. *Very* sophisticated.'

I said, 'I forgot. When I wouldn't let him go the bastard swore at us in English. Something north-eastern. Gateshead or Newcastle.'

Charteris didn't say anything. He'd gone white. Then he spoke quietly to Cummings. He said, 'Peg the bastard out, Sar'nt.'

And that's what they did. The military often seems to have a monopoly on cruel and unusual punishment. Two squaddies spreadeagled the poor sod in the middle of the field, and secured him with tent pegs, and Charteris threatened to have a tank driven over him. I remember the tank was named *Rachel's Dream*.

Charteris said, 'Come over with me, Padre. Maybe he'll speak to you.'

When we were at Lammers Charteris squatted down to speak to him.

'This is the way it works, old boy. I will signal the tank forward. It will move very slowly. Its starboard track will run right up the middle of your body. The first pain you will feel will be the pressure of it on your inner thighs, then it will crush your balls. It's all downhill from there, I'm afraid. I understand that your head will stay alive until the tank runs over it. That will take about five minutes if my driver is very careful.'

Lammers was taking fast deep breaths to pump himself up. He spat.

'Won't say nowt.' He still sounded like a Northerner, but said to me, 'Give me absolution, Father.'

I said, 'You're a Lutheran. You don't need it.'

'I'm not. I'm a Catholic, Father. Please give me absolution.'

'No,' I told him.

'That's not allowed,' he squealed. 'You can't refuse.'

'Try me,' and we walked away.

Charteris said, 'That was a bit hard, Padre.'

CHARLIE'S WAR

I thought that that was a bit rich, coming from someone who was getting ready to drive a tank over someone else. He waved his hand at *Rachel's Dream*, its driver revved it unnecessarily, and began to inch it forward.

England strolled over to join us: he seemed to have recovered his composure. Cummings's driver doubled over to us and saluted. He'd been sent to look at what was left of Brond. He was out of breath, but reported, 'The town square has disappeared, sir. Just a bleeding great hole. There aren't many undamaged houses left. If the squadron had been driving through . . . well, they would have got most of us, sir.'

Charteris said, 'Thank you, Trooper. Get yourself a cuppa, and try to ignore the screams.'

James asked me, 'You were there. How much explosive would it have taken to do that much damage?'

'We used four-thousand-pound blast bombs called *cookies* in the RAF. One of *them* couldn't have managed anything that big.'

Charteris looked quizzically at me. James asked him, 'Didn't you know the bold Padre was in the RAF before he saw the light?'

'Wireless Op,' I said '. . . but now I've found Jesus.'

'Good job someone has.' That was Charteris again. 'Fuck knows where he's been for the last few years!'

Lammers had guts. He didn't shout until the tracks touched him. Then he babbled fast and loud. Charteris waved a stop, and James told us, '*My* side of the business, I think.' He took his time about strolling over. He returned about fifteen minutes later. Doug had come back, with char and a wad for

209

Charteris and me. James had filled half a dozen pages of his small notebook with that fine script of his.

He told Charteris, 'Three thousand kilos of high explosive under a fountain in the main square apparently – what's that in pounds? They emptied the village in the path of our advance: deliberately stripped it bare, and didn't booby-trap it with anti-personnel mines. Best result for Jerry was that we moved a field HQ in there. Next best was that we just advanced a column up the main street because the street was clear. Either way we would have been blown to bits. Our friend on the grass out there would have set it off from the church steeple.'

'Who is he, sir?'

'A Lithuanian SS man. Unpronounceable bloody name. Very well drilled in the Geneva Convention: expects you to treat him with respect and humanity. He was a merchant sailor before the war, sailing for a shipping line out of Middlesbrough.'

'Anything else, sir?'

'They've prepared three more villages like this. He gave me the names. Do you want to radio them forward?'

'Thank you, Major. What *did* happen to the people who lived here?'

'He genuinely doesn't know. They were gone before he arrived. He said that they were relocated by a *Sonderkommando*.'

'What's that?' I asked him.

'What we'd call *pioneers*, but they're really clean-up groups. What they're good at is disposing of lots of bodies.'

The tank had backed off Lammers for twelve feet or so. Even from where I stood I could see the relief on his face. He smiled, even as *Rachel's Dream* suddenly lurched over him. It was over in seconds. Cummings was back with us.

'Driver's foot will have slipped, sir,' he told me. 'Do you want to say some words?'

'No. I told you. That bastard can go to hell as far as I'm concerned.'

Cummings grunted. It may have been a little laugh.

'Why don't you stick around, sir? You're our sort of Padre. The lads could get used to you.'

I wanted to be sick.

Les slept through the lot. Even the explosion. As we packed *Kate* for a getaway I told him, 'I spoke to a Jerry today. I picked up a telephone in that village and was answered by a switchboard operator in Bremen.'

'Does the Major know that yet?'

'No; I haven't had time to tell him.'

'Do. It'll make him laugh.'

He didn't laugh. He wrote it down in his little notebook while we bounced down little Belgian country lanes. Les can't have been happy with the roads we were using, because his hands on *Kate*'s wheel had white knuckles. James said, 'Thanks very much, Charlie . . . only next time tell me sooner, savvy? These little things can be important.'

'Yes, sir.' I told him. Situation normal.

PART FOUR

Holland: April 1945

Twelve

Close to nightfall the Major asked Les, 'Where's our crossing point into Holland?'

'Between Arendonk and Reusel, I thought, Major. I'm pulling us back into the canals. There'll be units backed up everywhere and a lot of confusion. With a little bit of luck the border'll be so congested we can slip through like last time. OK?'

'OK, Private. You're the boss.'

From a Major, that. Les filtered into a column of big army trucks. James explained to me, 'The problem is that we've been moving north across the fronts of two Allied armies: both moving due west. We're not going with the flow. But at pinch points like this we can make it work to our advantage: we can slip in with a bigger mob.'

They made me swap over with James. I curled into the back seat-well and pulled James's camouflage cape over me. Les slotted into a convoy and we lurched along with it for hours. I woke with cramp in my right leg that made me want to scream. I managed to clamp my mouth shut.

James said, 'OK, Charlie. You can come out now.'

'Where are we?' I asked.

'Holland,' Les sniffed. 'Land of the Cloggies. Where the Cloggies live in the boggies. Why don't you two see if you can grab some kip: like last night?'

Looking back, it was Les who taught me to sleep in cars and moving vehicles. I've done it ever since; sometimes when I'm driving. The Major pulled rank and made me swap to the front again.

I don't know what time it was when I woke up. It was dark, and over in the east there was that glow on the cloud base. The flashes in it, like lightning, must have been gunfire. Les grinned to show he knew I was there, but didn't say anything. He hadn't shaved for a couple of days, and was as dark as a Greek bandit. After a few minutes a tune came into my head, and I must have started to hum it, or something. Les said, 'Haven't heard them for a while.'

'Who?'

'Flanagan and Allen. You were whistling "Free".'

'Was I? I didn't notice. Do you think they'll care? – the kids who come after us. Whether or not they're free? After all, it's why we went to war.'

'Did we? Your lot may have, but not mine.'

'But I thought you went to Spain in the Thirties, and fought Franco? The Major told me.'

'Sometimes the Major has a big mouth.'

'I *heard* that, Raffles,' James said from behind us, snorted, and turned over.

Les plugged on, 'I went to Spain because I was outta work, and I can drive anything. It just happened that I ended up driving for the Reds; they were the first I came across, so I came back in '38 an 'ero, because I'd been on the right side for once. I would a' driven for the first who'd asked me. It was just a matter o' luck.'

'I don't believe that.'

'My old lady says I joined up last time to get away from her.'

'Does she know you name your car after her?'

'Safer than calling it *Susie*, an' 'aving a lot of explaining to do when she finds out.'

'*Would* she? Find out.'

'Definitely. They always do. That's one of the rules.'

'Whose rules?'

'*Their* rules. Why do you think there's ten times the number o' men getting killed in this war as women?'

James said, 'That's bloody well *enough*!'

I was grinning now. Les switched tack. He said, 'I'm going to stop in about ten minutes and fill the tank, if you wants to stretch your legs. Then push on for another couple of hours. We can laager up away from the war for a couple of hours, then drive in to the rest area at Blijenhoek just as they're serving breakfast. Americans eat well.'

'As you say, Private.'

I spluttered, 'Just who's in charge in this damned car?'

They said it together.

'*You.*'

*

217

We got as far as Les said, when *Kate* chose where to stop by catastrophically deflating her right rear. Les three-wheeled her, coasting gently over the billiard-table Dutch landscape for a mile until he pulled her off the road and into a farmyard. Lights showed dimly from a shed, and cows made cow noises. They seemed friendly, but you never know.

'If women make noises like that, tell them you love them,' Les told us.

'Why?'

'It's one of the rules.'

'*Whose* rules?' That was the Major, playing bastard again.

Les told him, 'Don't take the piss out of the servants, Major. It isn't nice.'

Honours even, I'd say.

The Major's communication skills in Cloggie were much better than he admitted to anyone. He told me, 'It's all bloody coughs and grunts. Once you've mastered that you're home and dry.'

He went over to the lighted barn which had made sounds like an urgent cowshed. I told you earlier that he wore his old pistol on a lanyard. I noticed that he pulled it from its webbing holster and let it dangle at belt height as he strolled over. He was gone about five minutes. Les got fidgety. He hauled his Sten into his lap, and cocked and uncocked it, moving the slide. Then the Major strolled back. His pistol was back in its holster. He leaned his head in through the window.

'We can use that shed over there.' He pointed to a large dark space with sides of overlapping tiles, and a high, vaulted wooden roof. It was as big as St Paul's. 'I don't suppose that either of you knows how to milk cows?'

'Not the four-legged kind,' Les said.

James gave him the look, but I could see that they were going to chew over Les's attitude to the female of the species for the rest of the week. I shook my head. James added, 'Pity. That means we'll have to pay to eat. The farmer is away somewhere with a big orange triangle sewed on his sleeve: he's gone off fighting Jerry, now that Jerry's on the run. Not much different to the Frogs, really. Anyway, Mrs Farmer is in there . . .' He gestured towards the light. '. . . playing with the cows' tits, and she has a fine couple herself. Young, too – can't be above twenty.'

'Maybe I can learn,' I offered. 'It's about time I pulled my weight again.'

'Make sure that's all you pull, young Charles.' He had this wicked grin when he wanted it. 'Raffles and I will change *Kate*'s boots, and join you afterwards for an early breakfast.'

Milking for England. I wasn't too good at pronouncing her name: the first bit sounded like *Gerd* or *Gerda*, so I stopped with that. She had no English, and at that time I had no Dutch, but she smiled a lot, and giggled when I was clumsy. She washed my hands right up to my elbows with rough lye soap in steaming water, before she let me anywhere near her cows. They were big black and white bastards, who made soft cooing sounds like enormous pigeons. If they lifted their tails you moved aside smartly, because they shit like fire hoses. Big, splattery, khaki streams of the stuff, the colour of a brown job's uniform.

Gerd was short and stocky, with wide shoulders and hips. She had short, very fine blonde hair tucked under a milking cap. Its flat top was greasy, and smelled of cow. Her mouth was small, but her lips were full and smiley. Her eyes were huge and round, and a very dark brown – like those of the cows in her herd – and she was pale-skinned. My mum once described such a girl to me as *strawberries and cream*.

She sat me on a three-legged stool, facing a gigantic, grubby-pink udder and a handful of teats. She pushed my head gently forward until the top of it rested against the animal's flank. I felt its heat, and breathed in its rich, heady scent. Then, standing behind me, she reached over my shoulders for my hands, and guided each to a teat – the cow's, mind you – and with her hands over mine showed me how to pull the milk from a cow. It was a rhythmic motion, combining a squeeze, a sliding pull, and a caress. When the milk was hitting the wooden bucket in regular steamy spurts she laughed, said something in Dutch which sounded nice, kissed my ear, and moved to the next cow in the line of stalls. Her hips swung as she moved away. She finished her cow before I finished mine, and I saw her take her wooden bucket down to a row of steel churns, and empty it. She came back for mine, and because I hadn't finished the job, decided that more practical training was called for. She giggled. I shut my eyes, and breathed in the scents around me: the warm milk, the beast, and her; her breath on my neck.

She didn't stop giggling, but pulled my hands away when

the cow was empty: it didn't take long. Then she led me to another one. She emptied my bucket, and brought it back to me, pushed my head down against the new cow. My fingers already felt tired, but I was keeping up with her by the time we finished.

Then we washed again, although it would be days before I lost the smell of cow from my hair. She washed my hands and my arms, and my shoulders inside my shirt. She let me wash her in return. She stood with her eyes closed when I did this. The soap was gritty, but lathered richly in the soft water. The water was hot. Her body smelled of warm cow, and warm milk, and tasted of soap. The cows made low noises. We made low noises. She giggled again. *Why not?* I thought. We both came very quickly; one after the other. What if the war ended right here? Maybe a dairy farm in the Low Countries would be just the ticket.

In the farmhouse kitchen Les was asleep in a wooden rocker beside a brightly tiled floor-to-ceiling stove. You could almost see the heat radiating from it. He was snoring. The Major sat at the table. He had obviously dined from a great, orange-skinned cheese in the middle of it. I hadn't seen so much food in one place since the start of the war. There was enough bread, eggs, dried meat and milk products to bury a battalion. His small notebook was on the table – he had just finished an entry. He smiled his charming smile, and asked the woman, in English, 'Give him a good ride, did you, Miss?'

She looked mystified, but smiled back at him, and said, 'Ja, ja.' I'm sure that she hadn't understood a word of that.

James then gave her a string of Cloggie words. Her giggle

became a genuine laugh, and she replied. I asked him, 'What was all that?'

'I asked if you were a good pupil. She said you are the best pupil she'd ever had, and could I leave you here? She made me an offer for you. Apparently you have the makings of a farm servant.'

I felt tired. My hands ached. There was a high wooden chair across the stove from Les. I slumped into it and stuck my feet out. I felt the heat through the soles of my boots. Gerd and James nattered to each other in Cloggie. I wasn't jealous. She was my age, and wasn't likely to go with someone as old as him.

I must have slept. When I awoke something like light was creeping into the kitchen through the outside shutters, and they were still at it. Les was awake, and grinning happily to himself, his eyes on the stove, looking nowhere. You could tell that he was relaxed because he looked as if he hadn't any bones. He turned his head towards us slowly, and gave us a ghastly vacant grin. His eyes were stary. The windows were open, the lights were on, but there was no one at home.

I asked, 'What's the matter with Les? Is he ill?'

'No, it's the pills he takes: some to wake up, and some to sleep. This happens sometimes if they get out of step with each other. He turns into a large dumpling for an hour or so.'

'What does that mean?'

'It means that you're driving the car when we get out of here, Charlie.'

'Which you're keen to do, now that *you've* had breakfast?'

I pointed vaguely towards the crumbs on the table, and the heartily rogered ball of cheese.

'Christ no. I was just sampling some of the produce the Army's going to buy. I just agreed the contract with her.' He pushed his little book across the table to her, with his pen; a nice black and green marbled Swan, just like the Americans'. I'd have to get one of those. He Clogged her and she Clogged him, and she signed the bottom of a page under a row of figures. Whatever he said must have been coarse because he reached out for her tits whilst she signed. Whatever she said sounded even coarser. She got his wrists with hands stronger than his before he got there, and put them firmly back on the table top.

I suggested, 'Maybe we could hang around for a few hours; until Les is himself again.'

'Fancy a rematch?' Gerda was in my seat by the tiled stove, smiling at me over a deep wide cup of ersatz. It was a smile I found myself responding to. Les was leering at her in slow motion – he was really a bit creepy. 'I shouldn't think that that's such a good idea, old son.'

'Why, James?'

'One of her more amusing observations, whilst you slept off your labour, was how proud she was of getting through the war with only three doses of the clap. She got it first from a Fritz who raped her, and something else from her masterful Dutch husband who raped her for getting raped.'

'What about the third time?'

'Some lost Scotch soldier looking for his regiment, apparently.'

I had that sinking feeling. It probably showed in my face.

He said, 'Don't worry about it, son. Too late for that. Just give yourself a good scrubbing off – without breaking the skin – and hope for the best.'

'Ha bloody ha!' He gave me a sharp look; a ranker's look; so I sullenly added '. . . Sir,' and explained, 'You've just taken all of the magic out of it.'

This time his look told me that he thought I was a bleeding idiot. That was all right: I *felt* like one. As we left I remembered something that Les and my dad agreed on, and asked James to tell me how to say *I love you* in double Dutch. I held her by the shoulders and looked her full in the eyes. She smiled and giggled. I stumbled over the strange words a bit, but eventually got them out. I don't know what her response was, but it sounded nasty. That was after she barrel-housed me with a slap that almost broke my jaw. Time to depart.

Les wouldn't let go of his Sten, which worried me because he still wasn't right. He insisted on sitting alongside me in the front, rattling the bolt moodily. We drove in silence at first, along straight, featureless roads. Eventually he asked me, 'Why so forlorn, little man? You really *liked* her, didn't you?'

We talked about women in the way men do. Something between a boast and the confessional. I think that each of us had said more about himself than he had wanted to, because after that there was just the swish of *Kate*'s rubber on the arrow-straight road, and the growl of the big Humber engine. Eventually the brooding silence got to me, and I said, 'That was just like being back on the squadron. We seemed to talk sex all the time then. It feels like years ago.'

'That's because you had sex to talk about,' Les said. 'It must be that bloody blue uniform you Brylcreem boys ponce about in.'

'Jealous?'

''course I am. Aren't you, now that you're as scruffy as the rest of us?'

'Gerd didn't seem to notice.'

The sky we were driving into was a deep creamy yellow, and the poplars lining the road stood out against it as black. At one point I must have seen movement from the corner of my eye, and glancing to the left saw a familiar trio of American P-38s overtake us at treetop height a field away, flying in the same direction. I made eye contact with the nearest pilot. I think that Les waved to him. The guy just stared. I couldn't see his face, so why did I sense the malevolence rolling out of him? That was just as the furthest half-rolled out of their little formation, and climbed away forward.

Les grunted. Then he said, 'Wake up, Major . . . and get down behind the seat please.'

I asked, 'What's up, Les?'

'That bastard bears us ill will. I know it.'

'Don't be dumb, Les. They're on the same side as us. We've got bloody great white stars all over *Kate* for them to see.'

'Look, sir, just do what you're told for once.' He had wound down his window, and put two spare Sten magazines on the floor between his feet. The Sten was round his neck again. When he cocked it the click had an air of finality about it. 'You can argue the toss with me afterwards. If you see a black dot in the sky in front of us just weave old *Kate* from side to side as fast as yer can; but keep her on the road.'

'A dot like that one?'

'Yep,' he said, and half climbed out of the window and into the slipstream, sighting his Sten forward as if it was a rifle. Light twinkled around the rapidly growing black dot, like fireflies, and I started to weave *Kate*, with my foot jammed down on the throttle. Part of me was saying, *This isn't fair*. Another part of me was urging Les to kill the bastard. Les didn't shoot back. Bullet and cannon shells kicked up the road and ploughed the verges on either side of us. A sudden crash coincided with the car filling with tiny cubes of shattered glass.

James said, 'Oh my!' but it was muffled by his panzer cape.

By the time that Les fired, the aircraft having a go us at was clearly identifiable as one of the three Americans. I don't know how Les managed it, but in between the time that the Yank was within his range and passed over us, he got two full Sten mags off at him: I saw the pilot jink his beast left, right, left, and then jerk the nose up. I think that Les had either laid bullets on him, or scared him. After all, if you're trying to murder your Allies, you don't expect one of the bastards to murder you back, do you?

Les shouted, 'Don't stop; don't stop,' as he slid back into his seat, and immediately changed a third mag into his gun. 'I'll spot for you. Weave again when I tell you.'

226

But he didn't, because the Yank didn't come back. The actual attack was over in less than a minute.

Kate was full of pieces of glass. They tinkled like water in a stream as they fell from the Major's cape when he resurfaced. An American cannon shell or bullet had hit the mirror mounted on *Kate*'s driver's door, blown it through the driver's side window, and out through the rear window. When I got out of the car later I glittered with glass fragments and glass dust, like a snowman in a garden. I had a scratched cheek. That was our only honourable wound from the fight.

We pulled off the road at the next farm. It was deserted. The house had been fought through: it was pretty burned up. There were five mounds marked with crude wooden crosses by its busted front door. Three of the names and ranks were German, two were Allied: American I think. The Major and I stood off in a neglected field, and brushed each other down until the glass and its dust were gone. I remember particularly that he wouldn't let me rub my eyes, but cleansed them very gently with clear water from the farmyard pump. He said that if I rubbed them with glass dust I'd scratch the retinas. I probably owe him my sight. I did the same for him. We even had to comb each other's hair out, like a couple of girls. His hair was grey with dust, making him look like an old man.

Les, hanging half out of the car, and shooting back at the Yank, hadn't collected much glass. While the Major and I checked each other up, he cleared the crap out of *Kate*, and by the time we came back he'd got a brew-up going, on the desert stove he carted around in the boot. That was dry earth, or sand, mixed with petrol, and crammed into a large bully beef can. Once you lit it, it burned on a low flame until you tossed it out. I remember that fresh char in a big ally mug, so hot you could hardly hold it – with milk I'd probably pulled from a cow myself not long ago, and three spoons of sugar – as one of the finest cups of tea in my life. The right thing at the right time. Eventually my hands stopped shaking.

Some time Les asked, 'Anyone know what the fuck that was all about? Those bastards have been looking at us for days, just to make sure. Even the tankies said, *I wonder what they're looking for?* Remember? Is there anything I should know?'

I remembered, and I felt shifty.

'For some reason the Yanks haven't exactly taken a shine to *me*, have they? Look what they did to me in Paris. But I honestly don't know what I've done to them.'

'Nuffink,' Les said. 'Not official, anyway. You surely irritated that Snowdrop Lieutenant, though . . . what was his name?'

'Kilduff.'

'That's right. I'd be surprised he took whatever it was personal enough to order their bloody Air Force out after you. Anyway, how would he know where we were?'

I said, 'He could have worked it out. He knew where we were heading.' Then I gulped and took the plunge. '. . . and I phoned him from that telephone in Brond and pissed him off. It seemed funny at the time.'

Les went very still. Froze with his tea mug half to his mouth. When he moved he stood up. He said, 'I'm going to have a waxer in my char. Anyone else?' He produced a rum bottle from *Kate*'s capacious boot, and we all got a dollop. It was all theatre to disguise how angry he was. The Major got me off. He sloshed his fortified tea around in his mug and observed, 'There could be another reason. You remember when we first saw that flight of Lightnings?'

I said, 'Yes. There were four of them. Our first stop after Laon. They crossed that town square when we were at a cafe.'

Les recalled, 'One of them had a sun painted on it. He waggled his wings as he crossed. I thought he was a flash git.'

'One of us *said* so,' I told him. 'I remember.'

The Major filled it in.

'The Flash Git's girlfriend was the waitress at that cafe bar. She asked me about the obligations of Allied servicemen if they got local girls pregnant. I told her how to stake a claim.'

Les asked him, 'When did she ask you that?'

'While I was rogering her.'

He looked away in one direction, and Les looked away in another. Les took a deep breath, held it for a lifetime, and said, '. . . And her boyfriend never came back, did he? Only the other three. Yes: I can see that pissing off his pals!' He got up and threw the dregs of his tea into the hot can. They hissed like angry vipers. On the other side of *Kate* from us he opened the front passenger door, and slammed it violently shut. Then, across her bonnet, he said in a deceptively calm tone, 'One of you two stupid bastards almost just got me killed . . . and fer nuffin'.' No exclamation mark. No *sirs*. Less than full marks for sentence construction, but it was down-beat, which is why it drove home.

I looked at my drink, and did the same as Les, throwing the dregs on the makeshift stove. The snakes hissed again. I said, 'Sorry,' and felt it.

What surprised me was that James said the same.

'Sorry, old man.' Then, 'My mistake.'

Les said *OK*, but sounded subdued; and then we were back on the road. Les drove – to make up time he said – but I think that it was so he didn't have to speak to us. I understood: when I was a Sergeant in the RAF I used to think that most officers were stupid. I think that I must have begun to doze. I turned up the collar of my jacket to deflect the gale blowing through *Kate*'s cabin. James sat stoically upright in the back, his cheeks reddened by the icy blast.

I awoke with that dreadful start of your chin hitting your chest as your neck muscles finally relax. Les said, 'Blijenhoek about ten minutes. This is just about as far as we got last trip. Should be a checkpoint in about a mile.'

There was.

Thirteen

It didn't look like an R & R station for tired troops to me; it looked like a sodding battlefield. The checkpoint was a staggered twin-barrier job, with a nasty great Sherman tank looking down its 75 at you from the second one. There were too many soldiers about, and they all looked edgy. We were in a queue behind another staff car and three small trucks whose bodies stood high off their wheels. The front one had a big Red Cross on a white ground painted on its hood. The soldiers scurrying around it had Red Cross arm bands.

Les told me, 'Don't like this much. The war had missed here and moved on the last time we were here.'

'Is this Blijenhoek, where Grace might be?'

'No. This is Ganda. Blijenhoek's a few miles on. It's just a few houses around an old castle: quite pretty, if I remember it right. This place was all right when we were here last month.'

It wasn't all right now. Ganda had probably been a pretty hamlet, built on either side of a broad curve in the main road. All of the houses had been fought through. Snowdrops worked their way methodically down the vehicles. Les asked one, 'What happened to this place?'

His white helmet was a size too small: he had half a cigar, and did the trick with it; moving it from one side of his mouth to the other, then speaking around it.

'Fritz happened. This was the little brother of the Battle of the Bulge. The old man reckoned there musta been half a division of them. Kraut paratroopers. The hard guys.'

'When was that?'

'Say ten days ago. They ripped back through the R & R area down the road like a knife through butter.'

'Where are they now?'

'Holed up in a friggin' castle, laughin' at us.'

James decided it was time to put an officerly edge on the conversation, and made a mess of it as usual. He leaned forward and asked, 'Can we still go up there − to the rest area? We need a quick word with one of your tank commanders, if he's still there.'

The Snowdrop took in the Major's bits of brass, and threw him a quick and sloppy salute. James did the same. His was worse. The American said, 'You wouldn't be the Englishmen chasing 'cross the war zone after some English girl, sir? We were warned to watch out for a couple of Limeys − sorry, sir − and a priest.'

I suppose that there was no point in denying it; I still had the crosses on my collar. Les had been caught off guard for once. The American had a firmer grip on his tommy-gun than Les had on his beloved Sten. James gave his winning smile. The one that fooled nobody at all.

'Yes. Hands up. I suppose that's us. Only you could have caught us, Officer.'

The American wasn't amused. That was the downside. On the other hand he didn't seem particularly concerned. He told us, 'Would you mind pulling out of the line, sir. My officer will want a word with you. That way we can clear the traffic behind you. You can park it up over there, sir.'

He indicated with his machine gun. The end of the short barrel made circular motions which hypnotized me with fear. I was distracted enough to notice that it had a flat, round magazine, like you see in gangster movies. As he manoeuvred us out of the line, and over to the small checkpoint hut, Les murmured, 'Another fine mess you've got us into.'

James said, '*Sir*.'

'Another fine mess you've got us into, *sir*.'

The American Lieutenant who came out of the small hut was thin and tired-looking. He was talking on a battered portable handset as he walked towards us. He had red mud on his boots and trousers, and a tear in his wind jacket. He hadn't shaved for a couple of days. As he approached the car he didn't so much as glance at me or Les: he shifted the radio to his left hand, came to a nice attention, and flicked James a very neat salute. There always has to be an exception. James wound down the rear window: he was lucky he still had one. The young American asked, 'Do you mind if I get in, sir? It'll be more comfortable.'

A wrong-footed James: I could see it in his eyes. He said, 'I suppose so,' rather grudgingly, I thought, and moved to make room. The American joined him in the back. I turned to watch. So did Les. Up close the Yank looked like a bit of a fighter. He said, 'James Oliver. Provost Service, sir,' and held out his hand.

Our James said, 'James England.' They did the handshake thing.

The American said, 'I know, sir . . . and this is Private Finnigan,' He smiled at Les. '. . . and . . . your priest.' He didn't smile at me. 'I received a signal from Paris. They said to watch out for you, and give you any assistance you asked for: that's *within reason*, I expect, sir.' He tried a tired grin.

I asked him, 'Who did that order come from, Lieutenant?'

'Somewhere up high, I expect, Padre, although not as high up as the guy you're speaking to.' He gave me a smile then: one that was hard not to forgive. 'A Mr Kilduff sent the signal; you know him? He said to pass you through, and report back.'

'We met.'

'He an' I were at college together: law. I just spoke to him over a relay. He said that you and the US Army had got off on the wrong foot, Padre, but that it was behind us now. I guess that means that he got his arse felt, sir.'

He turned the conversation back to James, who said, lamely I thought, 'Quite. These things happen.'

I wasn't as ready to forgive and forget. The bastard had kept me padlocked to a bed for a day, and I still half suspected that he had a finger on that P-38 which tried to kill us.

England asked him, 'What *is* the situation forward of here?'

'Stabilizing, sir. A few days ago you wouldn't have liked it at all. This was supposed to be a back area. Colonel Gatcombe reckoned that at least half a company of Jerry parachutists counter-attacked across a river and the canal. Raids like this are just to slow us down, make us think, and buy themselves time to dig in. They'll fight us on the Rhine. That's what *I* think, sir.'

The Major gave his wry smile. I could sense him relaxing. He asked, 'What does this Colonel *Gatcombe* think?'

'No idea, sir. The Colonel started to pray as soon as the Krauts came over the hill: they've shipped him Stateside in a strong jacket laced up with tapes. The fight-back at Ganda was organized by a Quartermaster Sergeant and a black cook.'

'And they stopped a half-company of Paras?' That was Les.

'Well, Mr Finnigan. Maybe not a *company*. The Colonel might have got excited.'

'So can we go through to what was the rest area?' James asked. 'The Padre here needs to speak to a Lieutenant . . .'

'Grayling. Albert Grayling. *Albie.* I met him once at the American Red Cross Officers' Club in Bedford.'

'Yeah, Padre. Albie's there. Acting Captain now. They'll need to find him a few more tanks before he moves on.'

'Is he OK?'

The Yank paused before replying. He seemed like a straight guy.

'Yeah, Padre. He's OK. They've taken a hell of a pounding moving up to the river . . .' There was only one river on people's minds these days. 'He lost half the squadron, so they went into R & R to wait for reinforcement. There ain't much for them up here, but they've set up a half-decent bar, and a couple of chow tents. One of our Entertainments Officers

DAVID FIDDIMORE

found some films. There's a bathing unit up there as well. They were OK until the Jerry came marching down the road behind them. It spoiled their party.'

'That's happened to us,' Les offered. 'It never does seem fair, does it?'

I asked, 'So what are you telling us?'

'That you might find Albie and his pals are a mite nervous just now.'

'And a big mob of Germans are still in a nearby castle overlooking their position?'

'Not *overlooking*, sir; but near enough to make you feel antsy.'

The Major asked him, 'Is there any good news?'

'The Bath Unit, Major. They stood and fought: saved the day. When they ran out of soap, they threw facecloths and scrubbing brushes. The Jerry turned and fled.'

'Into the castle.' It was James again. '. . . and they're still there?'

'Yeah,' the American said, and suddenly looked his age, which wasn't much. 'It's a bit of a pisser, isn't it, sir?'

236

Fourteen

Oliver came on with us. There were two more checkpoints to pass through. The Yanks must have believed in capital punishment for the politically radical, because his directions to Les were peppered with *hang a left here*, and *hang a sharp right, now*. Once the idea was lodged in my head I snorted each time he used the phrase. He began to look at me as if he thought I was a bit touched.

James said, 'Don't mind the Padre: God puts him under pressure now and again.'

'To tell you the truth, Major, the Padre is going to be the only one of the three of you that's welcome down there.' He probably had an IQ of about seven. Command material.

I revised my opinion of him as we turned into the olive drab campsite we had come so far to find. It looked like a Boy Scout jamboree, but with mud. He said, 'I'm sure that we can find you a rear saloon window to replace the one you lost, but I'm not so sure of the one on the driver's door. We may just have to cut a sheet of Clear-Vu, and rivet it in. That OK?'

'Whatever you say, Lieutenant.' That was James. 'God

says we should be grateful for small mercies: I'm not going to argue with that; the Padre wouldn't let me.' He chuckled. The bastard was taking the piss again. He was also taking the piss out of God. That's not so clever. God has a really long memory.

Albie's R & R area had become tacked on to the biggest field hospital Les had ever seen. (He told me that later.) Tanks and armoured vehicles were holed up over a huge area that had once been a dozen fields on a gentle hillside. It was churned to buggery, and soldiers in fatigues with mud-coloured legs were moving around on wooden-board pathways. My old man would have felt at home in something that looked as much like a First War back area as this. There was no guard or checkpoint, just a field gateway on high ground: the camp stretched down away from you and above you, smothering the bloody hillside. It was the first bit of Holland I'd seen that wasn't flat, and I didn't fancy it one little bit.

Our Yank, Oliver, asked Les, 'Would you mind leaving your car up here, soldier? You're as like to get bogged in down there, as not. I'll send a Maintenance Unit up here to have a go at the busted windows.'

Les stuck it in close to the hedge, and we all decamped: he kept his Sten, and strolled like I'd seen him do before, with his arm resting on it, as if in a sling. When we reached wooden-plank pathways Oliver said, 'Welcome to Boardwalk City. The problem is that I don't know where Albie is likely to be. Would you mind if we split? If the Major and his driver would care to move down among the tanks, and ask for Albie's unit, I'll take the Padre up the hill to the hospital and the recreation tents. We could meet you in the Quonset – that's the bar, the wooden thing with the flag over it – in say, an hour. One of us should have had some success by then.'

I wasn't too keen, and it must have shown in my face. James said, 'Take it easy, Charlie. If Mr Oliver was going to arrest you, he would have done it by now. I wouldn't have stopped him.'

'Thanks.'

Les asked the American, 'I suppose that some of them down there will be rustling up their breakfasts around now.'

'I shouldn't wonder, Mr Finnigan: but if they aren't, I'll get you into the chow line up the hill.'

Les gave him a salute. It was worse than one of James's. He sort of touched the rim of his beret with his right forefinger: and that was it.

The main encampment was far enough above us for my knees to feel the strain. Oliver didn't try to make conversation, which I appreciated. The biggest tents had huge white squares with red crosses on them: they were the field operating theatres. There were two sorts of wards, he told me: those for lying in, and those for dying in. He thought it would show solidarity with my Allies to visit the latter before I moved on.

About a dozen people, surgeons, nurses, attendants and patients, erupted from one of the operating tents just as we reached it. You couldn't have mistaken it for a welcoming party. One patient was carrying his own drip, and still running. A nurse caught up with him, and took the drip. They ran on together, ignoring the mud. One of the docs must have recognized Oliver, who swore under his breath as the guy stopped, turned on him, and gulped, 'Thank the fuck you're here. There's a mad bastard with a gun in there.'

I couldn't resist it.

'There are mad bastards with guns out here, too; thousands of them. Haven't you noticed?'

The doc was a scrawny character, whose apron was covered in blood. He eyed me up and down, and panted, 'A Chaplain: even better. Maybe he'll listen to you.'

Me and my big mouth. A shot sounded from inside the tent, and its canvas near us was plucked momentarily outwards. When it fell back in place there was a hole in it.

Oliver told me, 'You can wait out here for me if you like,' and stepped up to the flappy thing that was pretending to be a door.

I said, 'I'll be safer with you: you're probably the only man here who knows what he's doing.'

I only said it to make him feel better, expecting him to refuse. He eyed me up doubtfully, said, 'OK . . . let's go,' and moved.

At the far end of the tented room there was a patient on a table. His big toe twitched spasmodically, as if he was waiting for someone to scratch it. He'd have a long wait; there were few doctors, nor nurses that I could see. Those patients who could had got on the floor under their cots. There were a few who couldn't do that, and most of those too far gone to care. One deranged-looking grunt was sitting up on one bed, with his back against a ridge pole. Three medics were kneeling on the floor, in the mud, in front of him. One Doc, one nurse and one SBA — a sick bay attendant. They had their faces close to the mud, and their arses in the air pointed at us.

Guns always look big in confined spaces, don't they? He was holding one of those bloody great .45s, and there was that brilliant tang of gunsmoke in the air. The square gun barrel framing drifted in our direction as we neared him. The Provo didn't hurry. No point in hurrying to get killed, is there? When we were so close as not to be mistaken Oliver asked, 'Arnold? That you?'

'They took my fucking leg, Jamie.' The gunman had one of those soft Southern voices. I could see through the sheet over his lower body that there was something significant missing.

'He would have died . . .' That was the doc in the mud. It came out as a bit of a whine. Then he farted. I knew how he felt. The patient told him, 'Shaddup. I weren't talking at you. You stole my leg.'

We were at the end of the bed now. The GI said it again, 'They took my fucking leg, Jamie.' Then, 'Who's the guy with you?'

'A limey Chaplain, a Padre.'

'They took my fucking leg, Padre.'

'You can get along without it,' I told him.

'You ever heard of a one-legged rodeo rider?'

'Hopalong Cassidy?' I tried.

I heard the Provo's breath going in with a whistle. It got so quiet that you could hear a pin drop. Then the GI laughed.

'*You* ain't no friggin' hymn-singer, that's fer sure. Why you wearing a gun, Father?'

'Old Testament, son; an eye for an eye, and all that jazz

. . . I didn't want Jerry getting the wrong idea about peace and brotherly love.'

'Should I be worried?' he asked me.

I heard my voice saying it, but it wasn't really me.

'I'm really sorry, Soldier. Sorry about your leg; but you've got a lot of people scared and worried in here, and there's a man on that table at the back bleeding to death because you have a gun in your hand. I may not be that John Wayne, but what I'm going to do is promise you that if you make me unbutton this holster I'll try to kill you.'

Who was I kidding? It was my newly acquired Luger I was talking about. I didn't even know how to fire the damned thing. Again, I heard that whistling sound as Oliver took a quick deep breath, and a muddy squelch as he stepped away from me.

Arnold One-Leg said, 'Hot-damn!' and then, 'You can stop whistling, Jamie, I was never going to hurt no one; you know that.' And then, 'They took my fucking leg, Father, and didn't even let me see it.'

'You put the gun down, and they'll fetch the leg.' I was actually resting my right hand on the holster flap. I don't know if I would have done it. He grinned, reversed his pistol, and handed it grip-first up to the policeman. The medics began to stir out of the mud.

I said, 'Someone had better see to the guy on the table. And bring this man his leg. I think he wants to say goodbye.'

I think that they were the first proper orders I ever gave. A bead of sweat ran down the small of my back. Oliver went with them. I sat on the bed where his leg should have been –

it was a bit tactless, but the sooner he got used to it the better. I asked the GI, 'What's your name?'

'Arnold Ripley. I'm from a small place called Houston. You won't have heard of it.'

'I won't forget it now, will I? I had to sit down so that the others wouldn't see my knees knocking.'

'Would you have dropped me, Father?'

'We'll never know, will we? I've never fired the damned thing.'

'Better learn, if you're going to go round threatening soldiers.' He gave a low moan.

I wasn't going to be dumb enough to ask if it was hurting. I said, 'I'll get them to give you a shot when they come back.' The words were out before I could call them back, but he grinned through the pain.

'You don't take any fucking prisoners, do you, Father?' Then, 'Yeah; better you don't do it yourself: you could hurt someone.'

The nurse and the SBA came back with James Oliver. Each of the three was struggling to carry a galvanized iron dustbin. Jamie waved me over. He said, 'Problem. We got bins full of arms and legs back there. Some of them are a bit smelly. No one knows which one is his.'

This was getting out of control. I felt like a pilot whose control lines had been shot away. I went back to the bed. I said, 'Houston, we have a problem. They have bins of arms and legs, and they don't know which one is yours.'

'What we gonna do, Father?'

'Like they do in the gangster films, son. Identity parade.'

He laughed between gasps of pain. They got all the legs out, and laid them across the end of his bed for him to see. Eventually he laid claim to a fine left leg. The one he'd lost was the right one, and in any case the leg he identified was clearly black. I said, 'That's not your leg, Arnold. It belongs to a Negro. It's not even the right side.'

'I know, Father, but I kinda like it. It's a good leg.'

'OK. What do you want me to do with it?'

He gave a little gasp again, and said, 'Just say a little something over it, Father. Put it to rest.'

I gave the leg the Twenty-Third Psalm, stumbling a bit around the bit that says *walking* through the shadow of the valley of death. The nurse cried a bit, and the SBA grinned as if he was about to lose his mind.

Arnold said, 'You kin take it away now,' and, 'You can shoot me now, Padre.'

The nurse moved away to a trolley mired in the middle of the tent, and came back with a syringe of pink fluid. Whatever it was it put Arnold out of it very quickly.

The SBA asked, 'You want to pray over all these bins, Padre?'

I told him, 'Not now, son. Just stack them up out back, and I'll creep round and say the words over the whole lot tonight.'

'You're the strangest bloody priest *I've* met, sir!'

'It's the training. They rush us through it these days. You don't have time to get the rough edges knocked off.' I was pissed off with having to explain myself all the time.

The nurse fussing around the bed nearest to the door flap

as we left was the pretty one in a traditional nurse's outfit we had seen running away alongside a patient and holding up his plasma drip. She straightened up, backed away from the bed and half turned – almost bundling into us. She blushed, said, 'Sorry,' and then looked angry. But not at us.

'Lieutenant?' Her voice came all the way from that girls' school in Cheltenham. Some posh Anglo who was here for the good works that would take pride of place in her war diary one day.

Oliver stopped and said, 'Yes?'

'I want to report that man I was with.'

'What did he do?'

'He handled me. Handled me standing up in the mud. Up against a post while I held his drip, and kept him alive.'

'Why didn't you run away, Miss?'

'If I'd dropped the drip he would have died.'

'I expect he had his reasons,' the policeman told her, and pushed me out through the door flap ahead of him.

Outside he asked me, 'Is your denomination allowed to drink? I could show you a good bar.'

We waded up to the Quonset hut. It was a lot larger than I had thought: about the same size as a village church hall, but not much more substantial than one of the large tents. It had been wood prefabricated in the USA in four-ply, shipped in pieces and erected on a small bit of America in the Netherlands. Even though it was relatively early morning there was a party going on: maybe fifty people. Thinking about it, it could have been the dregs of last night's do. A coloured pianist in a white jacket was doing the *Casablanca* thing, and among the few couples dancing was a nice-looking nurse dancing with an older guy. He was in clean fatigues that bore no identification flashes, and wore highly polished black shoes. I couldn't see his face. I noticed them because she had a tit out, and she danced with her eyes closed. She looked beat; I think that she was sleeping. If that sort of thing offends your sensibilities these days, I can't say I care. We had almost reached the end of the world: things were different out there.

A friendly waitress brought a couple of foaming beers to our table – no money changed hands. I asked Oliver about that.

'It would be immoral to charge for it, Padre. After all, the Army stole it in the first place. We stole some from the Kraut, and after that ran out, stole it from collaborators. This is Belgium beer: made by some order of monks. They been told to supply it for free until the war's over. I think Patton told them that, or maybe it was Ike.'

'Can they do that?'

'Padre, they tell me that *Ike wants* are the most important words in Europe right now. Cheers.'

'Cheerio,' I told him. It was good beer: strong and with a bleak yeasty aftertaste.

The dance was an excuse-me. A tall Sergeant excused the guy in fatigues, and the nurse didn't even open her eyes. I was beginning to think that I fancied a bit of a dance myself. Fatigues stuck an American cigarette in his gob, lit it expertly with a brass Zippo, and wandered over. His sleeves were half rolled: I saw he had an expensive wristwatch on his right wrist: probably German. His arm sported a new eagle tattoo.

My old man always used to wear his watch on the wrong side. He sat down, and waved the waitress over.

'Hello, Charlie.'

'Hello, Dad. Where's Uncle Tommy?'

'Up at the clinic. Getting something for his warts.'

'I didn't know he had any.'

'Before we came here he didn't have. I've told him that they're something else, but he won't believe me.'

'Are you still digging?'

'Yes. You still flying?' The look he gave the clothes I was wearing begged a reply.

'No. I'm driving. I'm trying to find that girl Grace I knew. Do you remember her?'

'What's she doing over here? I thought that she was just a delivery pilot for the ATA.'

'She was. It's a long story, but she was pregnant, got caught in a bombing raid in London where a lot of children were killed, flipped over and ran away. Some people think that she's out here somewhere, doing relief work. Maybe she's even heading for Germany.'

'Am I a grandfather then?'

'I don't think so. The child's probably not mine. Probably an American she knew before we met her.'

'Why do you want to find her?'

'I'm not sure that I do, any more. But I promised her I'd find her after the war, and it must be on its last knockings now. The point is that the RAF wants her, and her parents want her: *and* Winnie, if I believe what people tell me. All I have to do is find her, and take her back.'

'Her people rich?'

'Filthy.'

'You going to marry her so we can all live like nobs?'

'Six months ago I would have liked that. Now I'm not so certain. I might love her, but that's not always enough, is it? I'm not all that sure that she's worth loving.'

My father was never what you'd call a smiler, but he cracked one now.

I asked him, 'What's so funny?'

'Nothing, Charlie. I was smiling because I suddenly realized that you'd grown up. It was pleasure.'

Some time during our conversation Oliver left us to dance with the nurse. Her shirt was open now, and flapping loose around her waist. Oliver was stroking her as they danced. Her hands met behind his neck. Her eyes were still closed. The Negro was playing 'I Saw Stars', which I remembered as a Les Allen number from before the war. The slow piano made it really smoochie. The Sergeant was now drinking at a noisy table which included MOs and SBAs with blood-stained coats. Above them the bare wood beams which supported the roof were strung with lines of small, tired-looking Allied flags. Some wag had managed to tie a triangular swastika pennant into them.

Dad asked me, 'Cigarette?' as he pulled another for himself.

'Please.'

'Camels. In my war men *flew* Camels, not smoked them.'

He always liked puns.

'I seem to remember that some men smoked them too. Didn't Sopwiths burn pretty easily?'

'They all did, then. It was the dope on the canvas. I should have asked you about your burns. You're obviously a lot better.'

'Some American doctor spread something on my shoulders in a hospital in Paris. I hardly notice them now.'

'. . . and we can't keep him away from the bints,' James England said, and flopped into the vacant chair. Les pulled one up to another side; cornering us. James held his hand out for a shake. I told Dad, 'This is Major England: I'm travelling with him.' I told James, '. . . and this is my father, Henry Bassett.'

'Nothing to do with the liquorice allsorts?' Les asked him, also doing the handshake ritual. His hand held on to my old man's a fraction too long, and they were feeling where to place fingers and thumbs. 'I'm Les Finnigan. Their PFD.'

'What's that?'

'Poor effing driver; pardon my French.'

James had his book out. He said, 'I'll write that down. Have you noticed how we all excuse our bad language with *Pardon my French*? Anyone would think that the Froggies swore all of the time.'

Another round hit the table. I would have to be careful. That was the third this morning. Our policeman came back from his smooch, and dragged a chair up. I noticed that the music had stopped, and when I looked up the only two folk missing appeared to be the pianist and the dancing nurse.

James Oliver asked, 'None of us found Albie, then?'

My father asked, 'Is that the American tank commander you met in Bedford?'

'Yes.' That was me. 'How the hell did you find out about that?'

'He told me, about a week ago. We were drinking in a crowd, and got to exchanging folk we knew: you know how it is. Why is it that no one believes you when you tell them it's a small bleeding world?'

'Do you know where he is, Dad?'

'Of course I do. He's sitting over there waving at you.'

It was the noisy table. There were about eight people around it, and you couldn't see the tabletop for glasses. The dancing nurse was there now. Maybe she had been there all along. Albie was grinning at me; he had a new growth of beard, and waved a hand above his head. The three first fingers had been bandaged together. Even from that distance I could see that the bandage needed changing.

My dad walked with me. Albie got up and gave me a hug. That was embarrassing because he enveloped me, and my nose came up to about his left nipple. He shook Dad's hand enthusiastically.

'You found your Charlie, then, Mr Bassett?'

'Only because he was looking for you, Captain, and that girl Grace.'

'There you go. It's an ill wind blows nobody any good.' The way his tongue was wrapping itself around his teeth I thought he did well to get that out. When he grinned I saw that one of his incisors wasn't there. He noticed me noticing it, and held up his right hand for inspection. As well as the bound-up fingers, the top inch of his pinkie was missing. It looked very red; like a recently healed wound.

'I'm leaving bits all over Europe, Charlie. I soon won't have enough to ship back home.'

'What happened to your fingers?'

'The small one was shot off: didn't feel a thing. Broke the middle one. Just lashed the others on either side as a splint. Been meaning to get it fixed up for days.'

The nurse was sitting alongside him. Up close you could see how tired she was. She reminded me of Les when he got his pills out of sync: the lights were on, but there was no one in. She wore no lipstick, and for some reason that touched me – I wanted to look after her. I asked her about his fingers. She took a long time to reply. Then she sighed and said, 'He'll get gangrene. We've told him that. I don't think he cares.' She spoke as if Albie wasn't there.

Albie asked her, 'How long before you're back on duty, hon?'

She made a production of checking a small watch which hung drunkenly on her collar. It all happened in slow-mo.

' . . . 'bout three hours. Back shift.'

'If you'll give me a quarter hour to talk to my friends here, I'll walk you back to your tent, and after that I'll walk you on duty, and you can fix my finger.'

'You just want to fuck me.'

'That, too.'

'OK,' she said.

Albie asked me, 'Are you following Grace about?'

'Yes. Do you know where she is?'

'She won't like that.'

'I promised her.'

'She still won't like it.'

Dad was coming back from the bar with the waitress. They each had a tray of beers.

I told Albie, 'You're right. I know it. But I haven't any choice. The RAF sent me.'

'What the fuck's it got to do with the RAF?'

'You didn't use to swear.'

'That's before the Kraut shot things off me, and killed my pals. I'm serious – what the fuck has it got to do with the RAF?'

'Actually, very little. That's the way their world seems to work. My boss tells me to go and do something. In reality he's repaying a favour to someone he owes, who's repaying a favour to someone he owes, who's repaying a favour to someone he owes. These are all personal favours: nothing to do with King or Country. It's person to person inside their business. Am I making sense?'

'What are you trying to say, Charlie?'

'That I could be working for the Jerries, and never know it. It depends who wants the favour done in the first place.' I said it again: probably the first time I faced facts. 'It's the way their sort of world seems to work.' If it sounded sort of lame, it was because it was.

'Whose world?'

'Spies,' I told him. 'I think.'

'Fuck . . . *off*, Charlie!' That was Albie.

'Charlie boy, what sort of a mess have you got yourself into?' That was my old man. They really helped, didn't they? I felt about ten years old again, exposed and foolish.

Albie told me, 'You missed her by about a fortnight. She crossed with us, ditched us in France, and then caught us here, after we were shot up again. She was here before those bloody Krauts came back through us.'

'She was OK, though?'

'Yeah. She had an orphan child with her. Wet-nursing it: I heard my folks talk about women wet-nursing other people's children when I was a kid. Never saw it until now. Still has nice little tits.'

'Do you know where she went?'

'No. She hung around us for a few days, but I didn't get to talk to her a real lot.'

'Don't worry about it. Talking a lot isn't what Grace does.'

'She took a fancy to one of the guys in the squadron. She might have told him more than she told the rest of us. All I know is that she was looking out for some mob of mad Frogs who believe that everyone has the right to medical care, regardless what side they're on. They say that medicine is like a religion: it has no boundaries. Apparently the Top Brass don't like them too much.'

'Will he talk to me, this guy? Grace's friend?'

'Who wants to find her, as well as you?'

'I thought I told you: her parents. They're VIPs. That means that the Prime Minister wants her found as well because he's a friend of the family . . . and I sort of got the short straw. Short guys do.'

Albie grinned.

'OK. I'll talk to him.'

'When?'

'See you back here tonight or tomorrow.'

He hooked his good hand into the nurse's armpit, and helped her to her feet. In the course of that his own chair fell over backwards. She smiled. It was a self-indulgent smile that said she had a secret. Either that or she was pissed to the eyeballs.

I asked, 'What do I do till then?'

'If you don't need a Doctor yet, grab a little R & R. It's what this place is for.'

I didn't like the word *yet*.

I went round and picked the chair up. Dad was helping a waitress clear the table back to the bar, so I gave up resisting and sat down with strangers. I'll have to revise that. There was a mixture of olive drabs and white coats. One black-face white coat studied my face, and said, 'Hi, Charlie Bassett.'

I said, 'Mr McKechnie,' as his name came back to me. 'Simmer, wasn't it?'

'Well done, Charlie, you have a memory for names. You should have been a policeman.'

'I thought that *you* were a policeman. Kilduff is looking for you.'

'He'll never find me. This is too obvious a place to look. The best place to hide a doctor is in a hospital.'

'The last time I met you you weren't quite a doctor.'

'Am now. Out of the shitehouse and into the shite.'

'What happened?'

'When I saw that you and your people could fuck the system, I decided to blow. I left the Lieutenant an anatomically accurate description of what he could do with my job, and just came out where they needed a doctor most — they don't care where I come from here, as long as I can cut. They like my style. They call me *the Cutter*. There's a cutter in every unit. The last one here was minced by a mortar round the week before I turned up.'

'I'm still looking for that girl.'

'Miss Emily, or your Grace what's her name?'

'Grace. I leapfrogged over Emily. Your Captain Grayling saw Grace more recently than Emily did.'

'That's good, because Miss Emily was here, then she got a few days' leave. I think that she's gone back over to England.'

'Did she know that I was looking for her?'

''course not. Why would anyone tell her *that*, Charlie? You still a pretending Padre?'

Fuck them, I could manage without help. I reached across the table with my glass of beer. He met me halfway. I said, 'Cheerio. I won't tell on *you* either.' We clinked.

'Cheers, Charlie . . . and I note that. You going liberal? Growing up on me?'

'That's what Dad said this morning.'

The devil of whom I had spoken was back in a chair alongside me, arguing the toss with the thin Sergeant. He twitched round when I tugged his sleeve.

'This is my dad,' I told McKechnie, and, 'This is my friend Dr McKechnie, Dad. He helped me in Paris.' OK: so that was stretching it a bit.

'. . . he's gonna give me a hand when I find Grace.'

I might have imagined it, but I sensed McKechnie's fine brown face becoming a couple of shades paler.

Five minutes later a wet SBA banged in at the door and shouted, 'Cutter here?' across the echoing hall.

McKechnie snapped alert, and responded with a, 'Yo. I'm here,' and threw his hand up.

'You got a bad arm up in Number Three, sir.'

He said, 'OK, brother,' and moved up and out.

I murmured, 'Good luck,' not meaning him to hear me, but he turned, and flashed me a brilliant smile before scampering out into the rain. I forgot to tell you; it had begun to rain. Eastern Holland should twin with Cambridgeshire: they have that in common. The roof of the Quonset was thin boards and tarred cloth. The noise of the rain was like being inside a side drum during a Gene Krupa solo. The SBA who'd come for the Cutter stepped over to the bar and had a quick one. It started as half a glass of something clear, but the barman stirred a spoonful of HP sauce, a spoonful of honey, and some salt into it.

The old man saw me watching. He said, 'Bourbon. They can do a good dark rum as well: a touch heavier with the HP, brown sugar and a dash of bitters.'

I saw the SBA swallow it in a oner, and shudder, before making for the door. I got a glance of rain bouncing off puddles outside as he left.

I asked, 'What is it?'

'Medical-grade alcohol. Ethanol: good with tonic water, and lemon, or lime. They call it an E & T. Lemons are not too easy to get, but we had a couple of lorryloads of limes last week. God knows where from. Anyway, the babes love an E & T. They dance on the tables.'

'Babes?'

'Sorry, son. The women. Everyone talks American over here.'

'Why?'

'Because they're paying for the war now, didn't anyone tell you?'

It must have been McKechnie's use of the word *shitehouse* that did it. Not long after he left to go to work my lower bowel performed a serious ritual of summoning. The barman gave me directions, which were outside and on to the boardwalk, turn left, walk the length of the Quonset until I reached the canvas field latrine. He'd have an E & T on the bar for me to try when I returned. I didn't walk; I ran. It was a large latrine: wind and water proof, if a trifle draughty. The usual thing – a long, narrow pit with a smooth pole along it lengthwise. You hung your jacksie over the pole and watched for splinters. In front of you was a heap of dirt, and an entrenching tool – so you could cover your spoil afterwards. There was an entrance at each end; for men and for women. They were labelled *Cats* and *Dudes*. I went for *Dudes*. The only thing was that they led to the same space. While I sat there balanced on the pole a woman SBA in fatigues came in, and squatted the woodwork about ten feet to my right. She smiled as she dropped her kecks, and opened a Forces newspaper.

She said, 'Oh, hi, Father,' when she noticed me, and turned back to it. She had a nice smile and a fine, white backside, but that was it for me. The romance was gone. The paper squares were cut from newspapers, just the same as in the UK . . . and the same bastard had got there before me, and stolen the cartoons. I slipped into role when I was covering my turds. As I sprinkled the earth on the rich faecal stench reaching up for me, I noticed the resemblance to a burial.

'Ashes to ashes, and dust to dust . . .'

I'd learned that from a Kid Ory number – I think that it was 'Oh Didn't He Ramble!' I must have spoken aloud, because the girl laughed. When I looked her way she was looking back, and said, 'Practising, Father?' then went back to her newspaper.

I could never have fancied her anyway.

Back in the bar I dropped the E & T straight into my stomach to get the latrine taste away from the back of my throat. Then I went over to where Les and the Major were building a glass mountain at the table between them. I'm not quite sure what happened to the rest of the morning. At lunchtime a great crowd of folk drifted through on the way to the mess tents. Some of them stuck. I lost James and Les and my dad, and eventually found myself at a table with a couple of GI captains called Harry and Salvatore, who wanted to tell me how they first met. When we ran out of conversation they told me about the Krauts holed up in Blijenhoek Castle: which is what I had stayed to hear.

Fifteen

The problem with the castle was that while Jerry couldn't break out, we couldn't get in. It was built like the proverbial brick shithouse, and sunk onto old granite bedrock. All the conventional ammunition that had been fired at it had bounced off: that included the huge 155mm shells lobbed into it from miles away. A few days earlier a section of fighter-bombers had tackled it with AP rockets, and left one of their mates flame-grilled in a field nearby. That really pissed them off: they came back later that day with a couple of five-hundred-pound bombs each. Those bombs, striking virtually horizontally, dropped clouds of pulverized brick dust into the moat with no effect on the stone inner. They might as well have used spears, or bows and arrows on it. A company of Scots from the Lowland Division had had a go twice, like medieval siege troops. It took a full day's truce to allow the Jocks to collect their bodies from the moat and surrounding meadows.

So now it had settled down to a regular siege, only nobody knew how much food they had in there, nor ammo, nor how long it would go on for . . . nor how many of the bastards there really were, come to that. The problem the damned place posed, apart from turning Uncle Sam's favourite R & R camp into a General Hospital, was that just beyond it, the main advance on the Rhine had ground to a halt. The Generals didn't want to race ahead with a pocket of nasty Germans in their rear, waiting to dash out and roger them from behind.

I asked about bombing the bloody place into submission, and was told that that was an option in two weeks' time. It was down to the USAAF, who were still running the daylight stuff, and that was the earliest they could put a significant number of birds over the castle.

Later they walked me down to the woods in the lower fields, from where I could see the action. There were soldiers in shallow scrapes spread at the edge of meadows which sloped down to an improbably wide moat, and a castle that looked just the way you don't want a castle to look; if you are on the outside. It was grey, massive, a bit battered, but unbloodied. I fell out of love with it at first sight. From time to time a mortar round from the castle would drop among besiegers, causing niggling casualties. There were two carried out in the period of time I watched. The Americans shrugged. One of them said, 'I don't like to watch good men wasted, but, what the hell; they ain't ours.'

That was exactly how I felt about the Kraut.

I left the guys there, rubbernecking, and taking souvenir photographs for their friends back home. You might not think that my interest was professional, but truly it was: all the time the Army wasn't moving, neither were we. Grace could be moving further into Germany; by the hour for all I knew.

Back in the bar I limited myself to a single E & T, and asked the barman who was really in charge of the war around here. He directed me to a big Leyland command lorry in a field about a mile away. It was so perfectly camouflaged that you couldn't mistake it for anything other than perhaps another Leyland command lorry. I hoofed it.

There was a Lowland Division Colonel drinking scented tea at a portable map table, under a canvas awning stretched out from the lorry. He was the first soldierly Brit I had seen all day; he was in full khakis, which had been neatly patched in places, indicating that the Colonel had been around a bit. I paused on the periphery, then threw him a decent salute as soon as he noticed me. An overweight ADC looked as if he was on an intercept course, but the Colonel waved him back, and beckoned me forward. I gave him the *Good afternoon, sir*, and my name, service and service number. He said, 'Whatever you want, Pilot Officer Bassett, my first instinct is to have you arrested. You look bloody horrible, even for the RAF. Where did you get that bloody jacket from?'

'A Yank gave it to me, sir, after another Yank had stolen mine. It suits what I'm doing.'

'And that is?'

'Driving around Europe looking for an important lost someone, sir.'

'Under orders, I take it?'

'Yes, sir.'

'Whose?'

Time to use my weight.

'Ultimately, the Prime Minister's, sir.'

'Oh,' he said moodily. 'Another one of those. There's bloody hundreds like you around at the moment. I'll be glad to get the war over with, and get back to proper soldiering.' There was something the matter with that somewhere, but I couldn't put my finger on it. He waved the fat ADC over, and asked me, 'So what can we do for you?' The ADC had a pad and a pen, like a secretary. I shut off the image of him sitting on his Colonel's knee.

'Nothing, sir, at present. Thank you.'

'Oh. I see. Courtesy call. Good of you. Carry on . . . with whatever you've got to do.'

When I didn't move he gave me an eye lock, with a quizzical expression fixed to his face. I decided to talk before the muscles locked up.

'I rather thought of offering something to *you*, sir. How would you like to lose that fucking great castle in the valley, sir?' Interest. He waved the fat man away again: he walked backwards away from us, slightly bowing, like a courtier in the presence of royalty.

The Colonel said, 'Interesting. Go on, please.'

'I thought a couple of Lancasters with a couple of cookies and eight one-thousand-pounders apiece would crack the place open for you. It will be a pity if you have to wait a fortnight for the Yanks to do it, sir. Then there's the problem of American bombing.'

'What problem?'

'They'll clobber your target OK, but they'll do it with at least a squadron, from a very high altitude. They will drop more than a hundred bombs, and some of those will fall as far as five miles away. It's the way they do things these days: they call it overkill. You'll have to pull back every living thing around five or six miles from the target to guarantee no casualties.'

'. . . and you think we can do better than that?'

'Yes, sir.'

'I have asked the RAF, of course, but they say *No: it's an American job*. Have you any reason to imagine they might change their minds?'

'Yes, sir.'

'Why?'

'*I'll* ask them, this time, sir. Sorry, sir.'

'. . . and that will make a difference? I realize that you're in the same club, of course, but . . .'

'You have nothing to lose, if I try, sir.'

'No,' he said. 'I suppose not.'

He had to give it the pretence of some thought, so as not to lose face. Then he said, 'OK. I've got one of those special RAF listening stations in a radio van parked round the back. See if you can use them to connect through to whoever you need to speak to.'

I'd heard of those types, and rather approved of them. They were RAF corporals and sergeants who connected into a special intelligence source somewhere, and told generals to piss off now and again. They were the best source of battlefield information the Army had, so it had to put up with them. This quartet of sergeants wasn't terribly impressed with me, but couldn't find a decent enough excuse to refuse to let me use their gear to speak to England. I gave them Cliff's name.

I gave them the telephone number for the Guard Room at
Tempsford, and another fall-back number Cliff had given me.
I think that they would have kicked me out, but that fall-back
number clinched it. The senior Sergeant recognized it. His
mouth got all twisted, as if his tongue had turned to worm-
wood, and had started to lick itself. They told me to hang
around, and that they would call me.

I walked back to the command vehicle. It was the fat ADC
at the table now, smoking a curved pipe. He motioned me to
a chair across from him. I produced my straight billiard, and
accepted a fill of dark tobacco. The sun had broken clear
again. There was a travelling chess set on the table.

When he finally came on the line Cliff sounded tetchy, but
his voice in the heavy black handset was as clear as if he was
in a room with me,

'What do you want?'

'Hi, Cliff. Nice to hear you too. I've missed our little
chats.'

'Fuck off, Charlie. What do you want?'

'I want a couple of Lancs, with a cookie and eight one-
thousand-pounders in each. I want them to crack open a castle
full of Jerry Paras on the Holland and Germany border;
tomorrow at the latest.'

'Why should I help?'

'It's holding up the brown jobs' advance, and I think that
Grace might already be on the other side. Heading off into
Germany with a band of mad sods.'

'Nazis?'

'No; doctors and nurses.'

'What's the difference?'

'The point is, Cliff, I am moving behind the advance with James and Les, and the advance has stopped. If Grace is already on the other side then she's getting away from me. Do you understand?'

'Yes. Let me think about it for a minute.'

He thought a minute; then he said, 'I'll call you back.'

'That's what I thought, Cliff. If Winston can't whistle us up a couple of Lancs what's the point of him being Prime Minister?'

I heard him give his little coughing laugh, and momentarily remembered the Cliff I had liked when I first met him.

He said, 'Don't get too good at this lark, Charlie. I might have to keep you on.'

I was called back to the little Austin radio van half an hour later. Cliff asked me, 'Can you give me the coordinates for this place you are responsible for killing?'

I liked the *you are responsible* bit. I said, 'I'll hand you over to someone who can, as soon as we've finished.'

'OK. It's ordered for 10.20 your time tomorrow morning, and just to make sure you take requests like this seriously, I've asked your old squadron to do it. It's going to be your mates up there being shot at, and there's bugger-all on paper. They're going to love you when they find out it won't even count as a trip for them.'

'Thanks, Cliff. What do I need to do now?'

'Nothing. Make sure that the brown job leader has pulled

265

all his people more than a mile back from the target, and has a company ready to go in and mop up as soon as the RAF's finished. Anything else?'

'I should confess that I didn't tell you that the RAF had already been asked, and had turned the job over to the Americans, who were going to do it in a fortnight's time. There might be some political knee trembling.'

'Thanks for confessing that. I should confess that I already know.'

'We'll both need a priest at this rate.'

'I've already got one, haven't I?' He gave that odd little laugh again. 'What about those coordinates?'

'Wait one,' I told him, and handed the handset to the RAF Sergeant alongside me, telling him, 'Give this officer the coordinates of that bloody castle. The RAF's going to lose it for us.'

The Sergeant surprised me. He said, 'Yes, sir,' before he took it from me.

By mid-evening the bar was nearly empty. I asked McKechnie. He said, 'Steak night. In peacetime this always used to be steak night in the officers' mess. So they kept the tradition going for the R & R areas.'

'You mean there's steaks on the menu?'

'Hell no, buddy. Just some grey and pink stuff the Scotties serve up. What are you drinking?'

'Ethanol,' I told him. 'I could get used to this stuff.'

'Don't. Stick to beer. It will leave you a few brain cells.'

'Bad as that?'

'Worse. Where are you kipping tonight?'

'Hadn't given it a thought yet; and I don't know where the guys I came in with have got to.'

'Can you remember the number seven?'

'Sure. That's my birthday.'

'That's the number of the tent I'm billeted in. Sleeps fifty. There's at least twenty empty cots right now. That's where you go if nothing else has been arranged.'

I waited until James, Jamie, Albie and Les were half cut before telling them that I had laid on an air display for the following morning. The word spread like gonorrhoea in a monastery.

The LD Colonel sat alongside me on the boardwalk in front of the Quonset, and his ADC stood behind us. The Colonel had a pocket watch he kept consulting. The ADC sniffed a lot. He had a radio operator with a field set by him. It was an interesting piece of kit, but far too big and heavy to lug around for long. We paid a dollar each for our chairs, and the first E & T. As much coffee as we liked came for free. I needed the damned stuff to un-fur my tongue. I had slept in old tent number seven, but had little idea how I got there. The water I had washed in was cold, and had a petroleum rainbow floating in it.

The weather over the target couldn't have been better for day bombing: it was clear, and a lazy grey. Ten miles north of us a bank of thin cloud hung like a sheet in the air: our aircraft would fly out of it. If the guys in the castle hadn't got radar, or weren't talking to someone who did, they wouldn't know

267

what was about to hit them. The castle was about three miles away in a low natural amphitheatre. I could see it above the line of trees I had skulked in the day before. McKechnie was about four chairs along from me: he had his boots and socks off and was passing the time trimming his toenails with an enormous fighting knife, and crooning. It was a Benny Goodman number: 'Sing'. I could smell him from where I was sitting. Someone would have to speak with him about that. My dad was a few seats after that, making friendly conversation with the girl I had first seen him dancing with. Uncle Tommy sat the other side of her looking glum. That was good: at least he was back to normal. Right at the end of the second row to my right was a little guy with slicked back dark hair wearing faded RAF blues. I was sure that I had seen him somewhere before, but couldn't be sure where because his back was to me all of the time.

I kept my fingers crossed because I was still thinking that Cliff might let me down. I think that that was why the LD Colonel and his retinue were seated around me: if the RAF didn't show I'd probably be on jankers before lunch. I jumped when the Adj tapped me on my shoulder, but it was only to offer me a fill of pipe tobacco to settle me down.

'Thanks, I will. I've always hated waiting for something to happen.'

'Don't see why, old boy. In my experience the RAF is late for just about everything it does.'

'Thanks again. I'll remind you about that when we've lost your castle for you.'

'Do. I shall be properly contrite. The Colonel will offer you a medal, won't you, sir?'

The pipe tobacco was heavy and sweet: I drew deeply on it, and filled my mouth with cool smoke.

The Colonel said, 'Command wouldn't wear it, but I'll ask the French. They have the next sector, and they'll put you up for anything. Very good at medals, the French.'

Les was hiding behind James England. I heard him grunt, 'Fuck-all good for anything else.'

'Hark,' the Colonel's Adj said, '. . . the herald angels sing . . . and lot's more than two of them, Mr Bassett. Look out for the black crosses on their wings everyone, and get ready to duck.'

Nobody took him seriously because the first planes through the veil of cloud were six Spitfires, flying at no more than two hundred feet. They echeloned into line astern, and took turns at hosing the castle with cannon fire. Lights twinkled along their grey and green wings, and puffs of grey dust appeared about the old masonry. The radio operator had two pairs of bins: he handed me the smaller. They had been made by Zeiss.

The Spitfires hadn't intended to do any damage with their cannons, it was just a wake-up call to the poor sods inside. A statement of intent. *Overture and beginners*, my old skipper would have called it. The Lancasters came through the veil a bit higher. Say two or three thousand feet. That's still not very high. If you fuck up at that height you can hit the ground in less time than it takes to fart. Which is probably exactly what you're doing as you hit the ground. They had more

Spitfires with them: they had to weave from side to side to get their speed down to that the Lancs were trundling in at.

There were three Lancs, not two: thank you, Cliff. Two of them climbed into a circle at about another thou – say four thousand feet. The leader flew a wider loop, and came straight back onto a bomb run. It was odd for me: I'd spent my operational tour flying Lancs by night – mainly over Germany – but I'd never seen one actually dropping bombs in daylight; not observed it from the outside, that is. I was surprised how steady it looked: my experience had been that of having been bounced about a lot on the bomb run. There was no opposing fire from the castle; perhaps that was something to do with it. It dropped two bombs: big cylinders with flat ends – no tail fins. It was curious; they rocked gently, and weaved slightly as they tumbled – like children being rocked to sleep by a parent.

The Colonel asked, 'What are they?'

I answered without taking my lenses from them: tersely, probably, 'Cookies: four-thousand-pounders. Eight thousand pounds of high explosive.'

'Poor sods,' James murmured just before the bombs disappeared into the castle. Bang on, both of them; but then you don't miss much from that height – like a chicken laying eggs. What appeared to happen was this. The bombs disappeared. After a pause of maybe a couple of seconds the castle walls seemed to expand briefly, and then fall back into their original shape and configuration. Now the castle looked more or less the same, but was fatally damaged. It was skewed. A pall of fine brown dust and thin smoke, hundreds of yards high, hung in the thin air above it in a squat column. Then the sound of the two almost simultaneous detonations reached us like a double thunderclap. The audience clapped too, and cheered. I had a funny feeling in the pit of my stomach. I hadn't really thought much about what my bombs had been doing when they reached the ground during those long months over Germany. All of a sudden I didn't want to.

The two circling Lancs gave a couple of turns to let the pall begin to clear, and then one of them pulled away for a run. It was like watching a cobra gear up for a strike. Again, it was a finely executed run in – the bombing standard on the squadron had improved since my day. I counted the bombs away. There were twelve of them. Shark-shaped, with fins to steady them into their dive. Before anyone asked me I said, 'Thousand-pounders.'

James didn't say anything this time, but I heard him grunt.

Three of the bombs fell outside the walls of the place: two in open fields, and one in the moat. The one in the moat threw up a great curtain of water hundreds of feet high, which hid from us what the nine that hit inside were doing. I saw their great flashes of red and orange and yellow behind the veil of mist, and could see the shimmering ripples of blast in the rainbow-laden air above it. The blast effect intrigued me. It was like invisible rings visible, and spreading outwards and upwards. As the shit cleared I could see that the castle was altered even more. It was still more or less the castle shape and size, but the whole of its profile had spread out.

The radio behind us burst into life. The communicant appeared to be shouting in a very highly pitched voice. The

271

W/Op answered in rapid, fluent German, then he told the Colonel, 'The enemy requests permission to surrender, sir.'

'I like that,' the Colonel told us. 'Very Germanic. Asking *permission* to surrender: we would have just thrown our hands up, and got on with it.'

'Sir?' the W/Op prompted him.

'Tell them *By all means*, and to stay put until I've worked out what to do with them.'

The third Lancaster had pulled out of the circle. The Colonel told his ADC, 'Give them the gun, Harry.' Then, 'Pity they dragged their bombs here all for nothing.'

The ADC fired off a Very Pistol too close to my right ear for comfort, and dropped a huge blue light in the sky. The pilot of the Lanc was a comedian. He did the run as if he'd not been given the scrub signal, and at the last minute, instead of dropping his eggs, waggled his wings and went off low across country. Two Spits followed him, weaving from side to side. The Colonel turned and looked at me.

He said, 'Very good, RAF. That medal: which one had you in mind?'

I was prevented from answering by the Negro pianist. He had a white batboy's jacket on, and had come to stand behind us. He was counting aloud. He got to sixteen.

The Colonel asked, 'Sixteen, George?'

'Yes, Colonel. Sixteen souls climbing up to heaven through the smoke.'

'If they had about a hundred or so Krauts in there,' the Colonel told me, 'that's maybe fifteen or sixteen per cent of their establishment. We've gone rather easy on them really.'

I decided that I didn't like the cold-blooded bastard, but it was all a bit late for regrets, wasn't it? He who laughs last, and all that.

The Colonel sent his ADC down later in the morning to take the surrender. We had had to wait until the Press Corps arrived. A company of hard Hun Paratroopers opting out of the war was bound to make all the front pages. There were a hundred and fifty of the Allies' finest down there to meet them. Probably twice as many Press people as military. And a load of guys rubbernecking. That included me: I'd just won my first land engagement, after all, and still had *To the victor the spoils* on my itinerary. When the heavy wooden gates of the castle pulled back the first thing that came out was a trickle of smoke. Then a white handkerchief tied to the muzzle of an old Mauser rifle. When nobody shot at that, a head in a grey ski cap bobbed out and back a few times. Then a scrawny Captain in dirty greys stepped out, and onto the causeway over the moat. He did a dozen paces on his own before the LD ADC stepped up to meet him. The first thing they did was shake hands, reminding me of sketches I had seen of Livingstone meeting Stanley. Or was that the other way round? The German gave the ADC his rifle with the white flag. (That explained the unfortunate front-page photographs the next day, giving the impression that we were surrendering to *them*.) Then the Kraut turned back to face the door, and waved his men out.

By that time I'd moved in close myself, and could hear what was going on. I counted the Krauts out onto the causeway. I'll swear none of them was over nineteen years old. Spotty teenagers mostly, hungry and tired in Para smocks too big for them. Their mixture of weapons looked as if they'd come from a museum. Including the middle-aged Hauptmann sixteen of them surrendered. George had got the number right, but the wrong way round – there were only sixteen of them left.

The ADC shook hands with the Captain again, and said something that sounded diabolically like, '*Sprachenzee Anglische?* Do you speak English?'

The Hauptmann looked pained; as if he'd failed an exam. He smiled apologetically and said, 'A little. Only a little.'

'You have many wounded?' That was Harry again.

The small German looked mystified,

'Nein: no, only these.' He indicated his rag, tag and bobtail street gang, who were carefully laying their weapons on the causeway. They had an inordinate number of potato masher grenades for so small an army; I remember that. The mortar that had caused the casualties I had seen the day before looked like a home-made job: it had started life as a drainpipe. Harry tried again.

'You have many dead, then? Many kaput?'

The Captain looked even more mystified, if that was possible: I didn't know if it was the question, or the hotchpotch of lingo it was posed in. He shook his head.

'No. Only these.'

I don't know when it began to dawn on us that the little Kraut was walking out with precisely the number of men he went in with. One of the Press Corps guys scrambled up onto the causeway. He gave the Kraut officer a cigarette, and asked him, 'You are Paras? *Fallschirmjägers?*'

'Nein. *Volkssturm.*'

'Never heard of it, matey.'

'People's Army. You call it the Land Defence Volunteers in your country, I think.'

'Fucking hell.' That was Les. He'd crept up on us. 'It's the Home Guard.'

That was what we struggled to come to terms with as we moved away from the embarrassment as quickly as we could. This motley crew of a man, and a few boys in pieces of uniform too big for them, had held up the Allied advance for almost two weeks, and killed dozens doing it. And we'd had to throw a dozen Spitfires and three Lancs at them before they gave up.

'It's just occurred to me . . .' I said to Les.

'. . . Yes, I think I know what you're going to say, sir. It's not going to be as easy to get to Berlin as Winston thinks, is it? Don't you think that someone should tell him?'

'Tell the Major,' I said. 'He can do it. Perhaps, for once, they won't shoot the messenger. Anyway, he's had it far too easy for the last week or two.'

'Don't be too hard on him. He never asked to go soldiering . . .'

'. . . and this isn't soldiering, Les, and what's more, you bloody know it.'

'It's not my fault, either, sir.'

'I didn't say it was.'

We climbed the rest of the way to the Quonset bar in a sort of baffled, humpy silence. The Colonel was standing at the bar with a couple of senior medical types. I tried to ignore him, but he spotted me, and turned to say, 'All fixed up, Padre. You'll get a Croix for this lot.'

'Hardly worth it, sir, for smoking out one man and Jerry's Home Guard.'

'It's definitely medal material, Padre. Sixteen Jerry Paras walked out alive after a gallant defence. There must be hundreds dead over there. I'll get you to pray over the rubble before you move on.'

'There aren't any bodies, sir. There's no one there.'

'Atomized, dear boy, by pin-prick . . . sorry, I meant pin-point . . . bombing. Your old squadron, I understand.'

He'd obviously been talking to someone, and had then had a few.

I said, 'Sir, it is my opinion that sixteen men went into that castle, and sixteen marched out. I can't in all conscience accept a medal for bombing the shit out of a Home Guard patrol, and missing them.'

'That's where my military experience comes in, old boy, so listen carefully. I'm the Colonel . . . and you're apparently a Padre, savvy?'

'Sir.'

'I agree it appears as if a patrol of Jerry's Home Guard has stood us off for a fortnight, and killed a good many good men. But *that*, the military mind tells me, is plainly impossible. So far?'

'So far, sir.'

'So there must have been another hundred or so Paras in there as well.'

'I see, sir.'

'Everyone knows that Paras fight to the death: so that is what this lot did, almost to the man. So far?'

'So far, sir.'

'. . . and if there ain't any bodies and body parts, it must be because they were blown to smithereens by our RAF friends. Atomized by devastating bombing. A great success for the RAF. I'm sure that you understand.'

'I do, sir.'

'. . . and that if you accept the Frenchy's little medal with dignity and grace, it will bring honour and credit to you and your squadron, and everyone will know that it must all be true, because the Froggie is very parsimonious with his awards.'

'I thought that you said he gave them out to anybody for anything?' I mislaid the *sir*; I suspected that he was already too pickled to notice.

'That,' he said, 'was when I was being unkind. Now that you have opened up my castle, I am benevolence personified.' He grinned a bleary grin. '. . . and just a wee bit squiffy. Run along now, and save a few more souls.'

I was getting damned tired of this religious lark.

I had to bloody go through with it. It must have amused James, because he sided with the LD Colonel, and ended up bloody ordering me to attend an investiture. Les summed it up with, 'A Brylcreem boy dressed in the clothes of all the other Services, and at least two nations, and disguised as a bleeding priest, getting a French medal for killing a hundred Jerries who never existed: this is a *good* war!'

They sent a retired French General of my father's vintage

to present the medal the next morning. He was even smaller than me, and wore a uniform straight out of the Crimea – red pants, a blue jacket and a flat-topped peaked cap that looked suspiciously German. He needed to stand on tiptoe to kiss my cheeks and his breath smelled of Parma violet. Normally I'm not bad at picking up languages, and at least my French was fairly fluent, but his staccato machine-gun delivery, punctuated by the occasional *mon brave*, kept beating me down the leg side.

The Colonel had lined a few of his brown jobs up with anyone else who wanted to gawk in an open square, with me in the middle. James stood alongside me, ramrod-straight in a cleaned uniform. Out of the corner of my eye I could see my dad – he looked really chuffed. There were one or two nurses, including the one who had held the GI's plasma drip. She had long rolling waves of chestnut hair like someone else I had known. McKechnie wasn't there: he was cutting a Kraut who'd owned up to a shrapnel wound. With James alongside me, like a best man at a wedding, I felt a bit of a drip. I felt like a bit of a fraud too, but in my head I rehearsed what we eventually learned to call the Nuremberg Defence – I was only obeying orders.

I hadn't expected Lee, although she seemed to turn up in my life every now and again, so I wasn't surprised to look up and see her smiling at me. She was with her pal Dave Scherman, and a naval officer wearing a grunt's winter parka. Lee had her arm through his, and looked happy. She gave me a discreet waist-level wave when she saw I'd spotted her. The hand she waved with had a small camera in it. George, the coloured pianist and barman from the Quonset, was there in a full infantry Lieutenant's colours, and James Oliver had forsaken his white battle bowler for a smart fore-and-aft forage cap, and had polished his shoes.

After suffering a few more kisses and hugs I let the silly old sod pin the medal on to my battledress blouse. Just over one of the neatly mended bullet holes which had done for my predecessor. A small firing party fired three volleys over our heads, almost as if they were burying me. Then it was back into the bar for a spam sandwich and E & T reception that they'd put on for us. The mud clung to my boots; I remember that. I had a shiny cross on my chest, and its small leather-worked case in my pocket just to prove it. I waited for everyone to file into the drinks emporium in front of me, and I went in with the last man. Lee gave me a brief kiss as she moved past me; plumb on my lips. I was trembling and it wasn't with emotion – not that kind of emotion, anyway. It was the sort of emotion I now recognize as fear.

You see, I've seen dead men walking, before. I've told you that. I want you to get that straight. I don't believe in ghosts, but I've seen men wandering about long after they were dead: that American patrol in Brond was an example. OK, so when I'm face to face with something I don't believe is there, I tremble. Got it? And when I saw a dead man in that small open square that morning I got a little jittery. OK?

It was the little guy in the faded RAF blues I'd noticed the day before. Not being a man to put off the inevitable, I waited for him at the door and, feeling a bit dumb, the first thing I said was, 'Hi, Pete. You're dead.'

Sixteen

'Hi, Charlie. Surprise, surprise.'

'Am I dead too?'

'Don't be a focking idiot, Charlie. You would have felt it. I am pleased for your medal.'

I ignored that.

'So you're not dead either?'

'Not at the moment.'

'I got your car and your radio.'

'I am pleased about that too: I was scared that turd Marty Weir would have them. He was always on the lookout for number one, wasn't he?'

'Marty wasn't so bad.'

I reached my hand out and touched his shoulder. I could feel his bony clavicle. How else is a clavicle expected to feel, except bony? Pete: Piotr: the Pink Pole. He felt real to me. Les stuck his face out of the door.

'What's the matter, Charlie? You in love again?'

'No, Les. Just an old pal. We used to fly together.' And, 'Les this is Pete. Pete, Les.'

They just nodded at each other. Les said, 'That's all right then. Don't keep them waiting long. You're the guest of honour, or what passes for one, and the Froggie General is wolfing all the bleeding sandwiches.'

Pete and I sat on chairs outside the door. Pete offered me a Lucky. No matter where we were he could always get hold of Lucky Strikes.

After we lit up he said, 'We got some catching up to do, and no time. You stick with that pipe and tobacco that girl gave you?'

The girl had been Grace.

'Most of the time; but you're right – no time: stick to essentials. Why aren't you dead any more? Did God give you a reprieve?'

Piotr laughed.

'You're very English, Charlie. You know that?'

'No. Pete; the last time I saw you alive we were climbing into *Tuesday's Child*. I dogged the fuselage door shut, and you checked I'd locked it. You did that every trip. It was our ritual.'

'That's right. I don't remember a lot about that trip. I remember calling out a small town in Germany to Conners so that he could check our drift. He was pleased. He said we were bang on.'

'That was on the way back.'

'Right. We were in Belgium, near Ostend. Nearly back to the Channel.'

'What do you remember next?'

'Two things. An extreme concussion . . . pouff!! All the

lights went out. My turret wouldn't move, neither would the guns. I got an electric burn from the breech of one. What was it; night fighter?'

'Lightning. We were bloody well struck by lightning. It knocked me out for a few seconds. I think that it earthed on the trailing aerial, and came in through the radio. I could feel the electricity arcing across my teeth before I passed out.'

'I worked out for myself that the second one wasn't the Kraut . . .'

'No. It was our own bloody Ack-Ack. Some trigger-happy bastard. He bracketed us, and then put one underneath.'

'Not underneath you, Charlie; underneath me. Focking bastard!'

'What happened?'

'Blew the bloddy turret away, didn't he? What height do you think we had?'

'Not much: no more than a few thousand.'

'Bloddy turret fell to pieces around me.' He did it again. 'I pulled the ring and the bloddy parachute harness nearly tore my balls off. They swelled like cricket balls the next day.'

'Pete: you didn't have a 'chute. I found your 'chute in the aircraft later. In its rack.' Then I remembered. 'You kept an extra one in the turret with you. One of those small ones for low jumps. Just in case you never got back into the plane.'

'I used to sit on it, like a fighter pilot. Sometimes it's good to be small. Isn't that so?'

'Yes, it is. Isn't it? How far did you fall?'

'Fock knows. The canopy goes bang, above my head. I jerk to a stop. I scream because my balls are in a vice, and then my feet are on the ground. What was it the comedian you like to hear always said?'

'*Just like that?*'

'Yes, Charlie. Just like that. And I am in Belgium. That was months ago.'

'I know that was months ago. Why the fuck haven't you come back? Everyone thinks that you're dead.'

'You need a silver bullet to kill me. What happened to you?'

'We never flew again. Brookie screened us away from flying. Had a great party. I met Glenn Miller before he was killed.'

'Everyone met Glenn Miller.'

'Suit yourself.' Bollocks. I wouldn't tell anyone else; I was tired of being taken for a Greek. 'Anyway. They split the crew. Grease was officered before that last trip, and went home to fly the Canadian prairies. He got really odd about it: didn't want to go. They got me at my next posting, and sewed a ring on my sleeve. Marty, Toff and Conners all sodded off to OTUs and OCUs, and Fergal went to the priests' school. He'll remuster as a Chaplain or Padre. Did you know that Marty carried a Gideon Bible with him on every trip we did? He got us to sign the flyleaf before we split, and then gave it to Fergal. Because you weren't there to sign I printed your name above mine.'

'Who got *Tuesday*?'

'Brookie did. I think that's why he retired us early: so he could get his hands on a better kite. It didn't work though . . .'

'How is that?'

'*Tuesday* never liked him. She crashed and burned him a couple of days later: only the tail gunner got out.'

'*Tuesday* liked tail gunners.'

'No: she just liked us.'

'Where they send you?'

'Tempsford: just down the road. Special Duties squadron . . . a very odd lot. They seemed to fly when they liked.'

'That was a bad break for you.'

'Not really. I had a ground job . . . but then I played silly buggers; scored a trip as a spare prick in an old Stirling, and the bastard crashed and burned on take-off. Burned my neck and my chin and my shoulders.'

'I wouldn't have noticed.'

'That's good, Pete. Now tell me *properly*. Why haven't you come back?'

'Charlie; since I join your focking Air Force I been shot at by Krauts and English fliers, shot at by secret policemen, chased by service policemen, locked up in your English prison for painting the tits of an English girl in the Polish colours – which I never did – bounced around Germany freezing to death in the back of a Lancaster bomber – and lastly shot down by our own guns. You tell me, Charlie. If you were me, would *you* go back to England if you had the chance to bugger off?'

I leaned back against the Quonset, and breathed a huge sigh of pleasure and relief. Pete said, 'You didn't answer me.'

'I can't. You're right. No clever man would go back to England.'

'Charlie,' he asked me. 'What happened to you? You're

wearing a half a sailor's suit, an Army top and a Yankee flying jacket. You joined the mafia?'

'Is there a Polish one?'

'Not yet. Not until I make one. Me and that Yank Tommo. He says he knows you.'

'That's right. Is he round here?'

'Somewhere. I'll tell him.'

'So, you're OK? *Really* OK?'

'Sure, Charlie. I'm a bit careful these days, but really OK. I even got a regular girl.'

'Would I get to meet her? If I stuck around, that is?'

'She's in Hamm.'

'That's in Germany.'

'Yeah. I only get to go home to see her at weekends.'

'Have we got that far yet?'

'Some of us have, Charlie. Don't worry; the regular Army will catch up one day. Your friend Tommo has bought half of Munsterland already. I help him with the language. His basic Kraut is OK, but he has no dialect.' Then he said, 'Go inside, Charlie; your friends will be getting anxious. I'll pick you up in a couple of days.'

'How will you know where I am?'

'I'll ask a friend.'

'Pete . . . I take it there's nothing particularly legal about what you're doing?'

'*Erwacht* Charlie. The Kraut is collapsing. There is no legal over here: there's just do what you want. Go over there and fill your boots, just like the rest of us. To the victors the spoils.'

'That would make a great name for a film after this lot is over,' said James. The bastard had come creeping up on me again. '*The Victors*. I think I'll write that down. Who's your pal?'

Pete and I stood.

'Pete. This is my Major, James England. Pete used to fly with me, James.'

England glanced at the Poland flash on Pete's shoulder.

'You're not the foreign johnny that seems to get into every district just in front of me, and buys up all the food before I get there?'

'No,' Pete said. 'Must be some other Pole. Goddam race of goddam thieves.' Only Pete could say that without smiling.

'Pete was shot down and evaded. He's making his way back.'

'Would he like us to help him?'

'No.' That was me. 'He's shifting all right for himself. I'm coming in now. Are there any of those sandwiches left?'

'Les and your old man are standing between a plateful and Mon Général, but I'd get a move on if I was you; the ravenous old sod will outmanoeuvre them before long.'

Pete was already moving unhurriedly away. He said, 'So long, Charlie. I'll see you later.'

When they handed me my first E & T at the bar I realized that although Pete had commented on my scarecrow's mix of uniform, he hadn't asked me very much about what I was doing. That was interesting. I wandered over to the piano with a couple of spamwiches in one hand and a hefty drink in the other. The pianist was playing a local arrangement of 'In the Mood'. He smiled white tombstone teeth at me and said, 'Nice medal, boss!'

We both knew what he meant, and grinned at each other. Pop danced past with his nursie: I thought that it was early in the day for her tits to be out again. It was the first time I noticed what a good, light dancer he was – up on the balls of his feet. As he passed he mouthed, 'Off tomorrow,' to me.

'Where to?'

'Home.'

James danced past like a bear in wellies. It was the first time I noticed that he couldn't dance at all. He had the girl from the latrine in his arms. He took his tongue from her ear long enough to say, 'Make the most of it Charlie. Moving on tomorrow. The girls won't like you where we're going.'

I looked around for Lee and her pals, and couldn't see them. Maybe I had imagined her. Albie was in a group with some tankies and James Oliver. He held his drink in his left hand; his right was buried in a sling. I asked him, 'How's that finger?'

'Dead and gone to heaven.'

He produced the right hand. The bandage wasn't there; neither was the middle finger. Not even a stump. There was just a neat plaster covering the gap between his first and ring fingers. I asked him, 'Will that be a problem?'

'Not unless I want to be Pad-u-wreski, or a New York cab-driver. Old Tits-Out was right as usual: gangrene or some-thing. Bloody McKechnie had it off before I had time to whistle "Marching thru' Georgia". I whistled the Last Post instead.'

DAVID FIDDIMORE

'He's turning into a good cutter. I'm pulling out tomorrow.'

'So am I. I'll be across the Rhine in two days.'

'Do you believe that?'

'Why not? The Brass have got it wrong so often that they're bound to be right sooner or later.'

'Do you think that my medal party is going to last long?'

'All day. Eat, drink, and be merry, Charlie . . . for tomorrow we die.' We had used that excuse on the squadron.

'Not you, Albie – you'll just lose another bit. Seen Les?'

'He was tapping up some American supply side Sergeant last I saw him; doing a deal down near the rattlesnake.'

'What rattlesnake?'

'That fat bastard of a diamondback that bit Pete Wynn last year. It's in a glass box at the far end of the bar. There's a table beside it which is a good place to be if you don't want no other company.'

The rattlesnake and I were acquainted. I had met it on a USAAF base in England where its guardian, a Red Indian, used to let it roam free. I went to the farewell party they threw for their squadron's Major. His name was Peter Wynn, and I had counted him a friend of mine. The Indian was killed over Lübeck, and Wynn got it in the arse from his snake when he went to clear the Indian's kit out. I wished the snake dead, but Wynn hadn't blamed it, and made everyone promise to keep it going. It was going to be a particularly well-travelled reptile. The snake recognized me. It raised its head about an inch off the sand in its big Plexiglas box, and gave me a lazy rattle with its tail. Its eyes twinkled at me. In a human being you would have taken that for good humour: with the snake I wasn't so sure.

Tommo shared the table with Les. When the snake spotted me Tommo said, 'She likes you. Siddown why don't yuh?'

I put the words back together the right way round, pulled out a chair, and sat between them. I asked Tommo, 'Wynn's snake; does it have a name yet?'

Tommo leaned forward, and put his finger against a row of small white matchstick men painted on the glass at the top of her box. There were five of them, just under a neatly painted Restaurant sign. He said, 'They call her Ace, now. She made five kills.' He tapped the little men as if he was counting them off. At his third tap Ace struck savagely. Poison ran down the inside of the glass screen. I was surprised to see that it was clear. 'I guess she don't like me so much,' he told me.

We shook hands. I was pleased to see him. The loose strands of my recent life were being drawn together on a muddy hillside in Holland. All I needed now was Grace walking in through the door, looking a million dollars and turning all the heads. She had that effect when she turned it on. There was a stack of black and white six-by-three girlie pictures on the table between Tommo and Les. They seemed to be all of the same girl. She had wavy, dark lustrous hair, and was putting her naked body through startling contortions on what looked like a dark velvet bed cover. She was stunning; somewhere between sixteen and twenty, I thought. I couldn't tell. I asked, 'Who is she?'

Les said, 'Dunno. They're American. I took them off that

bloke who fell under the tank a few days ago. What do you think?'

I turned a few of them this way and that, as if I knew what I was doing. She looked as if she could be your next-door neighbour's daughter. I said, 'Nah: not my type. Sugar and spice. She won't amount to much, will she? She's too skinny, and her tits are too small.'

'Charlie's wrong,' Tommo said simply, and, 'I'll buy. How many you got?'

'Just these, and he never had the negs. There's eighteen of them.'

'A dollar each?'

'Suits me,' said Les. 'Can I have that in coffee and fags?'

'Sure thing; only I take my cut then.'

'When didn't you?' I asked Tommo. 'I still haven't forgot what you were asking for bog paper during the bog-paper famine.'

'Business,' Tommo told me, 'is business, even between friends.'

'As one friend to another, how d'you get back over here? Weren't you retiring and leaving the war? The Pink Pole just told me you could get in and out of Germany, even though we're not there officially yet.'

I noticed he didn't answer the first bit. He said, 'You seen him, then? Cute, ain't he?'

'I wouldn't call Pete cute. His eyes glitter like that bloody snake's. So do yours come to that. The three of you were made for one another. What are you doing over there?'

'Buying Germany before anyone else gets it. There are

thousands of people ready to sell where they live, for protection, food and dollars. We got all three. You still got any of that money I changed for you last year? Money you can invest?'

'About a thousand, say thirteen hundred quid. Why?'

'Before I answer that, Charlie, let me point out a significant cultural difference in our backgrounds. To an American a quid is a hard piece of tobacco that you chew, and then spit out. It makes everything in your mouth the same colour as your shit.'

'Pounds, then. Thirteen hundred pounds. Why did you ask me?'

'I can get you a small hunting estate in the Odenwald for that.' He pronounced it *Urdenvald*. 'Lovely bloody country.'

'What about the legal stuff? Deeds of ownership.'

'Piece of piss. The Krauts are very good at that. They might be running out of bread and cheese and bullets, but they're up to their ears in lawyers, and still keeping the paperwork going. I own a piece of Germany as big as New York State already. Perfectly legal.'

'I bought a large town house from him,' Les told me. 'In Stuttgart. Eight bedrooms.'

'Is it still standing?'

'Yep,' Tommo told us. 'And what's more, it's insured against war damage now.'

'What insurance company would be mad enough to insure houses in Germany against war damage?'

'Mine would.'

'Mine as in *mine*?' I asked Tommo. 'You have an insurance company?'

'That's right. Me and Lucky.' I didn't think that I really wanted to know who Lucky was. 'It's a reputable old Washington company. You don't have to give me the money now. Just give me the nod.'

I laughed, and said, 'Why not?' We shook hands on the deal.

Tommo said, 'Congratulations, Charlie. You now own an ill-used, but largely intact mansion – more of a large farm, really – in Morsberg, and about four hundred and twenty acres. Schloss Felgensee something or other; it's all on the deed. There are two foresters' cottages and a keeper's lodge.'

'How do you know all this is for true, Tommo?'

'It's what me and my officer are over here doing: acquiring property for the US Army.'

'And you just help yourself at the same time?'

'American tradition, son. It's in our entrepreneurial nature.'

'They don't call it theft?'

'Not as far as I know.'

'Glad I met you again, Tommo.' I raised my glass to him. I noticed that it was nearly empty. Ace rattled at me warningly. I decided that Ace was too masculine a name for something as bad-tempered as that. Inside my head I added an 'l' and an 'i', and found myself with *Alice*.

A few drinks later Tommo gave me a worried look. We were on our own. Les had wandered off. Tommo said, 'I left you two kitbags to store for me. They safe?'

'Locked in my car, locked in a garage, behind a safe house in London. It's owned by the Major's mob, whatever that is, and run by Les and his brothers: there are bloody hundreds of those. If they were Masons they'd have their own lodge.'

'Like the K. It's safe then?'

'Absolutely. What's in them?'

'About two million bucks. Working capital . . .'

I blew alcohol all over Alice's Restaurant. She rattled at me again, but it was a friendly sort of rattle.

'You told me it wasn't illegal, you bastard.'

Tommo looked uncomfortable.

'It isn't. Not strictly. It's deals like this. I own property in England too. It was a steal. Prices started to fall as soon as the Kraut started to bomb shit out of you. So I bought something.'

'What did you buy?'

'I think it's called Buckinghamshire. Then my government made me an offer for all the produce coming off my land there, and began to send me money for it. I cashed their cheques because the bank would have become fiddly, and pushed the cash into a couple of kitbags. Then it sort of accumulated without me noticing, and then my posting back to the US caught me on the hop. Sorry.'

It was a funny bloody story. I moved my hand, slowly moving my glass across the table. Alice's eyes moved with it. Her tongue flicked in and out.

'How are you going to get it out? Isn't there something called Exchange Control?'

'How easy would it be to get our hands on it: say, if I sent someone?'

'Ask Les. They're his brothers. I dare say he could arrange access.'

'For a percentage, you're saying?' There was a wince in his voice.

'I should imagine so. You said it yourself: business is business.'

'So I did,' Tommo said. 'But I don't always have to like it.'

The next morning saw us back in *Kate*. She had new Perspex windows riveted in place; at the back and in Les's door. The Major and Les had taken their own advice, and made a night of it. James looked ill, and Les tired. Two girls I'd never seen before turned out to wave us off.

The lane outside went to Germany. I had expected Dad or James Oliver, or someone to be there to see me off. Not a fucking chance. England groaned and asked, 'Where did you get to last night, Charlie? I didn't see you.'

'I was overcome by the emotion of the investiture. I sloped off early to bed.'

'On yer own?' That was Les.

'Yes; more or less.'

'You can't do more or less. Either you were on your own, or you weren't.'

'There was a nurse in the next bed but one from mine. The one between was empty. She was changing when I came into the tent. She didn't seem to mind.'

'Pretty?'

'OK. Someone who would be nice to know for a long time.'

'Shag her?'

'No. We lay on our beds, and talked until about two. Then she went to sleep.'

'What was her name?'

'Dunno. I forgot to ask. She was gone by the time I woke up. Back on duty I expect.'

'Why didn't you ask her for a shag?'

'I don't know. But there must have been a reason.' I was being truthful, but I don't think either of them believed me.

I busied myself filling and lighting my pipe. Shortly after that the car was full of its thin blue aroma, and Les was whistling 'Lili Marleen'. James had fallen asleep, his head to one side, and his mouth drooped open. He was snoring. I thought about the girl from last night, and must have smiled. Les stopped whistling 'Lili Marleen', and grinned slyly at me. Then he started to whistle 'I Fall in Love too Easily', which was a song that that fellow Sinatra had started to trouble us with.

Eventually he yawned and said, 'Roman road. Spot 'em a mile off, can't you?'

I told him, 'Probably not. Grace said that most of the straight roads had already been here for a couple of thousand years before the Romans arrived. All they did was lay stone surfaces on top of the old straight tracks they already found.'

'Then what did the Romans do for anyone?'

'Baths. I suppose. They built a wall to keep the Jocks out. That wasn't bad.'

'Didn't they wear dresses with purple stripes most of the time, and bugger little boys?'

'Sounds like my old school,' James told us. I hadn't realized that he was awake.

'They weren't terribly good with women.' I remembered the stories about Boudicca and her daughters.

Les could be very persistent.

'So they did bugger-all for us, really?'

James said, 'Every type of fruit you eat graced a Roman tongue before yours; every building built has got a little bit of Rome in it; every road leads to Rome, and every European army since the Romans marches in the Roman step.'

'Like I said, Major,' that was Les again, 'they did bugger-all for us. Why don't you write that down in your little book?'

PART FIVE

Germany: April 1945

Seventeen

There was no border post. Just two pork-chopped tanks which had been shoved hurriedly to one side, one in each ditch on either side of the road. One was a British Cromwell, in an elegant overall charcoal black: its turret lay upside down in a field fifty yards away. The other was a Jerry; a Mark 4 Panzer. Les stopped between them. When I wound down my window I smelt the dirty, sweet scent of the monster I had met along the Bois de Boulogne.

Les said, 'Close it up again, Charlie, it pongs out there. I think that I should be saying *Welcome to Germany*, but the Boss has been insisting on demonstrating his navigation skills for the last half-hour, so we could be effing anywhere. Back in France, for all I know.'

An hour later we rolled into a small German town. That was just a day after the French gave me a Croix de Guerre I hardly deserved. What I remember of that first Jerry town is that the men were too old or too young to be soldiers, and that they looked at me with loathing when Les and I surprised them. They scuttled around heaps of rubble making less sound than the rats. Some of the women we saw walked with hands on their backs, as if massaging away pain. I tried not to notice that. There was a small girl of about twelve with a ripped dress. She froze, and began to tremble as soon as she saw us; tears started to roll down her face. We found a boy with wire-rimmed specs who took us to his father's house. The local Bürgermeister.

I sat away in a corner. The Bürgermeister's wife must have been pretty not so long ago. She brought Les and me substantial glasses of a heavy, white wine each. She had a tight, worried smile. I listened to James questioning her husband, a thin, nervous old man who wrung his hands as if he was washing them. I needed time to think. I needed to think because I realized that at least a quarter of the conversation I overheard was in German, and that I quickly began to understand it. I also realized that the same had been happening to me in France and Holland. Maybe some people are just good at that sort of thing and don't know it until it happens to them. Perhaps it's like having an ear for music. I think that Les had realized it was happening to me too, because he raised his glass, and grinned a silent toast. The boy tugged at Les's sleeve, and asked, 'Can I have a cigarette, Tommy?'

I spent the night in the Bürgermeister's daughter's bed. She didn't need it any more. A couple of days earlier some soldiers had murdered her with a flamethrower, after they'd finished with her. Turned her into a carbonized statue, kneeling in a burnt-out room like a black Madonna. James said that it happened that they were French, but they could have been in anybody's army. The family buried her in the evening, in a shallow grave in a small cemetery. She was wrapped in a quilted bed cover, which stank of kerosene before she was halfway there. Half a dozen old folk turned out to help. One old lady, in particular, wept a mountain, although she made no noise. The boy told me later that she was the school-mistress. James had us go with them. After they laid her in the hole the Bürgermeister looked at me. He and his wife didn't ask anything: they just looked at me. I saw that Les was also looking keenly at me. I murmured the Lord's Prayer, and the group followed me in German, the cadence of the lines moving up and down like music heard over water. Finally I bent to take a little soil, but the girl's mother took it from me and did the honours. Either that was the German way, or she knew that I wasn't quite what I was cracked up to be.

James put his hand on my shoulder as we walked back down to the house; sometimes our boots scraped on the cobbles. He spoke two sentences, which were, 'Nicely done, Charlie.' And, 'Thank you.'

I just hoped that I'd done the right thing. It must have been all right, because I didn't dream that night. I slept with my hand on my pistol, remembering the last conversation I had had in the Quonset bar the evening before.

Albie had lurched up with a smaller man who he leaned against. He was all tact, Albie. He said, 'This is Gumshield. Gumshield is a fast featherweight. He wins us lots of money, so don't shoot him.'

Gumshield started, and gave me a worried look. He had a Douglas Fairbanks moustache and sticky-up salt-and-pepper hair. And an interesting variety of facial scars. I guessed maybe he wasn't so fast after all. I asked, 'Why should I?'

'Gumshield's the guy I told you about. He was Grace's regular poke over here.'

It didn't feel as bad as I thought. He had a voice five registers too deep for his size, which made him sound vaguely ridiculous. He said, 'Sorry, bud. I thought she was unoccupied. Never took a Padre's girl before.'

'Don't worry. You were probably right the first time. What Grace never is, is occupied, that is . . . and I'm not used to being a Padre yet, anyway.'

'You don't mind then?'

'I didn't say that. I don't mind as much as I thought I would.'

'That's good.' That was Albie. 'We can all get another drink in then.'

I OK'd that. I asked Gumshield short questions, and listened as he gave me long answers. He had a tendency to ramble. Albie looked bored, and scratched his hand a lot around the space of his missing finger. The back of his hand looked red and angry. What it had amounted to was that Grace had shared Gumshield's field bag for a few days, while she waited to hitch up with a group of renegade Red Cross doctors and nurses. They had already tried to cross into Germany a couple of times, and had been sent back with fleas in their Gallic ears. After Grace had hooked up with them Gumshield had a feeling that they'd made it. Albie bellowed a long rolling thunder of a belch that could have stunned a cat, and agreed with him. They were mainly Frogs, they told me, but there were a couple of long-haired Eye-tie drivers from somewhere, and a beautiful blonde German nurse they were bound to have trouble with. They were travelling in a couple of well-stocked US White-type armoured ambulances. They were headed north-east, Gumshield told me, to a place called Löningen. What was in my mind was the map I had studied earlier. It was one of Les's maps. In my mind's eye I could see that Löningen. It was on the road to Bremen.

When we turned out of the gate Les had asked me, 'Where to, Guv?'

'Isn't that up to the Major?'

James told us, 'Not really. As long as we're not far behind the front there's work for us anywhere.'

So I said, 'Let's go to Bremen.'

I grinned at Les, and he turned and grinned at me and the Major, who told us, 'Don't take us anywhere we're likely to get bombed. That would be irritating.'

I'd lied to them about the girl in the tent. We hadn't talked for three hours. More like one. Because I had been otherwise occupied for a couple. Somewhere around 2300 McKechnie had found me alone at a table. I was glad that Albie and Gumshield had scarpered back into the fray. I was just beginning to want to kill the little boxer anyway. McKechnie said, 'Crack your face and smile, bud: I've got the night rounds to do. Have you seen the inside of one of our butcher's shops yet?'

'I was in that one where that fellow Arnold was sticking up the medical crew with a .45, remember?'

'No. I didn't know that. He wasn't one of mine. You comin'?'

I saw another side of the black bastard as he moved from cot to cot. His words were firm, and his hands were gentle. He said some of the guys were dying. I sat and held the hand of one. He was an older man about thirty-five: a Scot from Peterhead who had got his bullet pointlessly assaulting that bloody castle. He asked me, 'Will you hear my confession, Father?'

'I'm not a Catholic. I wouldn't properly know how to. I don't think that the Pope would pay that much attention to me.'

'That's OK. Will you say something?'

'If it helps.'

'Do you know the Pilgrim's Hymn then? You should know it; it's a good Proddy hymn.'

'I think so.'

For once my blessed memory worked. I murmured the old, cracked words to him. He held on tight to my hand. Then he turned his head away from me and said, 'I confess that I'm feeling unco wearied tonight, Father.' Then he said very distinctly, 'Goodnight Jenny.' Then he died, and as he exhaled it seemed as if his soul went out of him with the breath. Just like that.

I hadn't been aware of McKechnie standing over me. He put his hand on my shoulder. He had spoken two sentences, which were, 'Nicely done, Charlie.' And, 'Thank you.'

So you can see that I was a bit choked as I walked away from that small graveyard in that small town in Germany and our boots slipped on the cobbles. Same words, and James shouldn't have said them. It may have been Goch, or it may have been Cleve. I never did find out what the name of the town was. Never asked James the name of it later, and I never did go back to look. I hated the fucking place.

That was something to do with the way we left.

I told you that the gun I bought in Laon was a Jerry Luger?

It had a long butt. That made it easy to go to sleep hanging on to, without pulling the trigger and shooting your foot off: make no mistake about it, that 9mm ammo was serious stuff. When I awoke there was a hand between my hand and the gun butt, and another over my mouth. Neither was mine. I could see a face close to me. Unsurprisingly it wasn't mine either. Kilduff.

He whispered, 'C'mon Charlie: time to go.'

Downstairs, by the light of a small kerosene pressure lamp on the table, I met the Bürgermeister, who looked worried, and James, who looked tied up. His wrists were tied together with bootlaces. Les's feet stuck out behind the settle he had been kipping on. James said, 'He's not dead. I don't know what the bastards did to him, but he's not dead.'

The big soldier we'd met before, also called Bassett, cuffed James around the ear hard enough to move him a foot sideways. I guess that that meant *Shut up until someone asks you to speak*, but Kilduff hadn't liked it. He shook his head. He told me, 'It was the Princeton squeeze. You just put a bit of pressure on the carotid and they go down like busted horses.'

'Do they wake up?'

'Most times. Usually with a headache afterwards.' I could have told them that leaving Les lying about and about to wake up with a headache wasn't their best option. But I didn't. They could make their own fucking mistakes. Kilduff added, 'And before you ask me anything else I gotta tell you again: it's time we were going.' He had an automatic pistol in his hand. I couldn't think of a good counter-argument to that.

The Bürgermeister still looked worried, but he managed to

slip me a little smile that the others didn't see. I saw Les's foot twitch. No one else did: I steeled myself not to react, and didn't. The two Yanks pushed us outside, and carried the kero lamp with them. There was another on the bonnet of one of those ugly little 4x4 trucks the Yanks ran around in, in '45, and another American leaning against the truck. He had one of those light machine pistols around his neck on a webbing strap. He was smoking a fag which stuck to his lower lip. Between James and me and Kilduff's truck was a heap of rubble in the road. It had once been a weaver's cottage. Now it was just a low pyramid of seventeenth-century stone rubble. It didn't obscure our view. I just wanted to give you the picture the way we saw it.

Kilduff and big Bassett were behind us; prodding. It was slow going because we had to avoid the bricks and tiles, which were strewn around the slippery, cobbled road as if a child had just scattered his play set in anger. The idea for *Lego* probably came from things we did to houses in the 1940s.

I think that we were still about forty feet away when Kilduff's driver suddenly straightened up, and grunted. From the light on the truck's bonnet I could see that he had an odd expression on his face. Something between surprise and a bad attack of heartburn. Then he collapsed to his knees, and his chin came to rest on his chest. He explosively spat his cigarette away: it dropped onto the road, and winked out. It was all very sudden. I was also aware of movement in the houses and ruins on either side of us, as if a pack of animals was moving through them in the dark. It's plain that Kilduff and Bassett Major hadn't spent time as front-line soldiers, because their reactions were a long way behind everything that happened next.

James was on my left, with Kilduff behind him. Bassett was behind me, enjoying prodding the small of my back with a machine pistol. They called them Burp Guns or something. I knew that he'd make me take off my jacket if he shot me, because he'd had his eye on it as soon as I came down the stairs. When their man went down, and the rustling started, they moved outside of us: Kilduff to the left and Big B out to my right. Then someone stepped into the road in front of Kilduff, and a church bell went off in my right ear.

There was some movement down by the cab of the truck, and its narrow beamed lights came on, giving us some weak illumination. The church bell was someone belting the other Bassett over the helmet with the full flat of a long-handled spade. It must have melted his brains, because he sat down immediately, with his feet splayed out in front of him. He dropped his MP, and made funny little gurgling noises. I immediately cringed, waiting for the spade to swing on me. The figure confronting Kilduff was the little girl I had seen earlier. She had her hand back over her head with half a brick in it. I suppose that it could have been something nastier. He swung his pistol her way, but he was going to be a loser all along. England slammed into him with his shoulder, and Kilduff started to stumble sideways among the bricks. The girl was good. She would have been a bloody good point fielder if Jerry ever played cricket. She could even hit a moving target. Her brick piece caught him on the forehead, under the rim of his helmet, which tipped forwards across his face as he fell.

James threw himself across the body to pin it down, and when the Bürgermeister's wife stepped up to put another spade against Kilduff's neck, with her foot on the blade's shoulder, that was it, really. Les slammed Bassett's helmet sideways with another mighty, ringing blow of his spade, and the policeman slipped sideways to lie on the road as if he was asleep. Although his eyes were open, and he was still alive. His right hand twitched spasmodically as if it had a life of its own.

Les said, 'My effing head aches. What did they do to it?'

I told him. He massaged his brow vigorously, and cut James's wrist cords with that horrible black-bladed knife of his. They should have taken that away from him.

From James there was, 'Thank you that man: I'd say *Many thanks*, Raffles; but how the hell did you let them creep up on us in the first place?'

There was this thing about Les: honesty, and syllable-specific accuracy when you needed it most.

'I was a prat,' he said, and, 'It won't happen again, sir.'

James wouldn't let him take it all on his own.

'I suppose it would have helped if Charlie and I had managed to keep our wits about us for a change?'

'No call for that, sir. You're officers.'

Kilduff made a little gurgling noise, quite similar to Bassett's sound effects soon after Les gonged him. Mrs Bürgermeister's leg was getting tired, and her weight was beginning to bear on the spade, which was beginning to bear on Kilduff's throat. James waved her away. He had taken Kilduff's pistol, and Les had Bassett's submachine gun. He kicked Kilduff to his feet, stuck his pistol in his ear, and cocked it.

'After you, Captain America,' he told him.

The truck's lights were killed just as we reached it. The boy with wire-rimmed specs was sitting behind the wheel. He had lit a cigarette from a packet on the dash. The American driver was on his knees with his hands in his lap. Like he was praying. His eyes were open, like Bassett's, but unlike him, he wasn't breathing heavily. He wasn't doing much breathing at all. To be frank, he wasn't doing any. There was a little trickle of blood from his mouth to his chin, and a little grin on his face. It was self deprecating; as if acknowledging that he'd done a stupid thing. I could go along with that: dying uncalled for is often a stupid thing. Kilduff gawked, and then he turned his head away.

He said, 'Aw shit; they killed him with a garden fork.' He retched, but nothing came up.

It was why he was still kneeling. The fork had slammed into him from the back. As he had sunk to his knees and then fallen back, its handle had lodged against the road, keeping him upright. The boy winked at me from behind the wheel. Then he blew on his fingers, the way you see the hero blow on his knuckles after a fist fight in a gangster film. I could have retched myself, except that it would have been impolite. I could still sense the people moving in the shadows on either side of the street. It was like hearing waves lapping on a shoreline you couldn't see.

I asked James, 'You think we're all right now?' When he didn't answer I added, 'Sir.'

I don't think that it was that. I think that he was pausing to gather his thoughts.

'I'm not sure I'd say that. I think that we're better off than we were half an hour ago when these bastards caught up with you.'

We were back sitting near the stove in the Bürgermeister's kitchen. The American Private Bassett was sitting awkwardly at our feet, his legs crossed. His arms were bound uncomfortably behind him: wrist to wrist, elbow to elbow. He was sweating like Niagara, which either meant concussion or a fractured skull. Or that he was too hot. His helmet was on the kitchen table: one side of it had been flattened by the power of the first blow he had been given, so I wasn't surprised that he still wasn't saying much. James tied Kilduff the same way. Then his wrists were tied to his ankles. I think that the Yanks call that hog-tying. Then they sat him in one of the upright kitchen chairs. I had this thought that Germany, despite its other problems, clearly wasn't short of rope. The Bürgermeister hustled his wife out of the kitchen with him, leaving the victorious Allies to discuss their differences. The kid walked in with three canvas rolls like sleeping bags, and dropped them on the floor.

He said, 'They were in their lorry.'

James sighed, and asked Kilduff, 'Are you sitting comfortably?'

The American looked wary, but he nodded. James said,

'Then we'll begin. Were you going to kidnap Charlie again, or simply kill him this time?'

'He's wanted.'

'By whom?'

'I don't know; the Brits anyway.'

'An Intelligence Officer named David Clifford is pulling the strings, isn't he?'

'You mean the tricky bastard from Tempsford? No; he's fucking well not. No, sir. If he hadn't interfered we would have kept Charlie first time round: I would have let you shoot that cat-house Colonel you found.'

'Try me again, Lieutenant. What's so important about Charlie that you follow him around with body bags?'

'. . . and I'll tell you again. The Brits want him stopped.'

'Stopped from what?'

'Doing whatever he's doing.'

'. . . and what is he doing?'

'He thinks he's chasing around the War Zone looking for some female who's run off with some doctors.'

'And isn't he?'

'Search me, bud. If that's not enough reason to off him, then he must be doing something else: something he hasn't told us about.'

Either Kilduff was never too bright, or he was in shock. But he couldn't take it back once he'd said it. There was a silence, but I'd hardly call it golden. That was my cue: it was time to take part in the conversation.

I said, '*Off* him. Does that mean . . .?'

'Yes.' That was Les. He didn't want to be left out, either. 'It means that this time you can forget about that gentlemanly *You're under arrest* crap: the bastard was going to take you round the corner and slit your throat for you.'

It was very odd. I actually broke out in a sweat, like the other Bassett.

The smashed-up house next door still had a cellar with a heavy wooden door in the pavement outside. Les dragged the Private to it, whilst James and I manoeuvred Kilduff. Kilduff swore a lot. When I held the lantern over the gaping door the first thing I saw was the other soldier's body sprawled at the foot of the ladder. Somebody had used their initiative. Both the others went in on top of it with sibilant thumps that were somehow more sinister for their lack of drama. Les said that there was no other entrance. He must have checked up when I wasn't looking. Back in the Bürgermeister's house there was a damp spot in front of the stove, which rapidly dried.

I said, 'We'll have to decide what to do with them. If their orders to kill me are legitimate – I mean legal – they haven't technically done anything wrong. If they're not they should be arrested and court-martialled.'

Les said, 'You're beginning to sound like a nance, Charlie.'

'Leave it out, Les.'

James showed us a rare sad smile. He said, 'Sorry, chaps: not your business . . .'

I said, 'I . . .'

And he cut me off with, 'I mean it, Charlie. This is where I pull rank. Not . . . your . . . business. OK?'

'Thank God for that, sir,' Les told him. 'I thought that you were losing your touch.'

Then James asked me, 'Would you mind getting the radio in here from *Kate*, Charlie, and rigging it up? I might as well make my daily report early. At least for the civilians here, the war is over, thank God.' I was sure that they just wanted me out of the way.

The settee that Les had slept on was big enough for five. After I had rigged the radio for them, running the aerial to an outside drainpipe, I dozed there. Les and James muttered to one another across James's little notebook, and then James hunched over the set and punched out his tunes for at least an hour. His Morse hand was far better than the airmen's I'd trained. He was quick and clear. He used his one-time code, so it was all meaningless crap as far as I was concerned. Les left him to it, and took the other end of the settee: soon he was snoring. His Sten was in his lap, and a spare mag on the arm alongside him. I took care not to move snappily. Finally James yawned, and stopped rattling the Morse key. He asked me, 'Have you realized yet that the people here are two days from beginning to starve? If we don't get the basics up here, malnutrition, typhoid and cholera will do in four months what your lot couldn't in six years.'

'What's that?'

'Push the German race to the edge of extinction.'

This was too much to get around that early in the morning. I told him, 'I'm not sure that I agree with that. I mean, I'm not sure that I want that to happen.'

313

'Nor do I, Charlie, which is why I'm in the right job. Unless there's a problem, half a dozen lorries will roll in here tomorrow with enough to keep everyone going for the best part of a week. They will be headed up by a Quartermaster Sergeant who will take up residence, probably with the prettiest girl in the place. After that it will all be routine. The Bürgermeister will still be the Bürgermeister. Some of the policemen who ran away will return. Normality. None of them will ever have been Nazis; not even the English Quartermaster Sergeant.'

'Where will *we* be in two days' time, then?'

'We will have moved on. To the next town. Les will be worried about keeping me alive . . .'

Les snorted, and mumbled, 'Don't count on that.' Then he started snoring lightly again.

'. . . and you will be closer to your pretty lady. Is she pretty, by the way?'

'Sometimes. There's something special about her: like an *It girl*.'

When I had opened my eyes James was still asleep. He had joined us, and was slumped sideways, his head resting on Les's shoulder. When he sat up I asked him, 'What are you going to do about Kilduff?'

James yawned. Les and I copied him. It's catching: I just yawned again as I wrote that.

'See if he tells us who wants you chopped, if he knows, and then I suppose it's old Hammurabi's Hypothesis. Have you heard of that, Charlie?'

'I heard all this cock before,' Les said to neither of us in particular. 'All it means is that we're going to have to kill the beggars.'

That seemed sad, this close to the end of the war. It was another of the things you didn't say.

They must have been waiting to hear us stir. Mrs Bürgermeister busied in with something approximating breakfast. It was potato soup, and potato bread. When we finished James gave the Bürgermeister a form he had filled in for him. It came from a small loose-leafed pad, and the Bürgermeister had to sign it as well. James kept a carbon copy. Then he took the Bürgermeister outside. They walked up and down in animated private conversation.

Les said to me, 'The Major has just given him his appointment as a military-approved Mayor. It will probably last until they get round to proper elections; could be a couple of years. It's a very important piece of paper. It means that he stays top dog. If he's a good man we benefit from that.'

'Is he a good man?'

'Fuck knows. He must have been a Nazi to have held down the job in the first place. Don't worry: we've been dealing with Nazi Froggies and Cloggies for the last few months. The bottom line is we only appoint the ones who know how to run things. I'm going to give *Kate* the once-over.'

I stowed the radio. While I was doing it the boy came in and sat at the table and watched me with his owlish eyes. I noticed for the first time that his spectacles had been broken at the bridge, and repaired with copper wire wrapped in a tiny coil.

He said, 'It was an honour to meet you, Mister Charlie.'

'It has been my honour, too.' I decided to try something. 'Not long ago we heard that Jewish people were being rounded up and placed into camps. Is that true?'

'Yes. My mother was one. The Bürgermeister saved me from the camp. My family were there.'

'Where was that?'

'Here. Just outside of the town. It's empty now.'

'Are there many camps?'

Maybe I'd learned a thing or two from the Major after all. I began to sense that my single questions were wearing him down; showing me something under the skin. He looked at the table. His fists clenched and unclenched. I did it again.

'Are there many camps?'

'Yes, many. Every town this size has a camp. There are more than a thousand of them.'

'That means . . .'

'Yes, sir . . . tens of thousands of Jews; hundreds of thousands . . . maybe millions. And not only Jews . . .'

'I wasn't sure I could believe what was in the newspapers.'

'You may believe,' he told me, and looked up. The eye contact scalded me. 'You have our permission.'

'Why did they take you in?' I asked him a little later.

'I don't know. I didn't ask them.'

When I recounted the conversation to Les he said, 'Effing obvious isn't it? Effing insurance policy.'

*

That depressed me. Les's occasional cynicism sometimes got to you that way. *Kate* was parked about twenty yards along the road, on the Greater Germany side of town. We were all stowed and ready to go. The boy was standing on the passenger-side running board, set to guide us out through the ruined streets. Time for goodbyes. I felt strangely older than when I'd arrived, and couldn't get used to the idea that that was less than two days ago. We stood near to the heavy pavement door to Kilduff's cellar. Mrs Bürgermeister gave me a hug: women have always found it easy to hug me – it's because I'm small, I think. Her husband shook my hand; firmly, but for too long. Les and the Major had already been through the formalities.

Les then grinned at us, and taking the woman's arm walked her to the cellar door. He handed her something. I didn't see what. Then he bent and lifted the door about a foot. I heard Kilduff immediately. He must have regained his cockiness, because whatever he said ended in *fucker*. The Bürgermeister's wife had two small American Mills bombs in her hands. It was what Les must have given to her to hold. Women don't waste time when something unpleasant has to be done: have you noticed that? She didn't give Les the grenades back: she pulled the pins on both of them, and dropped them in. Les dropped the big trapdoor with a bang. The woman turned and smiled at us, as if she had done something very naughty. We hot-footed it to the other side of the road, Les dragging the woman behind him.

There are two things from the Forties that I will remember

all my life. One is burning Lancaster bombers at night. I have seen those at every firework display I have ever attended: I try to avoid them these days. The other is the noise that Kilduff made then. Even though I can remember it exactly, I still can't tell if it was anger or anguish. It was a screaming howl that began before the bombs exploded, carried on afterwards, turning into a higher and higher-pitched screech, like a noise I have described before. Like the sound of a cat drawing open claws down a glass window pane. Higher and higher. He went on and on. The cellar door lifted momentarily with the force of the blasts, giving me a glimpse of hell. There was a gout of smoke before it thumped back into place . . . Kilduff's voice was still there, making a noise no human being should be capable of. Then the building above suddenly collapsed, filling the cellar beneath. We got further back, quickly, in order to escape the choking cloud of stone and plaster dust. Kilduff had stopped. There were rumbling and creaking sounds as the rubble found its level. Finally that stopped too.

'Told you, sir.' That was Les to James.

'What?'

'Bad job, that house; jerry-built.'

He didn't even laugh at his own joke. Neither did we.

As we drove away I asked them, 'Two things. Was Kilduff going to kill me, and if so, why?'

England said, 'Yes and no and money.'

'What does that mean?'

'Yes he was going to kill you, but not necessarily alone — he was prepared to bury the three of us if he had to — that's what really teed me off.'

'. . . and the money?'

'He expected to pick up three thousand dollars for it. Some-one really wants you off the job, old socks.'

'Who?'

'Do you care?'

The bastard was right. He usually was.

Eighteen

We crossed the Rhine near a place called Emmerich. Don't even ask me what bloody day it was. What I disliked was the number of knocked-up Sherman tanks standing forlornly in the fields. I wondered if any of them was Albie's, and what chance he had had of even making it that far. The bridge was prefabricated of metal, and swayed with the water streaming beneath it. The water looked an ugly brown, and moved fast: we seemed to be too close to it. *Kate*'s wheels fitted into parallel tracks, like tram rails that dragged us into Germany. A sign on the far bank read *Welcome to the 1000 year Reich, and you didn't even get your feet wet! Courtesy of the HD*. The D was formed on the last upright stroke of the H . . . the letters ran into each other.

I asked Les, 'Who's that?'

'Bloody Highway Decorators. Highland Division. The HD. Pushy Jocks who can't resist leaving their mark on every place they get to first, just to tell you.'

'Like cats or foxes pissing on trees, I expect,' James told us, and that was that. I thought that they were being a bit hard on them. The cats, I mean.

The Rhine had loomed large in my imagination. Now it was just brown and brutish, had the consistency of an open sewer, and was behind us. The next town we got to was like many I saw in Germany: houses reduced to their component parts. The number of straight roads away from the ruined towns was unnerving: it was as if the road-builders couldn't think in curved lines. The up side was that Les could work up to a fair old gallop, provided we stuck to roads that showed signs of having recently been visited by the Army, and pretended that no one had invented the landmine yet. The down side was that if a fighter or a Jabo caught us in the open, and decided to invite us to tea, there was nowhere to hide.

I saw a couple of American Thunderbolts in shiny unpainted livery and invasion stripes – we weren't even bothering to paint the damn things any more, there was so little opposition. They were low to the ground and looked pregnant, with a bomb apiece, drop tanks and wing-mounted rockets. When they saw us they canted over in a flat circle that brought them behind us again, and about two hundred yards over to the left. Then they flew alongside for a few seconds. I could feel the hairs on my neck lifting, but the nearest pilot gave me a dazzling grin full of teeth, and a wave. Then they streaked off into Germany.

Les said, 'Those things do almost four hundred miles an hour.'

I said, 'I think that one of McKechnie's brothers just waved to us.'

'Black boy, was he?' That was the Boss. 'I've heard that they have some of those. Good job, really: much steadier under fire.'

Les asked, 'Why's that, Boss?'

'Fuck knows. Maybe they got a bigger dollop of raw courage than the rest of us when God was handing round the sweeties.'

'You believe that?'

'No. They're the same as the rest of us, only maybe they've been so badly done to they have something to prove. Turn left at the next major crossroads.'

'Why's that?'

'Bremen's north of us. At the moment you're pointed towards Berlin. The Reds would be awfully peeved if you reached it first. Not to mention the fact that we must be catching up the front echelons pretty quickly: another few miles and we'll be somewhere where the Jerry will want to have a pop at us.'

I turned back to look at him as I spoke. 'We are in their country after all, Major. Maybe they feel they have cause.'

'I expect you're right. I expect that that's what that policeman thinks.'

Les was already slowing up as I turned back, still asking, 'What policeman?'

'That one there,' Les said. 'I think he wants us to stop.'

There was a man standing in the centre of the arrow-straight road with his left hand extended palm forward to us. He wore a dark blue uniform with silver buttons, and white gloves. Apart from the silly hat he could have been a London copper. His hat looked a bit like an infantryman's helmet from the Napoleonic Wars: it was tall and black and shiny, with a gleaming silver badge on the front. It had a narrow black shiny peak, but the effect was spoilt by its crown, which sloped

from back to front. It made him look as if he'd stepped from
the pages of Toy Town. His car didn't help. It was one of
those funny black VW things that look as if an elephant has sat
on the boot and then wandered round to sit on the bonnet.

Before we stopped completely I heard the nasty little
ratchet sound of the Major cocking his revolver. He asked,
'Les. Why are you stopping?'

'I wish I could give you a sensible reason, Major, but the
truth is, out of curiosity.'

'Fair enough. But if I have to kill the bastard, on your head
be it.'

By then we had pulled up a few yards short of the man and
his little car. I couldn't see the copper's reinforcements either;
there was just this dead-straight road, the copper and his car.
He walked to Les's side of the car, taking his time. Les had to
open the door in order to speak to him. His Sten must have
been in plain view.

The policeman said, 'You are English?'

Les replied, 'Yes. Support troops. We bring food and
medicines to the civilians after the Army has moved through.'

'That does not concern me.'

Did all the bastards in Germany speak perfect English? And
if so, had they done so for years, or was it a fairly recent
phenomenon practised in the face of the inevitable?

'How can we help you?'

'By paying your fine at the next functioning police office
you encounter. I will not insist on this occasion that you divert
from your route to pay it in the nearest police office: you
must be in a hurry – invaders usually are.'

He was a man in his late forties. His respectable moustache was laced with grey. His eyes twinkled. Either he was as scared as I was, or he found the whole thing amusing.

Les grunted, and asked, 'What fine?'

'For driving at over the permitted speed. You passed a large black and white circular road sign a kilometre back. What was on it?'

'The number forty,' I told him, leaning over Les, who gently pushed me back, 'and a lot of bullet holes.'

'The bullet holes do not concern me. The numbers do: they state the maximum permitted speed at which a vehicle may travel. I am glad it is still there. You were travelling much faster than that. I calculate that you were exceeding seventy kilometres an hour. I will not permit that.'

Les was one of those guys who loved arguing with coppers, no matter where, and no matter about what.

'How do you know that?'

'If you look behind you will see seven trees alongside the road. I have measured the distance between them. I start my stopwatch as you pass the first, and stop it as you pass the seventh. From that, and the distance covered, I calculate your speed.'

'Have you always been a policeman?' I asked him.

'No. Only since the war was declared. Before that I was a teacher of mathematics.'

Les gave a deep sigh, and said to nobody in particular, 'Fuck it. He's jobbing me for speeding.'

'His calculation is likely to be correct, Les,' I told him. 'He's a maths teacher.'

'Too right!' That was the Major. 'Guilty as bloody charged, if you want my opinion.'

The policeman's face would crack if he ever smiled.

'Fined many people for speeding this morning, have you?' Les again.

'Three vehicles . . . and one for driving on the incorrect side of the road.'

'I suppose that you have measured the width of the road as well?'

'Yes, I have. The road is seven metres at this point. There were also two Americans in fighter aircraft,' the policeman said, 'but they would not stop when I signalled them.'

'I wonder why.'

'Les,' the Major said, 'cut to the fucking chase, and ask him how much the fine is.'

Les gave him the *You must be kidding me* look, but before he could open his mouth the policeman told James, 'It will not be necessary for your driver to ask me again, Herr Major. I heard you the first time, and, unlike our glorious leader, I am neither deaf nor a fucking idiot. The fine is ten DM.'

'Right.' That was James. 'May we pay you instead?'

'No; you would pay in forged notes. I am not an expert, Herr Major.'

'What about English money?'

'English no; Scottish, maybe. I was informed that Scottish moneys are difficult to forge.'

'Give him a bloody dollar, anyway, Charlie. He's earned it.'

It wasn't quite as simple as that. We had to wait until he

had walked back to his car, had written out a speeding summons for Les, and brought it back. When he reached over Les to hand it to me he gave me our first smile. Then he said to Les, 'Please be careful, driver. Now the war here is over, there are policemen with nothing to do, and many small townships that will feed their people from the proceeds of court fines. Do not get caught again.'

Les put on the wisecrack face. He said, 'Look, Jerry. I don't know how to say this best; but in case you didn't notice, you've just been invaded. There won't be any courts, except Allied ones, and they'll be fully tied up trying Jerries like you for crimes against people an' dumb animals.'

Our Jerry wiped his smile off, and went dead serious on us.

'You are very wrong, Private. No matter what *is* lost in Germany, we will not lose our courts of justice. The spirit of Germany lives in its courts, and we Germans are the most litigious race in the world.'

'You haven't met the Americans yet,' James told him.

'I'm sure that we will get along well with the Americans.'

'I'm sure you're right,' James said.

Nobody seemed to know how to finish the encounter. Les did it. He'd kept *Kate* ticking over. Now he did it: *bang* neutral, *bang* first gear, and let her roll. The policeman stepped back and saluted.

'That man had balls,' James told us.

'Yeah, but they were between his ears.' That was Les. 'He won't last the week.'

*

'Charlie, I'm not going to stop for another of those bastards. Lean out the window an' wave your gun at him, and don't drop it. Maybe he'll get out of the way.'

Another day, another dollar, isn't that what the Yanks say? In our case it was the same bleeding day, and likely to cost us another bleeding dollar. There was another vehicle parked on the roadside, and I could see someone in the road trying to wave us down. I couldn't make out if they were civvy or military. When I could see I told him, 'No. We know this guy. It's Tommo, remember? He sold you that house in Stuttgart.'

Les gave me a warning look as we slowed, but it was too late. James had already picked it up.

'What's that, Les? Are you buying a bit of old Germany? Fallen in love with the place so quickly that you're already planning to move in as soon as the shooting stops?'

It was the only time I saw Les properly embarrassed.

'Just a little free enterprise, Major. Someone like me doesn't get that many chances.'

'No offence meant.'

'None taken, sir.'

But you didn't have to be a mind-reader to work out that some moral judging had gone on there, and Les hadn't come out of it as clean as he'd like.

'My cousin used to have a place in Stuttgart before the war, but he was bombed out of it. Perhaps you'd rent yours out to him afterwards, if he wanted to come back.'

'I'll think about it, sir,' Les told him. It was a way of saying *No ruddy fear*, without face being lost all round.

'Thank you, Raffles.'

Tommo strolled over. He looked far from comfortable himself. I expect it was something about being out in the daylight. What made it worse was that Pete lounged nonchalantly in the front passenger seat of their jeep, and that Alice's Restaurant was on the back seat. We drew up alongside them. I opened the door. Pete grinned wickedly at me. Alice's head was buried in her coils; I don't know whether she was looking at me and grinning, or no. The Major stuck his head between ours. That made it a five-way conversation, which didn't always make complete sense.

I asked Pete, 'Why have you got the snake with you?'

'Someone knocked the case over at Blijenhoek. She escaped and bit the pianist halfway through "Moonlight in Vermont". Everyone was very pissed off.'

'Pianist pissed off?'

'I expect so. Dead, also. This snake doesn't goddam miss. Should have been a goddam sniper. Either snake goes, or snake dies. Tommo made some promise to some dead Major in England that he looks out for the snake. We're looking for what's left of a zoo. They got them in Bremen, Hamburg and Berlin.'

'No zoo in Berlin,' I told him. 'We bombed the fuck out of it.'

'That's good. They got Russians in Berlin soon. I don't want to be around no Russians; they won't like fellows like me.'

The Major asked, 'Tell me about Les's house: this buying and selling lark. Anything in it for me? Some bijou gingerbread house on the edge of a Bavarian forest would do; somewhere to take the girlfriend for a dirty weekend.'

Tommo took him at his word.

'I expect that I could fix you up, sir, given a few days. Furnished or unfurnished?'

'The former, I expect. Is this quite legal?'

'Why does everyone ask me that?' Tommo bleated.

'Your reputation precedeth you, I expect,' I told him. 'Why did you stop us?'

'To bring you the news, courtesy of the new Polish American Forces radio network.'

'What's that?'

'Me and Pete. The real estate business is too easy: too tame. We're going to start a commercial radio station.'

'I'm interested in business,' the Major told them. 'But what does commercial mean in that context?'

'It's financed from its own income.'

'And that is?'

'Small-ads – like the front page of the London *Times*: that and the accumulating values of its registered assets.'

'It has a lot of those, does it?' From Les.

'Mainly properties in Germany and England. It's all tied up. I'm not as well off as people imagine. Not like Pete here.'

The Major asked Tommo, 'How much would it cost for me to catch up with the rest of you?'

'Five hundred quid.'

'Is that what you charged Private Raffles here?'

'And Charlie,' said Les. 'He's bought a small estate near Frankfurt.'

James didn't say anything to me, just gave me a big

reproachful look. All wet eyes and turned-down mug. It didn't move me, but I told him, 'Didn't think you'd be interested, sir.'

Tommo told him, 'Les paid a lot less, and Charlie a lot more. Charlie bought a lot more. He's got an estate as big as your Hampstead Heath. But to answer your question properly: no, they didn't pay the same pro-rata I'm offering you; they paid less. There's different rates for officers: higher rates.'

'Charlie's an officer.'

'Wasn't when I met him; an' he don't look like one now. Looks like some sort o' gypsy.'

'Thanks, Tommo.'

'Don't mensh. I don't suppose you want a snake?'

'Thank you, but no. Why *did* you flag us down?'

And: 'How did you know we were on this road?' That was Les.

'A clever friend with friends, who owed me. They triangulated on your last broadcast, and we worked it out from there. We been waiting here a couple of hours. I fill my pants every time I hear a plane go over. I was never meant to be this close to a real war . . . and I told you, we flagged you down to give you the *news*.'

'What news?'

'That you're hot. Someone in the dirty circle has put the word round. There's a price on you. Three grand no questions to the man who brings home your head. All the seriously bad guys are talking about it. A year ago I would have thought about it myself.'

'Thanks again, Tommo.'

'You know some scruffy Lieutenant called David Clifford? A bit of an older guy?' Pete asked me.

'Yes.'

'Good guy or bad guy?'

I had to think about it. Les answered, 'Good guy, we think. It's difficult to be sure. Why?'

'Arrived at the 'Hoek a few hours after you left. He was asking. I think he's good: he'll catch up with you eventually if he wants to.'

'What was he saying?'

'He asked me to tell you he had arranged a plane to get you out. All he needed was for you to tell him where from. He said to forget everything else; it's time to go home and save your skin. I think I believed him. Maybe.'

'What did you say?'

'That I never heard of you. But that I would be sure to pass the message on if I ever met you. Then he starts buying drinks for the black fellow they call the Cutter. I think that they also call him Keck, which is something like his name.'

'What did he say?'

'They got drunk together, and Keck offered to circumcise your Lieutenant for free. I heard that bit. I missed what Clifford said back to him.'

'Why?'

'Because he was running too fast. He knocked down Alice's Restaurant, the snake bit the pianist, an' you know the rest.'

Les asked, 'Where did she bite the pianist?'

Tommo replied for himself this time, 'Behind the piano, where he was hiding.'

'No; I mean, where on his body?'

'Oh Christ; on his bum. You know that snake's got a thing about arses?'

'Sounds like some fellows I went to school with,' James told us. It seemed to kill that line of conversation, if you'll forgive the pun, and anyway he'd made that joke before.

Tommo pushed a couple of old oiled-cloth envelopes at me. He said, 'These are the deeds to your place, an' Les's too. Don't lose them.'

Les asked, 'These are legal?' again.

'They are deeds of sale and possession, made out by the best surviving Jerry lawyer in Frankfurt. Transfer entries in your names have been made in the property and land registers. Now: do I have to say it again, or would you like it set to music? You're landowners now. Legally. God loves you after all.'

'God, and Tommo Thomsett. Thank you,' I told him, and asked, 'Where's Grace?'

'Up beyond Löningen somewhere, I heard. They were slowed down because of a fight over the other bird they got with them. One of the Eyetie medics ended up in hospital . . . and then we shanghaied him to work on the wounded. Apparently he says he's only going to sew Krauts back together again, so they beat him up a bit and slung him in the can. Lucky he wasn't whacked. Some politician had to intervene to get him out again . . . you believe that?'

'Why not? Anything else I should know?'

'Lee Miller's up here somewhere. She took pictures of one

of those concentration camps, and the Army's trying to get them back off her to prevent them being published.'

'Why?'

'You seen one of those camps?'

'No. Why?'

'You will, an' then you'll know why. I ain't being coy; it's jest best you see for yourself.'

'What's Lee doing about it?'

'She's on the run; heading for Munich – the Army ain't got a chance.'

'What else?'

'Cliff's in zone, an' worried about you.'

'I know: Pete just told me.'

'He's using the call sign Ratking, an' listening in to the Major's daily callover. He won't butt in until you call him to get you out. If I had to trust him on a scale one to ten, I'd rate him at six or seven, I think.'

'Pete didn't tell me all that. Thanks. Who put a price on my head?'

'Us Yanks,' Tommo told me. ' 's funny: I always thought you was on our side, Charlie.'

'So did I.'

'So someone must have told us to do it.'

'We figured that out for ourselves. Who?'

'Someone who don't want you finding Grace, nor her kid maybe.'

There it was at last. I had needed someone to say it out loud before I could believe it myself.

'It would have to be someone close,' I told him.

'So why don't you give up and go home?'

'I have another appointment to keep in Bremen now; and Grace is the excuse I need to keep going.'

'I could arrange an escort for you. People I trust, with a lot of firepower.'

The Major butted in. They call his sort of butting in an interjection.

'Very kind, but no. Anyway, I ask myself, why should you help our Charlie here? In my country we use this proverb about not trusting Greeks bearing gifts.'

'Point taken, Major. I don't like Greeks either. I like the Eyeties though: good sound criminal stock. I look after Charlie because he's part a my family. Like the other guys I mentioned. He does me favours, an' I do him favours. Favour for favour.'

'And they're all strictly legal.'

'Naturally. So is this where I have to start to get humpy, and ask you what the fuck your problem is . . . sir?'

'I don't have one, Master Sergeant. Take no offence.'

'And you still want a cottage in . . . Bavaria, you said?' He pronounced it Barr varr ey . . . ah. It sounded very exotic.

'If that's not too much trouble, old boy.'

'Nothing's ever too much trouble for me to do; for people in my family, that is . . .' At least he spelled it out clearer to James than ever he'd bother to do for me.

Les asked Tommo and Pete, 'Is there anything else we need to know before we push on?'

'I heard that every Snowdrop who had contact with Charlie

in Paris has done a runner: AWOL. Probably an exaggeration. I think that that is making us Allies a bit unhappy about you.' When I didn't respond he added, 'That's a black Sergeant you call the Cutter, a PFC named Bassett – the same as Charlie – and some Lieutenant. I think his name was Kilduff, or something like that. I know all about the Cutter, of course – in fact I rather like the guy – but I don't suppose you know anything about the other two, do you? They were supposed to be on your trail. That Snowdrop Oliver at the 'Hoek is all fired up about them. First they come into his patch without a say-so. Then they start missing their radio schedule. You have a bad effect on policemen, Charlie.'

Les said, 'If we come across them alive we'll let you know.'

Pete always thought the worst of me. He smiled across a tiger smile that meant, I don't believe a word that any one of you has said so far, and said out loud, 'Your pal Albie Grayling: the tank commander. He's up in Löningen now, and laid up for a couple of days. He'd like you to look him up when you get there.'

'How'd he get there already? How'd he get past us?'

'He didn't stop to hobnob with the enemy at Goch, like you did.'

See what I mean?

Ten minutes later James asked Les to stop the car.

'Get in the back with Charlie. I need to think. So I'll drive.'

Les tucked himself into a corner, and closed his eyes. He asked me, 'We all just joined the Mafia, didn't we?' but it wasn't a question.

335

Nineteen

When you get to hell it will be on your right. And from a distance it might look like any other Army camp. It was on our right, off one of those arrow-straight Kraut roads. On our left – the west – there was a wide canal, its surface rippled by a persistent wind. When the sun was on it, it glinted like cheap diamonds. The ground had been cleared on our right for about a mile. Behind that the black forest started: it was as long and as deep as you could see. *Kate*'s tyres hissed on the tarmac. I opened my eyes as I sensed the Major slowing us, and asked, 'Where are we?'

'The last place was named Lunner or Lune something. It was knocked about a bit.'

'Why are you slowing?'

'Tanks . . . and something a bit odd over there on the right. What do you think?'

I could see an enormous fenced-off area, high wire and dark wooden huts. It looked a bit like the R&R area at Blijenhoek. As we cruised slowly past the parked-up tanks no one tried to stop us. James pulled up at a place where a well-used earthen track left our road at right angles. They weren't tanks, by the way, but Priests or Sextons – self-propelled guns: that is 25-pounder guns mounted on a Sherman tank chassis. Canadian jobs, crewed by artillerymen, not tankies. There was one young soldier sitting by the side of the road crying his eyes out. A Captain with a wall eye was bending down to put an arm around the kid's shoulders. I could see a couple of the Sextons up at a big wired gate: where the track met the wire fence. There were knots of people moving about. I saw the first guard tower. I said, 'It must be a POW camp.'

James shook his head and said, 'I don't think so. Hop out, Charlie, and find out what's going on.'

The gunner Captain looked up as I approached. He looked ashen; shaken, but I couldn't see any casualties. I didn't salute, and he didn't care. He held out his hand for a shake, as if he needed the reassurance of touch. He scanned my ragged kit, and lingered for a second over the small gold crosses in my lapels. The sun caught them from a break between the heavy white clouds, and for a moment they gleamed. He said, 'I'm glad you stopped, Padre. We need your help.'

Les had left *Kate* by then: his nose always troubled him. He and I walked up the track to the camp.

What they tell you about birds and animals staying away from those places is not true. There were crows. Hundreds of black crows. Maybe a thousand. When they were disturbed from what they were fighting over, they made a wheeling shadow in the sky. I won't tell you anything much about the place. What I will tell you is this.

*

Les was forty-four when he died in 1958. His war had caught up with him. One of his groups of wounds was shrapnel he picked up from a shell-burst at Dunkirk. He used to laugh that he was wounded three times, and that each time was in the arse. He once told me that the only thing he deserved a medal for was being in every retreat the Eighth Army ever made. It accounted for most of the arse wounds. The shell pieces were in his backside, his back and shoulders, and in his head. They never dug out a piece in his head, and when he was forty-four it killed him.

We'd stayed in touch; more or less. I was living in South Hampstead in London by then, and Les had been reclaimed by his tribe in Belmont, just to the south of smoky London. I visited him the day before he died, but the timing was accidental. The brain tumour and the strokes had smashed up his mind by then. Kate gave me a peck on the cheek, and said that he was upstairs; that he hadn't got up yet. When I approached the bedroom door I could hear him weeping and moaning, and mumbling to himself. I couldn't help remembering the able and funny man I had once known. When my time comes I hope that it's quick; not dirty, like that.

I went into their bedroom − the small double bedroom overlooking the back garden he had begun to love. He was sitting on the edge of their high bed, in his striped flannel pyjamas, staring at the full-length mirror on the door of the dark wood wardrobe. He was gibbering. I sat beside him, and hugged him; realizing for the first time how pitifully thin and wasted he had become. Eventually he calmed down enough to tell me that the sick and emaciated people we had seen in the camp were there in the mirror; calling and beckoning to him. They were calling him to join them, and for the first time in his life he was truly afraid. He had seen his own reflection, and his scrambled brain, doing its best to make sense of what it saw, gave him back the memory of 1945, and that bloody horrible camp. Corpses and living corpses, wearing striped prison suits like pyjamas. Those, and the black crows. That's enough. What we saw in that camp, he saw again on the last full day of his life. I've always thought that unfair.

James stopped *Kate* again a few miles further on, and turfed us out of the back so he could radio. A jeep was on its back less than ten yards away. It had lost three wheels and its sump guard was blackened by fire.

Les said, 'It wasn't a mine: there's no hole in the road: just that black flash mark. I reckon some kids got him with a panzerfaust.'

'What's that?'

'Like an AP grenade with a rocket up its arse. One-shot jobs. You fire it and chuck it away. In France we found a couple of sixteen-year-old kids who had cycled from Germany with them strapped to their crossbars. They had been captured by the Paras.'

There were three wooden crosses at a field boundary near it. One had an American helmet on it. Les leaned against *Kate*'s bonnet; I sat on the running board. He smoked about five of his cigarettes; one after the other. I smoked my pipe. Its smoke was sweet and cool. It cleaned my mouth. The sun broke through, and stayed. Light danced on the rippling water of the canal, moving around a partly submerged barge. There was a floating bundle lodged up under the barge's counter. It may have once been a man in a grey uniform.

Inside *Kate*, James rattled and rattled at the Morse key: you could sense his change of style. You could sense the urgency and the frustration. When he finished and backed out, Les asked him, 'You got through, sir?'

'Yes. I told them. I asked for Medics and food and clothes. They said they'd send a bulldozer.'

'What for?' I asked him, and immediately thought, *I've done it again.*

Les said, 'Don't be a prick, Charlie. It's for digging the graves.'

I asked, 'Will we get to Löningen tonight?'

Neither answered me. James scuffed the toe of his boot in some dirt on the road, deliberately dirtying it. Eventually he sighed, and asked, 'Sorry, Charlie. What was that?'

'Löningen. Will we be there tonight?'

'I doubt it. I don't know how far the fighting's gone.'

Les said, 'We could sleep in *Kate* tonight: I suddenly don't fancy any company.'

James once had this theory that all three of us died out there, but that our bodies kept going somehow, until God could be bothered to pick us off one by one.

Twenty

The first thing I said to Albie was, 'Where the bloody hell is your hand?'

He was sitting in a conservatory in a sanatorium that had been taken over by the Medical Corps. It was just outside of Löningen. There was glass missing, but Albie was out of the wind, with his faded canvas collar turned up. He looked pale: his face was a sort of white waxy colour. The end of the sleeve of his jacket right arm was pinned closed.

'Caught my sleeve in the turret ring, and tore my hand off when we traversed. You should have seen the inside of *Marlene*: she looked like Custer's Last Stand. Every time I moved my arm the blood sprayed like a fountain. I got Donny all over his face.'

He gave his great *arf, arf* laugh as if losing a hand was a great joke.

'OK,' I said. 'Who's *Marlene*, and who's Donny?'

'*Marlene* is my new tank. Not a Sherman: she's a fast bitch of a medium they call a *Chaffee* so I'm in love again. I didn't

DAVID FIDDIMORE

know we could make them like that. We reckoned, paint the name of a Kraut singer on the turret, and they're less likely to take a pop at her.'

'You may be wrong. Most Jerries reckon that Marlene is some sort of a traitress: you could call it *Beethoven*, or *Valkyrie*. The Krauts go for that sort of thing.'

'Yeah, but then my own people would whack me, wouldn't they?'

'How long you been here?'

'A day. I lost the hand yesterday, or maybe the day before that.'

'So what happened to it?'

'Told you. Turret ring. I'd already lost the feeling in it – that damned gangrene stuff I suppose. So I saved the Cutter a trip down here.'

'Is that as far as it gets?'

'Yeah. Sure. I get to keep the rest. I might get it fitted with a hook, like in pirate stories. They want me to sit here a few days and make some blood, and then go home, but I got other plans. I aim to see Berlin. I got this far, didn't I?'

'Yes, Albie. You did. When I first met you in Bedford I didn't think you'd get off the beach: you didn't seem to know too much.'

'War's a harsh mistress,' Albie said gravely. Then, 'I read that in a book somewhere. It's piss, isn't it?'

'I met Tommo another couple of times. He's got a better take on that. He thinks the war's a rich mistress.'

'Good old Tommo. I bought a house off him.'

'Where?'

342

'Some place called Goch. We drove around it to preserve the real estate.'

'I think we've been there. It was a bit knocked up.'

'Not my house: it once belonged to the Bürgermeister. He's run off.'

I let that pass. I asked him, 'You told me about *Marlene*. So who is this bloke Donny you sprayed your blood at?'

'My gunner. He sits beside me in the turret. He's a good engineer too. He was a Scotchman once; now he plays a guitar pretty good and sings folk songs for us. Brings in all the loopy ladies at parties. You can hear the knickers on the slide every time he opens his Irish mouth.'

'Uh-huh . . . I thought you said he was a Scot?'

'He was: he just don't sound like one. He likes this place. He says he's gonna take his stage name from it after the war. Donny Löningen.'

'I don't think that that sounds quite right.'

'You're being picky, Charlie, but I'll pass that on.'

'I saw one of those camps,' I told him.

'Yeah,' he said. 'I did, too.'

We didn't speak of it again.

Les came in and stood behind me. He said, ' 'morning, sir,' to Albie, and gave him something that might have once started out to be a salute. 'You had some more bad luck, then?'

'It could be worse; I jack off with my left, so that's OK.'

I asked, 'Jack off?'

Les told me, 'Wank.'

And James, who'd slithered silently in from somewhere said, 'Masturbate. Have you asked him about Grace?'

343

'No, he hasn't, but he may.' That was Albie still in there.

'You've seen Grace?'

'Yes, but not to speak with. She was with that group of foreign medics we talked about, when they were rounded up by your Redcaps for getting in a fight. They kept them in a prison tent up to their fannies in mud. I saw them as they were carted away, and loaded into the back of a lorry.'

'Did she still have the child?'

'I think so. The big German girl who started it was nursing a baby, and I don't think they got two.'

'When was that?'

'Yesterday; day before. Ask the guys. I wasn't being too sensible after I lost my hand.'

'Where do you go from here?' I asked him.

'Bremen and Hamburg. I gotta see Hamburg. It's the most complete medieval city centre in Europe.'

I chose not to tell him what we'd done to Hamburg a few months ago. I asked him, 'Are you OK up here? Isn't this the British sector?'

'Yeah, but I was lucky. The Brits haven't anything as fast as us, so we're sorta out on loan: hired guns. I'll see you in Bremen then? It's all moving rather quickly now.'

'Not if we see you first, Albie,' I told him.

Outside, James passed some comment on Albie's pasty colouring, and asked me what I thought.

I called it the way I saw it. 'He's dying, isn't he?'

'By inches,' Les said, and we fell about laughing. That's how it was.

James told us, 'At least you're closer to Grace again.' Then he asked, 'Didn't your Yankee gangster say that one of her travelling companions had been put in hospital, and then dragged out by the MPs and banged up? I wonder what happened to him?'

Les stopped, and offered us fags from his beret. It was the first time I had seen the Major accept.

Les said, 'I suppose that you could go all Majorish again, sir, and shout in somebody's face until they tell you.'

James said, 'Do you think that it would work up here?'

They both looked at me. Les asked, 'Charlie?'

'We've got nothing to lose,' I told them, and threw in, 'An' I'm bloody hungry. We could find some grub, maybe, at the same time' . . . for good measure. The ideas seemed to go together quite well.

There was a small, well-ordered camp of decent-sized canvas tents that looked as if they kept the wind and water out. The MPs' post was in the centre of a field of mud that had once been a football pitch. There were two jeeps with full weather equipment, and a Dodge personnel carrier, parked between their tents. James led us in a wade over to the largest of them. As the mud built up on my flying boots they became harder and harder to lift: I was in danger of stepping out of them. I was pleased to find that they were our own proper MPs: there wasn't a Yankee Snowdrop in sight. The senior man was a Sergeant with knobs on. He explained that he had had a Warrant Officer once, but that the guy had been driven back to safety with some kind of exhaustion. I forgot myself and said, 'Right-hand fatigue: bloody officers are all the same.'

The MP looked startled. James told him, 'Don't mind the

Padre. He was a Sergeant himself, not so long ago. He forgets himself from time to time.'

The MP looked doubtful. He said to me, 'I'm sorry, Padre. You're the first Chaplain we've had up here for a while, and I didn't expect you to sound like that.'

'That's OK, Sarge. I was only given the short course: they left me with the wrong vocabulary.'

He had winced when I used the word *Sarge*: they probably had a special name for his rank in the Military Police. But at least I was speaking with a policeman and a Non-Commissioned Officer who could understand a five-syllable word. Wunderbar. James showed him some sort of identity card I hadn't seen before. It had diagonal red lines superimposed on everything else. It must have said that we were gods newly descended from Olympus, because the MP visibly stiffened in every sinew.

James did the friendly officer bit, and talked about a bit of this, and a bit of that. None of it seemed to make sense to me because it was about football, which is about as tactically interesting as trees growing. The Sergeant, whose name was Arnisson, said that he followed the women's game, and that in Sheffield, where he came from, it wasn't unusual for a crowd of 25,000 to turn out to watch two teams of women footballers kicking the shit out of each other. He'd shown us to camp chairs: Les stuck his feet out, and closed his eyes.

'We've been on the road for days,' the Major told the MP, 'trying to catch up with a group of doctors and nurses trying to get through the lines to help the Jerries.'

The MP said — and there was a glint of triumph in there

somewhere – 'I knew that there was something dirty about that lot . . . at least one of them was an Eyetie. He stabbed a Geordie with a scalpel, all over some Jerry woman travelling with them.'

'She was a looker, I suppose?' James.

'Too bloody well fed for this end of the war, if you forgive me for saying, sir. Big everything: like those Viking women you get at the opera.'

I hadn't a fucking clue.

'*Valkyries*, Charlie,' James explained to me. 'Didn't you tell your friend with the one hand to paint that on his tank?'

'It's a brand of sardines,' I told him. 'My dad used to like them.'

'Probably still does,' James said. Then he asked the MP, 'What happened?'

'They abandoned the Eyetie, sir: stole away like thieves in the night. Took a good few armfuls of medical supplies, and a Corps bicycle, come to that.'

'What happened to the Italian?'

'The rude soldiery gave him a bit of a kicking. He was in the small field hospital at first. We heard that the doctors and nurses here were making too much of a fuss of him. He was one of theirs, after all: a member of the Lodge – the ancient and honourable society to promote the interests of medical personnel over all others. It was medicine crossing frontiers, and all that guff. Do you think we'll ever get free medicine the way they tell us, sir?'

'If we do, it probably won't be worth having . . . so what did you do?'

'I sent a couple of lads to fetch him back over here, where he belonged, or put him to work. Fucking criminal. Begging your pardon, sir.'

'Were you gentle with him?' James asked.

'Very, sir: I have no idea why we got the phone call.'

'What phone call?' I've told you before: I just can't resist it.

'The phone call from our Brigadier at the HQ in Fromme, sir . . . telling us to release the prisoner on parole.'

'And what did he say?'

'To put my fucking prisoner back in the fucking hospital if I didn't want to end up there my fucking self, sir. They were his exact words.'

'Where is he now, your prisoner?'

'Back in the hospital; filling himself up on hospital rice pudding, and touching up the nurses, I believe, sir.'

'Would you mind if I asked him some questions?'

'He won't give you the time of day, sir,' the MP told me. 'But be my guest. Ask him as hard as you like.'

Les yawned, sat up and looked like an alert and loyal soldier. There must have been a reason for it. He asked James, 'Excuse me, sir. Would it be OK for me to ask if there was the possibility of us joining the next food queue? I'm starving. I'm sure that you and the Padre are as well.'

James turned to face our host again. All he did was raise a friendly eyebrow like a semaphore signal. The Sergeant shrugged, and said, 'It's only bully and mash, but you're welcome to it, gentlemen.'

There wasn't a proper Officers' Mess, so James and I were put to a table by ourselves in the Sergeants' dining-out tent. The difference between our table and those of the five sergeants we shared the canvas with was that the cook wiped down the sauce bottle before he placed it between us. The Big Man was right: it was Mash and Bully, capital M, capital B. Les was shipped off to eat with the Ordinaries. I've seen him and James do that before. Then they compare notes when they get back together. It gives them a definite edge. James and I didn't have anything to bring to him this time; the sergeants didn't speak much whilst we were there. It was as if we were Untouchables who had wandered into a high-caste wedding breakfast by mistake. The only thing I really remember was the tea. British MPs make the best cup of char in the world. Afterwards the Major asked his driver – just to put them into the Army's preferred context, 'Did you learn anything, Les?'

'Two things. First that you can recognize the German bird the fight was over because she looks like Jane. That's Jane with a decent herbaceous border.'

'What was the other thing?' I was in this too.

'That you'd do better to forget your Grace, sir. She's shagging anything that stands still in front of her for long enough. She was probably the real reason for the fight: she's always trying to put one over on the German bird.'

'She doesn't sound too different from before.'

'And don't that make a difference?'

I felt suddenly tired.

'Not in the short term, Les. I'll get her back for them, if I can: it's as if I owe them and her something. After that, I don't know.'

'They're good at that, the moneyed classes,' James told us. 'Making people like you feel obligated.'

'You'd know all about that, I suppose, sir,' Les snarled. It was that snarly edge to his voice that killed the easy feeling we had been enjoying.

We met Albie at the door to the sanatorium, at the top of wide shallow stone steps covered by a long Victorian glass awning. It had survived, miraculously intact. He was leaning against a small soldier. His crutch had black, stand-up hair a cap would never sit on, and a cheeky smile. I asked Albie, 'Did you know that that Eyetie MO was in here?'

'Not when you were here. I do now. I sent someone to tell you. They're probably still looking for you. This is Donny.'

Donny grinned, touched his brow and said, 'God bless America, Father.' He had a strange musical, grating voice. Albie had been right. You could have taken him for Irish.

'He will, son, He will . . . I shall ask Him personally.' Then I asked Albie, 'You off?'

'Yeah. Before I lose anything else.'

His colour was better. Fractionally. Les told Donny, 'You look after him, son.'

Donny replied, 'Yessir.' Maybe he knew something about Les that we didn't.

James could be very good when he tried. We had to walk round, through or over about five levels of medical administration to meet the Italian. Then he was in a small room having a party. In order to get to the room we had to walk through a long airy ward of serious wounds. We were assailed by groans. One boy in a blue shirt called out, 'Over here, Chaplain,' to me as I passed.

I said, 'Don't worry, I'll see you later,' and, 'I won't forget.'

What I haven't forgotten is the smile he gave me as he settled back on his pillow. A nurse in a grubby green apron and tennis shoes ran past us, the length of the ward. She had a bedpan in one hand, and a mess of soiled bandages in the other. One of them unrolled, and trailed behind her like a bridal train. There were five people in the room apart from the Italian patient. Two guys and three girls. They were all drunk. The patient was sitting upright on the bed conducting them in a slurry version of 'I'm 'enery the Eighth, I Am'. He wasn't drunk. He was something else. His eyes were bright and fevered. I've seen that in pilots who were living off Benzedrine. Blue Bennies. The older of the two doctors was about forty. He grinned at Les, who grinned back and said, 'Fuck off. Fuck off the lot of you.'

The Doc was a bit of a trier. He tried, 'This patient has special clearance. You can't . . .'

Les introduced his Sten with an impressive rattle.

'An' now you've got special clearance: to effing well clear off. You can leave the room, or end up lying on its floor. Either way is OK with me.'

One of the girls giggled, and the Italian said, 'It's OK,

Dennis. You can go. They can't do anything.' From his speaking voice you could have sworn that he had been to the same school as James. James gave a quick, interested smile.

The older man was Dennis. He swayed when he stood up. His mouth dropped open as if he was about to protest again. James held his finger to his own lips. The gesture said *Ssh*. He whispered, 'Better you don't, old son. Keep a bit of hush; there's sick people out there.'

They filed out behind each other; weaving slightly. One of the girls was a short redhead. I'm partial to a bit of short redhead when I get the opportunity. This one gave me a cheeky grin as she squeezed past. They all had slightly fixed smiles. Les sat on the end of the Italian job's bed, and grinned his wolfy grin. He hadn't uncocked the Sten. The patient moved away from him, until the bedhead stopped him. Les moved closer, and said, 'What's your name?'

'Albert Long.'

'And I'm Victor Emmanuel the third. Try again.'

'Alberto Longhi. Why do you need to know?'

'So we know what to put on your stone . . . if we have a disagreement.'

The Italian looked down at the sheets. He muttered, 'We will have no disagreement.'

'I didn't quite hear that. What did you say again?'

'We will have no disagreement.'

'I'm pleased about that,' Les told him.

All this gave me time to size the Eyetie up. He was tall: as tall as the Major – and slim and muscular. His skin was a nice tanned brown: he must have come from that bit of Italy where a man's job was lying on the beach with a drink in his hand. You could see that because he wore his gown open to the waist to excite the little girls; he had no chest hair. The stuff on top of his head was too long, too black and too greasy. For my taste, that is, but what do I know? No matter how tall he was, he was still a gutless little prick. My Uncle Ted use to call people like that skinless sausages. I've always thought that that captures the idea rather neatly. Les stood up and let the spring down on the Sten.

James sat where Les had been, opened his notebook and uncapped his pen. He asked, 'Now, where shall we begin?'

I leaned against the door frame. Alberto answered James's first question by saying, 'I claim my rights under the Geneva Convention. I do not have to tell you anything: I am a doctor . . .'

Les was looking out of the small room's small window. He made a restless sound and a restless movement. He said, 'Listen, Alberto. In England there is a very famous music hall turn. His name is Stanley Holloway.'

'Maybe I have heard of him.'

'Do you know what a music hall is?'

'Of course.'

'Well. This Mr Holloway has a famous monologue. It is called "Albert and the Lion".'

'Why are you telling me this?' You could feel the cockiness growing in the bastard again.

'Because in the story, lad, the lion *eats* Albert. I want you to remember that when the Major asks you again. Do you think you can do that?' Les had delivered all this with his back

353

to us. The Italian shrugged, but he had stopped making eye contact again, so I suppose that it was enough. He told us about the vehicles they were travelling in, which we already knew. He told who they all were, which we didn't know, and what medicines and equipment they had managed to amass, which turned out to be surprising. We were looking at a small travelling hospital. They had bought a lot of their stuff from black marketeers, of course, and stolen or traded for the rest. He told James that they were heading for Bremen. Then they were going on to Hamburg, and then to Lübeck. Why Lübeck?

'It is where we will want to work after the war.'

'The Russians may well be in Lübeck.'

'Where else would a Communist want to work, except inside a Russian zone?'

'Fucking anywhere, I should imagine,' Les told him. He still didn't turn away from the window. I dropped in my tuppence worth for the first time.

'The English woman you call Grace Baker. She isn't a Communist.'

'Maybe she is,' Alberto told us. 'Maybe she's not. She won't go as far as Lübeck. She will go with my friend back to Italy: he has a small clinic.'

James glared at me for breaking in, but picked up my thread.

'He has a name? Your friend?'

'Carlo.'

Carlo: know thy enemy.

I tried again. 'They will expect you to catch them up: in Bremen. Where would that be?'

He shot a must I? glance at James, who nodded encouragingly. Then he said, 'The Hanseatic Hotel: it's just outside the docks. They took it for a hospital last year. They need people like me.'

I couldn't help it. I said, 'No one needs people like you. You're a fair-weather Commie who betrays his friends: I'll bet you were a Nazi when Musso was waving the flags.'

James spoke quietly. He said, 'Bravo, Charlie.' He wasn't the first to say that.

Alberto sniffed. 'I did not know them all that well,' he told us.

I don't know why the Italian upset Les so much. I think that it was his attitude. Les said, 'You make me sick. I don't know why. The only reason I'm not going to kill you now is because I can't be bothered, and it would get a policeman I know into trouble. That's all. That's all that's keeping you alive.'

'Your officer wouldn't let you.'

'His officer,' James said gently, 'would recommend him for promotion, and a medal, if he did.'

Les didn't leave it at that. He put on the earnest-toiler-in-the-fields face, which always unnerved me, and said, 'I do want you to believe this. I want you to ask in every town you go to, for the rest of your life, is there a small, curly-haired Englishman there; one who keeps his cigarettes in his hat?' He touched his grubby old black beret.

'Why should I do that?'

'Because if I see you again, I'm going to kill you.'

The Italian smiled. He had a brilliant, winning, playboy's

smile. The signorinas probably loved it. He said, 'I do not believe you.'

I gave them something. I said, 'Then you are very foolish.'

A shadow passed across the Eyetie's smile; but not for very long.

In the ward outside I found myself keeping to my word. I always like doing that. The kid in the blue shirt gave me his smile again. It was no different from the Eyetie's, except that it was genuine. Les and James wandered slowly on. The wounded boy showed me his right hand. It was under bandages, and looked a funny shape. I asked, 'Is that a Blighty one?'

'Too right, Father. Is it Father?'

'Padre will do. What did you do to it?'

'A Jerry cannon shell. Small job. Lost the little finger, and it smashed through the middle. I didn't even feel it for a few seconds.'

'I know an American tankie that that happened to. He's had a run of bad luck. First he lost part of a little finger, then his middle finger completely, then his complete hand. He says he's leaving bits of himself all over Europe.'

'Is he going home, Padre?'

'No. He says that seeing as he's come this far, he wants to get to Berlin.'

'I want to get to Accrington.'

'I think you have a better brain than he does, and a better chance.' Then I told him, 'I'm sorry, but I have to go now. Say hello to England for me.'

'I will, Padre, and thank you for stopping.'

I didn't turn to wave as I walked away from him. That was never my style. Even when I wanted it to be.

The nurse I'd seen doing the hundred yards earlier was at the far end of the ward, near the door I was aiming for. I could see James and Les stopped outside, waiting for me. She was still now, and had changed her grubby apron for a fresh green one. She had a good clean smile, and tired eyes. Most of Europe had tired eyes these days. I asked her about the boy in the blue shirt. She said, 'Oh, yes. Him. He's a nice lad, isn't he? Minor wounds in the hand, but gut-shot – very messy when they brought him in.'

'Will he make it?'

She sized me up to see if the truth was in order. I don't know what decision she reached, because she said, 'Fifty-fifty. No better than that.'

'Here's hoping,' I told her.

'Here's hoping,' she agreed back.

Les had been earwigging. He said, 'At least you could have said, God willing, Charlie.'

'I don't think so. I don't think that I have that sort of pull.'

As we walked down the steps to *Kate*, Les started again.

'Well. That explains that, doesn't it?'

'What?' James and I said it together.

'Free love. That's why your Grace will go with anyone. She's obviously a Commie, just like the Wop says. They're all for free love, that lot. That's why we lost in Spain. The Anarchists were OK, but your Commie couldn't leave off fucking for long enough to win the war when he had the chance.'

James said, 'That could be oversimplifying it, old man.'

And I said, 'That's just what those artists we met in Paris were like. They weren't Communists.'

''course they were. Common knowledge. Reds to a man. Perhaps that Redcap Sergeant was one: didn't he ask you about free medical care in the future, sir?'

'Yes, Les; but that doesn't make him a Communist.'

'They must be bloody everywhere. We'll be finding them under our beds next.'

'Reds under the beds? I like that,' James told him. 'Do you mind if I write it down?'

Twenty-One

When we sat in the car the penny finally dropped.

I told them, 'That American Police Lieutenant Kilduff, and his goon Bassett – they weren't looking for me officially. They were after the three grand. It was going to be a quick hit: there and back in two days – I'll bet they didn't tell anyone where they were going. Now the Yanks think that they're AWOL.'

'Well done, Charlie,' James told me, and, 'now: lean back, close your eyes and answer the questions I am going to ask you, without actually thinking about them. Shoot from the lip.'

'OK.'

'Given that there's a bounty out for you, *who* wants your head stuffed, and mounted on the wall over the fireplace?'

'Peter Baker. Either him or Addy, Grace's mum.'

'Well done. Why?'

'Because although they've changed their minds, I haven't turned back even though the op's been scrubbed. They don't want Grace back now, after all.'

'OK. Why did they want you to find Grace and the baby, to bring them back in the first place?'

'To get an embarrassing situation back under control. And at first they thought the kid was mine. That was OK – more or less. Then someone did the arithmetic: I was out of the frame, but several others were in. That includes bold Sir Peter, and might well shaft his hopes of promotion if it gets out. That's right, isn't it?'

'Don't ask the questions, Charlie. That's my job.'

'Sorry.'

'Now tell us why they've changed their minds and want to stop you, now that you're close to bringing them both home.'

'Because now they know what we know, and what they *didn't* know when all this started. She's heading east, and has no intention of coming back. They can live with that. Their problem has been solved, but Grace doesn't know it. She's still running, isn't she?'

'I warned you, Charlie. Two days' CB.'

'Sorry, Boss.'

'That's all right. Congrats, by the way; I knew that you would work it out – you have that sort of mind.'

I opened my eyes, and looked first at Les, and then at James. I asked them, 'What do you think?'

Les didn't say anything. He looked as if he'd just flipped over a stone and found something unpleasant there. After a pause James said, 'It's all pathetically fucking domestic, isn't it?'

Les fished a fag out of his beret and lit up.

The odd thing was that it didn't occur to me that I should stop right there, get on Cliff's plane, and fly home. Albie had said that he'd got this far, and now he wanted to go all the way to the Big City. I was beginning to understand how he felt. It must have occurred to Les and the Major, but they didn't say anything about it immediately either. We were close. It was a strange feeling.

Kate was alongside one of those ungainly looking American armoured cars with six wheels: we leaned in on her bonnet looking as if we were having a war talk. I took the opportunity to fill a pipe, Les smoked a few of the strands of string he had that resembled cigarettes, and the Major produced a thin black American cigar from somewhere. What he said was, 'I suppose that it only makes sense to push on, even though none of us seems to be conspicuously keen on it today.'

'You're supposed to be in charge, sir,' Les told him.

'I'd rather have a day off,' he said, 'but there isn't anywhere to go.' None of us said anything for a while, then he used one of those *decision-made* voices. 'Let's push on, and stop at the first place we find that hasn't been raped by rude soldiery, and has a bar.'

I suppose that that is the sort of reasoning the officer corps is paid for.

Just as I was knocking out the bowl of my pipe on my heel, a flight of Tempests went low over us, howling out their customary bellows of rage. I don't know why I chose to remember it then, but the pipe I was cleaning was my first and only . . . and Grace had given it to me. She went all the

361

way up to London to get it from a shop with which her old man had connections. It was only months ago, but was like looking back a million years.

The bar was just after a crossroads on a worn crease in one of James's prewar maps. He thought that the village was called Corne, or *Korne*. There was plenty of that around: the big fields were a dusty emerald green, and not too many of them had been arseholed by tanks. There were probably ten or eleven buildings along each arm of the cross, but because the countryside around was wide and flat and firm – good tank country – the village wasn't strategically all that important. The war had simply driven around it. One of those nasty little Dingo scout cars had turned a fetching shade of black and was still smouldering in a field close to the road. Its tyres had melted. The acrid smell of hot rubber bit at our eyes. A building at the very centre of the hamlet had had its corner lopped off by an inexpertly driven tank, and three-quarters along the west–east axis a knocked-out Tiger tank sat forlornly inside the blackened house into which it had been reversed. Its gun barrel drooped almost to the road. It was a big bastard, but not as big as the Elephant in the Bois.

Les said, 'King Tiger. Handy-looking thing, isn't it?'

I said, 'It looks bloody lethal.'

'Would be if the engines ever worked, but they don't: they piss out oil everywhere.'

Everything else about the village seemed to be conspicuously unwarlike and normal. There were people in the streets, and some children chasing an old car tyre: they just ignored us. We can't have been the first Allied soldiers they'd seen: a tattered Union flag clung to a telegraph pole, kicking in the breeze, and there was an HD sign daubed large on the gable end of a low thatched cottage.

'Mind the kiddies,' the Major warned Les. 'It's not their war.'

'Yes, Major.'

I don't know why it had taken me that long to get it, but *that* was when they slipped back into role: whenever we were on parade with strangers. It was like a blink of an eye, and Les and James became the driver and his Major. They ran a very good act.

The bar was the furthest building into Germany, which is precisely where I would have put it if I didn't want to share my best beer with foreigners. There were round wooden tables with rustic wooden chairs on the pavement outside.

The Major said, 'OK. Pull up here, Les.'

'I'm not sure about that, Guv'nor. I'm feeling a bit exposed.'

'Trust me,' the Major told us. 'This one's going to be all right.'

When James told us to get out, Les told him, 'I should cocoa,' and backed *Kate* into a small alleyway between the bar and the nearest cottage.

So James got out alone. It was the first time I had sided openly with Les. James thrust his head into the car window on my side and glared at us both.

'Gutless little ponces. What's the point of my being a Major if you won't do what I tell you?' And he stalked off to sit at one of the round tables.

Les asked, 'I wonder what we did to deserve that?'

I asked, 'James been served yet?'

'No. But you *do* understand that you can stop it right here, and get off free? You do get that?'

'Yes. But I don't think I can.'

'Why not?'

'I heard somewhere that Red soldiers play football with new-born kids. Probably crap; but I can't stand the thought of wondering if that had happened for the rest of my life — after all, if she knows I'm after her, I've virtually been used to chase Grace into their arms.'

'She knows, Charlie. But it ain't your fault, an' you heard the man: she might go somewhere else. South.'

'That doesn't matter. I ought to catch up: at least give her the choice.'

'Even if the rest of your life ain't so long because of it?'

'Don't worry about me, Les. I'm going to live forever.'

'I hate soldiering with men like you; you know that? Wanna fag?' Then, ' 'allo. Here we go. Fat man in a pinny coming up to the Major. He's gonna get it in the guts or in the guts. I hate soldiering with him sometimes.'

'What's that mean? In the guts or in the guts?'

'Beer or a bullet. It's what he does sometimes. Takes some effing silly chance.'

The barman waddled off. I saw him from the back. He had a tremendous arse: gold medal winner. He reminded me of those cows I milked in Holland. When he came back it was with three stone jugs of what I presumed to be beer, and a plate of something.

'Pickled cabbage,' James told us as we joined him, 'oh, my windy ones. And steins of pale beer. If this is where you go out, at least you go with a beer in your hand. Did you ask him?' The last bit was to Les alone.

'Yes, Guv. He wants to go on.'

'Told you. Stubborn little bastard.'

'I'm here,' I told them. 'You don't have to talk about me as if I'm not.'

'Then bloody well say something sensible for a change,' James told me.

The cabbage was vile; but beggars and choosers, you know. Another stein of beer came along, and the cabbage tasted better. There was sun on our faces, but a heavy low line of grey cloud crouched along the horizon of Greater Germany. Hitler was not having a good day. Les frowned.

I asked, 'What's the matter?'

'Dunno, sir. Something. Maybe it all looks too good to be true. The proper war's only a few miles up the road.'

'Is that what the rumbling is? I thought that was a storm gathering over there.'

'Guns. Plenty of them. Some poor sod is getting theirs.'

We watched James walking to and fro with the publican. The latter had the air of a relieved man. James's little book was out, and whenever they stopped pacing he wrote in it. Once he stopped to shake his fountain pen: he must be running short.

Les told me, 'Look. If it ever goes bad on us, and the Major and I don't wake up one day, make sure that you get his notebook, and get it back to civilization with you.'

'Why? It's only got lists of food in it, hasn't it?'

'. . . and the names of the prominent local Nazis, and Communists, who their contacts were in Britain before the war, and where their money and valuables an' the stuff they stole have been stashed. He's very good at food, but not half bad at the rest of it by all accounts. People talk to him.'

'Cliff's like that, isn't he? Is that what makes a good intelligence officer, then?'

'Not pissing folk off, sir, is what makes a good intelligence officer. Major James says you're as good as the next thing your contact tells you.'

'I don't understand.'

'With respect, sir . . . anyone can get information out of somebody once; what counts is when that somebody comes back to you with more information because he wants to.'

'And James is good at that?'

'The best, sir. Why don't you look at that now?' He nodded at our glorious leader.

The publican was earnestly explaining something. He had his arm around James's shoulder. A thought occurred to me.

'It won't happen, Les, but if it did, who would I give the book to?'

'You'd find lots of folk after it. Our friend Tommo and the peerless Pole would be after you a bit sharpish, I expect. They could use it.'

'What about Cliff? Would he do?'

'Aye. 'appen 'e would.'

I emptied my stone jug. The publican must have had half an eye on us all the time, because as I replaced it on the table he looked towards the bar and waved his tablecloth. The woman who served the next two pots was clean and whole-some-looking, if not pretty. Her thick hair was a dull, burnished blonde colour. She reminded me of France, and the type of woman James went for. Then she smiled, and her missing teeth made me think of France again, and the family from Laon.

I asked Les, 'OK, so we're up at the Front, doing what you came out here to do. What happens next?'

Les shook his head as if I was a pupil who could never remember his lesson.

'The same as we've been doing all the way through Froggie Land, Cloggie Land and Belgium. Clocking intelligence and signalling it back: don't tell me you never noticed?'

'I noticed, but I thought you were practising for now,' I told him lamely. 'What happens next? Tonight?'

'Major'll fix us up with digs, or we'll sleep in the car. I think it's been harder for the Major to fix up the three of us, than when we were just the two; although he ain't said anything. He'll sit in the back of *Kate*, code up his notes, and tap them out back to base. Then we'll eat if we can find some-one with something to sell.'

'And if we can't there's always spam and beans in *Kate*'s boot?'

'There you are, Charlie. You were watching all the time.' I was back to Charlie again. Les must have been relaxing. God was in his Heaven, and all was well with our twenty square feet of the world.

James worked his magic. We finished the day with a thin mutton stew, and mountains of powdery potato. You had to ask yourself how the Highland Division had managed to miss that, when they swept through a couple of days earlier. It made you wonder what else they might have missed. I know that it made Les tense.

We billeted in a detached wooden barn behind the bar. The yard between was rough-cobbled from coaching days. All of the accommodation was on the first floor. The ground floor was open, as if the building was on stilts. There was a neatly stacked log lump, a few roughly squared bales of straw, and room beside them for *Kate* if her blunt radiator stuck out. After we had eaten I noticed that Les went outside to her to run his maintenance checks. I took him out a piece of black bread and lard, pressed on us as a treat. He was working by the light of a small shuttered oil lamp sitting on *Kate*'s bonnet.

'You all right?' I asked him.

'No. Twitchy.'

'Any idea why?'

'If I had, I'd tell you and the Major, and we'd be out of 'ere, wouldn't we?'

'I'm sorry. I'll leave you to it.'

He had her plugs out, and was washing each one carefully in a small tin of petrol.

'No. Don't mind me. I get like this sometimes when we're

near the Front. I got this feeling for weaknesses in the line; I don't know how.'

'You feel that now?'

'Yeah, Charlie, and I've felt it every time Jerry has come back at us and we've been sent scarpering.'

I sat alongside him on *Kate*'s running board, filled and lit my pipe. If I didn't get some tobacco soon I would be suffering.

'What do you want me to do?'

'Make sure the Major knows I'm serious — sometimes he treats me just like I'm an old woman — and have everything you don't need for the night stowed in *Kate*. Just in case we leave in a hurry. That OK?'

'You're in charge.' I punched him lightly on the arm. The petrol slopped on his trousers. 'Sorry.'

It was dark by seven. The inn didn't have any other customers: probably because we were there. James helped the owners with the washing up, and gave the old man a paper that made him Chief of Police, or Master of the Municipal Sewer or something. There were a lot of bows and smiles after that, and the deal was sealed with a glass of syrupy, clear spirit that tasted of raspberries. I wasn't that keen: it stuck to my teeth. James had met it before. I noticed that he tossed it right to the back of his mouth. Then he wiped his lips on the back of his hand. The hotelier poured us another round of the thick stuff in little glasses, but made it plain that that was the last. He wiped a fat finger around the neck of the bottle to catch a drop, and put it in his mouth. We were sitting around a small fire on smaller three-legged stools in the small bar. Our landlady's cheeks were rosy: that must have been the heat. James was showing off for her. Were these people the enemy? It seemed ridiculous, but a week ago they *had* been, and if God's Grey Jerries came back, they would be again. Did Winston and Adolf ever sit with their feet to the fire, and wonder how it had ever come to this?

The crude sleeping accommodation above the first floor of the barn was a single room, entered through a hole in the floor from a wide wooden stair. Long ago the animal feed would have been stored there. Our hosts had built a simple raised sleeping platform across about a third of it, and a stack of thin pallet mattresses stood in a corner. A heavy rope hung along one wooden wall; over it about twenty things like grubby eiderdowns were draped. There was a wash hand basin with a rust stain in one corner, and a toilet partitioned off with plywood in the other.

The woman showed us around the facilities. She made up one bed by pulling one of the straw mattresses onto another and dropping a couple of the quilts on them. James tried his luck by pushing her face-first onto them, rolling her over and lifting her skirts. He can't have believed his luck when her legs opened so easily. I thought they looked plump and white and welcoming. Then she rolled over again, and gave him a haymaker around the side of his head that laid him on the floor alongside her. Then she offered him a big hand on the end of an arm the size of a ham, to haul him back onto his feet. Definitely nothing frying tonight.

When he asked, 'No hard feelings, old girl?' she plainly didn't understand, but laughed, so that seemed to be all right.

I asked her, 'What's this for?' and when she looked blank, used my hand to indicate the room we were in: you could have slept about thirty in it.

'Jugend,' was all that she would tell us. Then in accented English, 'Like boys. Boy Scouts.'

Les smiled, and nodded a thank you at her, but what he actually said, still smiling, was, 'Boy Scouts my arse! She's talking about the Hitler Youth I think.'

It didn't stop us sleeping.

Until about six, I suppose.

Twenty-Two

I was sleeping nearest the large hole in the floor through which the steps climbed, so I was the first that the big woman stumbled over. As she fell on me — which was like being knelt on by a horse — my arms went naturally to her waist: but this was no romantic assignation. She cursed, which I failed to understand, and pushing me away whispered hoarsely, '*Schnell, schnell,*' a couple of times. Then, summoning up most of her English vocabulary, blurted, 'The Boche are coming. *Schnell!*'

Part of me was thinking, *This is ridiculous, you* are *the Boche!* Another part was scrambling out from under her as quickly as I could manage it. That wasn't so easy. Les and the Major were quicker. They crowded the room's one small window that looked to the east. I joined them. The sky was dark grey, and shot with paler grey, and pale yellow streaks. There was just enough light to see the dark shapes, maybe about a mile away, moving in the fields — and a couple of small lights on the road. I learned quickly that there was no chance of beating Les and the Major when they were in running-away mode.

No contest. James actually managed to pause as he passed the woman, to plant a peck on her cheek. His turn of speed impressed me. She was still smiling as I tumbled past her.

I've explained that *Kate* was more or less at the foot of the stairs? For once we operated more or less as a practised team. James went straight into the back of *Kate*, Les behind the wheel, whilst I got to the front and swung the handle. The engine caught about one and a half turns on, and I scrambled in alongside Les as she moved out of the barn.

I suppose that there was always the temptation to race off west as fast as we bloody well could, but Les had done this before remember? He kept his head. Damned good job: I was gibbering by then. *Kate* had a fairly quiet motor: Les put this down to a big silencer, which he called a muffler. He nosed us slowly back up the alley alongside the inn, and did a forty-five-degree turn to port – that meant we were moving away from the men in grey who wanted their country back. He left the lights off, and moved us as fast as he dared without revving the old dear. That just left the lights on the road to worry about, and he reckoned that we could outrun them if the push came to a shove.

There's that Blake poem, isn't there? 'Tyger, tyger burning bright, in the forests of the night'? It was the wrong bloody day to forget it. As we came gently up to the section of housing into which we had seen the Tiger tank backed the day before, two small lights came on; narrow yellow bars across the road. From somewhere behind them came the ghastly clattering sound of a big diesel trying to fire up, and the gun barrel we had seen before almost stooped to the road began jerkily to lift itself. It was like watching a dead dinosaur come back to life. I began to dribble with fear as the bastard started to lurch spasmodically out of the front living room in which it had been parked.

James hissed, 'Right.'

Between two houses on the right was another alleyway. The question was, could we get into it before the bastard spotted us? The answer turned out to be *not quite*. The Tiger was turning to face us as we turned off the main road away from it. I reached for Les's Sten, which was on the floor between us. He had time to put his hand over it, and snarl, 'Don't be so wet!'

All James said was, 'Quickly. Forget the rest of them.'

I thought that we'd made it in time. The beast was three-quarters on to us as we turned into the black alley. Les knew differently. He growled, 'Fuck it!' and put his foot down.

This was an unmade road, and we were on a deeply rutted surface between house and garden walls. *Kate* bounced. I hit my head on her ceiling. If the big T was after us, and got into the alley before we could get out of the other end, then it was all over: even I was educated enough in the ways of artillery to work that one out. Les had to slow down for a turn at the end of it. We were at a T junction facing open fields, with a rough road running around the village stretching to the west and east. East was no good to us; it was full of unfriendly Jerries with guns. Les turned left and west. As he did that I looked over my shoulder and back up the alley. It was lit up with a bright flash that illuminated the house walls, and instantaneously the field beside us erupted. Then we were round. Les screamed; it was noises, not words. My teeth were chattering. I could hear James heavy-breathing like a man having sex. Les said, 'Fuck it!' again.

That was because the problem was the same. If the Tiger emerged from the alley and caught us on the open road, or in the fields less than half a mile from him, then we'd had it. It all depended on us being able to turn left again, back up into the village, before the Tiger came out of the lane we'd just exited. In theory we could travel faster, but not necessarily over a road as terrible as this. Les put *Kate*'s lights on: time for subterfuge was over, and besides, this next alley narrowed as we climbed it. I picked up Les's Sten. This time he didn't stop me. Les was scraping *Kate*'s wings on the house walls: she bounced like Tigger. I couldn't stop looking backwards for the great tank. We must have been three-quarters of the way up the alley before I saw him, and I thought it was all over.

But he made a mistake: it was a tight turn, and he hadn't made allowances for his gun barrel sticking out ahead of him, which didn't make the corner. He stuffed it into the garden wall. He had to back up, and swing again. He fired his main gun at us again as we turned out into the main street. The shell passed a foot behind the back window and at right angles to us, shrieking like an express train. I don't know where it went. You have no idea how quickly the mind works in situations like that. As soon as we turned back onto the main street I knew that we would make it: the Tiger couldn't possibly get all the way up that narrowing alley. Then there was one of those *Hey, that's not fair*, moments. There was some fairly slow popping, which I didn't at first recognize as the firing of a medium machine gun, and *Kate* shuddered. James said, 'Ow!' or made some noise like that, Les just gave a sharp intake of breath, and I felt a sudden dull pain in my upper right arm as the windscreen disintegrated away from us, and the window alongside me exploded.

Les said it for the third time, 'Oh, *fuck* it!'

I leaned out of the car window, looked back and saw a motorcycle combination about twenty yards behind us. It had yellow lights dancing over the sidecar. That was the bastard in there shooting at us. I gave him back a full mag of the Sten held loose with my southpaw, and screamed aloud when he suddenly turned left at speed, and hit a house front head-on. The best sound in the world is the smack of motorcycle and flesh against good old German stone.

Then it was just *Kate*'s noise, and the wind racing past my open window. It was getting light. How long had all that taken? Not much longer than it takes to write. I put the Sten on the floor. My whole body was shaking. That's when I saw for the first time that Les hadn't any trousers or boots on. Behind me James gave a quiet chuckle. Les soon joined him. Then I did, too.

Eventually Les asked, 'Major? He get you?'

'Just a graze, I think, along my thigh. It's a bit sticky, but there's nothing broken and nothing pumping. What about you?'

'In the arse again: I'm sitting in blood. Then it hit the seat frame before it went out through the glass. I think it got Charlie on the way.'

I realized that my upper right arm was numb. When I touched it I found a tear in my jacket, and there was some squishy stuff between my jacket and my shirt sleeve. James asked, 'How far back to Löningen?'

Les said, 'Thirty miles odd. With a bit of luck we'll run into friends before then. Some Canadians were moving out behind us. They could have a field medical team with them.'

'I can smell petrol,' James said. 'I don't know if they got the main tank or one of the jerrycans in the boot.'

'I'm not bloody well stopping to find out, sir,' Les told him. 'Not until there's ten miles between us, anyway.'

'Wouldn't have dreamed of asking you, old chap. Stop at the first thing that looks like a nurse. I think we need a maintenance team. Do you really think that one bullet got all three of us?'

'Pretty certain, sir. You all right, Charlie? You're pretty quiet.'

'Yeah. Fine. My arm feels numb. Will it hurt later?'

'Ask me again in an hour, sir. Try to stay awake.'

Les was doing a job on us, calling us both by the regulation *sir*. Don't let that kid you: he was the one in charge now. James said, 'I'm still worried about that bullet. Do you think they have new homing bullets, and that one went for each of us in turn, one after the other?'

It was such a stupid idea that we didn't answer him, so he mused, '. . . bloody magic bullet. I'd write that down if I could find my book, and *Kate* stopped leaping about.'

Les sounded almost fatherly.

'You write it down later, sir,' he told him.

The first thing that looked like a nurse was a nurse. We stopped at a checkpoint wooden barrier part of the way back to Löningen. We were pushed off the road to let a column of tanks go forward. A lovely khaki Bedford ambulance was on the other side of the road. A driver and a couple of nurses were enjoying fags alongside it. I got out of *Kate*, and stood upright by leaning against her bonnet. They laughed at Les, and pointed, when he climbed out, although men without trousers can't have been that unfamiliar to them. Then, when he turned away from them to help James out of the back, they must have seen the black blood caked on his legs and buttocks. That was when they stopped laughing, and ran between the tanks to help us. I bent at the waist to lay my head on *Kate*'s warm bonnet, and went to sleep.

The next morning I found a heavy machine-gun bullet in *Kate*, in the wheel well where my feet had been. It was an odd shape: it must have been tumbling and running out of steam as it struck me, because although it tore a gap in my leather jacket, it failed to break my skin. The squishiness I felt the night before was the pulpy bruise on my upper arm. It hurt like hell. They stitched up a small hole in Les's backside, and found him some trousers. They were bandsmen's pants in navy blue, with a red stripe down each outside seam. James wasn't pleased I found the bullet: it undermined the magic bullet story – the one he was already telling anyone who asked. If there was a bullet in the car, what took *Kate*'s windscreen out?

Later Les said to me, 'That bullet was tumbling when it reached you? Yeah?'

'Yes, Les.'

'Then it could have clipped you, blown out the screen without enough energy left to actually pierce it?'

'So it goes through *Kate*'s tank, along the Major's leg, through your bum, bounces off the seat frame, bounces off my arm and tears my jacket, hits the windscreen, breaks it, hits the door window, breaks it, and then bounces back into the car? Is that it?'

'I think so, Charlie.'

'Is this important?'

'Yeah. It's one of the stories you tell afterwards. Know what I mean?'

I didn't. This was still my first war. I hadn't had an afterwards. I said, 'Yes,' because a future was not something I wanted to talk about.

James hobbled up on a light cane stick he'd borrowed from someone, milking it for all he was worth. He said, 'I heard that the British tank squadron that passed through us last night got a bit of a doing in a valley the other side of Korne. I've got a feeling I know that valley. The Yanks are coming through in half an hour. Your pal Albie could be with them.'

He was. Well, most of him was, anyway.

It was a nasty flat-looking tank. All tanks are nasty tanks. As soon as someone opens a door you get that smell from them like a partly blocked latrine. The name *Marlene* had been painted out, and replaced with the words *past caring* and a sloppy exclamation mark. A forward hatch swung open, and thumped back against the armoured decking. It sounded like the tolling of a large church bell. A head popped out of the hatch, like a rabbit out of a magician's hat. The head was small, had brush-cut black hair, olive skin and slitty little eyes. I'm sure that we mustn't call them slitty little eyes these days.

The Major said, 'I think I see a chink in your armour, Albie.' When no one laughed he added, 'Sorry; I couldn't resist that.'

The oriental said, 'That's very funny. I haven't heard that one before.'

Albie was sitting on the turret turned towards us, with his legs dangling over the side. He had found a grey German officer's cap with a shiny black peak from somewhere. He said, 'He's not a Chink.'

I said, 'He must be a Jap then. Aren't we supposed to be at war with his lot?'

'Loyal Japanese. He's Japanese American: we got thousands of them. He must be all right because RKO sent him to me. He's a genuine film star. He's been in *Charlie Chan* films.'

'*My* name's Charlie,' I told the olive-skinned gnome. 'What parts did you have?'

'In most of the films I got to say *Yeth, Master*, or, *No, Master*. Then I died.'

He had a great, soft speaking voice that made you smile.

'I saw those bits,' I told him, 'and I thought you died very well. I thought that you had a great future in dying.'

Albie said, 'So did Uncle Sam. That's why he sent him to

me. My people are always dying. I asked for a professional, for a change.'

Then I asked Albie, 'What's his name?'

'*Ito*. We call him *Hero*; geddit?'

'Sorry?'

'*Hero Ito*. Hiro Ito. Isn't he King of all the Nips, or something?'

Then I noticed his eyepatch.

Les was faster than me. He asked, 'Sir? Albie?'

'Yes, driver?'

'What the fuck happened to your eye, sir?'

'I bashed it against the 50-cal magazine. The Cutter said that he'd take it away for me, because it would never work again. Didn't hurt that much.'

'Where is he?'

'Round here somewhere.'

As we strolled off James offered, 'You don't think that the Cutter is collecting enough body parts to assemble his own American, do you?'

He finished the sentence with a thunderous great sniff, which rumbled around his sinuses like the early phase of an earthquake.

I suppose that we now had the excuse to jack it in if we had wanted it, but in my case the choice was either going on to Bremen with them, or going to Bremen on my own. Part of me believed that Cliff had only set me off in pursuit of Grace because he thought I'd cock it up: he'd never thought I'd catch her – but at the same time he could turn to the Bakers and say, *We tried*. Now I was this close I wasn't going to stop, even if they wanted me to.

We waited for a day. We cleaned out *Kate*'s cabin, and Les bartered petrol for a replacement front screen. It came from a Vauxhall, so it didn't quite fit, but it was better than nowt. We couldn't do anything to the passenger side window, so Les stretched a cut-out flour sack over it, which he wedged in place with wooden pegs. He used two more tapered ones to seal the bullet holes in the petrol tank, tapping them firmly into place with a wooden mallet.

'Navy taught me,' was all he'd say about it.

When I told Les that they didn't have to stay with me he laughed. Then he said, 'I've a bigger pain in the arse now than you, Charlie, and I think that the Major wants to stick it out. Anyway something's gone wrong with our comms system, and I think he's keen to find out what.'

'I didn't know.'

'He's not likely to tell you, is he, sir?'

'What is the problem?'

'It seems like the stores he calls forward don't always get sent up; an' other things do instead. Some bastard down in the base store is altering his shopping list.'

James always had difficulty in saying nothing. Instead, he said:

> *'I keep six honest serving-men,*
> *(They taught me all I knew);*
> *Their names are What and Why and When*
> *And How and Where and Who . . .'*

I've told you about Les. He chipped in with:

> *'I send them over land and sea,*
> *I send them east and west;*
> *But after they have worked for me*
> *I give them all a rest.'*

Then he added, 'That was Mr Kipling, weren't it?'

James said, 'Very good, Les. Where did you learn that?'

'It was one of my dad's favourite pieces.'

They were just stringing me along, so I played the part in life God had fitted me out for: the dumb laddie.

'What does all that mean, Major?'

'It means, sonny, that somebody is rattling my chain. And I'm going to find out who, how and why. *Capiche?* So Raffles and I shall be with you for the time being. Do you have a problem with that, Pilot Officer?'

'No, sir. You're in charge.'

'Glad to have settled that.' He was unusually waspish; I suppose that his leg might have been hurting. I know that my bloody arm was.

Les asked, 'What about me?'

James grinned.

'Bollocks. You can be in charge, too. My second-in-command. Charlie can be the cabin boy.'

'Thanks,' I told them. 'I don't suppose that either of my COs would care to accompany me to a Canadian field kitchen a couple of fields away? They appear to have set up some kind of a bar alongside it. It has a stuffed moose's head on the ridge pole over the door flaps.'

That night we slept in the barn at Korne again, but weren't disturbed. In the morning our hosts turned out to see us away. Les gave them a couple of good dollars, and a handful of forged deutschmarks. The old man put a hand on my bad arm, and indicated the road we were to take. It eventually curved down into a valley, and disappeared. His wife gave Les a fat, wet kiss. James pretended not to notice.

Twenty-Three

It was a strong flat valley, and once in it another one of those arrow-straight roads ran from one end to the other. I couldn't remember who had won the argument about who built the damned things, but they were everywhere. The steep wall of hills to our right was densely clothed with pines. Between them and the road were fields of late winter feeding. That was good defensive country. James said that the northern Jerry fed his livestock on kale. I was partial to the irony taste of kale myself. James said that the first time German POWs were offered kale in England they refused it on the ground that it was animal food, and complained to the Red Cross.

The valley ridge to the west was flatter and closer, and clothed with good grazing grass. I could see a hill, or a further ridge, beyond it: perhaps it hid another valley. We seemed to be heading towards a distant forest of deciduous trees, without an obvious way through, but James and Les seemed to know what they were doing, and they didn't seem to be in a hurry . . . which pissed me off a bit. James took his eyes from the landscape, or his map from time to time, to scribble in his notebook.

When he said, 'Stop. Stop here, please,' in majorly tones, it did occur to me to wonder why. I couldn't see anything of significance for miles. Bollocks. He was away with the fairies again.

He said, 'Let's walk for ten minutes. All of us. It will do the pair of you good, instead of sitting around all day.'

Les muttered something about leaving someone to mind *Kate*, and volunteering himself for the duty. James said what I had been thinking.

'Bollocks.' Then, 'Who's in charge?'

I kept my mouth shut for once.

It was just as I had thought. As we moved gingerly on foot up to the west and north we were on dark, fine grass; like the South Downs around Hastings. There was thyme mixed in among it. We walked the walk, of course; James set a powerful pace as if he was in a hurry to get somewhere. Les was about six feet behind him, loping along with his Sten bouncing against his hip, and me a good ten feet behind him. We probably looked odd from a distance, if some Jerry sniper had a bead on us. James was taking a chance on the area being pacified, and I didn't mind him taking chances, as long as it wasn't with me. The ridge, which was our valley's west rim, simply looked into another: a shallower and more serious affair. It was more serious because there were dead tanks all over it — some square Brits, and some American light jobs. The Yanks looked low and fast and racy. They looked just as dead as the British Comets close to them. Les knew their flash, and said, 'Fife and Forfar Yeomanry. Scotch jobs. They have had a bit of a doing, haven't they?'

I looked quickly for Albie's *past caring* among the Americans. No sign.

James told us, 'I knew it! There was once a battle here.'

Les gave him the *If only you knew how pitiful you are* look.

'Would never have known that, sir.'

I added, 'No, nor would I.'

'Arseholes, the pair of you. Products of failed second-rate schools. I mean a *real* battle – swords against spears. This is where about eighteen hundred Jerries stopped a complete Roman legion dead in its tracks. One of the histories says that a year after, a man looking at this hillside from the tree line down there could be dazzled by the sun reflecting back from a carpet of white skulls. They weren't Jerries back then, of course, merely barbarians.'

'You're sure about this, sir? You ain't just making it up?'

'Absolutely sure. I've been wanting to visit here for years.'

'That's what you said about Agincourt and Waterloo, sir.' That was Les.

'When were you there?' I asked him. I was interested in spite of myself.

'Last month,' he told me. 'The Major has this thing about battlefields. He prefers the old ones to the new ones.'

'I'm not going to complain, Les. Bloody sight less dangerous.'

'Not always, Charlie. Look at this place. A good place to fight is always a good place to fight: different weapons, that's all.'

387

James had wandered off a bit, towards one of the Brit tanks. It had a great blackened hole where something nasty had gone in between the drive wheels. The track on that side had been thrown. All of its hatches were open, so unless it had been robbed in the last couple of days, some of the crew had got out. James abruptly lost interest.

'Let's go down there. That's where most of the fighting took place.'

There was the valley floor. It wasn't as deep as the valley from which we'd climbed, and followed a meandering stream fringed by bare trees. They were coming into bud and leaf. The earth seemed disturbed in a narrow line parallel to them; as if it had been ploughed. I wasn't sure that I wanted to find out why. The knocked-out tanks all seemed to be facing down towards it, as if they had come along the rim that we had walked over, and then turned down in open formation. James set off down through the ankle-high grass. Les hadn't the heart to let him go alone, and I hadn't the courage to leave them to it. James turned once on the short descent, to grin back at us. He was animated. Like a child.

And that's what *they* were like: like children.

The disturbed earth was a hastily dug trench. My dad would have done a better job than that. There were fifteen or sixteen dead children chucked around in it. It wasn't deep because they had tried to sink it too close to the line of scrubby trees, and had got into the roots. Don't worry, I won't go all soft on you. Tommo told me long ago: bad things happen: that's what wars are for – fade scene. They were soldiers, anyway. Little soldiers. Kids in their mid-teens away for their first and last adventure. They were dressed in bits and pieces of soldier suits, just like me and Les. Not only that, but the empty cartridge cases scattered around, and the fucked-up tanks on the hillside, seemed to indicate that they'd put up a hell of a fight before the tank squadrons had overrun them. I could see the crushed and churned areas of the makeshift trench, and the gaps in the trees where the tanks had crossed them. Some of the bodies were smashed. I thought that they looked like dolls tossed aside by a bored playmate.

James's voice was a thousand miles away. No one had ever sounded less like a Major. He said, 'Stupid, but I suddenly feel sick.'

It was too true, and too trite to be worth a response. We walked along the scarred earth, slowly, like visitors to a museum studying mildly novel exhibits. At the far end of the trench it fell back into the tree line. A boy who might have been fourteen, one of the youngest fighters there, was lying back out of the trench, as if he had been caught as he stood up. A grubby white handkerchief fluttered in a branch close to him. You never know. One of his arms was thrown back above his head as if grasping for the skittering cloth. His other hand, his left one, rested on his chest. His stomach cavity was as open as his dull eyes. So was his mouth. What had his last sound been like? There were flies. There are always flies, even when temperatures are too low to give them more than a day's life.

A boy of no more than five sat beside the corpse, his dirty little hand resting in the hand the corpse had placed on its chest. His little legs dangled in the trench. His head was bowed, chin resting on his chest, his back to us. He had a camel-coloured coat – I remember that coat – with a dark brown soft collar. He was as motionless as all of the others, and because he didn't move as the flies crawled on him, we knew what we were going to see but could not help ourselves. One of those nightmares you can't switch off.

The reality was worse than that.

I was closest to him. As I came up to him, and steeled myself to look, he moved. That was more shocking than anything else. He turned his head to look at me. His brown eyes were huge, in a small face as round as the moon. That was when Les said, 'Fuck it.'

None of us attempted to free him from the corpse he held on to. We sat on the grass in front of him, and spoke as if he wasn't there. James started it.

'Poor little sod. What do you think?'

'He won't make it on his own. He'll starve out here.' That was Les, replying. I wished that he hadn't. Then nothing; as if they had nothing to say. Then Les, as if there hadn't been a gap in the conversation.

'We can't bury them. It will take all bloody day.'

'I'll get some Pioneers up here. Don't worry, they'll be here in a couple of days.' James again.

I asked them, 'What about the kid?'

Then nothing again. What the bloody hell was the matter with them all of a sudden? Then Les, 'It would be kinder if this didn't go on for him, Charlie. Look at him. He can't even find his own food.'

'You mean, kill him, don't you?'

James wouldn't meet my eye. Les said, 'Look on it as being kinder.' He had almost repeated himself. Then, 'He wouldn't be here if he had anyone else.' The odd thing is that his voice sounded almost tender.

James coughed. I think that that was to hide his embarrassment. He said, 'Kinder. And pragmatic. You're right; he has no one to look out for him.'

Germany had bled with that argument for the last twelve years. I couldn't understand them any more. I said, 'Yes he has. He has us, for the time being. Us. Me.'

At least Les would look me in the eye. When he spoke he was almost whispering.

'Charlie, Charlie.' He was shaking his head, as if I was a stubborn child. I noticed for the first time that he had that horrible black-bladed knife in his hand. 'Will you fight me over it?'

'Yes. If you make me.'

Then nothing again. Then James: 'Why?'

'I've chased halfway across Europe to try to rescue a woman and a baby, haven't I? Maybe I'm not doing too well at it, but tell me where's the sense of saving one child, if I murder another one on the way to doing it?'

James said, '. . . or look the other way while someone else does the killing?'

'That too. People have been looking the other way in this country for too sodding long,' I told him. I saw Les drop his right shoulder, and said, 'Les, if you make a move towards the kid, I'll jump you. You'll have to kill me to get him.

I promise you.' I don't know what I sounded like, but I felt as if I was going to burst into tears. It was one of those moments. Les was suddenly like a Frog or an Eyetie, because he shrugged as if it didn't matter.

Nothing again. No one moved. Not a sound: then somewhere a bird was singing, and James sighed, 'Les is right, Charlie, but I'll pull rank for you. Just this once. I'll do that if you promise to dump the kid at the next village we get to.'

'All right. Fine.'

James asked, 'Les?'

Les looked away from us. Somewhere into the distance. His hands were empty. 'Aye,' he said, and, 'OK.' I wish I could say that he sounded relieved, but I'm not so sure.

The kid didn't speak as I lifted him away from the corpse, and carried him away from whatever he had seen there. He weighed nothing. His coat sleeve was stiff with someone else's blood. James had some sort of pidgin conversation with him as we climbed away again over grass that shone like dark-green glass. It was something like, '*Muter?*' The kid shook his head. James thought that he hadn't understood, and asked him again. The kid shook his head again. James realized that he meant *no*.

'*Fader?*' The kid shook his head.

'*Bruder?*' The kid squirmed in my arms suddenly. I almost stumbled. He pointed back over my shoulder.

Les spoke for the first time since his grudging *OK*. He said, 'Don't worry kid. We'll see they look after your brother,' and he touched the boy's cheek and hair. Then he walked ahead of me.

*

Back on the low west ridge of our first valley we could see *Kate* down on the road, and something else behind her. We all crouched. Les swung his Sten forward. He grunted, 'Company.' Then, 'Anyone got any ideas?'

I shook my head. James said, 'Your speciality, old boy. I'll leave it to you this time.'

It was another sign that James and I had been at different kinds of school. My lot would have called that a cop-out. Les turned to me, and grinned. I had noticed before that when he bared his teeth they had a feral look about them.

'Keep the kid's head down. If it goes wrong and you get hit, try to fall on him.' I think that Les always had this urge to action. No matter how low he got, anticipation of loosing off a mag or two from his Sten always lifted his spirits.

James asked, 'What about me?'

Les said, 'I was thinking of an open-order advance, if that's all right with you, sir? Give me about twenty yards on the left; then give me ten yards start, and watch where yer step. You move off to their right. If you hear me yell, hit the deck; I've better long sight than the pair o' you.' And, '. . . and you look after your new son,' he told me. His grin told me something else. It told me that he suddenly found my situation amusing.

He asked the Major, 'Time to go?'

James nodded, and Les lifted up and took a step to the left. He was correct. I wasn't as long-sighted as he was. I could see something small up *Kate*'s derrière, and maybe a dark figure on the road. Maybe the figure waved. I had about five minutes during which to watch them as they worked their way carefully down, moving further apart: they had done this before. It showed. The further they were from where I crouched, the deeper in grass they seemed to sink, until eventually they appeared to be wading waist-deep. All that time I reflected on the decision I had made about the boy who was hugging deep into my neck: if I hadn't stuck my oar in, there would have been three men moving down to *Kate*: not two. Anyway, it was sweat for nothing. As Les passed the halfway point he suddenly rose up and waved to the Major, and waved to me. It was clear that he was calling us down. By the time I got down to him with the kid it was clear to me why. I still hate those bloody awful little Volkswagens. It was the maths teacher who'd given Les a speeding ticket, days before. His uniform was still immaculate. The shiny black peak of his Toy Town helmet was still shiny black. I don't know what had passed between them before I was up to them, but I heard the policeman say, in his clipped English, 'I do not suppose that you have paid your penalty yet?'

Les told him, 'I don't suppose I have. We haven't been anywhere near a manned Police Office. We were at a place named Korne, but your Panzers chased us out again.'

'Korne was ever a lawless place. Anyway, the Panzers have gone away – before they ran out of gas. Are you going on to Bremen, sir?'

I don't know why Les answered him. Force of habit, I suppose.

'Yes. Eventually.'

'You will probably find a Police Office there.'

'I suppose that we will. What about you?'

'I suppose that I will stay here. At present the people need a policeman; and when they no longer need a policeman, they may need a teacher of arithmetic.'

The Major asked him, 'Am I allowed to wish you good luck?'

'Only after you have told me why you are stealing that child.' He nodded my way.

It was my turn, 'I'm not. We found him. There are loads more of them over the hill, but they are all dead. How many more fourteen-year-old soldiers do you have left to fight your war for you?'

There was a flash of something behind his eyes. He said, 'How many do you need?' Then, 'I wondered what had happened to them.'

'They fought our Panzers. It looks as if they did very well.'

'Some of them were once my students.'

Les sniffed. He said, 'So maybe they won't need a maths teacher after all.'

The copper didn't seem to have much more to say. He came to attention, and gave a terribly smart salute. His vehicle left a trail of thin, blue smoke which was blown away on the breeze.

Les told me, 'You missed your chance. You could have given him the kid.'

'He didn't want him, did he? Otherwise he would have asked. Do you think the kid'll mind if I put him down? He's getting a weight.'

I put the child down. He stayed by me, but shuffled from

foot to foot, looking very uncomfortable. I tried again: I asked Les, 'What's the matter with him? Can't he stand still?'

Les laughed. He took the kid's hand, and walked with him to the edge of the road. The first dandelions were beginning to show in the margins. Les unbuttoned himself, and pissed on them. The kid looked on with obvious interest, then pulled up his short trouser leg and did the same. The stream was so long and so strong that I wondered how long he'd been holding himself in. When Les walked him back to me the kid studied me for a couple of minutes. There was no malice in that look, but nevertheless he went back over to Les, and held his hand up. Les had no choice. He asked James, ''ow far to our next stop, sir?'

'Don't quite know, old chap. Twenty miles or more. I seem to have made a bit of a mess of today, haven't I?'

''ow far back to Korne, then; for the third time?'

'Ditto. But about ten miles I'd guess. Why?'

'That publican and his missus. They seemed like good people: we could leave the kid with them.'

'Good thinking that man. Your Mr Kipling always said that the NCO was the backbone of the British Army.'

'I'm not one, Major. I'm a humble private soldier.'

'I could always promote you.'

Les positively twinkled. He said, 'And I would turn you down. I can do without extra responsibility.'

Les said, 'Have you ever had one of them nightmares where you're stuck in a maze, and can't get out: every time you reach the way out you're back where you started?'

I was driving, and the kid was cuddled up asleep on Les's lap, which would be a problem if he needed to go for his Sten in a hurry. James was in the back working on his lists: occasionally he'd give a snort as if he had discovered something.

'Yes, Les. I think so.'

'I think that this is one of them. Every time we head away from Korne we end up coming back. Like bloody yo-yos.'

'Or boomerangs.'

'Yeah. Do you think that we died a couple of days ago, and this is some kind of Never Never Land we'll never never escape from?'

Cliff had used similar words months ago. Never Never Land was always close to your tongue in '45. It was one of those puns that meant anything. James looked up and grunted. Time for an upper-ranks contribution.

'I can think of people I'd less like to get stuck there with.'

Les told him, 'There was something the matter with the grammar of your last sentence, sir. Not up to your usual standard. Try again please.' Then he said to me, 'Slow her down, Charlie; Korne's over the next hump.'

We had climbed up again, out of the valley that time forgot, and for the second time in several days arrived at precisely the point from which we had set off. James hugged the publican, and called him *Otto* as if they were old friends. Otto's wife hugged Les, and then hugged the kid and hoisted him over her shoulder, and the kid hugged her back, so all was going more or less to plan. James began to explain to them what was going on. They were speaking Kraut, and too

397

fast and too gutturally for my expanding vocabulary. Occasionally I picked out the word *Charlie*, and whenever I did they all stopped talking, and looked at me. A couple of times the looks were soft and emotional, and a couple of times they were stern and hard. What the fuck had I done this time?

I asked James, 'What's going on?'

He said, 'Frieda will tell you.'

The woman gave the kid over to Otto as if she was tossing over a small sack of vegetables. Then she came up to me and hugged me. We were more or less the same height, so that was all right. Then she kissed me on both cheeks and on the mouth. Then she stood and gobbled at me like a turkey for five minutes. I couldn't work out if I was receiving a benediction, or being ticked off. I would describe her as a fluid speaker rather than a fluent one. The fluid was a haze of spittle droplets that seemed to hang in the air between us. Halfway through she suddenly fished down the front of my shirt, and pulled out my worn RAF identity discs, and paused to copy my name and service number onto a small order pad, with a stubby licked pencil. Eventually I got the kisses on the cheeks again, before she curtsied, and stepped back to stand alongside her husband.

'Didn't understand a word of it,' I said to her, and smiled. What else was I supposed to say?

James looked very shifty. He said, 'Had to come to a compromise, you know?'

'No I don't. What have you let me in for?'

'She'll take the kid for the time being,' he said, 'providing we pay for its upkeep.'

'That's OK.'

'There's more.'

'Tell me the worst,' I asked him.

'For some reason she thinks the kid's from somewhere called Brittel. I think that's about a hundred miles away; further to the east. She says they'll contact someone they know in Brittel. If they find one of his relations they'll pass him back.'

'That sounds OK, too.'

'They don't want an extra mouth to feed permanently.'

'What does that mean?'

'If they can't find anybody, they are going to dump him outside the nearest Army base, with a label around his neck bearing the service number and name of one of us. We'll get him back.'

'And you said she could have mine?'

'That seems fair.' That was Les putting his oar in. 'It was you that talked us into lifting the little bugger in the first place. No point giving him to me. I've plenty of my own.'

'What about James?'

'The Major's a confirmed bachelor. He'd never manage. Nah; if it comes down to it Charlie, he'll be much better off with you.'

'He'll have to find me first.'

'Isn't that what your girl Grace said to you? Isn't that how you ended up here in the first place?'

I said, 'Fuck the lot of you.'

I broke my golden rule. When we walked back to *Kate* I couldn't resist having a quick look over my shoulder. Frieda had the boy again. She raised his arm to make him wave to me. I waved half-heartedly back. I heard her spit out a stream of Kraut, and picked up *Papa* and *Englander*. I asked, 'What was that all about?'

Les said, 'She told him that you may be his new English father, and come back for him soon.'

I looked again. The little bugger was smiling at me. What else could I do? I grinned back at him. Les told me, 'He's got a little dark patch under his nose. That's where the moustache will grow. Just like Hitler. What will the people down your street think when you get 'ome and bring 'im wiv you?'

I didn't answer him because there were tears in my eyes. There were tears in my eyes because I had imagined taking him home to my little sister Francie. She would have adored him. So I suppose that I did what Francie would have done anyway. I was almost at *Kate*'s door when I grunted, 'Forgot something,' to them, and, 'Won't be a min.'

I hurried back to Otto, Frieda and the kid. I fished out my tags, and pulled off the spare. We always had to wear the two. One was to be tacked on to your grave marker, and the other sent back to your unit. It was nice to find something useful to do with them instead. I put the spare in my jacket pocket – I'd find a string to wear it on later – and hung the other around young Adolf's neck. I got another slobbery kiss from the woman for the gesture. This time I didn't look back; that was too difficult. Les put an arm around my shoulder and squeezed, avoiding the tender part. I don't think that that sort of thing came too easily to him. He said, 'Proud of you, Charlie. That was nice,' and, 'I'll drive.'

James was already in the back with his notebook open. I don't think that he even noticed. I reflected on what Les had been willing to do a few hours ago.

Twenty-Four

We made it through the valley in a oner this time. At a Y junction at the end of our valley there was no village smithy under the spreading chestnut tree. It was spreading its new green mantle over an ageing AEC Matador lorry instead – the four-wheeled type, with the soft back. The lorry had that unmistakable sulky look that machinery adopts when it breaks down. The driver, old RASC like Les, was standing beside his cab looking perplexed. He had a fag behind his ear. I waved to him. He nodded back. In the ditch about thirty yards away – up the road we weren't meant to take – one of those little Jerry jeeps was on its side. It looked otherwise unharmed. The driver caught my glance, nodded towards the wreck, and said, 'Don't. It's wired.'

I never argue with Yorkshiremen: they get too much pleasure from usually being right. I said, 'Thanks,' as Les and I walked over to him.

James stayed put in *Kate*. Les must have felt secure: he left his Sten on *Kate*'s driving seat. It was National Nodding Day because he nodded too: up at the lorry. It had the name *Obadiah* lettered neatly in Gothic on a plate above the windscreen. Les asked, 'What's up?'

'Iffy diffy. That's the third I've run this war. I dunno what he does wi' 'em.'

'Why don't you get rid of it? There's some good new Bedfords coming in.'

'Naw. *Obi*'s taken me up over Italy. Might as well finish it with him.'

Our own esteemed driver poked one of his big pink fingers into the soft canvas canopy covering the lorry's load.

'What you got?'

'Socks. Winter woollen socks, and coffee, tea and some boxes of medicines.'

'Bremen?'

'Yeah. You?'

'Yeah.'

Les pulled at his lower lip. Then he asked, 'When did you get your orders?'

'Yesterday. I understand that there's a foreign gentleman riding up at the front end, with one of the armoured divisions. Fielden, our gaffer, says he's an RAF pilot who was shot down and evading. Somehow he established contact with the QM's base area, and is calling forward the needful. He coulda gone 'ome before now, but he's riding the back of a tank all the way to Berlin.'

Les grunted. Then he said, 'Some fellah.' The way he said it made you glance quickly at him.

'Good job he took it on.' That was the driver again.

'There's supposed to be an intelligence officer up here some-where, but it looks as if he got lost.'

'Did he now?' Then Les asked, 'You OK?'

'Yeah. We were in a convoy of six. The Master called through for us from his jeep. Recovery's on the way.'

A mile or so further on we pulled over, and chinned it all out to the Major. He said, 'Your *bloody* Pole, I suppose, Charlie?'

'We don't know that, but if it is, it looks like he's got your job, sir. I wonder why they think you're lost? I know that your signals are getting out. Do you want me to check the suitcase again?'

'No. I'm getting acknowledgements and sign-offs back.'

Les mumbled something. I didn't catch it. James explained, 'If some bent bastard has paid off the soldier receiving my call-over not to pass it on to anyone else, then I am *lost*, aren't I? Who else knows where I am?'

'I wish you wouldn't keep calling him *my* Pole.'

'Then bloody do something about him. Get him off our backs. It's more than my job he's stealing. Look at the bloody silly load that wagon was carrying. Why had it got socks and beverages, when today's urgent need is probably flour, potatoes, powdered milk and blankets?'

'I don't know, James, but I suspect you're going to tell me.'

'Because they all command best prices on the black market *today*, you silly little man. It's just like the stock market: different products command different premiums in different places at different times. The laws of supply and demand.' He thought that Pete was substituting his own stores requests for ours, and then hijacking them. After that he went into a sulk, and wouldn't say any more until we had put another ten miles on the clock.

We stopped for a brew. Les said, 'Major,' with deliberate gravity. 'Do you think we should go back for him? He won't have an effing chance if the wolves fall on him.'

'Too late, I suspect. Not our business anyway. Police stuff.'

'Pete wouldn't do this,' I offered. 'It's too sloppy. He wouldn't do anything he'd get caught for.'

'That's all right then. No point in going back and getting into trouble, is there?' Then Les said to me, 'Five bob. Five bob says that he nicks the lorry, and kills the Tyke.'

We shook on it. We were bloody well going to retrace our tracks again, weren't we? Conscience is like being attached to life by a bit of elastic: it always pulls you back to somewhere you'd rather not be.

Back at the Matador we found Pete, of course, but with a couple of blokes and a great Thornicroft tank-recovery vehicle. That's a six-wheeled crane with all-wheel drive, big enough to lift and tow a tank. In the Army's world, big is *big*.

Les said, 'I wonder if I keep *Kate* long enough if she'll grow into one of them?'

I said, 'There's Pete.'

'Glad you're awake, Charlie.' That was James again. He sounded bitter. 'Are you going to get him to go home and leave us in peace, or shall I simply shoot him?'

I said, 'Hi, Pete. Fancy meeting you again. I thought you were away with Tommo, printing money.'

'Tommo's met another *Mädchen*. One with legs as long as the Suez Canal, and tits like pyramids. I can't get him out of bed.'

'What are you doing then? The Major thinks you're back in the black market, and stealing his stores.'

'I told you I'd be OK: they've joined me up in the police to keep me out of trouble until the war in Europe is over: can't be long now.'

'You gotta be joking.'

But he wasn't. He pulled out one of those little cards with the red stripes on it to prove it. James butted in, 'I was going to arrest you, but changed my mind when I remembered that your partner might still come up with a nice little German property investment for me.' He nodded at Pete's pass, and asked, 'That thing genuine?'

'Yes, Major, it is.'

'Explain. Make me believe you.'

Pete shrugged. He said, 'OK.' It sounded like *ho-kay*. 'I try. Poles in exile congregate with other Poles in exile, so for several years I associate freely with my country's political representatives in Britain. That also involved me with your black market, because most of them were up to our necks in it. You say it like that?'

'You could definitely say it like that, Pete,' I told him.

He continued, 'It was a hobby. Now I'm supposed to go home, but your police have a big black market blowing up over here. Also they want to keep an eye on me because I am a Pole with interesting political connections. They solve both problems by signing up one to solve the other. That was a very English solution: I think that your Mr Clifford may have put in a word for me. I am not stealing your stores, I am finding out who is. I am a military policeman, Polish Division.'

I said, 'We call that a poacher turned gamekeeper.'

'I like that phrase, Charlie. I will try to remember it.'

'Get the Guv'nor to write it down for you,' from Les. 'He's good at that.'

'When it's all over I will return to Poland and join the Resistance. Maybe I told you that already.'

Les said, 'Ain't it a bit late for that?'

'Resistance against the Russians, friend: the Germans have already run away.'

Les looked perplexed, 'That don't make sense. Didn't we go to war to free Poland in the first place? The Russians may have got there before we did, but you can't believe we'll let them keep it?'

Pete did what he always did if he was being asked to reveal his serious side: he took the piss.

'If Poland is returned to the Poles,' he told Les, 'I will personally see that you get a medal from my country after the war.'

One of us had to bring the conversation back. Me.

'We thought that broken-down lorry had been set up to be hijacked by you and Tommo, and sold into the black market.'

'And you left him? That was kind. You used to be braver than that when I flew with you.'

He always knew how to put his finger on the button.

James admitted, not too gracefully, 'You're right, of course. That's why we came back.'

'I know. The British always do the right thing in the end,' Pete told us.

He had a tall Redcap sergeant, and a nifty jeep with side screens and all of the gear. This man strolled over banging his stick against his knee. Why do they all do that? He saluted very smartly, which embarrassed us all over again, and asked James, 'Excuse me, sir. You would be Major England, sir?' James smiled, and slouched something like a salute back. The MP continued, 'There are some folk a bit worried about you, sir. No one's reported your signals for several days, and anyway you're supposed to be about two days north of here . . .'

Les's face flushed suddenly. You never knew in advance what was going to trigger his anger. I held my hand up to James, hoping he would just keep the guy going, and dragged Pete into the lee of the Thornicroft.

'What's happening to the Major's signal traffic? He's radioed it in, getting an acknowledgement, and then bugger-all happens. This is the second time we've been told he's off contact.'

'What do you think?'

'Some bent bastard is cutting him out.'

'You want me to fix it?'

'Just like that?'

'Just li' that.' Both of his hands were held at waist height, and extended parallel to the ground. It was that comedian's catchphrase again. We'd used it on the squadron. It made us both laugh.

I said, 'Thanks, Pete.'

'It's not a problem.' Then he paused, and gave me the look. He said, 'Why don't you and your people toddle off now, and leave me with *my* problem.'

'What's that?'

'You guessed wrong about this lorry being abandoned to the black marketeers. It's the rest of this focking convoy we've lost. Five lorries, a jeep and twelve men, including a Lieutenant Fielden who won an Olympic silver for running something before the war. Everybody's panicking except Pete. Situation normal.'

'Who's stealing the stores?'

'Some bad Czech with an unpronounceable name. Pete will fix it.' I suddenly remembered his characteristic way of speaking of himself in the third person.

'You want us to fuck off, and leave you to get on with it then?'

'It would be best, Charlie. I fix the Major's radio traffic, OK? See you in Berlin, OK?'

'. . . and now you're really a policeman?'

'Yes, but only for a little while.'

Ah hell. Bugger him. I tried to tell James and Les. Les sniffed. James said, 'I know. We heard you – I've a phone call to make, I think.' James wandered off to Pete's jeep.

'Where the hell does he think he's going to find a working telephone in this part of Germany?' I wondered.

'You found one a few days ago. I guess he's guessed that the Redcap has a field telephone rigged in his posh jeep. Wanna fag?'

*

409

'You *believe* the coppers, old man?' James asked when he drifted back.

'Every time I do,' I said, 'they lock me up in prison, or handcuff me to a bed. It's not very encouraging.'

'What your Polish johnny says is more or less right. Seems there's some Czech airman ripping the arse out of the black market by getting his supplies sent up by the Army for free, and I got caught in the middle of it. He's upsetting all the proper racketeers, so Charlie's Pole has been recruited to sort him out. Apparently this guy doesn't need to steal our stores; we *deliver* them to him. You ever heard the like? He calls small convoys forward, pretending to be folk like us, and has the stores out of them.'

'I think it's confusing. I don't know who's on our side any more.'

Les told me, '*No one* is, Charlie.' He waited a full thirty seconds before he spoke again. 'No one ever was. Are we going to bleedin' Bremen, or what, sir?' he asked me. 'It seems to me to be getting further away from us every day.'

Twenty-Five

It bloody rained, and we got stuck between a column of muddy Brit Sherman tanks and a small convoy of smaller Morris trucks full of troops. There were about ten of them being shepherded by a Dingo scout car, and each contained about ten men. The tanks didn't stop for nightfall, but outside yet another small German town the infantry did. So did we.

I helped James whilst Les brewed up. I rigged his aerial for him; looping it over the highest branch I could reach. He held his earphones up to one ear only, which meant that I could listen in to the other earpiece. He had done that before when he was worried about signal strength, and his keying. He needn't have worried. I told you he had a good hand. His signal was all encrypted, of course; so it meant bugger-all to me. So was the acknowledgement from the other end, and the brief message that followed it.

Then the operator sent something in clear. He or she sent *Tuesday's Child*, which brought me out in goose bumps. The Major signed off and put the 'phones back in their rig in the suitcase lid. He looked tired. Asked me, 'What did you make of that, Charlie?'

'Different hand, different operator. The way someone uses a Morse key is like a signature. You only have to hear someone once, most of the time, to be able to recognize them again. Ever since we set out the guy you've asked me to listen to has been the same person. This guy is someone different.'

James said, 'OK . . . and now tell me about *Tuesday's Child*; it wasn't in my briefing anywhere. It doesn't mean anything.'

'It does to me, James. That was Pete's way of telling us that he fixed your communication problem. *Tuesday's Child* was a Lancaster bomber, one of the best. Pete and I completed our tours in her.'

'OK . . . Where is she now?'

'In hell with all the others. She crashed and burned the day we gave her to another crew. Bad bitch.'

'*Tuesday's Child*?'

'That's right, James. Grace. We named her after Grace.'

'I see.'

He didn't, and I hoped that he never would. He asked me, 'You *Tuesdays* stick together then? After you finished flying together?'

'Don't know. Pete's the only one I've met so far, and I thought he was dead.'

'Are you pleased that he's not?'

'Yes. Yes I am. What's this about, James? What are all the questions for?'

'Just asking,' he said. 'Just interested.'

I didn't believe him either. Life's not that tidy.

That night I retuned the suitcase for them. The noise came out of a neat speaker the Krauts had built into the lid. We sat around Les's fire, which threw out a surprising heat. It wasn't far from our small tents. *Kate*'s back door was open, and from the suitcase we listened to Johnny Mercer doing 'GI Jive', and Louis Jordan doing 'Is You Is, or Is You Ain't My Baby?' Later there was a Glenn Miller hour from Paris. Probably from that bloody club the Americans captured me in. Dinah Shore had flown in, and was doing 'Stardust' with them. Somewhere a few miles up ahead people were fighting and dying at the arse end of a bad war, and Dinah was singing 'Stardust'.

They told you lies when they said that the worst things to be seen on the march across Europe were the concentration camps, and what was left of the people who had lived in them. They weren't the worst things – and I know because I saw three camps, and there were things even worse than that.

They never told you about the big German cities. The big German cities laid flat. The big German cities full of dead people . . . or how we invented the microwave oven fifty years before its time, and flung whole bloody communities into it. I've told you before: I was never afraid to ask the questions.

We drove through a small town. Every house, shop, office or tenement I saw was smashed and burned. Two churches had been spread about a bit, but the cinema had managed to remain intact in the town square. Maybe that was a pointer for the future. The town hadn't only been bombed: I thought an army had fought its way through it. There were no people and no stray animals, except a thin fox I saw rummaging in a shop window with smashed glass. The smell of burning seeped inside *Kate*, like stale cigarette smoke clinging to your jacket after a night in the pub.

The Major said, 'I think that they used to have a car factory here,' as if that explained everything.

'I've been to the briefings,' I told him. 'We would have crapped all over it even if it had only made prams.'

There was a GI standing on our side of the road at a crossroads just the other side of the town. He wore a scarred chamberpot helmet, a weatherproof coat, and had a big two-strapped pack thrown over only one shoulder. His back was to us, and the hand held out with its thumb up was brown. He turned and smiled when we stopped by him, and held out the hand to me. I had to open the car door to speak to him. We did the ritual: touched, grasped and shook. I liked his open smile, and hoped he wasn't on a runner again. I said, 'Hello, Cutter.'

'Hi, Charlie, Les. Hello, sir.' He gave James a cursory salute and the Major attempted a return serve. All James did was succeed in knocking his cap off. He cursed, *Damn*.

I asked, 'Are you running again?'

'No, Charlie. Same as you, travelling. Under orders this time. They liberated Bremen yesterday, and they have a field hospital that's going under.'

'They ordered you to *walk* to Bremen?'

'Shit no. There was a motor bicycle, but I wrecked it. I ran into a dog the other side of town. Pity. It looked a good dog. It was certainly the *only* dog they got left.'

'See any people?' That was James.

'Nossir. I guess they all evacuated. Someone else's problem now.'

'Wanna lift? We're going that way too.' That was Les.

'Yes please,' Cutter said. 'You want me to ride in the back with the General, or up front like the enlisted men?'

'Charlie can sit in the back,' Les said. 'I want you up here where I can keep an eye on you.'

Cutter rode with his pack and helmet clutched possessively into his lap. I asked him, 'What do you have in the pack? Booze? Silk knickers for the Fräuleins?'

'The tools of my trade, Charlie, and that ain't *them*. I've as much penicillin as they'd let me have. If we flogged it I'd be worth my weight in gold to you today.'

'Not that you'd ever sell?'

I'd gone too far. There was a bit of a sulky silence, and then the Negro said, 'What's the point of my cutting folk if I can't keep them alive with the proper drug afterwards?'

I said, 'Sorry,' and meant it.

A while after that the Cutter asked, 'You boys mind if we stay in touch while we're all still in Bremen? I don't know what it's gonna be like up there. They may not like me.'

In a cobbled dairy yard on a hill closer to Bremen we found five British Army trucks. They were all time-expired AEC Matadors, just like *Obadiah*. They were parked neatly along-side each other, burnt to a crisp, and still smoking. The rubber smoke made my eyes water. We had slowed up, and then stopped to rubberneck, when we saw a jeep on its side in the ditch outside. When we walked over to examine it we could see that the jeep had heavy-calibre bullet holes in its cracked windscreen, and bullet slashes on both of the front seat cushions.

There was a small, deserted cheese factory – two rooms in a two-hundred-year-old shed – alongside the dairy. Behind it we found fresh graves, with identity discs hanging on the rough wooden crosses. Some of the crosses were surmounted by British helmets; another bore an officer's soft cap: half of it had been torn away, and it was stained with blood.

James was with me. The colour left his face. He lifted the cap, and then said, 'Bollocks,' softly. Like a whisper. Then he flung it away from him. He prowled the yard with his revolver in his hand; Les with his Sten. There was no one there to shoot at, of course. The Cutter seemed the least moved.

'We in trouble?' I asked him.

'No. They're long gone. It takes three hours to burn out a truck as thoroughly as that.'

I'd forgotten that he'd been a policeman once, and cops know things like that. James and Les searched the sheds and the house. The Cutter told me, 'Wasting their time. Does your Major still have his radio?'

'Yes,' said James. I swung on him, scared. So did the Cutter. James had come from nowhere. He said, 'Sorry,' and, 'Yes, I do have it. Why?'

'I wondered if you might think to send a signal to Charlie's

friend Pete. I understand that he's a policeman again, just like
I used to be.'

'Again?' I asked him.

'Yes. He was one before the war, didn't you know?'

'Bollocks,' I said.

'Precisely,' James said.

Why hadn't we known that?

McKechnie and Les left us to it. In the house Les got a
brew going. James said to me, 'I'm flying a bit blind here, old
son: sending a signal to an operator who appears to have been
substituted for my regular, by your flaky pal.'

'. . . because your own operator was playing against you,
James. Trust me.'

'Maybe . . . and maybe we'd better go back to *sir* until this
bit's over with.'

'OK, *sir*. It's your call: forgive the pun. We can either
report this, and the law can still catch up . . . or *not* report it,
pass by on the other side, and maybe they never will.'

'*Pass by on the other side*: isn't that sort of what your pal
accused us of before?'

'Yes. We're good at it, obviously.'

'You want me to call him up, don't you?'

'Yes, sir.'

'Fine.' It wasn't. He was pissed off. He sounded as if he'd
eaten bitter aloes. James sprayed a short burst of Morse. He
had encrypted it, and assured me that the essential detail was
there. I wasn't reassured. He had asked the operator to
forward it urgently to *Tuesday's Child*. That was neat. We only

waited ten minutes for a response, which was Morsed back in clear as, *Tx. KKK50*.

James showed me, and asked, 'What the fuck does that mean?'

'It's either Pete, or someone who reads old prewar RAF shorthand. It says, *Thanks, I will formate on you in 50 minutes*. Pete will be here within the hour.'

'. . . and pigs fly.'

'Stop grumbling, James. Sir. Come and have a cuppa. We'd better not tell the Cutter about the *KKK*. He'd take it very personally.'

The room in which Les had discovered a working stove was in what had once been a small farm kitchen. On the way there I said, 'At least they gave them a Christian burial.'

'The Czech is probably a Catholic,' James told me. 'They can be strict about these things. Why don't you go and say a few words over them? Just in case no one else has.'

'You know I'm not a proper parson, sir. So it won't bloody do.'

'I'm the bloody Major, and you're the bloody Captain, and that's all there bloody is to it! So do as you're bloody well told, and go and get your *bloody* book.'

The only good things to happen were that they joined me at the gravesides, didn't take the mickey, and said *Amen* in all the proper places. I don't know why, but at a grave of one of the driver privates I became suddenly convinced that the occupant had a young family. I made a picture of them in my mind. Horsing around, unaware that they no longer had a dad. I suddenly couldn't go further. My voice went away somewhere, and James stepped in and finished it for me. When we did caps on, and walked back to the office, James grasped my upper left arm, and guided me as if I was a blind man.

But I was still pissed off with him afterwards — with this public school thing of wanting to give all the orders, and still wanting to be one of the boys. Besides; it was my sore arm that he had grabbed. I took the char Les offered me: it was in a big chipped mug he'd found — it held about three-quarters of a pint. He'd also slapped a generous waxer into it: brandy this time. I think that he had the contents of a small off-sales bar in *Kate*'s boot. Anyway, I walked outside with it. I've told you that it looked as if the cheese factory had once been part of a small dairy farm? Its muddy yard was cobbled. I walked across it to the old farm fence away from the main road: I didn't intend to go into the field beyond, but I suppose that Les was keeping an eye on me anyway, because he wandered up behind me. Leaning on the fence. The tea in the mugs steamed.

I said to Les, 'When I'm an old man, and telling stories to my grandchildren, do you think I can say I fought my way across Europe with you and the Major?'

Les flicked his fag-end into the field. I could smell the brandy in the tea.

'Not much fighting so far, but yeah, why not? You could say that. Why?'

'Because the only people I've helped kill so far are three Yanks. People may not want to hear about that.'

'Yeah. I can see that, but the bastards deserved it.'

'Yes, they did. But you *do* see what I mean?'

'I do, mate . . . but what's worrying you then?'

'All these bloody coppers, I expect. Wherever I've gone since I left the squadron I've had coppers of some sort at my heels. It started when I saw Pete shoot a copper while I was *still* on the squadron, and helped him to get rid of the body. There was also another body he'd brought back to the squadron with him from London. There was another one: a bastard of a catering officer on our station, who was knocking about the kids who worked for him.'

'So that's another three, as well. Do things in threes do they, your lot? You killed 'im too, did you?'

'No. I didn't kill any of them. Pete shot the copper because he was going to shoot me: I'd caught him rummaging through Pete's gear. It was to do with the death of some Polish general in an air crash.'

'Sikorsky, that would be.'

'How did you know that?'

'I think you'll find it was in the papers. You didn't kill this . . . catering officer, then?'

'No. By then Pete was in the black market, and so was *he*. I don't think Pete did it. I think he probably asked someone else on the squadron to do it. They drowned him in an old field latrine.'

Les fished a cigarette out of his beret and lit up.

'You really don't let up once you start telling it, do you, Charlie?'

'I was just worried about the coppers. I'm worried that they are still trying to rope me into this.'

'Anyone else know about this?'

'Mr Clifford. And anyone he's chosen to tell.'

'Do you think that you've killed any Krauts in the course of your private little wars?'

'Bloody hundreds I expect. I dropped bombs all over them, remember?'

'You got nothing to worry about then, 'ave you? You scored more goals than own goals.'

'It's not a bloody game.'

Pete was beaten to the draw by a jeep and an ambulance, which came from the Bremen road. That surprised me; they must have been better organized up there than I thought. The jeep slithered into the courtyard, and disgorged its driver – a stylishly dressed Major. He saluted by waving a leather-covered swagger stick at his cap, which had a leather peak. Les took no chances, and gave him something like a salute. So did I. He said, 'Major Hendriks. Ira. South African Military Police, but don't get in a lather . . .' He had that nasal SA drawl I've always liked, '. . . I'm not a proper police-man. I do the science.' He said African as if it was spelled *Efrican*.

'Like Sir Sydney Smith in England, sir?' Les.

'Yes, Private. Well done. You've got some bodies, and burned-out lorries for me, I understand.'

I was tongue-tied, so it was Les again.

'Our Major's inside, sir,' he nodded to the dairy office. 'And the tea he's drinking's not too old.'

'Thenk you, Private. What's the matter with your Captain?

Don't he speak?' I think that he was just trying to break the ice.

'He's just a Chaplain, sir. Only talks to God these days.'

'Oh, I see. One of those. Carry on.'

After he sloped off I told Les, 'Supercilious bastard.'

'I would agree with you, sir, if I knew what it meant.'

There was a driver and three SBAs in the ambulance; a neat little Austin job. The SBAs climbed out of the back with spades at the ready. Les showed them where the graves were, and watched them get to work while he smoked fags with the driver. That is to say he listened. He never passed up the opportunity to find out what was what in the other people's war.

Soon after that a small Yank communications aircraft, still covered in black and white Normandy stripes, landed on the road outside. Pete was keeping his word; it had taken him less than fifty. His uniform had silver tabs added to its shoulder boards, red flashes to the collars, and he wore a flash black-peaked cap with some silver braid around it. Like the SS. Both James and the South African who went out to meet him paused, and saluted. After a few words with them that I failed to catch he walked slowly over to me. I asked him, 'What the fuck have they done to you, Pete?'

'Colonel Pete. They made me a Colonel.'

'Who?'

'The Polish government. They want their soldiers to have some clout at the conference tables of the victorious.'

'What exactly do you mean by that?'

'I told you: the Reds are going to be in charge for a long time. I go home in this uniform they sling me in a camp. I go home dressed as a miner, or a welder in the shipyard – maybe I'll stay safe, an' make trouble for them.'

'Why go home at all? Why not stay in England?'

'Not a focking chance, Charlie. Can't you see the way the wind is blowing? The English won't let Polish soldiers stay, the Reds will say *Please send our gallant heroes home, so we can lock them up in the empty concentration camps*, and the Brits will only be too glad to get shot of us.'

'Why do you think we'll betray you?'

'You betrayed everyone else for hundreds of years. Am I so different?'

'Somebody told me you were a policeman back in Poland. Was that true?'

I suppose he took a few seconds to think about it. Then he said, 'Yes. That was true. Are you happy now?'

The wind got up from somewhere: it blew the smell of burned rubber from the lorries around us. The sky was leaden. Les was watching murdered men being exhumed without turning a hair, and James was off fretting because Pete had ignored him, Major or no Major. I said, 'This is a stupid conversation, Pete. Go and talk to James; he'll only take it out on me and Les if you piss him off.'

'OK. Thanks for telling me you'd found the lorries. People don't tell the cops nothing these days.'

'*Anything*. They don't tell the police anything . . .'

'Nothing,' Pete insisted. 'They tell cops *nothing* . . .'

423

'Nor would you,' I told him. 'Not when you were on the other side.' Then reality checked in, and I added, '. . . only you were never really on the other side.'

Bugger him. Bugger the lot of them. I wanted to find Grace and say my piece; make sure that she was all right, and then go home. For the first time in my life, I thought, I had a decent plan. When we gathered up, and went out to *Kate* we had to skate close to the American plane. I think that we called the type a Cricket. The pilot grinned, and raised a hand to me as I moved past. It was Tommo. He was in a flying jacket. He looked shagged out. I thought briefly about Cliff; how come so many of these types had learned to fly? The Cutter was commandeered by the SA Major, who wanted to do a quick and dirty autopsy on the bodies. Hendriks promised him a lift into Bremen as a reward. The black man looked very unhappy as we drove away and left him.

The Cricket zoomed low over *Kate* an hour later. They would be in Bremen before us.

Twenty-Six

'You forgot those two Jerries on the BMW, didn't you?' *Kate* was labouring up a long twisted hill. The Major had assured us that we would be able to see Bremen from the other side. I'd already worked out that what I had originally thought were thick cumulus storm clouds was in fact a broad column of smoke.

James asked, 'What?' and sniffed the air like a gun dog. He must have been dozing.

A jeep pissed past us as if *Kate* had been standing still. Mud splashed back from it. Les cursed, because since we'd changed *Kate*'s windscreen the wipers didn't work.

Les again: 'He was worried about not having killed enough Jerries before the great reckoning up began. He doesn't want to face the Great Architect in the sky with all his pluses in the wrong column. He'd forgotten those bastards on the motorbike, and is still worried about the Yanks we had put down.'

James asked, 'What Yanks? Can't seem to remember any.'

'Nor can I, sir.'

We ran without speaking for thirty minutes or so. *Kate* sounded sweet. We crested the hill, and saw the southern

425

suburb of Bremen for the first time. It was about fifteen miles away. Les said, 'Journey's end, Charlie.'

A few miles on, in a small hamlet the size of Korne, we were pulled up at a roadblock manned by bored-looking squaddies. There were half a dozen vehicles parked up off the thoroughfare, waiting to be passed through. James got out for a look-see. A squaddy saluted. One other started to, and then bent over and vomited. James raised an eyebrow and waited. It was the first time I'd seen him do either. The saluter apologized.

'Sorry, sir. He's got some sort of stomach problem.'

'I can smell it from here, Bombardier' – he was good at unit flashes – 'I'd say his stomach problem came in tall brown glass bottles labelled *Wein*.'

The saluter straightened. His face wore a *game's up* expression.

'Sir.'

But James ignored the vomiter.

'So what's the hold-up?'

'I think that things are a bit chaotic down there, sir, so they want everyone held back until the MPs have got control again. There are three armies loose in there at the moment.'

'Brits and Canadians, and . . .?'

'I understand that an American tank unit got in there somehow, sir.'

'Are there any exceptions to your instructions? We really do have pressing business . . .'

'They left me a list, sir.'

'Could you check it for a Major England, Mr Finnigan –

my driver — and er . . . Pilot Officer Bassett? He's my passenger.'

'I could, sir, but . . .'

His eyes flicked sideways to his drunken companion, who was sitting on the ground by now, hunched over a .303, cradled in his lap. James leaned over and lifted the rifle away. He said, 'We'll hold the fort for you.'

The gunner nodded. He stepped sideways through the hole they'd knocked in a cottage wall. It was their makeshift guard house. I got out to stretch my legs. I'd already filled my pipe with sweet nutty tobacco. Now I lit it. I asked James, 'What's afoot, sir?'

'I don't think they want us to see what our brave soldiery are doing to the citizens of Bremen. Matey is off to check his list of bodies who may be passed through. I said that I'd man his post.'

'We could just sod off.'

'That would be unsoldierly.'

'I think that you make those words up, sir.'

'Sometimes. But I always write them down afterwards.'

Kate had once been identical to the staff car which drew up. Unlike *Kate* it still had all the right windows, was unbattered, and it had obviously had a wash that morning. Its driver, when he hopped out, was immaculate. He went to attention in front of James, who put him at ease. James appeared to be enjoying himself. The new driver must have at-eased in a particularly soggy spot. I could see that he was slowly sinking into it. The new Humber suddenly swayed as somebody heavy shifted inside. A rear passenger door opened, and a portly Colonel stepped out. He had a nicotine-stained moustache the size of a small broom. He said, 'Sod it man, he's only a *Major*, just *shove* him out of the road!'

The Corporal turned white, but he didn't move: James had the gun. James looked at the fat man, who said, 'Hello James.'

James said, 'Hello Freddy.'

'Still causing trouble?'

'Still bumming your fags?'

'No. Grew out of it. Got married. Three children, one grandchild. You?'

'No. Didn't get round to it. Do I have to call you *sir*?'

'If you like. In front of the oiks. Didn't you have an exceptionally pretty sister?'

'I still have. She's worn quite well, sir.'

'Your man's got his mouth open. Gaping.'

'I've told him about that before. He's a parson and a grammar school boy.'

'Explains it.'

'That's what I think, too.' James turned to me and offered, 'This is Colonel Sir Frederick Hastings. He was a consultant surgeon at St Bartholomew's Hospital before the war. Before that he accompanied the Royal Veterinary Corps into Afghanistan in the Twenties and Thirties. He is probably the world's most knowledgeable living expert on battlefield injuries. Sir Frederick is on the Surgeon General's staff.'

I saluted, and stepped forward – careful to stay clear of the soft stuff.

'We were at school together. Freddy was in the Upper School when I was still a nymph.'

The Colonel took out a huge pocket handkerchief, and emptied the contents of his nostrils into it. The bogies seemed to flow on for minutes. After a flamboyant wipe he asked James, 'What *is* the hold-up?'

'Bremen hasn't been pacified yet.'

'Balls. Any fighting Germans are miles away. It's all over bar the weeping.'

'I don't think that the Germans are the problem, sir. It's the Canadian Army fighting the British, and both of them are fighting off some Americans.'

'Can my man move yet? His boots have disappeared.'

'No, I don't think so. I feel like Horatius at the bridge.'

'Would it make any difference if I gave you an order?'

'No, sir: I know my duty.'

'Thought so. You always were a silly beggar . . . Harrington?'

The driver said, 'Yessir?' He tried to come to attention in the mud, but it didn't work. His feet wouldn't obey his head, and he swayed alarmingly. I thought that he was going to fall.

'You'll just have to stay there until this is sorted out. Don't upset the Major. He was a crack shot in the ATC.'

The guard slipped back out through the wall. He saluted the Colonel and James. Both responded. He told James, 'None of you were on the list to be passed through, begging your pardon, sir, but I've spoken to a Major Hendriks, who vouched for you, sir. You're free to proceed.'

'What about Hastings and Harrington?' The Colonel asked reasonably. 'We on your bally list?'

' 'fraid not, sir.'

'Thought not. Who *is* on it?'

'There's a Bernard Montgomery and a Brian Horrocks on it, sir. It doesn't say their rank.'

'No. Of course not. Silly bally names. Wonder who they are.' He seemed to notice the squaddy sprawled on the ground for the first time, and asked, 'Well: seeing as I'm staying, apparently, I suppose that you'll want me to look at that fellah. He'll die if we don't do something for him.'

The soldier was breathing in slow rattly draughts, each further apart than the last. The Bombardier responded with, 'That would be very kind, sir. I'll get someone to move him inside.'

'Don't bother. My Corporal will do it. What's he standing in, by the way?'

'Road drain, sir. Caught a couple of the lads out before we realized that it was full of mud and shit. Sir.'

The Colonel touched his sinking driver on the shoulder.

'All right, Harrington. Carry on.'

After we moved off downhill Les told James, 'If he was an old school chum you could have used your influence with Mr Hendriks to get him cleared through as well.'

James didn't reply for a six-beat: he was sprawled across *Kate*'s rear seat with his hat tipped over his eyes. Then he said, 'I told you. He's on the Surgeon General's staff. He'll be heading for the same hospital as McKechnie and Charlie, and taking over. I thought that Charlie could use a few hours' *grace*. Pardon the pun.'

Twenty-Seven

Bremen was very odd. Right from the start. Some parts of the suburbs were almost untouched by war. We had driven through a large park where people were strolling. Three drunken sailors were trailed by a tail of inquisitive children and acquisitive young women – all out in Number Ones and Sunday-best dresses, despite the chill wind that came from the north-east. That was a metaphor for Germany that year: a chill wind from the north-east full of Russians. It was one of the things for which I was unprepared: the chill wind, I mean – I'd had plenty of time to think about the Russians. Then there were bits of the city simply missing. Whole blocks a half mile by a mile. The roads were still there – cratered, but cleared by the methodical Kraut – but where blocks of flats and tenements had stood, there were pyramids of stone and brick. Some of the pyramids had narrow paths cleared through them: they would have followed narrow streets and paths before the war, I'd guess. Where leafless trees or wooden posts remained – and there weren't many – they were covered in tiny, handwritten notices . . . *Ilse is now with her parents in*

Baden . . . Madelaine and Freya have moved to Bassum, Uncle Otto was killed in March.

I noticed one of those cellar doors in the pavement, open alongside a mountain of rubble. People moved in and out of it, blinking as they came into the light; moving slowly. None of us in the car spoke much. I had come looking for a city, but parts were only a red desert. A rusty mist of brick dust danced in the air like a dust storm, and blanketed everything. A woman pushed an old high pram. She had waved to the car as we cruised past. She was wearing a fashionable dress with a short fur jacket, and a jaunty black pillbox hat. And a surgical face mask. The baby in the pram wore one too. It didn't wave as we cruised past. And there was that smell, of course: it even got inside *Kate*.

Les broke the spell.

'Crossroads. Scotch soldiers over there. Which way do we go?'

Then there were the other places. Where the walls of the buildings still stood: more or less. But instead of containing functioning houses, flats, offices and businesses, they were filled by rubble and burnt or smashed beams, and open to the sky. Buildings with a wall cleanly removed so that you could see the contents of the interior: like looking into doll's houses. One three-floor house had a top-floor bedroom, now open to the weather, with bright yellow patterned wallpaper, and a bed with a green and red eiderdown. It was like a garden in the sky. There was a red cross daubed crudely on its front door. I asked, 'What's that mean? Plague?'

James: 'No, that will come next month. Probably cholera

and TB . . . and syphilis, of course, once the Frogs get here.' He'd been snotty about the French ever since spending a night in one of their cells. He went back to his thoughts, and they were probably too lofty for the likes of me and Les.

Les said, 'The red cross means *unexploded bomb*. A Jerry we had a couple of months ago told us that. It explains why there's anything still left in that house.'

There were more folk moving around in these recognizable ruins. The roads were more heavily cratered, and the craters hadn't been filled in with rubble, as they had been in the areas of total devastation. A lot of infantry soldiers as well, thankfully all belonging to Scottish regiments, and not dressed in field grey.

One road we attempted was so badly cratered that we couldn't move forward. Les started to back *Kate* up. A young brown job Sergeant with a Gateshead accent came sprinting from the cover and threw a sloppy one at James, although it was to Les that he spoke.

'Would you mind backing up as quick as you like, chum, and getting off the street? Then I'll explain what's going on.'

The Good Soldier Finnigan. The Sergeant seemed a clued-up type, even if he was in a Scottish regiment. Les backed *Kate* between two shagged-out houses without roofs. The infantryman said, 'Thanks. You were in harm's way, and all that.'

James: I haven't seen any fighting Germans yet.'

'Neither you will, sir. It's those fucking Canadians. It's like the gunfight at the OK Corral down there.' He waved vaguely

433

in the direction we were travelling. 'Where were you hoping to get to, anyway?'

James asked, 'Charlie?'

'The main telephone exchange, and the hospital in the Hanseatic Hotel. Doesn't matter in which order. *Befehl ist Befehl.*'

'Meaning?' Then he spotted my collar crosses and added, 'Sir.'

'An order is an order. It's a German saying. They use it to explain something about themselves.'

'You speak German? Good. It will come in handy.'

That was a bloody laugh, wasn't it? Les thought so: he smiled.

The Sergeant then said, 'You'll never get the car through. The Canadians are using anti-aircraft guns and mortars against anything that moves; particularly if it's khaki. Someone has told them they've been infiltrated by *Werewolf* units dressed as British soldiers. My boss has said that Horrocks has threatened to call up air support if the fighting doesn't stop soon. You wouldn't want your transport to be caught in the open with a Tiffie up your arse. Begging your pardon, Padre.'

Then he examined James's old prewar street map and showed us where we were, and where the telephone exchange had been, and hospital was. The telephone exchange had fallen down after one of the American daylight raids a few days previously. Les put *Kate* in somebody's front room and stayed with her. We followed the Sergeant for a couple of minutes to find his platoon HQ set up in another. A spiky Highland Lieutenant confirmed our position, and showed us on his charts where the Canadians and the Americans were. As we left the little platoon he observed, 'You've got a bit of a problem with the car. I don't suppose you'd care to wait until the rough stuff's died down?'

'How long is that likely to take?' I asked.

'About this time tomorrow would be about par for the course once the Allies start shooting at each other. I don't suppose you can wait that long?'

'No.'

'Then you'll have to leave your wagon. You'll never get any closer in that. The roads are fucked up. Full of big holes, burst water mains, and swimming in sewage in some places: don't forget to take your tablets. You can leave your car inside the house next door, and then proceed on foot, although you'll have to leave someone with it. Otherwise all you'll have left when you get back is a bag of bolts. They'll steal everything. The telephone place is about two miles away, and the hospital another mile or so beyond that.'

That was that, then. Except.

Except that when we moved back into the space between the houses there was a jeep parked in front of *Kate*, and Cliff was sitting on its bonnet talking to Les. The bastards actually looked pleased to see each other.

Addressing a superior officer as if he's a bit of dog dirt you've found on your shoe is called insubordination. It's what I did then. The only surprise was the grudging look of approval Les shot my way. I snarled at Cliff, 'And where the *fuck* did you spring from; Fairyland?'

He ignored my tone, and lack of respect. I don't suppose he wanted to charge me.

'Your Pole's aeroplane. He gave me a lift. We landed on a big dual-carriageway road around the town. Did you know that foreign bugger outranks me now?'

'Only in the Polish Army: I'm not sure that it actually exists.'

'Hello, Cliff,' James said, and (meaning me), 'Hasn't he turned into a rude little sod?'

Cliff grinned. His grimy moustache twitched. I've told you before; he was actually another who it was impossible to dislike when he smiled. He said, 'Must be the company he's keeping.'

Les took a cigarette from his hat, and lit up. I tried again with Cliff.

'How did you know where I was, sir?'

'They told me. The same way my message got to you. You *did* get the recall, by the way?'

'They told me I could stop, and come home. Having chased Grace and her baby into the arms of the Russians I can come back now.'

'Then why haven't you?'

It wasn't as easy to answer as all that. We were standing on big grey flagstones between the smashed houses. Two aircraft roared by at house height about two hundred yards away. They flinched automatically. It was the engines that told me.

I said, '*Mossies*,' and didn't even bother to look up from the brick dust I was scuffing with my boot. Then I answered, 'I never wanted to chase Grace away. I might even still want her back, which sounds stupid, but it's true; you don't stop loving her because she's shagging somebody else. Loving someone doesn't depend on them loving you back.' I think that I embarrassed everyone with *that* revelation. I needed somebody on my side. I asked Les, 'What do *you* think, Les?'

It was very odd. It should have been me who sounded tired and defeated, but it wasn't. It was Les. He sighed, 'You reminds me of meself when I was young.'

'When you were twenty-one?'

'No: when I was sixteen.' Then he asked me, 'You still want to find that 'ospital?'

'Yes. Yes, I do.'

Les just said, 'OK. I'm on for it.'

Cliff's neat little mouth turned down at the sides. Out bloody voted; I knew that he wouldn't pull rank, but he had a last try.

'If you don't stop now I can't guarantee to keep you out of trouble once we're back in Blighty.'

'You never could, sir,' I told him.

I used the *sir* again because the negotiation was over. But it didn't turn out like that. James came over majorish, and insisted that Les remained there to guard *Kate*. Having manipulated the rest of us into scrambling through Bremen on our hands and knees, Les actually looked a bit smug about being left behind.

*

437

After an hour at the crouch or on our bellies, we slid into a bomb crater, only to find it already occupied. There was a single infantryman – one of ours – and four scared civilians.

Cliff said, 'Bloody fine foxhole, this. Any port in a storm.'

A mortar round or light artillery shell landed up about fifty yards away. I crouched under the shower of mud and brick pieces it threw at us. I said, 'I think you've said that to me before, Cliff. At least, *someone* did. About a woman.'

'Begging your pardon, sir,' the soldier said. 'It's not a foxhole. Not a proper one. It's a bomb crater. The Americans gave it to us a couple of days ago – that's why the heap of bricks is still warm.' Another Scot: it was their sector now.

'What's that smell?' I asked. There was this thin, familiar smell. Once it was in your nostrils it never seemed to go away.

'I thought Les had taught you that.' From James. 'It's what dead people smell like. Your lot probably did it.'

There was another dull thud of a nearby explosion.

Cliff asked James, 'We've shared a foxhole before, haven't we? Where was that?'

'Caen, I think: it must have been in July or August. Les got shot in the arse again.'

'Excuse me, sir.' It was the Scottie again. 'It *isna* a foxhole.'

Cliff said, 'Does it make a difference?'

'Aye, sir, it does. A foxhole wouldnae been large enough for the eight of us. I woulda denied you entrance.'

'With that horrible rifle?'

'It would be sad if it hae come to tha', sir.'

There was something about these bastards who wore khaki,

carried guns, and walked everywhere: when they made threats you tended to believe them. The eight of us were me, James and Cliff, the Scottie, two women and two children. The children were both girls of about ten. One of them had fair hair and wore a pink plastic patch over one eye. There was a pad of grubby cotton wool behind it. Most of the time we clung around the sloping sides of the bomb crater. From time to time the Scottie scuttled out to the bottom of the depression to check on the meal he was cooking, and slot more wood into the solid fuel stove that stood there. It had a short chimney that smoked a clear thin smoke you couldn't see from six feet. It must have once been in a kitchen in the pile of bricks alongside us. Something evil was bubbling in an enormous greasy black saucepan on it. Lying around it were piles of broken wood ready to feed its red maw, potato peelings and empty bully cans.

The Scottie had told us, 'It's for them. They haven't eaten for days . . . ye can have what's left over.'

'If you're the *Stovie* man,' James told him, 'we've followed you around for weeks. Aren't you trying to rejoin your unit?'

'Yes, sir. We have a nice phrase from where I belong, which is *part and part.*'

'What does that mean?' James got out his book and scribbled it down.

'In my case, sir, it means that I am trying to catch up with my platoon, but not too quickly. I prefer cooking up feasts for lost civvies.'

Cliff told the Major, 'That sounds like your sort of soldier, James, why don't you adopt him?'

We all ducked instinctively as another round went off. Nearer this time, I thought. The girl with the eyepatch whimpered. One of the women – who had a lock of blonde hair escaping from a scarf tied over her head – hugged her. Mother and daughter, I thought.

'We've chased your bloody feasts across Europe,' I told the Scot.

'And now he's probably saving lives with it,' James said. 'Potatoes, corned beef or spam if they're lucky, is all that anyone will be eating here for months. At least someone's showing them what to do with it.'

The Scotsman looked mollified. He said, 'I put in a handful of ground oatmeal when I can get it: you can stir in a great gobbit o' clotted cream if you hae't. The kiddies go for that.'

'Will you give me your recipe?' James asked. 'I'm going to open a restaurant in England after the war: it could be a novelty dish.'

The Stovie Man said that the Canadians hadn't got any heavy stuff, so they were using Bofors light anti-aircraft guns to keep our heads down, and he said, '. . . an' they're being a bit half hearted about it. I don't think they want a proper scrap. I'm thinking they're waiting for someone to come and sort it out. Just like us. Excuse me a minute . . .'

He slid down to the stove at the bottom of the pit, and returned with two ally mess tins of grey and pink goo, which he handed to the kids. Every time I saw it, it had a different consistency. This time it looked like jellied dogs' brains. They scooped it out with their hands, wolfing it down like, well . . . wolves. Maybe they were the *Werewolf* soldiers the

Canadians were worried about, disguised as ten-year-old girls. They had nearly finished the food before he got back with two more, on big wide soup plates, for the women. One of the plates had lost a great chunk of rim. The girl with the eyepatch held her mess tin back out to him. A Bofors shell exploded with a sharp crack maybe a hundred yards away. The Scottie smiled at her, but shook his head.

He asked James, 'Can any of you speak the lingo properly, sir?'

'Les and I can get by; Charlie's still a bit green . . .'

'Les is not here,' I reminded him.

'Then that leaves me, I suppose. What did you need old boy?' James.

The soldier smiled at the women again before he asked, 'Can you tell them that there *is* more food, but that it would be wiser to wait half an hour before their second helping. I'm thinking they ha'en't eaten for a couple o' days. Too much in one go will mak 'em sick.'

James said, 'OK, soldier . . . I can manage that.'

He turned so that he was facing them, and said about three sentences, speaking clearly and slowly. Both women smiled weakly. Eyepatch pulled the outstretched mess tin back, and cradled it to her body. There was a rattle of small-arms fire which seemed further away. A single multi-engined aircraft droned high overhead.

I said, 'The firing's getting further away. Are you ready to move on, James?' I wasn't going to call him *sir*, sitting in a bomb hole waiting for the next shell to catch us.

'Give it ten, old son . . . let 'em get a bit further.'

I rolled over to face Cliff. He was about six feet from me. He had his revolver in his hand. He had had it in his hand since we'd left Les with *Kate*. I still don't know who he didn't trust – me, the Canadians, or the odd scraps of Scottish soldiery we came across from time to time. Most of those had been in cellars, shell holes and bomb craters just like the bloody Somme battles thirty years earlier. Cliff must have picked up on that, because as I turned to him he said, 'Don't you think that this is *the better 'ole*, compared to our last one?'

'Don't know what you mean . . .'

The Scot guffawed, and James gave his silly little giggle. The Scot told me, 'Dinna mind them, sir. *The Better 'ole* was a musical entertainment from the *First* War. My father took me down to Glasgow to see it. To the music hall. You're too young to ken that.' Sure enough; he was closer to James's and Cliff's age than to mine. Then he started to hum, and then quietly croon a song that I took to be connected to it. It was 'What Do You Want to Make Those Eyes at Me For?' Possibly not the best thing to be singing to a ten-year-old girl who maybe only had one left, but she didn't understand the words anyway. She smiled at him through her fear, and hugged her mess tin closer, as if it was a doll.

I asked Cliff, 'Will you be straight about something with me, sir?' Perhaps the truth would make me strong and joyful. Pause. Maybe five-beat.

Then he said, 'Only possibly. There are always other considerations.'

This time the five-beat was mine. I could always choose not to ask.

First of all I told him, 'The Major and I have already worked out that I'm not supposed to catch up with Grace and bring her and her baby back to England. I'm supposed to chase her into the welcoming arms of Mother Russia, where she and the baby will disappear into the snowy wastes for ever.'

Cliff eye-wrestled with me: he didn't blink. I asked, 'Did you know that when you sent me out here?'

'No, Charlie. I didn't.'

'Would you have still sent me if you *had* known?'

'Yes, Charlie. I rather believe I would.'

'What *did* you know?'

There were three rifle shots. Two from in front of us and far to the right, and one answering shot from what I presumed was our side. It seemed even further away.

'What I told you: although I suspected that there could be alternative plans that I knew nothing about.'

'And you didn't ask?'

'Always better not too, old son.'

'And you didn't think to mention that to me or James?'

'No. I kept it nice and simple, my ear to the ground, and my eyes wide open. For what it's worth, I think that the Bakers actually wanted them found and brought back to begin with. It would have been messy, but they could have dealt with it. Then, when Grace moved so determinedly east, another solution presented itself.'

'Did you ask the Americans to stop me?'

'No, it must have been them. It's how it works in old man Baker's factories. He compartmentalizes: keeps people and their tasks in separate boxes. The person making the bullets in one part of the factory doesn't need to know about someone rifling gun barrels in another. The parts only come together in the gun.'

'I'm not sure that I understand . . .'

'Power, old boy,' That was James. 'Keep what the individual knows to the minimum, but know the whole picture yourself. No one can challenge you then, and you get to do whatever you like, because no one else knows enough to do it better.'

'. . . which is why he told the *Yanks* to stop you, but didn't tell me. It wasn't about not telling you, it was about not telling *me*. So that I couldn't disagree with him, or learn enough to start worrying at it, and work out what's what. Do you see that now?' Cliff.

'Maybe.' I didn't respond immediately; then, 'Two more questions.'

'No promises.'

'OK. How did they get to the Yanks?'

'Probably through that Captain that Addie is shagging. I don't think that he's done much flying since he took up with the old lady. He probably knew someone who knew someone, and so on. All of a sudden the Yankee police all over Paris are falling over themselves to lock you up.'

'. . . and does Grace know that someone's chasing after her to get her back?'

'Almost certainly. Someone must have tipped her the wink. That's why she's on the move all the time.'

'Does she know it's *me*?'

'That's another question. And a particularly stupid one.

You said *two* questions.' I let that hang, and Cliff eventually said, '. . . anyway, I don't know that. This all seemed so simple when I waved you off. How did I get to be hiding in a bomb hole in Germany explaining myself to you?'

He sounded tired. Almost as tired as James's old street map looked. James glanced up, folded it and said, 'See that spectacularly large heap of masonry over there?' He gestured vaguely to the north-west. 'That once could have been a main telephone exchange.'

The Scottish soldier said, 'There must be two or three cellar doors around it. There's folk under there: I've seen civilians diving in and out.'

I borrowed his helmet, and cautiously poked my head over the lip of our crater. No one shot at me. The heap of rubble was about fifty yards away: a mixture of brick and stone the shape of the long barrows you can still see in Wiltshire, but about a hundred times that size. The original building must have been as big as the Bank of England. There was another bomb hole just this side of it. I couldn't hear any fighting. They must have run out of shells for their Bofors, or were saving them for afters. When I slid down, and gave the Scottie back his helmet, I told James, 'Fifty-yard sprint, to another crater just alongside it.'

Cliff had put his pistol away, and had been prodding the ground thoughtfully with a three-foot length of half-inch piping he'd pulled from the crater wall. He said, '. . . and if they've a Bren zeroed on the space between we won't get halfway. I have a better idea.' He had finished tying a grubby white handkerchief at the end of the pipe. Then he stood up, and was immediately head and shoulders up, with his flag hanging limply above him. 'Let me get halfway before you follow.'

James wasn't that stupid. He let him get to the rim of the next bomb hole before he moved us. The Scottie came with us. We crouched, and moved fast. I asked him, 'What's your name?'

'Alan. Sanderson. Gordons.'

'I'm Charlie, and that's James and Cliff. We don't belong to anything.'

James turned for a half-pace, and gave him a nod. A Sunday stroll.

Our new pal asked, 'What's the matter with your army, sir? D'y' hae no use for ranks?'

I explained, 'It's the work they do. Sometimes things get mixed up. I'm just along for the ride.'

'That's my first mistake then, sir. I thought that they were looking to you for their orders.'

'We are,' James told him. 'Charlie just hasn't worked that out yet.'

There was a foot of water in the bottom of the new hole. Cliff was up at the face of the crater. The heap of brick intruded into one side of it: I suppose that the water was burst main pipe – it looked clean enough.

'What I want to know before I get my boots wet,' James told us, 'is what that bloody horrible rustling sound is. Sounds like rats.'

That's when I noticed it myself. It was the noise that your boots make when you kick your way along gutters full of dried leaves in autumn. I bent to the bricks to listen, and then I heard them. Voices. The murmur of many voices. We needed a breather anyway, and I hadn't actually worked out what I intended to do – stroll down the cellar steps, and ask if anyone knew Ingrid Knier – always remembering to spell it with a K.

I asked Cliff, 'Whose baby did Grace have then? It wasn't mine, or any of my lot. We came along too late.'

'That leaves an American flyer, and the old man, doesn't it?'

'And once they worked out Grace might have had her stepfather's baby, they changed their minds about getting her back? I wonder if they ever played Happy Families when she was a kid?'

When Cliff eventually responded he asked, 'What are you thinking now?'

'I was thinking *What a cock-up*. Sir.'

Cliff sniffed. So did James. It was probably some public school coded message.

Alan said, 'There's still no shooting,' and, 'I can see one of those cellar doors from here. It's one of those big double wooden ones, like they have in front of the pubs on Rose Street.'

I said, 'If we wait until the next time they open it, James and I can drop down there – I'll need you because of your German, James – Cliff, you could stop at the doors: watch our backs, and Alan you can cover us all from here.' None of them said anything so I added, lamely, I thought, '. . . unless you can think of anything better?'

447

'Unfortunately, no.' That was James. I had forgotten that he actually knew why we were here, whereas the others didn't. 'Shit or bust, eh?'

I could have thought of better similes. Cliff asked me, 'Who do you expect to find down there?'

'Just one of my contacts, sir.'

He gave an amused little smile, and said, 'I was right about you, young Charlie. You have promise. Only been out in the field a few weeks and you're already building your own little network. Nice stuff.' I suppose that that was better than him knowing the truth.

You wouldn't believe the number of wide, worn, red-brick steps that led down from the cellar's doors to its floor. I nearly choked on the smoke from small fires, candles and oil lamps, and nearly gagged on the smell of unwashed bodies, and what would have been sewage if there had been a connection to a sewer.

Two teenaged boys had come up to scavenge, and we were up alongside them as they were closing the flat doors. As usual, James was on them before they heard him. Cliff had stayed with them at the top of the steps. I stopped counting the steps at fifty. The murmur of humanity died progressively as more and more of them saw us. I carried my Luger in my right hand. Remember that I'd already seen what their Home Guard could do at that castle in Holland.

Funnily enough, it didn't *feel* dangerous. As we descended James whispered, 'Remarkable. Bloody remarkable.'

'What is, sir?'

'This place. Enormous. Roman bloody brickwork.'

'Not that again.'

' 's true. Water cisterns I think. I saw this in Istanbul before the war. They must have just built the telephone exchange on top of it.'

It wasn't a nineteenth-century cellar at any rate. It was a series of huge vaulted brick caverns supported on massive brick pillars as far as the eye could see. The floor, where I could see it, looked dry and sandy. People were gathered in groups. Families? I wondered. Neighbours? Near the bottom of the worn steps an old lady caught at my ankle, and asked in English, 'All right now, Tommy? War finished?'

I said, 'War finished for you, Mother. War nearly finished.'

To make sure that she understood James repeated me in Kraut, and we stood, still not at floor level with them, and watched his words move from group to group. There were absolutely no soldiers that I could see; just women, children and old folk. My brain registered a couple of children crying, and a woman sobbing close by. James murmured, 'What next?'

I nearly replied, *Fucked if I know*, but retreated a step or two up from him, and looked out over the crowd. They had joined up, silent now, pressing closer to the steps. Cliff's voice boomed hollowly down to us, 'OK down there?'

'Fine. You?'

'Yeah.'

Still they didn't say anything. Still a couple of children cried, and still a woman in the darkness sobbed. I used the thirty-foot voice.

'Is Ingrid Knier present? Is Ingrid Knier here? K-N-I-E-R.' I hated the incongruous rhyme. I wasn't trying to be funny.

James repeated it, and then said something else in Kraut. There was an odd experience of watching our words rippling out through the crowd, like a shock wave. Nothing seemed to happen. James murmured again: he said, 'Long shot anyway, old man,' and coughed.

Then I sensed some sort of movement that started at the back of the crowd. It parted as a figure moved forward, closing up again behind it. Bloody silly really, but I found that I was holding my breath.

The woman who stepped to the front spoke very quietly, but everybody in that place could hear her: one of those pin-drop moments. She didn't look up. 'Here is Ingrid Knier,' she said. 'I am her.'

She was small – even smaller than me – but roughly the same age, and dressed in baggy grey overalls, under a soldier's jacket which had had its insignia and buttons removed. She had long dark blonde hair. I couldn't say from where I stood whether she was plain or pretty, because a gash across her right cheekbone had been very roughly stitched: it pulled her face out of shape. She tried to smile but couldn't make it.

I said, 'I'm Charlie Bassett. Do you remember me?' I'm always coming up with original chat-up lines. It sounded ridiculous, but I couldn't think of anything else.

'Yes. Of course. Pilot Officer Bassett. I did not believe that you would come here.'

How do you explain yourself to a girl you've never met, in front of a crowd of a hundred or more? I felt a lot of tension leaving me. I wondered what I was doing with a gun in my hand. I didn't mean to sound pompous as I said, 'I don't make many promises, Fräulein Knier. When you know me better you'll know that if I do, I *keep* them.' I was particularly pleased to have remembered to say *Fräulein*.

James murmured, 'And if I'm not mistaken it's your doing just that sort of thing with your Grace last year that got us here in the first place.'

The woman moved forward, and stood up to the step below me, alongside James. Then she turned outwards, and spoke in German too fast for me to follow. One of the old men clapped, and another couple of the women began to sob. I asked James, 'What did she say? I couldn't follow it.'

'She told them that you'd made a promise to her to come and save her from the Russians, and that now you are here with your Army. She told them that they are safe.'

That's when the noise came. It was almost as if they all began talking at once. Their voices filled the cavern.

'Fucking hell, James, what have I got us into?'

The crowd didn't exactly disperse. It just moved back out into its component parts. I sat down on the step. James sat alongside me. Ingrid sat about two steps down. After a suitable pause James said, 'I hope that you don't mind me observing this, but now it seems to be my sort of a problem, rather than your sort of a problem.'

'What do you mean, sir?'

'Well, these people *are* starving, aren't they?'

'Are they?' It hadn't occurred to me. I asked the girl, 'When did you last eat?'

451

'Yesterday.'

'What did you eat?' That was James.

'Soup. Everyone had a bowl of soup.'

'What was in it?'

'Cabbages: six cabbages and a few potatoes. The boys did well yesterday.'

'Between a hundred people?'

'Two hundred and nine,' she said. She pronounced the words very precisely. 'It was two hundred and eight, but a baby was born yesterday. It is not old enough for soup.'

'No,' said James, and, 'Six cabbages between two hundred people, Charlie. They had a bowl of flavoured water.' Then he asked Ingrid, 'How long have you been down here?'

'Twenty days.'

Then he said to me, 'I'll have to radio in. Get some trucks in here if the Canadians let us.'

The girl Ingrid had been following the conversation — probably better than me.

'But you will need to go away . . . to bring help?'

'Yes.'

'You cannot use our telephone?'

'Is it still working?'

'Of course. It is the Deutsche Telephone Company.'

When she led him away I experienced an emotion I hadn't met properly since my school days: jealousy. I sat and watched the crowd. They watched me back: she'd told them I was their saviour. It was a curiously uncomfortable experience. He returned alone.

'Food and blankets here by close of play today, provided the Canadians agree to stop shooting at us.'

'You're beginning to sound like a Major again: you didn't sound like one when we were in the bottom of those bomb holes.'

'I suppose I am really.'

'Then it's *sir*, again?'

'For the time being, if you don't mind, Charlie.'

'My pleasure, sir.' As long as he didn't try to pull rank on me over the girl, that was all right by me.

'Would you mind cutting up the stairs to Cliff, and getting him down here?'

'No problem, sir. What shall I tell him?'

'Tell him that there's a live telephone switchboard down here, one of the last that's left in Germany . . . and he can listen in to some of the calls that are still being made between the remains of Jerry's armies and their commanders, in what's left of Germany. Still time to win him a medal for initiative. Your girl Ingrid is going to be busy.'

I had nothing to do. My brief experience of being in charge hadn't prepared me for relinquishing it again. The girl Ingrid, who I had never truly expected to meet, threaded her way back between the groups. She sat on a step beside me and took my hand. It was the sort of gesture I remembered of my sister. Did that show on my face? Eventually she said, 'I did not say *Thank you*. Thank you.'

'I didn't do anything.'

'You came.'

'I explained that. It felt like a promise. I keep promises. Don't Germans ever keep promises?' Even for me, given her circumstances, that was a bit bloody brutal.

'Germans do; *men* don't.'

Me put in my place, wasn't it? I wanted to change tack.

'I expected I might find you, and maybe a few others hiding down here . . .'

'. . . and instead you have a multitude to feed.' She sounded pleased.

'The Major says that the loaves and fishes will be here before nightfall.'

'I didn't know that you were a priest.'

'I am not. I'm just an ordinary man in a priest's jacket.'

She didn't say anything for a time, but didn't let go of my hand either. When she did it felt cramped, and I rubbed and squeezed my fingers together. She spoke very quietly as if she didn't want anyone else to hear,

'Sorry, Charlie Bassett. I thought that if I let go, you might disappear. I am afraid that I will awake, and not know what else to do except wait for the bombers again.' Then she said something in German that I failed to understand.

I asked, 'What was that?'

'I said that your Major was a very good man.'

'*I* think so.'

'He values you also.'

'I *don't* think so.'

'You are wrong.'

I asked her, 'Is this our first argument?'

She didn't understand the joke but laughed at it anyway.

She asked, 'When will you go?'

'I don't know. Tomorrow probably. The Major will want to stay until his food and blankets are here. Tomorrow the fighting will have finally stopped. I have to visit someone in a hospital in the Hanseatic Hotel, in the docks, do you know it?'

'No. I know where it is. You will find many people there also. Their telephone link failed.'

'Of course. It was not Deutsche Telephone Company.'

'Now you are making sport of me.' Her face set like concrete.

'Now I am making sport of you.'

'So, I will go.' She moved to get up. I pulled her gently down again by the arm.

'No. Please stay.'

She looked directly ahead, and smiled a little smile: as if she knew a secret.

'I was making sport of *you*.'

'I know,' I said, 'but I wasn't sure.'

Again there was a pause, but I didn't feel uncomfortable. Ingrid said, 'The other officer in the RAF uniform . . .?'

'Mr Clifford. Yes?'

'Yes . . . he asked your Major who I was. Your Major said that I was *Charlie's bint*. Does that mean anything?'

'Now you are making sport of me again.'

'No. Tell me.'

'The Major was making a mistake. It is an old Arabic word. *Charlie's bint*, means *Charlie's woman*. He made a mistake.'

When she spoke again her voice was small, and so quiet that it could have been the voice of a child. I had to lean close to her to catch the words. She said, 'No. He did not make a mistake.'

Charlie's little heart stopped.

We had visitors. I scrambled up the steps with James close on my heels. Alan's voice had floated down with, 'Soldiers, sir. Those Canadians, I think.'

James just carried on past me. 'Don't move, Charlie, I'll handle this one.'

The South African, Major Ira Hendriks, stood in the light. His immaculate uniform was a little muddied about the edges. We could see that he had a pair of white undies tied to the end of his leather-covered cane. Either they were some girl's, or he was a very peculiar man indeed. At about fifteen feet James said, 'Close enough, Mr Hendriks,' and, 'I thought you were some kind of a policeman.'

'I am. But to do my sort of policing you need all the medical stuff first, so I'm also a qualified doctor. I have another doctor, and two Corpsmen with me. Can they come down too?'

'What about the bloody Canadians?'

'That's all calmed down a bit. They've pulled back to the docks . . . apparently a barracks full of Jerries has surrendered to them there, so they have their hands full anyway.'

'How did you know we were here?' James was obviously pushing it a bit.

'Apparently your ranker phoned my ranker. We were at

the hospital. He said that you were stuck out here with two hundred refugees, and needed help. Can my . . .?'

''course they can, old chap. Pleased to see you again.' He stuck out his hand for the ritual. Explanation accepted. Pax.

One of Hendriks's people was a black man in the arse-end of an American provost's uniform. He had a green operating theatre gown over one shoulder, and was carrying a small case. I said, 'Wotcha, Cutter!' as he walked up.

He said, '*Wotcha*: that's *English* for something I suppose?' and, 'I brought you a drink.' This was as we walked down the steps. He gave me a half-bottle of bourbon.

'Thanks. Does that mean we can get through to the hospital now?'

'You can walk it in thirty minutes, although I wouldn't try it. You'll end up down a hole with a broken leg. There's a lot of unexploded ordnance lying about as well.'

'Grace Baker still there?'

'She was when I left.'

I don't know what I had expected, but it was as if all of the air had been suddenly punched out of my body. The silence spread around Hendriks's people as they reached the lower levels, and the people got a sight of them. Especially the Cutter. Ingrid stood up to face us. I said, 'Tell your people that they are doctors: from the hospital. They can help the sick and hurt. They will not harm anyone.'

She turned away from me, and spoke aloud. By this time the Cutter had reached her. When she had finished speaking he reached out, and turned her face gently into the best light, and told me, 'I can tidy that up for a start.'

Ingrid looked a little panicky. I told her, 'He is a friend — *my* friend. He is a very good doctor. We call him Cutter.'

She gave him the eye, and said perfectly, 'You will not cut my head off?'

Cutter said, 'No. It's far too pretty for that.' His teeth gleamed in the light.

I went to find James. He said, 'It's a funny old bloody world,' about nothing in particular.

'Yes it is, Major. I wonder what Les is doing now?'

'Lugging your bloody supper around,' Les said. He was above us on the steps, and fifteen feet back. 'Where d' y' wan' it?' He had a rations box on each shoulder. It would be full of tins of corned beef.

You can trust an officer to be ungrateful. James said, 'I thought I left you to guard *Kate*?'

Les said, 'You can trust an officer to be ungrateful, can't you?' Then, 'I left an Ordnance Corps type with her, sir. It was as far as your lorries could get. They needed me to show them the way across your brick field. There's six of us will make two journeys each — it's about a twenny-minute stroll if we're careful, now nobody's shooting at you — that will give you just about enough grub for tonight. They'll get the rest through tomorrow. You'll have to make do without the blankets for another night.' James didn't say anything. Les went on, 'I trust that's all right, sir?'

James didn't say anything. Not at first. Les put the boxes down when he reached our level. I helped him with them. Then James reached out and touched him on one shoulder.

'Of course it's all right, Les. Thank you. Thank you very much.' They both grinned like a couple of bloody Spartans.

After a couple of trips Les went back with his squaddies. Alan produced a couple of blankets from his pack, and spread them a few steps down from the doors, then closed up and battened us in for the night. I can still remember his face, half lit, high above us. He was smiling down at James introducing a circle of middle-aged Fraus to the mysteries of the Stovie as if he had been making it all his life.

Alan called down, 'An' dinna ferget the handful o' oatmeal, sir.'

James waved back. He said, 'I won't, Sergeant.'

That took seconds to sink in.

'Beggin' your pardon, sir . . . I'm no Sergeant.'

'You will be, when you get back to your regiment.'

I had tucked myself up against a wall, in the dark. I had expected it to be cold or damp. It wasn't. It was dry like the floor. Ingrid found me there. She squeezed alongside me, and pulled a heavy, old curtain around our shoulders. She hooked her arm tight through mine, and put her good cheek against my shoulder. We took a good couple of medicinal sucks at the Cutter's bottle of bourbon. Her closed eyelids looked purply blue in the half-light. I closed my eyes.

Twenty-Eight

I guess that I awoke at about dawn. My left arm, with her right wrapped through it, had gone to sleep. She had half turned towards me during the night. My right arm was stretched across my chest and hers, and my hand was inside her grey ovies, against an amazing breast. She stirred as I removed my hand. There weren't many people moving about . . . an uncanny quiet, disturbed by snores, and the occasional low murmured conversation. I was still rubbing the circulation back into my arm as I reached the steps. James was at the bottom of them smoking a cigarette: the smoke smelled like Turkish tobacco.

'Morning, sir.'

'What O, Jeeves.'

'You should save that for Les.'

'Yes. Sorry old man. I keep forgetting that you had the operation.'

'The operation?'

'Made into an officer; they scoop most of your brain out – must be an operation. Didn't you notice?'

'No, sir. I didn't notice.'

'That's how you can tell; once they take your brain away, you never notice. Fancy breakfast?'

'Yes, sir. What's cooking?'

'Dampers: flour and water pancakes. We still have loads of flour, and a big tin of jam for the kids: Les will bring the rest up today.'

'How long will what's on your lorries keep these people going, sir?'

' 'bout four days, if they're careful. But that's not the point. There will be a Supply Sergeant along as part of the package. He'll have a radio man with him, and between them they'll organize it into a regular supply run.'

A shadow fell over us. It was Les. I looked up. Bright sun was pouring through the opened cellar doors, and I could only see him in outline.

'It's been the Major's major contribution to war theory so far: instead of drawing all of the DPs together in hundreds of thousands, in 'uge camps and feeding stations, the Major worked out that we can save more of them by coping with smaller numbers in the areas we find them, using field kitchens. Two or three hundred at a time . . .'

'*DPs?*'

'Displaced persons. Remember that one; you're going to hear a lot of it for the next few years. Europe is full of them.'

' 'morning, Les,' James said. 'You're right: the next few years will see the biggest demographic changes in Europe since the Stone Age.'

'Demographic?' New word for me.

'The numbers that tell you where and how people live.' Even bloody Les knew it. Then he apologized. 'If you hang around the Major long enough, you get to pick up long words.' Then he sniffed. I didn't mind.

We climbed up into the sunlight. Blue sky and big fluffy clouds. A bit of a nip in the air. Like Pearl Harbor. Sanderson had washed and shaved, and was now going through a routine of callisthenics. Les sat down on the top step and examined Alan's rifle, which was stowed in a narrow sack, like a holster. When the Scot came up, pulling his shirt on over a surprisingly clean singlet, Les asked, 'What is it?'

'.303 Ross Rifle. Canadian job. Best sniper rifle in the theatre.'

'That you? A sniper then?'

'A marksman. Yes. I lost my taste for it eventually.'

For the first time I noticed the dull khaki badge sewn on his shoulder under his regimental flash.

There was a jeep parked at the cellar entrance: a jeep with a big black radio bolted into the back, above one of the wheel arches. A ghastly duet warbled back at us from it: it was 'A Pretty Girl Is Just Like a Melody'. Les said, 'It's good, ain't it? I got tired of all that Yankee stuff. This is coming from a British Forces station somewhere in 'olland.'

No one answered him. Eventually James said, 'Whatever *happened* to Anne Ziegler and Webster Booth?' and before anyone could answer asked, 'Anyone seen Cliff?'

I offered to be the search party, and as I descended the steps again I heard this: James — somewhat reproachfully I thought, 'Whose jeep is it, anyway?'

Les, 'Our'n.'

'You didn't give them *Kate* in return?'

''course not, sir. What do yer take me for?'

I heard Alan stifle a snort. Privates didn't talk to Majors like that in his mob.

Les went on, 'I gave them fifty of Charlie's dollars, an' a couple o' thousand bad occupation DMs. *Kate* would never have made it across to here, an' I think the jeep'll get us across to Charlie's 'ospital without walkin'. I was thinkin' of *you*, sir.'

'That's a load of old bollocks.'

'Sir.'

I found Cliff in a smaller vaulted brick space, at the very back of trog city. He was sitting at a bench topped by a surprisingly large, modern-looking frame of telephone switch-gear. He had stretched his arms on the bench, and cradled his head on them. I noticed that his shirt cuffs and collar were frayed, and that he could do with a haircut. He wasn't anything like dead.

Ingrid appeared at my shoulder: she moved as sneakily as James. She had something black and steaming in a cracked mug.

'I brought him coffee. Not real.'

Cliff sat up, and groaned. He looked at me on one side of him, and the girl on the other. She put the mug down close to his hand, and said, 'It is not real.'

He smiled. He said, 'Neither are yours, Fräulein Michelin.'

'I do not understand.'

'Don't worry love, bad English joke. Especially bad with

463

your boyfriend standing alongside me.' He yawned and stretched. 'Did I go to sleep? Must be getting old.'

I asked him, 'Did you hear Hitler?'

That seemed to bring him up short. He said, 'Thank you for the coffee, Fräulein. Do you think you could find a cup for my friend Charlie here?'

What he was saying was, *Sod off because I have something to say to Charlie that I don't want you to hear*, but he was doing it politely. Ingrid was brighter than either of us, when she said, 'Of course,' and turned to leave, she wasn't talking about the coffee either.

I said, 'What is it?'

'Do you remember what I told you about Adolf a few weeks back?'

'Yes. I wasn't sure that I believed you then.'

'You'd better, because the old bogeyman died a fortnight ago; peacefully and in his bed. Uncle Joe doesn't want it announced until the Red Flag is flying over Berlin. The war stops when he stops: not before.'

'And we agreed?'

'. . . At Tehran. Sorry.'

'Does James know this?'

'Of course.'

'And how many others?'

'Maybe twenty Brits. No more. I don't know how many Yanks. We won't have told any of our other Allies.'

'But you've just told me. Why?'

'I don't know, old boy. I have a feeling about you. I just wanted to break the rules for once. Not very scientific, is it?'

I said, 'No,' just as Ingrid came back to us. She held out a mug of *ersatz* to me. It was identical to Cliff's: even cracked in the same place. That made me smile.

I said, 'You haven't brought one for yourself.'

'*No.*' I wondered if she would smile more frequently as I got to know her better.

'You will share mine,' I told her.

She said, 'I thought that too.'

Cliff said, 'You'd better watch that one, Charlie. She'll checkmate the lot of us.'

She did smile for that. She recognized a compliment when she heard one. She insisted I take the first sip. The acorn coffee was bitter, and clung to the back of my palate. That's exactly when I fell in love with her.

Ingrid and I sat on the bottom step. Every time I turned to look up at the doors I could see motes of dust dancing in the light. There was just a slight tang of wood smoke from the brazier. Our shoulders were touching. I filled and smoked my pipe. An old man propped himself on an elbow to watch me. Ingrid coughed, but not because of the tobacco smoke: it was one of those coughs that clear your throat when you are about to say something dangerous.

'There is an old Russian lady. She is here with her two grandchildren. She is determined not to be taken by the Russians. Isn't that strange?' She pronounced the words as *Roossian* and *Roossians*.

'Sounds like a good idea to me. Would you stand around and wait for the SS if the boot was on the other foot?'

'Please?'

'. . . if you were in the same position as her?'

'I see. No. She told me something.'

'What was that?'

'She said to be careful. That it is too easy to become involved with someone who has been of great service to you. Someone who has perhaps saved you.'

I let that hang in the air for half a minute.

'She sounds like a wise old lady.'

'Is that what you think?'

'I think that it is possibly too easy for a man to become involved with a girl he has never even seen. Just a voice on a telephone.'

She let that hang in the air for half a minute; then, 'Why are you going to the hospital: is that as a result of a promise also?'

'Yes it is. Several promises.'

'A woman, also?'

'Yes, an English woman. She was in an air raid in England, became unwell and ran away to hide. First she ran to France, and then in Holland and now in Germany. She saw many dead children, you see, and was pregnant herself . . .'

'*Your* child?'

'No.'

'I have seen dead children.'

'I thought that: sometimes you have sad eyes.'

She took my hand, and drew invisible signs on its palm with her forefinger.

'You promised to marry her, this woman?'

'I once asked her to marry me, and she laughed. Then she said *Yes*, but only after the war, and only if I could find her. It *feels* like a promise.'

'So you will find her, and marry her, this woman?'

'No. I will find her, and ask her to release me from my promise.'

'That is because you stopped loving her when you met me?'

She could have been mocking me. Was she laughing at me for being insincere?

'No. I think I stopped loving her even before I spoke to you. Loving her enough to marry her, anyway. It is like having a *memory* of having loved her.'

Big pause. I racked my brains to work out if anything had been lost in translation. Then she asked, 'She had a child?'

'Yes, I believe so. I have heard reports that there is a baby travelling with her.'

I watched the dust again, dancing in the shaft of daylight.

'If you no longer love her, why are you going to meet her?'

'A promise is a promise. I also promised Mr Clifford that I would find her, and ask her to take the baby back to England.'

'*His* baby then?'

'No. He made a promise to her parents.'

'So many promises.'

'Yes. So many promises.'

Her finger on my palm stopped moving.

'Will you make me a promise?'

'No.' She looked away from me, but I hadn't finished. 'I do not have to. I am here.'

I couldn't bear the way the old man stared at me. I knocked out my pipe, refilled it with tobacco, and offered it to him with a box of matches. He sat up eagerly, and shared the smoke with a man alongside him. He was even older, if anything. While I watched them smoke I told her, 'Would you believe that I might already have a child; a *German* child?'

'You had a German lover; already?'

'No. Not already. I found a little boy — with a lot of dead German soldiers. One was his brother.'

'What did you do?'

'I gave him to an innkeeper's wife. I promised her that if she could not find his people, that she could send the child to me.'

'You told me that you don't make many promises, Charlie Bassett. I think perhaps you make too many.'

'Did your wise woman tell you that?'

'She did not have to. I am here.' It was a soft voice, and full of promise.

The men finished my tobacco, and handed the pipe and matches back. The older of the two spoke in rapid northern German.

I asked Ingrid, 'My German's not that good. What did he say?'

'I am not going to tell you.'

The old man laughed, and spat a few more words. They sounded coarse. When he smiled his front two teeth were missing. I remembered the French family again. There must have been homeless front teeth scattered all over Europe.

'He lost his wife in an air raid a week ago. She was eighty-two. It was their wedding anniversary.' I smiled at the old man then. I left her at the bottom of the steps, still chatting with the two old men.

Les asked me, 'You ready then?'

He had the jeep radio tuned to a news broadcast. Something about the RAF attacking German merchant ships trying to escape from Germany with SS soldiers on board. The commentator could obviously see the weapon strikes, and was getting very excited — as if he was describing a football match.

'Yeah. Thanks. As much as I'll ever be.'

'Mr Clifford coming?'

'No. I don't think so. What about the Major?'

'Yeah. I'll give him a whistle. He's sitting down the steps with that Scotch guy he promoted. They're exchanging recipes like a couple of girls. You walked right past them on the way up.'

'I didn't see them.'

'Well; you wouldn't, would you? You got that glazed look in your eyes.'

He didn't have to whistle for James. The Major must have seen me climbing by, and followed me. He popped out of the cellar like the March Hare.

'What's that? Charlie in love? *Are* you in love, Charlie?'

'I don't know. It doesn't *feel* like love.'

'You're not an expert, old boy, compared to us: but explain . . . what *does* it feel like?'

'It just feels like it's all over.'

'What is?'

'The bit of my life that includes chasing girls, and that sort of thing.'

'. . . that sort of thing?'

'You know.'

' 'fraid we don't, old son.'

'Look, I don't want you to think I was a ladies' man, because I wasn't. It's just that I've had a few girlfriends — mainly in the last six months. And got used to . . .'

'. . . a bit of a poke when you felt like it . . .' That was Les.

I told them, 'It doesn't *feel* like being in love. It doesn't feel like any sort of emotion, except maybe a little sadness that things can't stay as they are.'

'Why not?'

'Like I said, sir. Nothing luvvy duvvy. I looked at Ingrid just now, and had this overwhelming . . . *knowledge*, I suppose . . . I just knew I had met the woman I was going to spend the rest of my life with. All over. No choice. Not any more. Sad really.'

Les said, ' 'strewth.' That was a word we used at the time. 'The slings and arrows of outrageous fortune.'

James said, 'Stop showing off. The boy's stricken.'

'That's what I meant, sir. Shall us get moving?'

Twenty-Nine

Lee Miller's jeep had had the word *Hussar* painted on the bottom frame of the windscreen; remember? Our new one had the word *Chasseur*. I wondered if they'd once been stable mates. Les drove, and the Major sat alongside him, his faded trench coat blowing out in the slipstream. Not that there was much of that; Les had to pick his way around bomb and shell holes, collapsed buildings and exposed, ruptured water mains. One of them plumed about twenty feet into the air, and a group of kids danced and played around it. They ignored us. The high brick wall of an area of dockyard had been laid flat by blast for a length of about two hundred yards. It still looked like a perfect brick wall, but built horizontally rather than vertically. Those odd French painters would have liked that. Submarines on cradles had become scattered pieces of scrap. One of the pieces was a more or less complete submarine conning tower, marooned on dry land. A red flag bearing a huge maple leaf flew from the periscope housing.

We had to turn inland again. Les knew what he was up to. The old Hanseatic Hotel was in a district of warehouses and dock workers' homes. At the end of one street of small houses there was a bomb site comprising a near perfect pyramid of bricks. Les stopped to let us see that as well: I wished he hadn't. It was topped by half a dead woman with an outstretched arm, like a bizarre signpost pointing east. Some wag had hung a notice on it. It read, *Berlin 200 miles*. There's no such thing as a joke in bad taste in the middle of a war. The radio warbled 'The White Cliffs of Dover': at least it wasn't that bloody Vera Lynn woman. Les grunted. He said, 'Someone should bury that before it begins to stink.'

He was right, really. It was just so much meat. I wondered if the kids we'd passed, playing in the water, had seen it. I wondered if some of them wondered where their mother was. Les took us perhaps another quarter-mile. Then he stopped and switched off.

The Hanseatic Hotel towered above low warehouses – one had burned; its roof was gone. The hotel was an ornate, four-storey, square building made from pale red brick. Its cornerstones, lintels and window surrounds were of a fine light-grey ashlar. Flagposts jutting out over the road carried Red Cross flags. They occasionally cracked in the breeze. In the yard between it and a warehouse painted with tarred black paint I could see a dozen ambulances parked randomly, whilst their crews stood around with cigarettes. A large seagull paced up and down the rain channel at the edge of the warehouse roof. It had a piece of blood-stained bandage in its beak, which it shook periodically. It was like one of those civilians they showed you on the newsreels, waving small flags as their liberators drove past.

As we waited, a driver in olive-green pants and vest got into a US ambulance – one of those new Dodges – drove out, and turned away from us. He was as small as a boy; I saw his pale arm as he waved. Les waved back. I didn't have it in me to do the same. Three wide grey steps, a double iron door, painted black, but now chipped and shrapnel-scarred, framed by two square columns of grey ashlar. Both door halves stood open. There were people on stretcher trolleys in what had been the lobby in better days, and a bustle of activity in any direction you looked. Three men in different-coloured fatigues sat behind what had been a reception desk. They looked dog-tired. One, in surgical green, asked me, 'Is it all over out there? They stopped fighting?' He was American.

'Yesterday. Didn't they tell you?'

'No time. The people just keep on coming. The Krauts equipped this place for five hundred patients; we got a thousand. They just keep on coming.'

'I think that the city actually fell two days ago.'

'No one told us. They never do.'

There was a tug at my sleeve. When I looked round there was a small woman standing alongside me. I know what you're thinking, but you'd be wrong. It wasn't Grace. It was a nun; one of the nursing orders. Her white pinafore gleamed like a light in the dark. She said, 'This way,' and tugged me gently again. When I didn't move she repeated, 'This way. They are waiting for you.'

James didn't play the officer any more. He gave me an encouraging smile and a nudge. Les had turned to look at me. He gave me a curt nod. I left them there, and followed her.

We walked. The stairs were polished white-grey stone, as were the corridors. I could do hospitals; this was my fifth since leaving the squadron. Two wide corridors crossed each floor like a crucifix. They had opened up the top floor to four large wards and slipping between them along the corridor was like walking a cloister. Following the nun was like experiencing that sinking feeling you had when you were summoned to the Beak's study at school, without knowing what you were supposed to have done. Grace was somewhere along here, and instead of skipping my feet felt heavier with each step. How to start? *Sorry for chasing you?* or *Did you know it was me?* Don't be an arse, Charlie, of course she did. *Do you still love me?* Did she ever?

Grace me no grace. No Grace.

The room I followed the nun into was thirty feet across. I'd already began to think of her as a large white bird, and myself as a scarecrow flapping in her wake.

No Grace.

The lighting was subdued. Fifteen or so people: maybe more. Chairs arranged in rows of about ten facing a makeshift altar. A crucifix had been painted on the wall above it. Close to it an RAF Sergeant lay on a stretcher trolley: the thing the Americans call a *gurney*, I think. He was propped up on his elbows, smiled, and gave me a nod. The nun turned round, gave both the tarnished crosses on my blouse collars a polish with the balls of her thumbs, then surprised me by giving me a brief kiss on the lips. I don't know what order of nuns she came from. The quick pressure from her body told me it might have been the Mary Magdalenes. Unworthy thought, Charlie. I regretted it immediately.

She said, 'You are the first.'

'The first what?'

'The first priest here since the others ran away. That was two weeks ago. Bless you.'

'. . . and you, Sister.'

I went to the guy on the trolley. He lay back, and stretched out a hand for shaking. I think that the British took the handshake around the world. I noticed that he hadn't shaved for a few days. He noticed me noticing, and rubbed the back of one hand over his dark chin: it made an odd rasping noise. He said, 'Not much water for the last few days, Padre,' and, 'My name is Ross. I'm from Fife.'

'Charles Bassett. I'm English, although my father lives in Glasgow now. I've never been to Fife.'

'I've been to England,' he said. 'You'd like Fife. In places it's just like Sussex: good farming country, and big broad-leafed trees. The girls are all good-tempered, and even the kirks have that English look to them.'

'The churches?'

'Aye.'

'What happened to you?'

'Stupid. Flew into a factory chimney. It was probably the last one standing in Bremerhaven. That took enough off my wingtip to upset Old Lady Gravity. I broke my ankles in the crash.'

'What were you in?'

'Tiffie. Typhoon. Popping rockets into Jerry merchantmen trying to slip out of harbour for neutral countries. They've only got small old ships left now: our rockets turn them inside out.'

'I'll bet they do. Who's this lot?' As I asked him I looked around the room for the first time. I guess they were pretty representative of what we found in each newly captured German city. More than I had first thought. Maybe thirty people. They didn't say much. The kids watched me with big reproachful eyes. Men and women; young and old; civilians and soldiers. Soldiers. I studied them. There were maybe five scattered around the room, all with oddly prominent bandaged injuries. Ross said, 'Don't worry about them, Padre. They're out of it. If the truth's told they're shitting themselves because they don't know what happens next.'

I realized that there was something he needed to know.

'Sergeant Ross . . .'

'Yes, Padre?'

'You *do* realize that you're going to be OK now? The fighting has stopped. The good Jerries have surrendered, and bad ones fled. The city is full of Canadians, and Scots like yourself. I've just left a man from Easter Ross feeding two hundred civilian refugees in a cellar about a mile from here.'

He lay back and looked at the ceiling, a forearm resting on his forehead. He smiled. It was like the sun coming from behind a cloud.

'I wasn't sure. I think I've been here about five or six days.

The shooting died away yesterday I think. Nobody tells you much, except Grace.'

'Who's she?'

'An English nurse. She's working with the French and the Italians. Does that make her a traitor, like Haw-Haw, do you think?'

'I'm sure it doesn't. Aren't doctors and nurses exempt from that sort of thing? What sort of woman is she?'

'The sort you fall for.'

He grinned. He didn't seem to mind. I stood at the nearest window. The hospital stood at the very edge of a one-mile destruction zone. This part of Bremen looked like a gigantic, smashed-up building site. You start with one of the most elegant skylines in northern Europe and a couple of thousand bombs, and work your way backwards to heaps of scattered bricks and stone, a couple of thousand large holes in the ground, and cap it with the stink of unburied bodies. They'd call that reverse engineering these days, I suspect. I did something stupid. Still looking out of the window I spoke what was on my mind: never a good idea.

'Mankind is very young,' I said. 'Scarcely out of the caves.' It sounded like just the sort of platitude an unimaginative priest might have used: as profound as last week's Yorkshire pudding. Maybe Ross thought so too. He asked me, 'Will you take a service, Padre?'

Bollocks! Funnily enough it was an easier prospect than facing Grace. I asked him, 'Do you think they'll want it?'

'Of course, Padre. Didn't Anna tell you?'

'Tell me what?'

The nursing sister told me herself. 'We moved all of the Christians in here,' she said. 'If anything bad had happened they would have all been together.'

Anything bad. For once I didn't ask a silly question.

'All the Christian denominations under the sun,' the Sergeant said cheerfully.

'So they won't mind me, then?' I asked him. 'I'm an independent hedonist.'

He made a whistling sound, and said, 'Don't get me wrong, Padre, but in my mob we would have said that that sounds very painful.'

'And I haven't any of my things . . .'

'We have a Book of Common Prayer, and a couple of hymnbooks. Theirs are in German, of course, but mine's English. It always flew with me.'

I don't know why I wanted to do it. I asked, 'Would you be satisfied with a short informal service? I say a prayer, and you could sing a few of the good old ones?'

It's the silly little things that sometimes get to people.

The nun asked, 'Can I say that the war is over?'

'For Bremen,' I told her, 'the war is over. Tell everyone you like.' After that they all began to speak to each other. In low voices, murmuring. No one used loud voices any more.

It felt oddly natural turning to face them with Ross's book in my hand. I should have felt ridiculous, but I didn't. I gave them three prayers, including a long one for peace on Earth, and good will to all men. Looking back on that, it may have been a bit hypocritical, but it seemed appropriate to the times. They gave me three hymns back, singing lustily at first. Everything went well until the last one: I chose it from among my memories of a whitewashed, corrugated iron Sunday school alongside our parish church . . . and all of a sudden the Germans couldn't sing because they were crying. Sister Anna's voice, and mine, and Ross's rang out in the little room, whilst all the rest of them mumbled. One of the soldiers came up and hugged me afterwards; tears were streaming down his face. I know that he wanted to speak, but something was stopping him. I didn't know what the hell was going on until James asked me, 'Did you plan that, Charlie, or did it just happen? Part of your magic?'

He had been standing at the doorway, and must have seen the end of my performance.

'Hello, James. I am afraid I don't know what's happened. They suddenly got very emotional.'

'It's you, you silly bugger, and the last hymn. Don't you realize that you've just had them sing the tune of an old German national anthem?' Then he said, 'Les wants you. You'd better come downstairs. You didn't meet your Grace?'

'No, but she's here somewhere. That pilot talked about her . . .'

As we walked down the marble stairs he said, 'You're getting awfully good with the bell, book and candle, you know.'

'Thank you, sir.'

'Maybe it should be your line in Civvy Street.'

'I don't think so.'

'Better than being one of Cliff's bloody spies for the rest of your life.'

'Fat chance of that either, sir.'

'Yes. Didn't you tell us you were off to Australia to be a sports writer?'

'That's right, sir. That's what I'd like. What's the matter, don't you believe me?'

All he did was give his strange whinnying laugh. Now what was so bloody funny?

There was a different atmosphere in the hospital: some cloud had lifted. Alongside the pain and the scrambling of medics and nurses from ward to ward there were some smiles too. I saw the back of Hendriks's head. He was dashing down one of the corridors like a sprinter: he didn't notice me. They must have had a radio in one of the wards, and it was that fellow Sinatra expiring over 'When Your Lover Has Gone' with Tommy Dorsey's band. I've loved that performance ever since. God sends you all these little messages, and you never pick up on them; you're always tuned to another station.

Les was sitting on a small marble bench in what had been the hotel lobby, oblivious to the noise and bustle. He had some people around him. One was a plump nurse with long wavy blonde hair like a film star. I knew immediately that this was the woman they had told me about. The German nurse on Grace's team who the men had argued over. If I hadn't just met Ingrid I could have seen why. Her uniform was white, clean and a little too tight. That's what my mother would have said, anyway. She looked startlingly well fed.

Even the heavier Germans I had seen had had their skins hanging off them. I knew that it was the woman because she sat alongside Les, and was cooing at the tiny swaddled child he held in his arms. The Scottie, Alan, stood by them. When he spotted me he said, 'Hello, sir. I brought your German bird over. She's outside.'

Great.

Les said, 'Meet Carlo.' He held up the baby for me to inspect. 'I think he looks like you.'

The baby was asleep. He had round red cheeks and pale eyelashes. I could see one perfect hand, and tiny fingernails.

'I've already told you. It's not mine. Where's Grace?'

'Gone, according to the abandoned Fräulein here. Gone off with some Eyetie, heading for Eyetie Land. She left you a baby and a letter. Congratulations. The baby's a good 'un, but I haven't read the letter yet.'

'Can I have it please?'

Les spoke Kraut to the Kraut. He told me, 'She has a name: Gretchen. Sounds like a fairy tale.'

She popped open a button on her top, and fished a creased envelope from her bra. The letter smelled of soap. It was a cheap envelope of coarse grey-white paper. It had *Charlie* on it, in Grace's big flowing handwriting. I walked away from them to read it.

Charlie

  Enough. Stop following me, please. That's what we agreed the last time we met. When I said before, that I'd marry you if you caught up with me after the war, I didn't expect you to.

*I meant it at the time, but don't any longer; if that makes
sense. Sorry. What do you think of Carlo? Having him was a
bad decision I made after seeing a bombed-out school in
London. That's what our bombs did in Germany when I flew
with you. Everything else followed on from that. No one
wanted me to have Carlo: not even you. Until Grayling told
me you were looking for me, I had good memories of you. After
that I was running away from you too. I'm leaving Carlo,
which really puts you on the spot. You can walk away from
him here, where he'll die unless someone takes him on, you can
go home and give him to Adelaide, and tell her that you did
half the job, which is better than none of it . . . or you can
keep him yourself. A load of old garbage, of course; I would
never leave him if I believed that you wouldn't do the right
thing. Grech has something for him. Bye,*

    Grace.

Bye, Grace.

Just like that. I read it through twice before I handed it to
James. He read it, and gave it to Les. Les had the child
balanced over one shoulder. It belched. A soft, damp sound. I
took the baby from him, and asked, 'Where did that German
girl go? The one who had the letter?'

'There.' She was talking to Alan.

'Ask her if she has anything else from Grace.'

'Why don't you ask her yourself?'

It was Les she smiled at when she popped another button,
and went fishing again. It was the other tit this time. Grace's
fibre tags with her name and number, on a leather cord. I

didn't know that the ATAs had tags: I'd never seen Grace with hers, naked or dressed. Les gave me back the letter. I folded it into its envelope, and buttoned it into the breast pocket of my khaki blouse alongside Grace's tags. The baby felt comfortable on my shoulder, and there was a curious tension in the air. It was as if I was supposed to know what to do next.

When I stood outside on the steps, with Les, the Major and the Scot, Alan, around me, Les popped the question. He asked me, 'What next?'

From near by came the sound of weird music. It was something between the sound of a barrel organ and the Northumbrian pipes. Ingrid stood at the foot of the steps wearing a thick topcoat that someone had given her. She was talking with Cliff, who had popped up from somewhere, and they were standing alongside *Chasseur*. There was a familiar small boy sitting in the back of it, alongside the big radio: he wore a camel-coloured coat with a dark brown velvet collar. Someone had tied a label to his sleeve as if he was a parcel. He looked cold and tired. Cliff was as interested in my reply as anyone. He cocked his head on one side, and looked up at me. I found that my voice wasn't shaking, nor betraying any emotion.

I said, 'That should be the bloody finish of it, of course. I'm not sure. This is where the rest of you get off, if you like.'

Ingrid pointed to the boy, and said, 'This is Dieter. You will remember him. It was confirmed that all of his relatives are dead, so he was sent to you.'

'That was quick. Does he know all that?'

'Of course. He believes that you are to be his new father. Did you tell him that, Charlie?'

'I may have done.'

She didn't reproach me. Not even with her eyes.

Les asked, 'What did you mean, *not sure?*'

'I'm not sure that I'm ready to finish this until I've actually seen Grace.'

Cliff looked away.

Les said, 'We'll need a car then, won't we?' just as James sat down very suddenly on the steps.

James sat down so quickly that for a moment I thought he'd been shot again. It was like the air being let out of a balloon. He put his elbows on his knees and his chin in his hands. That bloody music was on us, and James was crying. There was no grief or noise or anything embarrassing like that. The tears just ran down his cheeks. Poor old sod. He said, 'That's a bloody hurdy-gurdy. We've played them across Europe for four hundred years or more.'

It was always the damned history that got to him.

The sky was blue; pulverized brick danced in red columns in the air like dust devils. A line of people picked their way across our front, across the rubble and around the bomb craters. The civilian who led them was incongruously tall and thin. His legs moved with an angular deftness; like spider's legs. He was a walking scarecrow with some sort of dark visor around his forehead and over his eyes, and a dirty tattered trench coat, bleached white by sun and age. It can't have kept back an icy wind. The scarecrow carried a long wooden box around his neck on a heavy leather strap, and wound a handle on its side. It leaked the weird music I had heard. Partially sighted, I'd guess, he stumbled occasionally, but otherwise moved slowly and deliberately, almost as if he was feeling his way with his feet. The figure behind him had one hand on the musician's shoulder, and the person behind him had a hand on *his* shoulder, and so on. They all had dark glasses, or patches or dirty bandages on their eyes. Except one close to the tail. He had two old healed pits where eyes once rested. What it reminded me of was photographs I had seen of gas-blinded soldiers in the First World War. James was looking far further back than that. I squatted down alongside him, adjusting my balance for the child's weight on my shoulder.

'What's the matter, James? What is it?'

What he said was, 'Can't you see it, Charlie? We've bombed the whole *fucking* continent back into the Dark Ages.' He looked incredibly tired, and for once I thought about him, *You shouldn't be here: you're too old for this*. Les had known that all the time, of course.

'War, famine and pestilence,' I told him. 'At least you're doing something about the last two.'

My bones creaked as I stood up. The hurdy-gurdy man had stopped hurdy-gurdying, and shuffled on with his blind platoon. Maybe the fourth in line had heard my voice. I don't think so, because we were too far away. Anyway, he turned his face in our direction. He had a heavy bandage over most of his face, which covered his eyes. He wore a black eyepatch over that. He was a tall man in olive drab coveralls. He sported a German officer's cap, and a short leather jacket, cut not unlike mine. One of its sleeves was empty and pinned up, and it was blackened by burning or oil on one side. He walked with a marked limp that I didn't remember. He cannot have seen us: I don't believe that there was anything left to see with. I wouldn't have minded, but he was grinning as if he had put one over on us. They were marching in the direction that the dead woman's arm had pointed: *Berlin*. Faced front again, and limped on. I thought that it was Albie, and I never saw him again. You can read his name on the huge wall of the dead that looks out over the US Forces cemetery at Madingley, but I don't think that he died in Germany. I think that he made it.

The kid in the jeep must have been fiddling with the radio. A kid's life is a perpetual fight against boredom. Music exploded; shockingly real. Les said, 'I know that. It's coming from the ARC Grand Central Club in Paris. It's that black bloke.'

That was when I heard Sidney Bechet for the first time. The double-time march he played was 'Maryland, My Maryland'. I know that because I heard him play it live in 1952. What happened next was that the line of blind men picked up the rhythm. First they picked up the step of the march, and their shoulders went back; then they picked up the rhythm of the jazz, and they began to strut and weave a little. They moved away from us like a conga line, kicking up red dust, and disturbing the scent of putrescence that speared head-level across the rubble plain. It wasn't the country of the blind we were in; it was the country of the mad. I bent down to James and told him, 'It's OK: you can come out now, Major, they've gone: you're safe. We're back in the 1940s.'

He kept his head down. He wouldn't even look at me. No one else found it funny either. Black mark, Charlie.

It was Les again. He said, *again*, 'We'll need a car. Can we take *Kate*?'

'What about James?' I asked him.

It was Les who squatted down by him this time. He put a hand on James's shoulder. James twitched, but didn't look up, or say anything. The tears had stopped.

'The Major's fucked out. Aren't you, guv?' Les said. 'He's been fucked for days. He shouldn't have been sent out here again. Mr Clifford can arrange for him to be looked after, can't you, sir?'

Cliff nodded, but before he could reply I added, 'And Ingrid, and the boy,' I told them. 'You'll have to look out for them until I get back.'

Cliff smiled the tiger's smile.

'Any reason why I should, old son?'

'So that you can justify staying on in Germany for a few more months. It's where you want to be: Tommo always said that this is where it was all going to happen after the war.'

'I should imagine he was talking about organized criminality, old boy . . .'

'Isn't that what you do, Cliff, only on a larger scale?'

He dropped the insolent smile then, shrugged, pouted, but then switched it back on. He looked like a little boy caught stealing apples. His smile could be quite dazzling.

'OK. Why not?'

*

487

Later. Ingrid asked me, 'You have sold me to him? Is that what has happened?'

'No; I wouldn't do that.'

'You have *given* me to him then?'

'No, I wouldn't do that either. I haven't given you to anyone.'

'Do you want me to sleep with him?'

'No. I don't want you to sleep with anyone. Anyone except me. I want you to wait for me. Mr Clifford will look after you until I come back. You will look after the boy.'

'Can I trust Mr Clifford?'

'For the small things, *no*: for the large things, *yes*. He is a good man who pretends to himself to be a bad man.'

'Is wanting to sleep with me a big thing?'

'No. That will be a small thing. Keep your door locked at night.'

'Now you are making sport of me again. I have no door.'

'Yes, I am making sport of you again.'

'How long before you come back?'

'I don't know: months.'

'When will you leave?'

'Soon.'

We were drinking wine from small mugs. The bottle had come from *Kate*'s cavernous backside. It was a thick, heavy red that made me sleepy. We sat on stools either side of a barrel in a small vaulted alcove in the cellar. The old ladies had prepared it for us, and had screened it with a hanging threadbare blanket: an illusion of privacy. Dieter snored in a nest of coats against the wall. He had refused to take his own off. The luggage label on his sleeve bore my name and service number – nothing else. On the other side of the blanket screen the baby was awake in a crib made from an ammunition box. I could hear the blonde woman, Gretchen, murmuring to him. Eventually Ingrid asked me, 'Charlie, when are you going to have me?'

'I thought about now would be all right. Do you have a place?'

Her smile danced in the candlelight. She had a dimple on her chin. I noticed it for the first time.

'Yes. I can find a place.'

'Will the boy be all right?'

'He will be fine. Both your boys will be fine. Now they have a brave father and a clever mother. They will sleep.'

So did we.

We said our goodbyes in the cellar. The boy hung his arms around my legs and would not let go. He yelled, and I could not understand him. Ingrid and I knelt on either side of him, and put our arms around him.

'When I return,' I told them, 'I shall never leave you again.' It was an exceptionally stupid thing to say. She repeated it in German so that Dieter understood. In her voice the words sounded soft and loving. The yelling dampened to a teasing grizzle, and then stopped with a last sob. Before I stood up I realized that something odd had happened in my brain. I wasn't thinking *Kraut* or *Jerry*; I was thinking *German*. It's what happens when wars finish, and you start sleeping with the enemy.

*

The sky was blue, with puffy white clouds, as I strolled over to the smashed-up houses where we had left *Kate*. The stove had gone from the Scotsman's bomb crater. I hadn't seen him for a few days either: he had left as abruptly as he appeared. Moving on into Germany behind his battalion, I guessed: but never too close. He'd catch up with them just in time for the victory parade in Berlin.

James stood beside Les beside *Kate*. I hadn't seen much of him either. His flesh, where I could see it – his hands and face – looked yellow and bloodless. We shook hands with an odd formality. His hand felt icy cold.

'Silly, isn't it?' he told me. 'Do you think I've caught something?'

'Demob fever, I hope, sir. Did you hear that Hitler is dead? It was on the radio yesterday.'

'*Déjà* ruddy *vu*. I seem to have heard it before, but just can't seem to recall where. What are your plans?'

'Les wants to go back to Paris, and leave Grace's boy with Maggs. He says he trusts her; then we're heading south. Grace is travelling with an Italian who comes from near Siena: I'll start there.'

'Clifford has arranged a plane for me from Paris. Mind if I cadge a lift?'

'Of course not, sir.'

'Of course not, *James*.'

'If you insist.'

'I do. It's too late to pull rank on you now. You're leaving your bint with Cliff: do you trust *him*?'

'I think I do. I think that it'll be all right.'

'Why?'

'He trusted *me* with something recently, when he didn't have to. It's just a feeling.'

We pulled out onto the street past half a dozen five-tonners. A Staff Sergeant left off shouting at his drivers to snap James a smart salute. James nodded pleasantly from his place on the back seat, as if he was royalty. It was the third or fourth supply convoy since our arrival. When I glanced back a little later he was already sleeping.

Les told me, 'I went back to the forward depot yesterday; that's *funny*, isn't it? I wanted some spares.'

'Good idea.'

'I met that snapper of yours: the American woman with the cameras.'

'Lee Miller. What was she doing?'

'Same as me. Spares and petrol. She had enough booze to stop the Russian Army.'

'Good old Lee.'

'She was a bit pissed, and looked shagged out. A bit like the Major here. She was driving a ruddy great staff car about ten sizes too big for her.'

'She got a Chevy then?'

'Looks like it.'

After a longish silence he asked me, 'Where we going then?'

'Paris first. I wonder how Maggs will cope with the baby.' It was in its ammo box alongside James England. It seemed to sleep a lot, thank God.

Epilogue

I finished writing this book in the same place I finished my first one: sitting in the garden, with a rug across my shoulders to cut away the north breeze that curls over the forest and hill behind the house in September. I've told you before that I don't believe in ghosts. I've also told you that I've seen men walking who I knew to be dead. I don't do anything with these two opinions; I just let them snarl at each other across my brain from time to time. It won't be long before I find out for certain, I guess. The old lady who brings me my morning dram sees them more frequently than I do. Which is why I am surprised that she hasn't seen my most recent visitor. Today she walked right past her.

A big old plane tree sits at the far edge of the garden, in front of the house. Beyond it the hillside drops out of sight into the blues and greys of the Cromarty Firth. My visitor is sitting on the ground under the tree, looking out to sea. Her arms are wrapped around her knees, and she is wearing the same clothes I once saw her in: frayed fatigue pants, and a skimpy khaki vest that clings to her body. The other thing she is wearing is that smile that's maybe a smile, and maybe not. She doesn't appear to feel the cold. I suppose that means that she's gone, at last. It won't be long before we're all gone.

I don't care as much about that as I used to.

Springtime in Germany: a recipe, and a little history

Charlie Bassett's journey through northern Europe in 1945 has been a much more personal trip than any of those I flew with him from Bourn Airfield in *Tuesday's Child* in 1944 – I knew some of the men who actually did it, you see. There actually was a car named *Kate*, and they took her to Germany.

The airfield at Tempsford, which was the trigger of his headlong rush across the Low Countries, was once referred to by Winston Churchill as *the most secret place in England*. He was sandbagging, of course; there were far more secret locations than that – perhaps Tempsford was just the most secret place he felt he could trust us with. The function of the two squadrons that used it was flying personnel and supplies to agents and Resistance fighters operating in Axis-held territories. The aircraft they used were frequently unarmed, and the work was dangerous. It is to the RAF's great credit that it made room there for a few pilots whose personal beliefs conflicted with killing other human beings, but who still wanted to serve. Tempsford still has its pub, but another two that the aircrews used are now private houses, and the Hall is a corporate HQ. The village's best-kept secret is the small medieval manor farmhouse on the south side of its main street – it looks as if it hasn't changed in five hundred years. Everton village, just east of the airfield, has the Thornton Arms, the pub that Charlie knew; it still serves one of the best pints of bitter in England. A time traveller can lunch there, then walk almost from its front door, down the wooded footpath, to the skeleton of the airfield. There you will find sections of runway and perimeter track, a parachute store camouflaged as a barn, and a clump of trees, each planted and labelled in memory of an agent, or an aircrew, who didn't return. Waterloo Farm still endures, and the farm cottage at which Charlie was billeted can be seen from the track that spears past it.

Charlie set off for France from Croydon Aerodrome, which was the original London Airport – and a far more civilized terminal than the municipal toilet we built at Heathrow to replace it. Before the war one could see over the airport perimeter from the top deck of a passing bus . . . and that's how my mother and father saw a new squadron of Spitfires arrive in August 1939, and realized that another world war was imminent. The old man joined up a couple of weeks later. The prewar airport terminal has been sensitively conserved, and converted for commercial use. The visiting public are welcomed, and there is usually a display of artefacts and memorabilia demonstrating its history. A society has been formed to preserve and promote its heritage.

Sadly, the last time I looked you could no longer get a pint at the Propeller. The watering place of choice for many of the defenders of London in 1940 is boarded up and falling to pieces. Shame on the owners and the council; that should never be allowed to happen to a decent pub.

Charlie recalls the old prewar Imperial Airways biplane airliners that dominated the air route between Croydon and the Continent. Like most large aircraft in private hands, they were pressed into RAF service in 1939. One, named *Scylla*, ended up at Drem Airfield in East Lothian, Scotland – just twenty minutes' drive from where I write this. It was blown over and wrecked by one of our northern storms in 1940, and the fuselage, with its galley and first-class seats, turned into a dispersal hut for the pilots of 605 Squadron who were defending Edinburgh. They cut a glade into the woods close to their Spitfires, and hoisted it up on bricks. Who knows, perhaps a schoolboy poking through the thickets and woods around the old airfield will yet come upon its mouldering frame.

It is wrong to think of the newly liberated countries of Europe as *pacified* in early 1945. There were old scores to settle, and political tensions, centred on organized armed groups with incompatible ambitions, created deep fault-lines in societies – there were more guns per head of population in France in January 1945 than there are in Florida today. Young men from Resistance groups, who had grown up with no trade except fighting and sabotage, grappled with a similar problem to today's retired Provo or UDA fighter – *What do I do next?* The liberation of the Channel countries called into being a window of opportunity for the opportunists, and

DAVID FIDDIMORE

criminal opportunities for the criminals . . . and armies of
displaced people were beginning to move around Europe like
a legion of the lost. By 1948 there were few adults in the UK
who didn't know what the acronym DP stood for. It is not in
current use, even though mass movements of the dispossessed
have occurred throughout Europe, Africa and Asia ever since.
There were also the deserters – from both sides – operating
as individuals, or in gangs. Don't forget a few isolated or
lost Axis stay-behinds, who for a couple of months vented
their spleen by throwing hand grenades into cafes, and by
other acts of sabotage. An old man at an Algerian cafe in
Dijon once told me, *There were some bad losers!* and shrugged.
He said that in one particular street of restaurants, in one
particular month, there were so many incidents that the
local Gendarmerie started calling the establishments 'shooting galleries'.

The American war correspondent and photographer Lee
Miller wandered into my first book by accident, and I couldn't
resist bringing her back: Charlie seems attracted to independent women. Contemporaries still talk of the Lee Miller
cocktail she lugged around the Continent in jerrycans: it
consisted of anything alcoholic she could get, poured into an
empty petrol can, and given a good shake. When she reached
Munich she billeted in Adolf Hitler's apartment with her pal
Dave Scherman. They bathed in Hitler's bath, and used the
telephone there to call the Hitler house at Berchtesgaden
before it fell to the Allies. The call was answered, but they
didn't get the quote they asked for. My favourite photograph
of her is of her in that bath – her battered combat boots

alongside. She had been desperate to change her jeep, *Hussar*, for a larger more comfortable staff car, and eventually Dave did a deal for one. In a new Chevrolet she travelled through Germany chronicling the collapse and aftermath of resistance, into Denmark and through Austria and Hungary – where she was arrested by Russian troops – and into Romania. That's where she stopped.

I borrowed James Stewart for a few hours: he won't mind. He had a pawky sense of humour, and a distinguished war record as a bomber pilot. Sorry, Jimmy. As a film actor his range was wider, even, than those he rode in some of the cowboy leads he made so famous.

Soldiers' graffiti have been around for a couple of thousand years, but World War Two finally legitimized them. The conquering armies in the West – German, Russian, American, Italian or British – daubed every town they passed through. Allied soldiers used their unit signs or nicknames . . . and often topped them off with a humorous put-down, aimed at the friendly units that followed them. The Germans often used quotations from Hitler's speeches. The Brits, in particular, were also quite keen on comedians' catchphrases – like Tommy Handley and the mob from *ITMA*. I suppose that that says something about us. The British Highland Division was so notorious for signing the buildings they knocked over, and roads they wrecked, that other divisions of the Allied armies gave them the nickname the *Highway Decorators*. You can still see the HD sign which recorded their march on buildings in Italy, France and the Low Countries, although the paint fades with weather and the years. It is worth while reflecting the next time you overreact to the activities of a teenager with a paint spray can that he is only taking forward an art form from his grandfather or great-grandfather's generations. Charlie says it all the time – what goes around, comes around.

Shining massed searchlights against a low cloud base in order to produce an artificial daylight *did* occur, and was known ruefully as 'Monty's Moonlight', although Bernard Montgomery was probably not its originating genius – I wonder who was.

My parents' generation never used words like Spitfire, Lancaster or Mosquito. For them the aeroplanes were Spits, Lancs and Mossies. Possibly the more homely contractions made the killing they had to do with them easier to bear. Halifax bombers and transports, such as flew from Tempsford, were Hallibags, and Typhoon ground-attack fighters – like the one that the Fifer, Ross, broke – were Tiffies. Sherman tanks were Ronsons, but that was for another reason: too often the petrol-engined vehicles burned like the cigarette lighters they were named for. Those that burned their crews were said to have brewed up . . . just like making a pot of tea. Today's military has not moved away from the practice of having homely, friendly phrases to describe the most terrible of events. By way of a contrast, our stockbrokers and white-collar managers infuse their patois with aggressive and macho phrases that attempt to associate their office politics with trench warfare. Poor fools; if only they knew.

Not long ago some people in Glasgow opened a long-unused door on a floor above an amusement arcade on the Trongate, and found themselves standing in a music hall that had been lost since 1938. They had rediscovered the Britannia Panopticon, on whose stage an uncertain Stan Laurel had taken his first steps to fame in 1906. It had also offered an English actor named Archie Leach an early taste of the footlights. A society, the Britannia Panopticon Trust, has been formed to preserve and restore it, and some guided tours have been carried out. If that's your bag, try the internet. Maybe, in the slipstream of a generation that has pushed stand-up comedy back into the limelight, the Panopticon's time has come round again.

My father marched with the Eighth Army: he told me about how he and his peers would retune British forces radios to pick up German broadcasts, particularly in order to listen to 'Lili Marleen' sung by Lale Andersen in its original lippy German: I never hear the recording without thinking of him. Many of the popular British and American chanteuses of the time recorded cover versions, but they couldn't reproduce Lale's husky, haunted tone.

I first came across the remarkable Ross rifle when I was living in Easter Ross, and shooting targets at an old quarry with the Tain Rifle and Pistol Club, in the days of innocence before Dunblane. One Saturday the Secretary, John Macrae, stopped me by the boot of his car, and reverently began to unwrap a rifle from yards of velvet material. He asked me, *Have you ever seen one of these before?* It was an exquisite Ross rifle. The original Ross Rifle was designed by one of the Rosses of Balnagowan, an estate and castle just south of Tain in Ross-shire, at the turn of the century. As a military weapon it was superseded by the rugged .303 Lee Enfield, because it

DAVID FIDDIMORE

had a number of weaknesses, including the fact that its bolt can take out the shooter's eye if it is reassembled clumsily after cleaning. It has one saving grace that repays the care and love its sharpshooter devotees still lavish on it: in the hands of a skilled marksman it can consistently shoot the pips from a playing card at a quarter of a mile. It is a true sniper's rifle.

During the last weeks of the war the Allied armies at the point seethed with rumours of supposed *Werewolf Units* — allegedly well-armed groups of stay-behind fanatical Nazis dedicated to what we would identify today as acts of terrorism. There *were* such units, but not many of them: neither were they well organized or equipped. They mounted a couple of operations, but in the large scheme of things didn't amount to much. They were successful insomuch as the fear of them, and the steps taken to counter them, used far greater resources than their actual threat warranted, but in 1945 no one was prepared to take a chance with a Nazi. Charles Whiting's book *Werewolf* is an accessible account of their activities, and contains as much information as the general reader will need: a footnote to history.

The story of the dying soldier sitting on his bed in the Fifties and believing that he saw the victims of the concentration camps beckoning to him from his dressing mirror is true. I know: I was there, a thirteen-year-old sitting alongside him.

Finally: A state-of-the-art plateful of Stovies, and a fine pint of beer, can still be had for less than a fiver at the Halfway House in Fleshmarket Close, a narrow street of steps, behind Waverley Station in the Old Town of Edinburgh. For those of you that want to do it yourself, a typical Stovie recipe comprises 6 large peeled and cubed potatoes, a cup of milk, a tablespoon of salted butter, a chopped onion and a 12-ounce tin of corned beef cut into small chunks – with additional salt and pepper to taste. Drop the milk and potatoes into a saucepan, boil and simmer until the potatoes are soft – maybe half an hour. While the potatoes are simmering sauté the onion in the butter, in a skillet over a medium heat, until pale and soft. When the potatoes are soft, mix in the sautéed onions and the corned beef. Give it another ten minutes to heat through, and season with salt and pepper. Some recipes include a small poke of finely ground oatmeal, if it needs stiffening, or a serving can be topped off with a dollop of soured cream, or crowdie. *Bon appétit*.

I had anticipated that Charlie Bassett would bow out of my life with this story. However, the Russians are coming, and now I know that Charlie will have to fly again.